THE BORGIA CHALICE

Derek Wilson is a leading writer of popular history, biography and fiction. He has over thirty titles to his credit, including the internationally acclaimed *Rothschild: A Story of Wealth and Power*, *The Astors: Landscape with Millionaires* and *Hans Holbein: Portrait of an Unknown Man*. After graduating from Cambridge he spent several years travelling the world, working by turns as teacher, antique dealer, magazine editor and radio presenter, and he still writes documentaries and radio plays as well as serving as an Anglican lay reader. Since their three children grew up, Derek Wilson and his wife have divided their time between homes on Exmoor and in Normandy.

Also available from Headline are *The Triarchs*, *The Dresden Text*, *The Hellfire Papers* and *The Camargue Brotherhood*, further chronicles of Tim Lacy's investigations in the artworld.

The Borgia Chalice

Derek Wilson

HEADLINE

First published in 1996 by
HEADLINE BOOK PUBLISHING

First published in paperback in 1996 by
HEADLINE BOOK PUBLISHING LTD

10 9 8 7 6 5 4 3 2 1

British Library Cataloguing in Publication Data

ISBN 0 7472 5065 0

Typeset by Palimpsest Book Production Limited,
Polmont, Stirlingshire
Printed and bound in Great Britain by
Cox & Wyman Ltd, Reading, Berkshire

HEADLINE BOOK PUBLISHING
A division of Hodder Headline PLC
338 Euston Road
London NW1 3BH

The Borgia Chalice

PROLOGUE

The murderer handled the plain buff file lovingly, reverently, as though it were a crisp-lettered incunabulum from the workshop of Caxton or Wynkyn de Worde. Its owner would not have traded it for the rarest volume in the world's finest collection of early printed books. Every folio masterpiece, every treasured first edition had its blemishes and endearing inaccuracies. Here, within these bulging covers of anonymous beige, was perfection. The insoluble crime.

Slender fingers opened the folder. The murderer smiled a self-congratulatory smile at the sheaf of photocopies and cuttings clipped in precise order. The top page, beautifully printed in Renaissance Italian, was from Vespasiano da Bisticci's *Vite d'uomini illustri del secolo XV*. The translation followed. Light laughter filled the room as the murderer read the familiar text. Who would ever believe that a twentieth-century assassination had been conceived five hundred years before?

It was this same Pope Alexander who caused the celebrated Augsburg goldsmith, Georg Schongauer, to fashion a chalice of impious design and most unholy purpose. The stem of this costly, gold and enamel goblet was formed by three interlocked female forms, their feet resting – appropriately – on

1

a circle of writhing serpents which formed the vessel's foot or pedestal. Cunningly concealed within the elaborate carving was a mechanism which, when activated, released an instant poison into the bowl from the chalice's hollow stem.

Ever on the watch for treason among those closest to him, it was the pope's established custom to strike first and upon the slightest suspicion of disaffection. In the autumn of 1496 it was reported by his spies that three cardinals – della Chiesa, Montadini and Petrucci – were plotting against him. Alexander summoned them to his chambers and confronted them with their alleged crimes. They vigorously denied proceeding against his holiness in word or deed and on their knees besought some token of his favour. Laughing, Alexander bade them rise. 'I am glad these stories are nothing more than malicious rumour,' he said. 'Come let us drink to our continued friendship.' He had the chalice brought which I have described. A servant filled it with wine and his holiness drank deeply from it. He then passed it to the others who were present. Each, in turn, knowing the pope's reputation but thinking no ill could befall them since they had seen his holiness taste the wine, followed his example. Besides the cardinals, the pope's sons, Giovanni and Cesare, also drank from the cup. Within minutes della Chiesa, Montadini and Petrucci were seized with violent pains and, falling to the ground, died in great agonies. The physicians who were summoned to examine the bodies decreed that the cardinals had been poisoned but as none of the Borgias was in any way harmed they were unable to say how the fatal drafts had been administered.

Nor has anyone ever been able to resolve this problem.

The murderer luxuriated in the thought of a crime maturing for half a millennium. Waiting, like a great vintage, for a palate refined enough to appreciate its mellowness and subtlety. Waiting for the precise moment. Turning the collected leaves the murderer found a report from the *Daily Telegraph* of 21 October 1992.

Santori family in court uproar

Screams of 'I'll kill them' rang from the public gallery of Court Three at the Old Bailey yesterday afternoon. Several people had to be manhandled, still shouting, from the chamber before Mr Justice Grandisson could complete the sentencing of Gregor Santori, found guilty of criminal fraud. The accused seemed unmoved by the disturbance. He stood erect but frail as the judge ordered him to spend four years in prison.

The tone of high drama which has marked the seven months of this trial continued to its very end. In the early stages of the proceedings the jury and public were baffled by the spectacle of rival experts, put up by the defence and the prosecution, slanging each other from the witness box. Then, in July, Santori (51) collapsed in court and had to be rushed to hospital with a minor heart attack. That was followed by a strong plea from the defendant's family for the case to be dropped. The *Telegraph* took a lead in condemning Judge Grandisson's decision to continue wasting taxpayers' money in the pursuit of a sick man whose only alleged crime lay in persuading very rich collectors that the products of his own acknowledged genius were the works of long-dead masters.

When the trial was resumed in October it soon became known as the 'Borgia Chalice Affair'. The prosecution sought to convince the jury that Santori had faked a five-hundred-year-old 'death cup', reputedly made for the notorious Rodrigo Borgia, Pope Alexander VI. Santori produced a string of specialist scholars to support his claim that the magnificent, jewel-studded goblet, the centrepiece of many sinister poisoning legends, was genuine. But the jury accepted the evidence of a team of leading international experts assembled by the prosecution. Even so, it took the eight men and four women two-and-a-half days to reach their verdict.

Yesterday's public-gallery rumpus was caused by Santori's son Tristram (26) and daughter Guinevere (23), who have stood by their father throughout the proceedings, organizing a petition and mounting pavement demonstrations outside the court. The family's lawyer made it clear that he would be appealing against the sentence. Ms Santori wiped tears from her eyes as she confessed to media reporters her fears that her father would not survive more than a few weeks in prison. Asked whom her courtroom threats were addressed to she replied 'So-called experts' before being hustled into a cab by her brother.

What a remarkable talent Gregor Santori had possessed.

And how the art establishment had loathed him. Hypocrites! Predictable, closed-minded hypocrites! But the murderer had every reason to be grateful to the spokespersons of the artworld. It was their protective, ghetto mentality that had created the right atmosphere for a criminal triumph. Oh, their delicious self-righteousness! How well it was expressed in *Apollo*'s editorial of August 1993.

Private Grief, Public Concern

The death, in prison, of Gregor Santori is a tragedy for his family and for his wide circle of friends. It is not an eventuality that even his most ardent opponents would have envisaged or desired. We extend our deepest sympathy to all who mourn the passing of a fine craftsman, a dedicated scholar and a warm, ebullient human being.

Yet, let there be no crocodile tears. Eight months ago, Dr Julia Devaraux, Director of the Kurtheim Institute, and Mort Bronsky, of New York's Bronsky-Stein Gallery, made a cogent case in this magazine for labelling as a fake the so-called 'Borgia Chalice'. They concluded their article with these words:

'What should, in truth, be called the Santori Chalice is a masterpiece in the traditional sense of that word. In this single, virtuoso item Gregor Santori stakes an irrefutable claim to be ranked with the very best contemporary goldsmiths. That is not at issue. Nor, sadly, is it the point.

'In the world of private and institutional collectors, authenticity counts for more than genius. A secure attribution may increase the market value of a painting, a sculpture or a Renaissance chalice by a factor of ten or even more. That fact will always tempt owners, dealers, 'improvers' and downright fakers to manufacture provenance, to forge signatures or, as in this case, to fabricate artifacts. Every collector must take CAVEAT EMPTOR for his banner device but he is also entitled to expect the protection of the law. It is sad to see a man of Gregor Santori's skill and knowledge serving a prison sentence but the judgement was just and may deflect others from the paths of deception.'

The media has made much of Santori's constant insistence that the Borgia Chalice and other items in which he traded over the years were all genuine. It is a story that is destined to run and run and this month's sad news will not put an end to it. Authentication is a hazardous business and experts do make mistakes. There is not a major museum which does not have in its vaults objects now consigned to embarrassed obscurity which were once acknowledged by leading academics as respectable masterworks of impeccable provenance.

However, we must not allow sympathy for Mr Santori's family or indignation with the judicial system to cloud our judgement. The balance of specialist opinion about various items sold by Gregor Santori is clear, and potential purchasers of artworks deserve safeguards no less than buyers of second-hand cars and insurance policies.

The murderer flipped through the pages. Documentation

of a multiple assassination: method, timing, accomplices. The murderer laughed aloud. Innocent, unsuspecting accomplices! They had even posted advance notice of the crime. Yes, here it was in *Grinling's Monthly Review* of August, 1994.

The gold and enamel cup with cast stem and chased rim shown opposite must be one of the most frequently photographed examples of the goldsmith's art. The celebrated, or notorious, Borgia Chalice is the best known item of the Santori Collection which will be auctioned at our New Bond Street rooms on 29 September. This item was at the centre of the controversy which put a sad end to Gregor Santori's remarkable multifaceted career as goldsmith, collector and dealer in Renaissance and sixteenth-century silverware, bronzes and jewellery. Also included in the sale of 163 lots is the Shrewsbury Ewer, dating from c.1590 and carrying an estimate of £40,000–£60,000 ($64,000–$96,000). Among the items from the late Mr Santori's own workshop are several pieces of tableware inspired by sixteenth-century Florentine designs and three acknowledged copies of bronzes by Ghiberti and Riccio.

The controversy over the genuineness of the Borgia Chalice did not end with the court case. Though Grinling's are content to accept majority expert opinion that it is an extremely well-crafted piece in the German Renaissance style, further study and the application of new verification techniques may yet suggest otherwise. Whether this remarkable cup is the one in which Pope Alexander VI served poison to his unsuspecting guests or a modern masterpiece which caused one of this century's most controversial fraud cases, it will certainly attract considerable international interest.

The murderer sat back, eyes closed. It had all fallen into place so easily and been carried into effect so smoothly. Inevitable – that was the word. It described all art. A masterpiece of painting or music, even a Renaissance chalice – they seemed 'right' because one could not imagine them any other way. Every line, shade, nuance was in its proper place – genius and industry concealed by inevitability. That was why the Michaelmas Massacre was recognized, and always would be recognized as a work of art.

I

DEATH IN THE CUP

It is necessary for a prince, wishing to maintain himself, to know how not to be good, and to use this – or not use this – according to necessity.

Niccolò Machiavelli, *The Prince*

CHAPTER 1

Catherine Lacy stepped quickly across the pavement and stationed herself under the purple awning of Grinling's rooms while her husband paid the taxi driver. The rain which had been on and off all morning was in a very emphatic 'on' phase and she did not want any of it to spatter her black woollen suit. Its tailored lines emphasized her slender figure and Catherine noted the appreciative glances of a couple of men going into the auctioneers. Nice to know that she could still turn heads even though the big four zero was looming. Tim joined her, shaking droplets of water from his thick black hair, and they went up the steps into Grinling's wide foyer.

'Crowded,' he observed.

The spacious vestibule was dotted with little groups of people, several of whom the Lacys recognized. There was a cluster, two or three deep, around the counter where the catalogues were sold. Still more formed a reverse waterfall up the impressive staircase leading to the first-floor galleries.

'I guess we should have gotten here earlier.' Catherine's New England drawl had not been softened by eleven years' residence in Britain.

Tim glanced up at the famous Blitz Clock on the wall above the racks of recent sale catalogues. In 1940 it had been carried, still ticking, from the wreckage of the

11

auctioneers' original premises near the river and had been installed here when Grinling's relocated after the war, still bearing like a veteran's scar the wide gash across its enamel face that it had received in the bombing. Nine forty-three it proclaimed, defying contradiction.

Tim checked his watch against it. 'Quarter of an hour to go yet. We obviously underestimated the pulling power of the Santori legend.'

'I'll bet most of them are sightseers, not serious buyers.'

'Tim, Catherine! Great to see you!' The man who came up behind them and clasped their shoulders in a heavy embrace was large, ebullient and American. 'I didn't expect to see you here. Have you started investing the Lacy millions in Renaissance silver? If so, this is not the place to start. Prices will be going through the roof today.'

Tim evaded the question. 'Mort Bronsky!' He allowed his hand to be crushed by the New York dealer. 'We should be asking what *you're* doing here. It was partly your evidence that put Santori away. I can't believe you've come to gloat over the break up of his collection.'

'Hell no! I never wanted to see poor old Gregor sent down. I was gobsmacked when that judge handed out a custodial sentence. It really wasn't necessary.' Bronsky's affable smile faded to a concerned frown as the three of them moved towards the staircase and began to climb.

Catherine glanced sideways at her fellow country-man. She was never quite sure about the over-friendly Mort Bronsky. Somehow, his hail-fellow-well-met manner seemed too good to be true. 'Don't you think some people might regard your presence here as . . . well . . .'

'Bad form?' Mort laughed. 'Cathy, you get more

English every time I see you. But yes, I guess I'll probably merit a few inches in tomorrow's gossip columns. I certainly thought long and hard about coming. But they were very pressing and London always gives me a buzz . . .'

'They?'

'Grinling's, Tim. Very insistent they were. They want me to take part . . .' He came to a sudden halt on the top step. 'Sorry, guys, I'm going to have to take five. I'll catch up with you later.' The burly American turned and bumped his way back to ground level through the ascending throng.

Catherine looked at her husband with raised eyebrows. Tim grinned. He nodded in the direction of a small man standing in the doorway of the main gallery inspecting a full-sized bronze figure of Neptune and referring through rimless spectacles to his catalogue. 'There's the reason.'

Catherine studied the balding figure in immaculately cut suit and bow-tie. 'Who he?'

'Heinrich Segar – German academic; leading expert on Renaissance sculpture.'

'OK, I know the name, of course. I've even browsed through one of his books. Wasn't he another of the prosecution witnesses against Santori?'

'That's right. This seems to be quite an old boys' reunion. Except that Segar and Bronsky hate each other's guts.'

'Hence Mort's hasty retreat?'

'Right.'

'So what's the problem – professional jealousy?'

'Partly. They both make a lot of money out of advising top galleries and museums. That makes them rivals and they seldom seem to agree. If Mort says a piece is phoney the owner only has to wheel in Segar for the item in question to be given a clean bill of health – and vice versa.'

'But they both declared the Borgia Chalice a fake.'

'That's right. That went a long way towards swaying opinion in the trade generally and, presumably, the jury. People said, "If Bronsky and Segar both say the chalice is wrong, it must be wrong." He glanced towards the commissions desk at one side of the upper foyer. There was a short queue of people leaving bids or registering themselves as potential buyers. 'I must just go and sign on, darling. Do you mind going ahead and grabbing a couple of seats?'

'If I can.' She gazed into Gallery One – the Long Room – with its purple walls, hung today with nineteenth-century watercolours awaiting a sale the following week. The thirty or so rows of folding chairs were filling up rapidly.

Catherine squeezed through the throng in the doorway and walked towards the dais at the far end. She found a couple of seats at the edge of the fifth row but she did not sit immediately. Instead she dropped a newspaper and a catalogue on the chairs and gazed round, savouring the atmosphere.

She loved sale rooms. Whether in a plush London gallery like Grinling's or a provincial auctioneer's draughty warehouse, the same elements were always present – the buzz of expectancy; the nonchalant dealers feigning bored indifference; the rivalries masquerading as camaraderie; the bonhomie from the rostrum; the thrill as nodded bids bounced back and forth, pushing a lot well beyond its estimate; the breath-holding silence giving way to excited chatter as soon as the gavel fell; the eccentric characters these pieces of impromptu theatre always attracted; the chance to talk shop with friends and acquaintances who shared an appreciation of beauty and craftsmanship.

Yet today's event was much more exciting than even a major West End sale. The trials and tribulations of Gregor Santori had seldom been out of the media for the past two years and more. The long-running saga had the elements that news editors, feature writers and presenters of late-night arts programmes alike drooled over – a flamboyant central character well-known for wealth, extravagant parties and love affairs, a court case that had never lacked drama, a fraud scandal that did not cease to be controversial even after the jury's verdict had been given, a fabulous collection of early silver and jewellery – one of the best in private hands – and, at the heart of all the arguments and speculation, the Borgia Chalice, an object with a mystery and a romantic legend of its own. No wonder the reporters were here in force.

Looking around, Catherine noted two TV crews and recognized three broadsheet arts correspondents. A wiry little man was on the dais arguing with one of the Grinling's people about positioning his Walkman on the auctioneer's desk.

Catherine was suddenly aware of a commotion behind her. Both TV cameramen were focusing on something at the back of the room. In company with several others, Catherine turned.

The attraction was a large woman in her forties, heavily made-up and enveloped in a sack of wafting silk. She was attended – that was the only word – by an entourage of hangers-on who clustered round her as she progressed down the room greeting and being greeted, like royalty at a levee. Julia Devaraux was admired by many, loathed by many more but ignored by no one – her publicity machine saw to that. She was a woman of undeniable intellectual attainment with a string of degrees to prove it but she had early made the decision that academia presented too small a stage for her talents and had deliberately turned herself into a media celebrity. This she achieved by being outspoken, brash and downright insulting on a variety of issues from trends in modern art to women's rights, vegetarianism and nursery education. Currently she was writing a bitchy column for one of the upmarket weekend magazines and hosting a Sunday afternoon antiques programme, in addition to her day job as Director of the Kurtheim Institute of Art and Craft, Birmingham's scaled-down version of the V and A.

Catherine turned away quickly, grabbed up the catalogue and pretended to study it closely. She was too late.

'Catherine Lacy? Yes it *is* you. I knew it; I never forget a hair-do.' Julia's powerful contralto had a penetrating quality that might have been the envy of a La Scala diva. She leaned forward across three seated elderly ladies to grasp Catherine's hand.

'Hello, Julia, how nice . . .'

'What are you showing in darkest Wiltshire this season? It's high time I came down and did another piece on your gallery.' The *femme formidable* turned to declaim to the world in general. 'This little woman has one of the best eyes for talent in the business. She buries herself deep in the country but some of her shows are simply stunning and she finds such promising new material. Call my secretary, Catherine. We'll fix a meeting and discuss my visit.' The last words were flung over La Devaraux's shoulder as the cavalcade moved on.

Catherine sat down quickly, her cheeks burning. 'Female canine,' she muttered under her breath. She knew she was trapped. Like the elephant – an apt simile – Julia did not forget. If her office did not receive a call within a week, her secretary would be in touch with Farrans Court, pen poised over Dr Devaraux's engagement diary. That meant that Catherine would have to organize a lavish but health-sensitive lunch and subject her exhibiting artists to a couple of hours of instant evaluation and bombastically delivered judgement. The trouble was it would be very good for the gallery, which right now needed all the publicity it could get.

Back in the mid-eighties, before Thatcher boom had given way to Thatcher bust, it had seemed a wonderful idea for she and Tim to run separate businesses from the idyllic setting of a period residence in mid-Wiltshire. Catherine had turned the principal rooms of the late medieval manor house at Little Farrans into a gallery and arts centre where painters and sculptors – especially newcomers – could not only display their works but also meet with dealers, academics, collectors, critics, media reporters, school and college groups and the general public. The idea had worked well. Several artists who had made their debuts at Farrans Court had gone on to become well established and highly collectable. The house was now marked out as a favourite venue for exhibitions, lectures and seminars. The Farrans Festival, started three years ago, was already an important part of the region's social calendar. But Catherine had discovered that while laurels fade and fashion is as substantial as summer clouds, the expenses of running a business and maintaining a five-hundred-year-old mini-mansion were very solid, very permanent realities. One always had to be dreaming up new ideas to bring the punters in and not for a single day could one afford to neglect publicity. Catherine sighed. And that involved being nice to the Julia Devarauxs of this world.

Meanwhile, Tim had joined the knot of people registering their intention to bid. As he did so, a mid-thirtyish woman came through a doorway marked 'Private' and smiled as she recognized him.

'Tim?' Her eyebrows rose in genuine surprise. 'Surely you haven't come to buy.'

He laughed. 'Yes and no, Corinne.'

'And what's that supposed to mean?' She offered her cheek.

Tim appreciated the cool fragrance of her perfume as he leaned forward to kiss her. It complemented the image of efficient femininity Corinne Noble presented to the world. It was no mask. When she had arrived from Christie's two years before she had been the youngest department head Grinling's had ever appointed but her mix of adventurousness and expertise had quickly paid off in the Medieval and Renaissance European Paintings department. At a time when rival houses were struggling in a depressed market, Corinne had made some remarkable coups, substantially increasing the company's turnover and profit.

Tim lowered his voice. 'It means yes I'm buying – or trying to buy – and no I'm not buying for myself.' Before she could press him for further details, he went on. 'Anyway what are you doing here? Shouldn't you be beavering away upstairs among the anonymous Gothic masters?'

Corinne grinned and shook her close-cropped auburn hair. 'Everyone in the building's trying to look in at the Long Room. There promises to be high drama.'

'You're expecting ferocious bidding?'

'Not just that.' She gave him a broad wink.

'Stop being mysterious. What do you mean?'

'Aha! W and S, as my grandmother used to say.'

'Your grandmother must have been a very infuriating woman.'

Corinne laughed. 'She was. They say I take after her.'

At that moment the queue moved on and a bright young junior looked up from her papers. 'May I have your name, please, sir?'

Corinne intervened. 'Jenny, this is Mr Tim Lacy of Lacy Security. His credit is excellent and even if it weren't we couldn't turn away his business. These entire premises are guarded by gadgetry he's installed. If we upset him he may break in at dead of night and clean us out completely. Isn't that so, Tim?'

Jenny giggled. She handed Tim a paddle – a plastic board shaped like a small tennis racquet – and noted its number against the name she had just added to her list. 'That's fine then, Mr Lacy. No. 237.'

As they walked back towards the gallery, Corinne slipped her arm through his. 'Is Catherine with you?' she asked nonchalantly.

'Yes, so you'd better behave yourself.'

'As if I wouldn't.'

They paused in the doorway of the Long Room and eased their way through the crowd of dealers who preferred to stand at the back of the gallery where they could keep an eye on rival bidders; where they could be seen from the rostrum but not be watched by the seated customers.

They stopped for a moment, scanning the rows of well-filled seats. Tim said, 'Talking of security . . .'

Corinne feigned wide-eyed innocence. 'Were we?'

'Talking of security, what's happening about the new warehouse? We don't seem to have heard anything.'

Corinne looked away quickly. 'Isn't that Catherine along there, on the right?' She moved forward.

Tim laid a restraining hand on her shoulder. 'Have I said something embarrassing?'

'No . . . of course not.' Her self-assurance gauge took a sharp dip. 'It's just that . . . I'm sure you'll be receiving a letter very soon.'

Tim increased the pressure on her shoulder. 'Saying what?'

'Tim, these are board decisions, you know that. Personal feelings don't enter into it.'

'What you're trying to tell me – or, rather, what you're trying not to tell me is that Lacy Security is being cold-shouldered.'

She turned towards him, frowning, high colour suffusing her cheeks. 'Some of the top brass . . . Well, they've heard that Lacy Security's been having some problems and anyway,' she rushed on before Tim could react, 'they think we need something more than conventional security systems. You know the rate at which specialized art theft is increasing.'

'That's the first time I've heard Lacy systems called conventional.'

'Tim, it's no longer just a question of guarding priceless objects. Today's syndicates are violent and ruthless. Look at the Frankfurt raid last month: two museum staff killed. And a couple of weeks before that there was that ghastly affair in Barcelona: a guard and a member of the public gunned down in broad daylight.'

Tim removed his hand from her shoulder. He sighed. 'I see. We're talking thug patrols; ex-cons ready to turn any suspected break-in into a private massacre. Well, it's pretty obvious who's been feeding these ideas to your bosses. Saul Druckmann.'

Corinne shrugged. 'These decisions have nothing to do with me, Tim. Oh, look, it is Catherine. She's spotted us.' She waved and set off purposefully down the gangway.

Tim followed. As Corinne and Catherine greeted each other and shuffled chairs around so that the three of them could sit together he forced a smile to cover the anxiety that was eroding his normal relaxed self-confidence. He kept up his corner of the light-hearted conversation but his mind was elsewhere.

He had invested everything in Lacy Security. Not just money – everything. He had given up an army career in which he had been tipped for rapid promotion. He had been joined by a handful of colleagues who believed in his abilities, vision and enthusiasm. He had established a company which was small, flexible and fully conversant with rapidly changing technology. He had targeted the specialist world of public and private fine art and antiques collections. Within five years Lacy Security enjoyed an international reputation and a share of the market out of proportion to its size. He had bought Farrans Court, moved his office there from London and brought his new wife there. A couple of years previously the Lacys had taken on a new partner. Emma Kerr had joined the team with enthusiasm and put all her resources into Lacy Enterprises, the company controlling both sides of the business. All that he had built up, all the people that he cared most about – his wife and two young sons, his colleagues and their families – all were dependent on the success of the business, dependent ultimately on him. Up till now he had not let them down. But now . . .

Catherine squeezed his hand. 'Hey, snap out of it. We're here to gamble recklessly with someone else's money. Let's enjoy it.'

At two minutes to ten, Adrian Deventer, Grinling's M.D., personally took charge of proceedings. Under his expert directions the sale moved briskly. Mort Bronsky's prophecy was very quickly fulfilled: prices realized on most lots were well above the auctioneer's estimates. The computerized display screen above the rostrum was a constant flicker of changing prices enumerated in pounds, dollars, deutschmarks and yen.

'And now we come to lot 93, ladies and gentlemen.' A more concentrated stillness filled the room as Deventer's emotionless voice announced: 'Gold and enamel cup, known as the Borgia Chalice, in the style of the Augsburg Renaissance goldsmith, Georg Schongauer.'

Several cameras flashed and all eyes focused on the gleaming piece of precious metal as the aproned attendant removed the cup from a blue velvet bag and held it aloft.

There was a pause and the rostrum microphone picked up the sound of shuffled papers. Deventer smiled lightly at his audience. 'At this stage of the proceedings I am requested to read a short statement from the will of the late Mr Gregor Santori.' He cleared his throat. 'I quote: "The Borgia Chalice has unfortunately given rise to feelings of considerable bitterness. It is not my wish that these emotions should continue. I therefore stipulate that the chalice shall only be sold after a public act of reconciliation between my children and those critics who have most prominently cast doubt upon its authenticity."' The auctioneer paused briefly to allow the outburst of gasps and surprised murmuring to subside. '"I should like my son and daughter to drink wine from the Borgia Chalice with Mr Mort Bronsky, Dr Julia Devaraux, Herr Doktor Heinrich Segar and Monsieur Patrice Saint-Yves as a sign that all animosity between them is at an end." That concludes the relevant extract from Mr Santori's will. I am delighted to say that all those persons named by Mr Santori have agreed to take part in the little ceremony

22

he stipulated. Would they please, now, be kind enough to step forward?'

There was an uproar of excited conversation, heightened by a rush of photographers and TV cameramen to the space immediately in front of the auctioneer's desk.

Tim shook his head. 'Typical Gregor – a showman to the end.'

Corinne smiled. 'No, Tim, I think there's more to it than that.'

'What do you mean?'

'I've been doing a lot of thinking since we knew about this charade. According to the legend, Rodrigo and his sons drank from the chalice with some of their enemies – with fatal consequences for the latter but, mysteriously, not for the Borgias.'

Catherine looked puzzled. 'So this is a kind of re-enactment . . . But why?'

'I reckon it's a sort of challenge. These experts have all gone on record as stating that the Borgia Chalice is a fake. Santori insisted, right to the end, that it was the genuine article. So, now, from beyond the grave he's saying to them, "OK, put your life where your mouth is." If the cup is a phoney they have nothing to fear . . .'

Tim grimaced. 'But if it isn't they'll all drop down dead? Is that what you're suggesting?'

'Don't be silly, Tim!' Corinne laughed. 'Since the chalice has been here we've had it gone over by goldsmiths, metallurgists, locksmiths, antiquarians, spectro-analysts – every kind of specialist we could think of. There is no hidden mechanism in that little beauty; no way some other substance could be introduced to the wine. No, it's just Gregor's outrageous way of having the last laugh: he challenges his detractors; they have to accept; a refusal would be tantamount to an admission that they could be wrong; so they come and drink from the famous poisoned chalice; nothing happens. Of course nothing can happen – but I'll bet right at this moment their palms are sweating.'

Deventer had descended from his dais and was expertly opening a bottle of vintage Krug. He deftly caught the effervescent overflow in a crisp napkin and poured wine into the chalice held by his clerk. The four experts and the two Santoris stood in an embarrassed semi-circle. Deventer handed the cup to Guinevere.

Tim watched intently as the strong-featured young woman shook out her magnificent, shoulder-length hair, which had the colour and patina of ancient bronze. Hers was a forceful, Pre-Raphaelite kind of beauty, carried with a defiant, 'don't mess with me' air. If there was anything queenly about her it was more in the mould of Boudicca than Guinevere. She tilted the cup and took a long draft of the champagne. The glance she gave to Mort Bronsky as she passed the chalice on certainly did not speak of forgiveness.

The gleaming goblet travelled along the line – from Bronsky to Julia Devaraux to the French dealer with an exuberant sweep of fair hair, whom Tim had never met, to Segar, keeping as much distance as possible between himself and the American. Finally, Tristram Santori drained the cup. Tim looked with interest at the slim, dark young man who also possessed the strong family features – long, straight nose, wide-set dark eyes and slightly protruding chin. He had never met Gregor's children, although he had, four years before, spent some time at the craftsman's house and workshop in Hampstead, installing a new security system. Tristram and Guinevere had elected to return to their father's native country. They shared a flat in Florence where the girl did freelance translation work for publishers and her brother was with a firm of lawyers and had – or so Tim dimly seemed to recall – political ambitions. That was all he knew about them.

The little ceremony was over. Its participants dispersed. The anticlimax was complete – no one frothed at the mouth or fell to the floor in squirming agony. Someone near the front began a tentative clapping which might have been intended to be ironical but which was gradually taken up by the rest of the audience. Then, with Deventer back in his chair, the serious business of buying and selling continued. Whether true or fake the Borgia Chalice was about to find a new owner.

Giorgio Schiavoni was a light sleeper. In his business that was an asset. A boatman needed his wits about him all hours of the day and night. Thieves were becoming notoriously bold, even in Rome. Especially in Rome. It was not uncommon for villains to cut a mooring rope at dead of night and make off with vessel, cargo and all a man's livelihood. That was why, on the night of 14–15 June, 1497, Giorgio slept on his boat, with fore and aft cables holding her in the Tiber's current three clear metres out from the bank between Santa Maria Nuova and the Ponte Sant' Angelo. He lay rolled in his cloak on the small deck space in the bow, one hand tucked into his belt at the point where the sheathed dagger was fastened. For an hour or more after sunset he lay looking up at the stars, smelling the mingled malodours of the summer city, listening to the occasional clatter of horses on the bridge and the laughter of revellers on their way to and from the whore-houses. More than once he cursed his luck that he was not among them; that he was stuck here with his valuable load of cedar brought up from Ostia because a dithering client could not make up his mind about unloading. At last he drifted into sleep.

It was sixth sense rather than any actual sound that woke him. Body rigid and totally alert, Giorgio strained eyes, nose and ears. He knew instantly from the chill in the air and the silence of the city that it was the last hour of darkness. He grasped his knife, rolled noiselessly on to his side, then knelt till he could see over the gunwale. No movement on the bank. Mooring lines still taught. He scanned the river side. Nothing disturbed the Tiber's turgid surface. He was just about to cocoon himself again in his cloak's woollen warmth when a nearby shadow became divided, then divided again. Two men had emerged from the blackness of San Girolamo's Hospital. From the way they moved it was obvious that their activities were clandestine. They peered up and down the bank making sure that they were not observed. Giorgio kept very still. One of the men turned and waved an arm. From behind the narrow alley behind him a man emerged on a horse, a white horse. He was attended by two foot-servants who were steadying something which lay across his mount behind him. He rode it to the water's edge, down the slope the Roman scavengers used when they emptied the refuse carts. He turned it around and two of his companions lifted from the animal's crupper the burden which hung limply down each side. One either end of the heavy object, they swung it backwards and forwards twice. The third time they let go and it arched with a thick splash into the water.

The horseman raised himself in the stirrups to scan the river. 'Is it well in the middle?'

Giorgio heard one of the attendants reply. 'Oh, yes, sir.'

'There's something out there, floating. It must be his cloak. Get rid of it.'

Giorgio watched the four footmen gather stones and fling them at an object outside his field of vision. After a couple of minutes they appeared satisfied with their labours.

'That's it, sir.'

'Good.' The rider wheeled about and re-entered the blackness of the sleeping streets, followed by his companions.

Giorgio yawned. Some other poor devil caught up in a gambling row or a disagreement over a woman. He settled down to sleep away what was left of the night. Gentlemen's vendettas were none of his business.

It was only that evening, after the timber was off-loaded and he was spending part of his earnings in a waterfront tavern that he changed his mind. He overheard two Vatican clerks excitedly discussing the latest news. Pope Alexander's second son, the Duke of Gandia, was missing. His horse had been recovered from a street near the Cardinal of Parma's palace with a cut stirrup leather and his body servant had been found stabbed to death in the Piazza della Guidecca. That was the moment that Giorgio realized that he had information worth several ducats.

Bidding for the Borgia Chalice began at £300,000 and moved swiftly. Not until the half-million mark had been passed did the pace begin to falter. Some of Grinling's staff were receiving telephone instructions from foreign clients and it was one of these unseen potential buyers who was making most of the running.

'At five hundred and sixty thousand.' Deventer gazed across the hushed audience. 'It's against you all in the room. Have you all done at five hundred and sixty thousand?'

Slowly Tim lifted his paddle and held it aloft.

'Five hundred and seventy.' Deventer turned towards the telephone positions and received a signal from one of his colleagues. 'Five hundred and eighty thousand.' He looked at Tim. Tim nodded. 'Five hundred and ninety.' Again the enquiring glance towards the blonde woman speaking into her handset. All eyes were fixed upon her as she hesitated, awaiting instructions. She smiled and bobbed her head. 'Six hundred thousand, then, on the telephone. Are there any more bids?' He caught Tim's almost imperceptible movement. 'Six ten.' This time his fair-haired colleague waited several seconds before raising the price another notch. 'Six twenty. At six hundred and twenty thousand pounds. Have you all . . . six hundred and thirty.' He had caught Tim's gesture. 'At six hundred and thirty thousand pounds in the room. Against you on the phone.' This time the Grinling's woman shook her head. Seconds later Deventer crashed his gavel down and announced, 'Two hundred and thirty-seven.' A roar of conversation rolled across the room and Tim found himself gazing into a TV camera lens.

'You dark horse!' Corinne smiled at Tim with half-closed eyes. 'So, who's your principal?'

Suddenly she wasn't the only one asking questions. A jostling, elbowing group of reporters surrounded the Lacys. 'May we have your name, please?' 'Are you buying for yourself?' 'Did you expect to have to pay so much?' 'How much higher would you have gone?' 'Will the Borgia Chalice be put on display somewhere?'

Corinne grabbed Tim and Catherine by the arms. 'This way!' she shouted over the hubbub.

She led Tim and Catherine to a door behind the rostrum. She opened it and pushed them through, hurried them along narrow corridors to a staff lift. Minutes later in her top-floor office she perched herself against her desk. 'Phew! That's quite enough excitement for one day. So what's it all about? Is this a new departure for Lacy Enterprises?'

'There's no big mystery.' Tim smiled broadly. 'I'm just doing a favour for a friend who prefers to avoid the limelight.'

Corinne turned to Catherine. 'Were you in on this?'

'Sure thing – and boy was it ever fun!'

'Oh well, I know better than to press you for your client's name.'

'Press away,' Tim said. 'It won't do you any good.' He looked at his watch. 'I'm going to have to cut and run.'

'Not collecting your loot?'

'I'll leave that to Catherine. The sooner we get the chalice home and locked in the safe the happier I shall be.'

'Can't you even stay for the lunch?' Corinne looked genuinely disappointed.

'Lunch?'

Corinne explained. 'Just a little affair. We usually hold them after important sales. This is just a thank you to the Santoris and to some of the major buyers.'

'Well, I'm afraid you'll have to make do with the cleverest and most beautiful partner of Lacy Enterprises. I have an important meeting lined up.'

Corinne held up a hand. 'Don't rush just yet. We must

mark the occasion somehow. I've had a thought.' She went over to the outer office and had a quick word with her secretary. The girl hurried away along the corridor. When she returned, two minutes later, she was carrying a Krug champagne bottle.

Corinne held it up to the light. 'Just as I thought; they hardly drank half of it. If we hadn't rescued it the porters would have finished it off. Such a waste!' She found wine glasses in a filing cabinet and poured the sparkling liquid. As she handed the Lacys their champagne, she said, 'Well, I suppose the toast has to be: the Borgia Chalice and its mysterious new owner.'

They drank the excellent wine. Then Tim checked his watch again. He buttoned his overcoat. 'And now I'm afraid I really must be going.'

He gave his wife a quick hug. 'See you later, darling. Careful how you go with your expensive luggage. Good to see you, Corinne.' He flashed a quick smile, opened the door and strode briskly along the corridor.

Outside it was raining again and Tim had to wait a couple of minutes for an empty cab. As soon as he was settled inside he took out his mobile phone and patched in a number.

'Hello?' A cautious female voice. In the background Tim heard the monotonous beat of pop music.

'Good afternoon. I'd like to speak to Wes, please.'

'I'm afraid the boys are rehearsing right now. Could you call back . . .'

'Tell him it's Tim Lacy.'

'Oh, Tim, hi! He's been expecting you.' The voice was suddenly friendly. 'Hang on, I'll fetch him.'

After a short pause the distant drums and guitars jangled into silence.

'Hi there, man! Where you been?' Tim held the phone

away from his ear as the pop star's rich, enthusiastic bass boomed out. 'I been near pissing myself waiting on your call. Did you get it?'

'Yes, Wes, I got it.'

The shriek from the other end of the line must have been heard by pedestrians scurrying, heads down, against the near-horizontal rain. 'Fantastic! Wait till I tell the boys.'

'It was six hundred and thirty thousand.'

'Shit, I don't care about the price. I just want that beauty for my collection. Hang on there a second, Tim.'

Tim heard Wes Cherry relay the news to the other members of the band. He heard the hoots and cheers with which they received it. Then the black man was back on the phone. 'OK man. That's great, really great. I'll fly down first thing tomorrow to pick it up. You didn't split to the media, did you?'

'No, of course not.'

'Great! We want the mystery to build up. We're planning to centre the publicity for our next album on it. We're calling it *Poison*. What do you think?'

'Great,' Tim said with as much enthusiasm as he could muster.

'See you tomorrow, man. Look after my golden baby till then.' He gave another wordless scream before the line went dead.

Tim exhaled slowly. One satisfied customer. What was more important, a very healthy slice of commission – five per cent of six hundred and thirty grand. That should keep the bank manager happy for another month.

'Now for the less pleasant phone call,' he thought, as he pressed more numbers on the handset.

'Artguard. Mr Druckmann's office.' A very different kind of secretarial voice – hard and serrated.

31

'This is Tim Lacy. Put me through to Mr Druckmann, please.'

'I'm sorry, Mr Lacy, Mr Druckmann is in a board meeting. He won't be free . . .'

'Tell him that I'll be there in ten minutes.' Tim flicked the 'off' switch.

CHAPTER 2

Someone had had the bright idea of standing the Borgia Chalice on a makeshift plinth in the centre of the large circular table. Its broad bowl and slender stem of sinuously interlocking forms were reflected almost perfectly in the polished mahogany. It was flanked suitably by a luxurious escort of silver salvers bearing blinis with caviar, ratatouille-stuffed courgettes, fresh dressed salmon, avocado mousselines, cold cutlets accompanied with a madeira sauce, coulibiaca of sea bass, foie gras, venison croquettes, a variety of salads and with artillery support from a row of ice buckets bearing bottles of Bâtard Montrachet. Catherine eyed the spread approvingly, reflecting that Grinling's did not stint on their hospitality.

About twenty-five people had gathered in the large penthouse boardroom whose wide windows offered views of rain-swept roofs and snail-paced traffic. A dozen small tables lined the circumference and, in accordance with Grinling's tradition, they provided the stations for what was, literally, a movable feast. Guests and senior executives sat in threes and fours while the caterers circulated the dishes, but during the course of the meal everyone moved from table to table.

Catherine enjoyed the luxurious informality. She chatted with several acquaintances and met a couple of interesting fellow guests who had only been names to her before.

33

Her main concern was to stay as far away as possible from Julia Devaraux and, since the self-important woman was always instantly locatable by her large presence and loud voice, that was not difficult. She had just made good her escape from Adrian Deventer who, at close quarters, oozed unctuous insincerity and a Jermyn Street dealer who had bought two exquisite Renaissance bronzes in the sale and was holding forth on market trends, when a slim man wearing a magenta velvet jacket over a lime-green roll-necked jumper stood up and gestured to the empty chair next to him.

'Mrs Lacy, do come and share your triumph with me for a moment.'

'Delighted, Monsieur Saint-Yves.'

The Frenchman smirked coquettishly. 'Patrice, *please*, then I can call you Catherine – such a lovely name.'

'You're very well informed.' Catherine tried to keep the amusement out of her voice as she surveyed the Parisian connoisseur and art critic. Earlier, watching him take part in the little loving-cup ceremony, she had been fascinated by the crest of thick, slightly unruly fair hair that seemed out of place atop the features of a man evidently well into his fifties. She had tried to decide whether or not it was a wig. Now that she could scrutinize it at close quarters, she still was not sure.

Saint-Yves said, 'But you have just attained instant celebrity. Everyone is talking about the mysterious Tim and Catherine Lacy and wondering what they are going to do with the Borgia Chalice.'

'It is beautiful, isn't it?' Catherine diverted the conversation and gazed across at the golden goblet.

'Ah well, that depends.'

'On what, Patrice?'

'On whether you agree with Shakespeare: "Beauty is

truth, truth beauty. That is all ye know on earth and all ye need to know."'

Catherine smiled. 'Keats, as a matter of fact; "Ode on a Grecian Urn".'

The Frenchman made a mock bow. 'You know your English literature very well for a foreigner.'

She returned the compliment. 'You speak the English language very well – for a foreigner.'

He laughed – a sort of high-pitched gurgle. '*Touché*. You see, there are some expressions that are only possible in French.'

'I suppose what you meant about truth and beauty was that you believe the chalice is a fake and that, therefore, it cannot be regarded as beautiful.'

He shrugged good-humouredly. 'It is sufficiently beautiful to you or rather it is to the person for whom you act to pay £630,000 for it.' He looked at her quizzically but continued when he saw that she was not going to take the hint. 'For me it is a fraud, a fake, a sham, a piece of brazen dishonesty.'

'You're absolutely sure about that?'

'I have staked my reputation on it, publicly – and been threatened with annihilation for doing so.'

A waitress came up with a fresh bowl of orange and chicory salad. Saint-Yves helped himself. Catherine, whose plate was still well filled, declined.

She pursued the argument. 'But surely you agree that the chalice is a fine piece of craftsmanship?'

'Exquisite. Worthy of one of the best Renaissance masters.'

'Then surely . . .'

'Surely it doesn't matter who made it or when? Is that what you were going to say?'

Catherine nodded.

'But it matters very much. Art has a moral content. A painting, a sculpture, a golden chalice – whatever the article – it must have its origin in one man's genius. That is what makes it beautiful. Now, the Borgia Chalice is a copy, a pastiche. Santori thought he could play a joke on the art establishment. He read the only description of Pope Alexander's chalice that exists. He studied the four surviving pieces of Schongauer's workmanship. He combined this information with his knowledge of Renaissance craftsmanship and his own undoubted skill, and the result was the Borgia Chalice – a fascinating item but not an original masterwork.'

'But that's only the verdict of a handful of self-authenticating experts, and experts are notorious for disagreeing among themselves. Look at the Vinland Map. Opinion about that has been knocked back and forth like a tennis ball for thirty years. It's been X-rayed and given polarized light microscopy and electron diffraction and just about every test in the book. Yet some historians and scientists still insist it's a fake while Yale University believe they have the genuine article – the first map showing part of the Americas.'

Saint-Yves drained his glass and smiled at her over the rim, though Catherine thought he was struggling to sustain his good humour. 'I can see you don't hold us experts in very high esteem. I am the first to admit that we are not infallible but I hope that you would admit that we are at least a necessary evil. After all, if there were no system for authenticating works of art and antiquities, where would we be?'

'Perhaps we would all have to make up our own minds about the beauty and desirability of objects – and value them accordingly.'

The Frenchman pushed away his empty plate. 'I see you

are determined to deprive me of my humble li...
I wish you success in your avocation, my dear Ca...
and I hope the Borgia Chalice brings pleasure to it...
owner.' He stood up. 'And now, if you will excuse me,
I must deprive myself of your charming company and go
and talk to some of these far less stimulating people.'

Catherine sat alone for a few moments wondering
why it was that the flamboyant Parisian had got under
her skin.

'May we join you?' Her reverie was broken by
Guinevere Santori, her brother and a sallow young man
in faded denim with hair standing out, porcupine-like,
in multi-tinted spikes and wearing a single earring of
geometrical links worked in gold. 'I'm Ginny Santori,'
the handsome young woman said as she sat down. 'This
is Tris and this is Oz Karnham – everyone calls him
"O.K.".'

Catherine was immediately struck by the obvious bond
which existed between these young people. The body
language was not at all demonstrative but it was none the
less powerful for that. 'This must have been something of
an ordeal for you all.'

Tristram looked at her intently for some seconds, as
though weighing the question carefully. 'Actually, it's
been worse for O.K.'

His sister immediately expanded the concise reply. 'It's
the end of the story for Tris and me. The last act in the
grieving process. With the collection gone – especially
that bloody chalice – and an end to all the publicity, we
can finally put everything behind us and start living our
own lives. But for poor O.K. . . .' She laid a hand on her
friend's arm. 'It's been heartbreaking to watch everything
sold off.'

A waiter arrived to clear all the plates. He was followed

immediately by another bearing a tray with coffee, cream, sugar and cups. Automatically, Ginny reached for the jug and began to pour. 'O.K. was Dad's . . . Well, sort of apprentice, I suppose, although there was nothing formal about the arrangement. Dad knew right from the start that Oz was a natural. He's got a feel for precious metal and what can be done with it. So Dad decided to teach him everything he knew about gold and silver – old and new.'

O.K. shook his head. 'I'd never have picked up half what Gregor knew, no matter how hard he learned me.' The young man spoke with a strong East End accent. 'He was brilliant. No one understood metal like him – especially these poncing so-called experts.' He looked around the room with an all-embracing sneer of contempt. He leaned forward to fix Catherine with an imploring stare. 'You know he built up from nothing, don't you? Came over from Italy after the war, studied in the sixties; worked in one of the bigger studios; qualified as a master; registered his mark and started up by himself.'

Catherine nodded. 'Everyone knows the Santori rags-to-riches story.'

O.K. snorted. 'Huh! What "everyone knows" is a million miles away from the facts. They'd have ruined him if they could. They rubbished his designs, pinched his customers, tried to force him out of business . . .'

'Who's "they"?'

The young man leaned back in his chair, his resentment almost choking him. 'This lot. The establishment. The Goldsmiths' Company and their City mates. The critics. Other firms, jealous of his talent, his originality.'

'I see. I hadn't realized. So that was why he decided to specialize in antique silver and gold?'

Tristram explained, more dispassionately than his friend.

'He really loved it. He was fascinated by the ways craftsmen centuries ago had achieved beautiful, intricate effects with comparatively simple tools. He had an absolutely unerring eye for quality. So, over the years he bought and sold very adroitly. Then he discovered that museums and collectors would pay well for copies – extra pieces to make up a *garniture de table*, matching sconces or candelabra, replacements for stolen or damaged items – that sort of thing. That gave him his own niche in the market and he occupied it very successfully.'

'They never forgave him for that,' Ginny added. 'He was the nasty little upstart, the wop who'd beaten them all on their own pitch. They did everything possible to put him down. And in the end they succeeded. Poor Dad.'

'That must have made him very bitter.'

Tris shook his head vigorously. 'Oh, no, Mrs Lacy. Not at all. He regarded it as a game – a game in which he won round after round. He didn't care what people said about him. He just enjoyed his little triumphs. That's why there were all those parties. Every time he had a new acquisition to show off, like the Shrewsbury Ewer, every time he made an important discovery, such as pairing up Lord Buxton's anonymous warrior bronze with the Verrocchio in the Museo Nazionale in Florence, there had to be a dinner party or a big reception. It was like proclaiming his achievement with a fanfare of trumpets.'

Catherine smiled, remembering some of the television profiles and magazine articles that had appeared over the years. 'He was certainly a great self-publicist – right to the end. Did you know he'd organized today's little performance?'

Ginny answered. 'Not until our lawyer showed us the

will. At first we didn't want to go through with it. Then we thought, "What the heck, it's Dad's last photo opportunity," so we agreed.'

'Perhaps it was his way of helping you to put all resentment and bitterness behind you.'

'I guess so.' Ginny picked up the jug. 'More coffee, anyone? We might as well get our money's worth out of Grinling's, considering all the commission they've picked up today.'

Tristram slid his cup across the table. 'I'm afraid we're boring you, Mrs Lacy. We didn't really waylay you to give you a potted biography of our father. What we really wanted to say was . . .'

'Don't believe a word that frog bastard tells you,' O.K. interrupted.

The other man frowned. 'No, that wasn't quite it . . .'

'Yes it is, Tris,' Ginny objected. 'No need to wrap it up in lawyer's doublespeak.'

Catherine intervened. 'Look, you don't have to explain anything.'

'Yes we do,' Tris insisted. 'You bought the Borgia Chalice and you have to know that it is absolutely genuine. My father abhorred fakes. He would never have tried to pass anything off as genuine that he knew to be false. Saint-Yves, on the other hand, is a dedicated liar. He knows, always has known, that the chalice is what it claims to be. But he saw how he could use it to destroy my father. He knew that if he cried "fraud" others would follow. Well, that's all past now. Saint-Yves was one of the ones who killed Gregor Santori and I hope he can live with his conscience. We just want to warn you to take no notice of anything he told you.'

'Thank you.' Catherine looked at the three sombre young faces. 'I'll certainly pass that information on to the new owner. I wish I could tell you who it is but, for the moment . . .'

'That's OK.' Ginny stood up. 'We don't really want to know. Thanks for hearing us out. We've enjoyed meeting you. Say hello to your husband for us. Dad always spoke very highly . . .'

At that moment there was an odd confusion of sounds at the far side of the room. A contralto screech, cascading china, staccato exclamations, and a dull thud like someone dropping a sack of flour.

Everyone turned in that direction. Standing up, Catherine saw the recumbent, silk-draped form of Julia Devaraux attended by a group of anxious figures. The whole tableau resembled a tasteless mimicry of the pietà. How typical, Catherine thought. The wretched woman simply could not bear not being the centre of attention.

Then she felt a hand fix itself on her arm – tight like the bite of a rabid dog. She turned instantly. As she did so the grip loosened. Patrice Saint-Yves stood before her. Swaying. Both hands now clasped to his stomach. His face was red and contorted. His lips were moving but only throaty gasps were emerging. He glared at or through her with unseeing eyes. Then he fell.

Catherine stared down. She froze. Shock momentarily blocked appropriate reaction. One incongruous thought filled her mind. 'So, it *is* a wig.'

When they hauled the Duke of Gandia's body out of the Tiber in a fisherman's net there were a dozen gashes in his chest and abdomen and his throat had been cut. He was fully clothed and tied hand and foot. He still wore his jewelled rings, his gold-hilted dagger and the gems studding his brocade doublet. A purse containing thirty ducats hung from his belt. Whoever had killed the pope's favourite son had not done so for money.

The grief of Alexander VI, Rodrigo Borgia, was terrible to behold. Not that many did behold it. The pope shut himself up in the apartments he had recently renovated in the Castel Sant' Angelo, refusing food and comfort, receiving no friends, contracting no business. When the torchlit funeral cortège passed his window and crossed the bridge on its short journey to Santa Maria del Popolo the crowd of respectful and curious onlookers heard his cries of anguish.

Desolation slowly gave way to the desire for vengeance. The pope's recovery was fuelled by his determination to track down Giovanni's assassins. He sent his agents into every corner of the town, armed with swords and gold, to extract information about his son's death. Every day Alexander demanded reports from his men. Every day those reports amounted to nothing. Rome might have become a city of blind, deaf mutes for all anyone was prepared to reveal. The Borgia paced his rooms with mounting anger and frustration. Sometimes he stood for minutes on end staring out over the slums which erupted at the very foot of the Vatican's walls and oozed all the way down to the river. Somewhere amidst all that squalor and in the palazzos on the opposite hillsides were people who were privy to the secrets of the night of 14–15 June. Alexander knew why they remained silent. Why neither the allurements of wealth nor the threats of his men had raised a single reliable informer. It was fear. Fear not only among the questioned; fear also in the questioners. His own servants were not prepared to probe too far or too hard because of the Borgia's powerful, ruthless enemies. Some had, doubtless, even been paid off. Alexander fumed. What was the point of being pope if others in Rome comma[...] [...] than he? Was there no one who, for whateve[...] could rely on for stubborn loyalty in the face of u[...] No one with the brains, the cunning and the knowledge [...] Rome's festering underworld to discover the truth? That was when he thought of Fra Pietro Foscari.

'By nature the ground of man's soul is receptive to nothing but the divine Being, directly and without mediation.' With difficulty Brother Pietro traced out the Latin words, holding the much-worn little book of Eckhart sermons up to the narrow shaft of light. For about two hours every day, as the sun passed directly in front of the grating high up in the prison wall, he was able to read from the three precious spiritual works the guards had not bothered to confiscate. These were the most valued moments of his day, the moments that prevented his mind succumbing to loneliness, darkness and uncertainty. It was the uncertainty that was the worst. As a condemned heretic only one fate awaited him. But when? It was seventy-three days since the agents of the Inquisition had thrown him into this catacomb beneath the Castel Sant' Angelo. Pietro had carefully marked off the days on one slime-surfaced wall. Clearly those Dominican hell-hounds of the Inquisition intended to undermine his spirit. They wanted him to be led out to the stake a broken man, ready to recant in front of the people he had served as preacher, pastor, healer and friend for over two years. Well, they would not succeed. What was near starvation to a Franciscan, trained to survive on the most frugal diet? What was solitude to a man able to commune with God in his inner being? As for absence of light, how could that compare with that fearsome darkness of soul which blinded his persecutors? Brother Pietro fell to his meditations and his prayers.

Not for long. Well before the time for his midday crust the door clanked open and the duty jailer blundered in, hauled Pietro from his knees and thrust him up the broad stone stairs that led to the world of men. This then was it. No time to prepare for the final ordeal. Just a hustling through the crowded streets to the piazza where the piled faggots, the platform and the stake awaited. Wordlessly, the Franciscan was propelled along corridors and through a succession of doors. But the journey ended, not in a room where papal guards stood ready to chain him, but in a chamber where two servants in the Borgia livery stood beside a steaming wooden tub, watched by a thin, black-haired priest.

The man stared at the dishevelled friar with obvious distaste. 'Off with that ragged apology for a habit,' he ordered and the servants dragged the frayed garment from Pietro's body. When they had stripped him to the skin they half-led, half-carried him to the bath and plunged him into water that was hot and perfumed. As they scrubbed his emaciated torso and limbs, Pietro asked the priest what was happening. But the man, who now leaned beside a window and surveyed the proceedings with an air of detachment and faint disapproval, merely shrugged, as if to say, 'This isn't my idea: I'm only obeying orders.' After Foscari had been scrupulously cleaned, towelled and sprayed with rose water, he was clad in a new shirt, brown habit and sandals, then he was thrust into an armed chair to receive the ministrations of a barber. After two and a half months' growth of beard had been removed and the friar's tonsure freed from the matted, lice-ridden overgrowth of head hair, the priest told Pietro to stand up. He walked around the prisoner, examining him as one might a prospective purchase at a horse fair. Then he gave a grunt of

44

satisfaction and, with a curt 'follow me', he moved to the door.

Foscari stood his ground. 'Where are we going?'

The man turned in the doorway. 'Don't be impertinent, friar. It is for you to obey; not to ask questions.'

Foscari smiled and did not move. 'If I were a good son of holy Church that would be true but, as you know, I am a heretic and we heretics get all manner of strange notions into our heads. I wish to know where you are taking me.'

The priest sneered. 'Well then, heretic, I will humour you thus far: the holy father has sent for you. Why, I know not. In my opinion, burning is too good for your sort. But the pope as Christ's vicar is imbued with the Saviour's compassion. See that you do not abuse it. Come!'

They climbed to a higher level of the fortress-palace and walked through interconnected chambers and lobbies whose marbled floors clattered with the noise of scores of hurrying feet as clergy, scarlet-robed bishops and liveried servants hurried about their work. They stopped in an antechamber where a self-important secretary sat at an imposing table strewn with documents, and a dozen or so suitors stood in twos or threes waiting hopefully for their summons to the presence. Foscari's guide spoke to the secretary then turned and left without a further word or glance directed at the Franciscan. The secretary rose and half ran to the door behind him, a door glistening with polished walnut and applied panels of gilt-bronze. He knocked, entered and reappeared almost immediately. He beckoned imperiously. 'His holiness will see you now, Brother Pietro.'

Still bemused, Foscari entered a large chamber whose panelled walls were hung with tapestries. It was well-furnished with tables, chairs and carved cassones. On the wall to the right hung a large silver crucifix and before it an ornate prayer desk. The incongruous mix of piety and vulgar ostentation appalled the simple friar. He peered around but could discern no other occupant in the room. Then he saw the large window. It was on the left and it was full of blue sky. Brother Pietro was drawn to it irresistibly. He stood before it and gazed down on the river, the bridge, the narrow streets, horses, carts and people; people walking and running; people standing on corners talking; people shopping at market stalls.

'Freedom is a fine thing, is it not, little friar?'

Foscari turned, startled. Not a metre away the pope sat in a high-backed, cushioned chair facing the window. Pietro dropped to one knee and kissed the ring on Alexander's extended hand. It was not just the suddenness which prompted his reaction. He was overawed by the pope's presence. Pietro had come to despise the Vatican establishment, the corruption no one even bothered to hide, the notorious immorality of the Borgias and their entourage. Yet, face-to-face with the head of the Church, he was, despite himself, impressed. Alexander was tall, dark, bushy-browed; there was that about him which commanded, if not respect, certainly obedience. He left Brother Pietro kneeling for several moments before bidding him rise.

'Yes, little friar, how good it would feel to be walking in those streets, meeting old friends, watching children playing, boats on the river, birds in the trees. In less than an hour that freedom could be yours. On the other hand, you could be back in your prison cell, never to see the light of day until you make the short walk to the stake. I offer you that choice.'

Foscari turned his back on the window. 'Holiness, is the recantation of one poor heretic so important?'

'I said nothing of recantation, Brother Pietro. Of course,

if you abused my clemency by preaching abominable error under the very walls of the Vatican you would know what to expect. But I think you have more sense. All that I am offering you now is the opportunity to put the past behind you.'

Foscari returned the pope's gaze. 'Your holiness is very generous,' he said cautiously.

'I see from your face that you suspect my generosity may have a price. You are right. I want your help in this business of my son.'

'Your holiness should not have a son!' The taunt leaped from Pietro's lips before he was aware of it.

Alexander frowned. 'Don't preach to me, little friar! That is between me and my confessor. I have taken a personal interest in your case. Don't make me regret it.'

'May I ask why you are interested in me? Italy has many critics of the Church; many whose hearts long to see a return to holy living and simple preaching of the Gospel. Why should your holiness concern himself with me?'

Alexander stood and stepped across to the window and pointed. 'Because you know that – Rome. I have a full report of your activities since you came to the city. I know of your work among the sick and dying. I know that you are well read and that your preaching has stirred many to repentance. I know that the doors of palace and hovel alike are open to you and that some of the city's worst criminals have trusted you with their confessions. Above all, I know that you are incorruptible. You cannot be bought or browbeaten. For all these reasons I have kept you alive. I thought the day might come when I should have need of just such a man. That day has come. You will fearlessly seek out the perpetrators of this sin that cries to heaven for punishment.'

'What sin, holiness?'

'Why, the murder of my dear Giovanni, of course! Don't pretend you do not know . . .'

'How should I know, holiness, buried in a living tomb these last two and a half months?'

'Of course. I had forgotten. I must give you the facts that everyone else in Rome knows. Then you will see how important it is that these evil men are brought to justice. One evening in June a party was given for my sons, Cesare and Giovanni. It was at their mother's vineyard at Trastevere, close to the city wall.' He pointed downriver towards the wooded slopes of Gianicolo.

Foscari visualized the fair Vannozza dei Cattanei, the painter's daughter who, several years before, had enriched herself by becoming the mistress of Cardinal Borgia and about whom men still sang bawdy songs in the taverns of the Borgo San Spirito.

The pope continued, still pointing out the relevant landmarks. 'They left after dark, attended by a few servants and torch-bearers. They rode along beside the river as far as the Tiber Island Bridge. There Giovanni took his leave of his brother. He was, I suppose, bent on more pleasure – you know what young men are.'

'I know what the lusts of the flesh are, holiness, and that, for our soul's health, we must avoid them. Enquiry has, presumably, been made in the whore-houses?'

'Of course, but they either know nothing or are frightened to tell what they do know. Cesare tells me that the last he saw of his brother he was heading towards the Piazza del Pianto, in the Jewish quarter.'

Pietro raised his eyebrows. The earnest Hebrew money-making community was not the obvious venue for young bloods looking for a good time.

Alexander turned from the window. 'The next time anyone saw my son . . .' His voice faltered as he described the discovery of Giovanni's body. 'He looked like an angel when they had washed him and laid him out.'

The friar reflected that 'angel' was probably the last word anyone else would choose to describe the Duke of Gandia – a strutting, vicious, arrogant young man, exceeded in his capacity for deliberate malevolence only by his brother, Cesare. They were both, like the whole Borgia clan, glutted with the Church's wealth and the privileges which came with being the pope's relatives. 'And that is all that is known of this sad affair?'

The pope relayed the boatman's testimony. 'For the rest,' he concluded, 'Rome keeps its secrets secure – even from me. Oh, there is one more fact, though what it means I know not. On that evil night Giovanni was accompanied by a masked man. He attended the party and was much in conversation with my son. Cesare and his mother assure me that they have no idea who he was.'

'Is it not odd that no one thought to ask?'

'Would to God that someone had. But there is a sort of code among these young people, as I'm sure you know. Those who do not wish to be recognized in certain places or seen in certain company hide their identity and it is understood that nobody enquires too closely.'

'It is only evil that needs to cloak itself,' Pietro observed quietly.

'You see, then, that you are the only one who can find these assassins. People will speak to you and you will not be afraid to ask the right questions.'

'And I, too, could end up in the Tiber.'

'It is a quicker death than the fire.'

The Franciscan spent some moments gazing silently out of the window.

Eventually, the pope broke in on his reverie. 'Come along, little friar, there's no great tussle with conscience here. You will be free to continue your good work among the poor and, at the same time, you will be seeking the truth. Is that not a worthy endeavour?'

'And if I do discover the truth and if that truth is not to your holiness's liking, what then? I have undertaken such enquiries once or twice before and discovered things that everyone concerned wished afterwards had remained hidden. But once uncovered . . .'

'You need have no fear on that score. You will report to me alone and whatever you tell me will be treated in confidence. No one shall know of your activities – not my secretary, nor any of my staff. And if the message is unwelcome the messenger shall not suffer for it.'

'And your holiness will keep this investigation secret from your family?'

Alexander hesitated momentarily before nodding. 'Very well. Not my other sons, nor Lucrezia, shall know of your activities though, of course, they are as desolate as I at Giovanni's death.'

Foscari doubted that but said nothing. 'Well then, I am your holiness's to command.'

The pope was not sure whether or not there was a note of sarcasm in the friar's response but chose to ignore the possibility. He held out his hand. 'Very well, then. Away with you and God speed your labours. My secretary has money for you and on the table by the door is a letter of authority should you need it.'

Fra Pietro kissed Alexander's ring and moved back towards the door. Halfway across the rug-strewn floor he halted. 'Have your men interrogated Guido Lombardi?'

'Lombardi? I don't know the name.'

'The man's an ex-soldier and into every kind of villainy, including killing for money. There's little that happens among Rome's criminal fraternity that he doesn't know about.' Foscari spoke the last words almost to himself as he strode purposefully to the door, eager for the open, free air.

Tim hit the outer office of Artguard like a Florida hurricane looking for a township to flatten.

'Druckmann!' He stated the name to the open-mouthed receptionist as he strode past her desk.

She half rose, recovering quickly but not quickly enough. 'Mr Druckmann . . .'

'Will see me now!' Tim pushed open swing doors and marched into the corridor beyond. He made for the room at the far end and went in without knocking.

It was empty. The quilted leather armchair behind the wide mahogany desk with its neatly arranged piles of paper was untenanted. Tim glared round the office, furnished to convey reassuring opulence to potential clients. The thick charcoal-grey carpet matched the grey City skyscape beyond the wide windows. The matching hide chesterfield and solid armchairs suggested comforting stability. Tim felt like overturning them; hurling the brass desk lamp at the poor imitation of a Corot prominently placed on the facing wall; creating mayhem for the sheer hell of it. He turned, deflated, and was on the point of retreating when he heard voices coming from behind a door to the right. He stepped towards it.

It opened.

'Major Lacy. It's nice to see you but I thought my secretary explained that I was in conference right now.' The man who filled the doorframe was tall and thickset. A well-cut suit and regimental tie were incongruously at odds with the long, dark hair drawn back into a pigtail.

Tim observed that the jacket was so well tailored that the empty sleeve was barely noticeable.

'Well, *Sergeant* Druckmann – if we're using military rank – what I have to say won't take long.'

Druckmann exhaled a theatrical sigh and advanced into the room. He waved Tim to a chair.

Tim remained standing. 'You won't run Lacy Security out of business by spreading lies about us.'

Druckmann dropped into the swivel chair and leaned back. 'What bee have you got in your bonnet now?'

'I've just come from Grinling's. They seem to have got hold of the idea that I'm in some sort of financial difficulty. And they're not the only ones. In the last couple of days I've had three other clients wanting to know if it's true that Lacy Security is about to fold.'

The other man shrugged. 'You know what the grapevine's like.'

'I know how easy it is to spread rumours and I know who's been doing the spreading.'

'You're getting paranoid in your old age. People are quite capable of putting two and two together, you know. The fact is your outfit's out of date. The security business is changing. The era of clever gizmos is past. Nowadays every successful villain has a bevy of technical whizz kids working for him.'

'If anyone knows about the criminal mind it's you, Sergeant.'

A flicker at the corner of Druckmann's eyes indicated that the sting had penetrated. 'OK, so I've been a bad boy. Done a couple of years. But I used that time to advantage. I got to know a hell of a lot about the enemy – names, traffic routes, M.O's . . .'

'Where to hire muscle; how to run a protection racket; what syndicate bosses to get in bed with.' Tim advanced to the desk and glowered down at the man who wanted to drive him out of business. 'I'll go into liquidation before I sell out to a crook like you.'

Druckmann pushed his chair away from the desk. He looked at his wrist watch – very slim and very gold. 'That's your choice.' He stood up. 'My offer is a good one and it stands until the end of the month. Now you'll have to excuse me. *I* have a business to run.' He went back to the boardroom, leaving Tim in sole possession of the office.

The taxi ride back to the small Westminster flat the Lacys used as a London base was a slow affair. The traffic in Fleet Street was almost at a standstill and when the driver cut down to the Embankment it was no better there.

Tim sat back and tried to make himself think clearly, unemotionally, about Saul Druckmann. Not easy, particularly as he had a sudden niggling pain in his chest. 'Champagne on an empty stomach,' he thought. Hamburg 1973 – that was when he had first come across Sergeant Druckmann, S. Then Tim had been Captain Lacy, second in command of an SAS unit detailed to winkle out the remnants of a left-wing terrorist cell. It soon became clear that someone was selling the Red Brigade information about the movements of arms and ammunition. Everything pointed to Druckmann, and Tim had testified against him at a court martial. Somehow, the stocky sergeant had wriggled out from under a steaming heap of evidence. As things turned out he might have been better off in a military prison cell. Two weeks later his paymasters, believing themselves betrayed, sent him a parcel. That explained his missing left arm.

Tim forgot all about Druckmann but Druckmann did not forget Captain, later Major, Lacy. Soon after Tim started his own security firm the ex-sergeant came and asked him for a job. Tim turned him down with conventional politeness – 'no vacancy at the moment but we will retain your application on file'. Thereafter, scarcely a year passed during which Druckmann did not write or phone a couple of times just to keep in touch and to let Major Lacy know with what admiration his old army colleague was following his career. As harassment went it was pretty mild and apparently pointless. Only now was it obvious what Druckmann's years of stalking had been leading up to. Despite a couple of spectacular business failures and a spell in jail for fraud, he had worked his way up the ladder, apparently never short of financial backers, until he could elbow his way into the exclusive fine art security market. Motivated by greed and revenge, he had studied Lacy Security's methods and business contacts. For the last year Druckmann had been deliberately targeting Tim's customers, offering not only cut-price deals but 'extras' designed to appeal to the guardians of public and private treasures worried about the growing violence and expertise of art-theft specialists. How dim could people be? Artguard's customers might be reassured by Druckmann's underworld intelligence service and his not-easily-intimidated ex-con staff, but they would learn the hard way that poachers do not make the most trustworthy gamekeepers.

Tim's phone bleeped. He took it from his overcoat pocket.

'Tim, where are you?' Catherine sounded agitated.

'On my way to the flat. What . . .'

'Can you come back here – to Grinling's. Something terrible has happened.'

'What?'

'The four experts . . . the ones who took part in that charade with the Borgia Chalice . . . they're all dead.'

'Sorry, darling, the signal must be breaking up. I thought you said . . .'

'Dead! That's exactly what I said. They all collapsed at the reception – poisoned.'

'What about the Santori kids?'

'Right as rain.'

'But that's . . .'

'Yeah, looks like the remake of a "B" movie, doesn't it – *The Curse of the Borgias*?'

Tim tried to get his mind round the bizarre facts and wished that the pain in his chest was not distracting him.

'Tim, are you OK?'

He heard the note of anxiety in Catherine's voice and responded automatically. 'Yes, fine. Look, the traffic's pretty impossible but I'll get there as quick as I can. Not that there's anything I can do . . .'

'The thing is, darling, the place is crawling with cops, labelling things and putting them in plastic bags – including the chalice. Poor Wes is going to have to wait for his prize.'

'Damn! I've already told him we've got it. He's flying down to pick it up in the morning. Can't you reason with the police . . . I mean the chalice can't have anything to do . . . Oh, this is bloody ridiculous.'

Catherine shared his annoyance. 'It messes things up, doesn't it? I did try having a word with the top man but . . . well, they say it never rains but it pours. The officer in charge is Detective Inspector Edgerson.'

Tim groaned. 'That's not rain; it's a bloody monsoon. There's no way Edgy Edgerson will do anything to oblige us after that French business.'*

'Too right! He really enjoyed telling me to run along,

* See *The Camargue Brotherhood*

good little girl, and not get in the way of his
..'

'OK. See you soon.' Tim put the phone away. He called out to the driver, 'Change of plan. We have to go to Grinling's, Bond Street.'

The young man smiled at him through the driving mirror. 'Much more of this weather, sir, and I'll have to ask you to take a turn at the oars.'

Tim was too preoccupied to respond to the witticism. Edgerson was a cop who kept a rule book where his imagination ought to be; a man who let his feelings cloud his judgement – who felt nothing good for the Lacys. He would hang on to the chalice for weeks – months, out of sheer spite. No chalice meant no cheque from Wes Cherry. No cheque from Wes Cherry meant more explaining to the bank. And if the bank refused to play ball Tim might have to go, with his tail between his legs, to Saul Druckmann. Worse than that, he, Catherine and the boys would have to leave Farrans; their partner, Emma Kerr, would be lucky to get half her capital out of the business; George Martin, Sally and thirty or so others who had worked hard to build up the business would be at the not-very-tender mercy of Artguard. Tim gritted his teeth. 'No! Never!'

A sudden surge of agony carved through his torso. He folded, gasping, arms pressed to his chest. With sudden certitude he realized what the pain was. He tried to call out. No words formed in his closed throat. He lunged towards the glass partition. And knew no more.

CHAPTER 3

Foscari's obeisance was of the very briefest: his knees bent slightly; his lips brushed the pope's extended hand.

Alexander was equally impatient. Throwing his riding whip down on the walnut table and letting his cloak fall to the patterned marble, he slumped into an armchair. 'Well?'

The friar let his eyes roam around the pope's Vatican apartments, smaller than those in the Castel Sant' Angelo and bright with newly painted frescoes. 'If I am to serve your holiness effectively in this matter, I must insist on being allowed to do things my way.'

Alexander's heavy lids flickered. 'That's understood.'

'Then why did I find that Lombardi has been arrested and examined by three Spanish Dominicans, holiness?'

The pope's face registered surprise. 'The Inquisition?'

'Exactly!' Foscari stood firmly in the centre of the room, his slender frame swaying slightly, like a sapling. 'They claimed to be under your holiness's direct orders.'

'They were supposed to report to you. I thought they would be useful. They are experts.'

'Huh!' The little man grunted his scepticism. 'They have their way of doing things – the Spanish way. It may work with heretics and Jews. Not with a professional assassin like Lombardi.'

Borgia frowned, resenting his agent's tone. 'Boots!' He

stretched his long legs out before him and was gratified to see Foscari wince before dropping to his knees.

The friar grappled with the mud-spattered buckskin. He eased the pope's feet out of their sheaths.

Alexander wriggled his toes inside the scarlet hose. 'That's better. So, what did you get out of Lombardi.'

'I?' Foscari stood up rubbing his grimy hands on his habit. 'I got nothing out of him. Even Pietro Foscari cannot make dead men talk.'

Alexander sat up suddenly, back straight, deep-set eyes staring. 'What do you mean?'

'When I reached Castel Sant' Angelo, Torquemada's pupils had done their worst – and I do mean worst.' Foscari wandered over to a side table. Without bothering to ask, he helped himself from a silver dish of almond cakes. 'All they got out of Lombardi was a bucket of blood and piss. I don't know which of their elaborate instruments they used but they obviously went too far.' He nibbled the crisp confection and savoured its bitter sweetness. 'You can't torture information out of men like Lombardi . . . your holiness.'

Alexander chose to ignore the insolent tone of the two words, added almost as an afterthought.

His agent continued, talking indistinctly through a mouthful of crumbs. 'Someone who's been through the wars and served in the galleys doesn't scare easily. He's had a bellyful of cruelty, a mind soaked in horror, and a soul saturated with pain. The *domini canes* of the Inquisition were wasting their own sweat with their whips and screws and knives and branding irons. They might as well have been torturing that.' He waved an arm contemptuously at the polychromed figure of the Virgin in the corner of the room.

With a sigh, the pope hauled himself to his feet. 'So we

still know nothing about the man who ordered Giovanni's murder?' He towered over the little clerk who shrugged and would not be overawed.

'Nothing, holiness . . . Or almost nothing.'

'Almost?' Alexander grabbed at the word. 'Then you have found out . . .'

Foscari shook his head. 'Probably nothing of value.'

'Whatever it is, tell me!'

'Lombardi played with his tormentors; laughed at them. They admitted as much. They examined him for three hours and in all that time he only said one thing – over and over again.' He swallowed the last mouthful of cake and stared straight at his master.

'Well?'

'"Ask the pope." That's all he said. "Ask the pope about the Michaelmas Massacre."'

'What!' The word came out as a roar that made Foscari fall back a pace or two. 'Insolent pig! He deserved whatever the Inquisitors did to him.' Alexander strode across the room and poured thick malvoisie from a silver ewer into a goblet.

Foscari watched as the tall man drank deeply of the sweet wine. He noted the slightly shaking hands. 'You don't think Lombardi's jibe has any relevance?'

'How can it?' Alexander snapped out the question – a little too brusquely, in the agent's opinion.

'How?' Foscari shrugged. 'I only know the story everyone knows.'

'Lies! Deliberate calumny!' The pope refilled his cup.

'If your holiness can tell me the truth of the matter, perhaps we can see whether it has any bearing on your son's death.'

'If you want a suspect try Cardinal della Rovere. He is behind this business somewhere. He hates me ever since

I beat him in the papal election. He will do anything – anything at all – to harm me and those I love.' Borgia loosened his jerkin. 'It's stifling in here! Come!' He strode from the room.

They had been walking among the fountains and parterres of the privy garden for some minutes before the pope stopped suddenly by an arbour overhung with oleander. He lowered himself on the stone bench within and motioned Foscari to sit beside him. 'What do you know about this so-called "Michaelmas Massacre"?'

The thin-faced friar answered slowly, carefully. 'It occurred last September. Cardinals Montadini, Petrucci and della Chiesa came here for a meeting with your holiness.'

Alexander growled. 'They came to beg pardon for their treasons.'

'And your holiness . . .'

'I forgave them – freely, as Christ himself would have forgiven them.'

'And you drank wine together – you, the cardinals, Giovanni and Cesare – from a common cup.'

The pope nodded. 'And what is supposed to have happened next?'

'The cardinals died – poisoned, according to the physicians.'

'While I and my sons watched, quite unharmed?'

'So the story goes.'

'And by what witchcraft do people say that the Borgias can drink poison and not die?'

'Some believe you have a potion which renders you immune to all toxins.'

Alexander laughed. 'Any alchemist who could produce such a philtre would soon be the richest man in Christendom, would he not?'

'Some prefer a mechanical explanation.'

'Ah, yes. They say I have a chalice set with poisoned gems.'

'Or a chalice with a hidden compartment containing a lethal liquid, which can be released by means of a concealed device.'

The pope brushed at a fly hovering around his tight black curls. 'People want to believe that the Borgias are capable of every crime the wit of man can conceive, so they devise elaborate theories in order to dispose of inconvenient facts. That's the triumph of blind faith over reason.'

'Perhaps the Church has schooled them too well. A man's reason tells him that bread is bread. It looks like bread. It tastes like bread. It must be bread. "Not so," says the Church. "It's really flesh and bone because a priest has muttered some Latin words over it."'

Alexander allowed himself a sardonic smile. 'Would you pour your shameless heresies into the very ear of the pope himself?'

'The pope knows well enough what I believe.'

'Indeed he does, little friar.' Borgia's words now had a cutting edge. 'And don't forget it. For all your pretended stoicism, you've no taste for the fire. That is why you'll do my bidding in this matter and find the truth for me.'

'Then your holiness must conceal nothing from me.' Foscari's delivery was level, emotionless.

Alexander spread his arms in a wide gesture. 'I am not concealing anything.'

'About this chalice . . .'

The pope's mouth opened wide and a laugh rumbling up from the cavern of his belly exploded into the stillness of the garden. 'Oh, surely not you, too, little scholar. All those years at Paris and Pisa and you credulously

61

swallow a ridiculous story that probably had its origins in the taverns and brothels of the Viale Aventino.'

'Then no such chalice exists?'

'Certainly it exists. It is magnificent. It was made for me by the finest goldsmith in Augsburg. But a chalice is all it is. It has no subtle mechanism, no concealed inlet, no hollow stem filled with venom. If you need proof of that I'll have it brought to your lodging. You may examine it at leisure.'

Foscari frowned. 'Then how were the cardinals poisoned? They *were* poisoned? Or was that, too, a tale spread by drunken pimps?'

Alexander stood abruptly and began striding across the grass. As the friar caught up with him, he said. 'I don't know what happened to the cardinals – and you may believe that or not as you please. After our meeting they left, in perfectly good health. Later they celebrated mass together in my own chapel. Cesare and I had business at Viterbo. We set off before noon. The news of the deaths was brought to me there a couple of days later.'

Foscari thought, but did not say, How convenient. 'Was any attempt made to find the assassin?'

'Of course. Unfortunately, the most exhaustive enquiries yielded no result.'

They walked in silence while the friar mentally leafed through the meagre scraps of information he had gathered. Eventually he ventured cautiously, 'Supposing, holiness, just supposing that Giovanni was in some way implicated in the deaths of della Chiesa and the others . . .'

Alexander stopped suddenly and glared down at him. 'Don't be absurd!'

'Then let me put it this way: supposing someone *thought* that Giovanni was responsible for the Michaelmas

Massacre, then the motive for your son's death might be revenge.'

The pope nodded. 'I grant that that is possible.'

Foscari pursued the argument's logic to its conclusion. 'And if that person believed – as most men believe – that *all* the Borgias plotted the cardinals' murder . . .'

Alexander's eyes became narrow slits in his puffy features. 'In that case I think you had better find some answers – very quickly.'

Emma Kerr applied the last brushload of paint to the strip of wall above the kitchen cupboards and descended the step ladder. She dropped the brush into a bucket of water, removed the worst of the white emulsion and finished the cleaning process under the tap. She dried her hands and checked her watch. Six thirty-seven. Time for a long hot tub before breakfast. She crossed the sitting room and climbed the cottage's narrow staircase. Ten minutes later she lay up to her chin in hot water and bubbles. Still she could not relax.

Emma willed the tension to seep from her body, the tumbling thoughts to float free and leave her mind at peace. It was no use. The worries that had stolen her sleep were still there, vandalizing her consciousness. It had been some time after three thirty that she had given up the losing battle, thrown aside the too-hot duvet, and decided to re-decorate the kitchen on the grounds that if she had to be awake she might as well be usefully awake. The trouble with painting was that it did not require much mental effort. She had gone on turning over her problems – endlessly, monotonously, pointlessly.

'There must be something I can do!' Emma glared at the rubberized Daffy Duck perched beside the hot tap.

'So, do you expect me just to sit around and let my world fall apart?' He glared unhelpfully back.

Emma had been with the Lacys over three years. She had sunk all of a fairly substantial legacy into the business and thrown herself into it with enthusiasm. For the first two years it had been great. She was enormously fond of Tim and Catherine. She loved Farrans Court, the medieval-Tudor manor house deep in the Wiltshire countryside from which the two parts of Lacy Enterprises were conducted. Emma had enjoyed learning how Catherine ran the art gallery, how she sniffed out promising new talent, how she tailor-made a highly individualistic publicity campaign for each exhibition, enticing the right collectors and dealers from all round the world. Tim's work was equally fascinating. Emma knew that she would never keep up with the pace of changing technology in the security business but she could explain what heat sensors, infra-red scanners, print and voice identifiers, automatic screening devices and ultra-sonic alarms actually did – and that was what potential clients wanted to know. She had been fascinated to accompany Tim to major public galleries and to stunning private collections in magnificent houses and apartments, palaces and castles, mansions and yachts the world over.

But during the last year something had been going very wrong. It was not just business recession. Old clients had been not renewing contracts. Appointments were often cancelled, sometimes at the last moment. There had been five serious failures of Lacy Security equipment, resulting in losses and massive claims against the company's insurance. Tim and George Martin, his head of installations, were convinced that the systems had been sabotaged, but they could prove nothing. Now the firm was in real financial trouble and getting in deeper month after month.

Everyone at Farrans had been working flat out the whole summer – advertising, touting for business, phoning possible contacts, falling over backwards to maintain good customer relations – but the situation was no better. A few more weeks – six at the most – Tim said, and they would have to start cutting staff. But if it came to that it would not stop there. Everything was in jeopardy – the business, Farrans, her capital, a whole way of life.

Coming on top of all that, yesterday's events were devastating. Catherine had phoned in the evening. In a tone as close to hysterical as she ever got she had announced that Tim had had a heart attack. It was too early yet to say how seriously ill he was but, of course, she would be staying in London to be on hand. Would Emma mind holding the fort? Catherine would phone again as soon as there was anything to report.

That news had deeply upset her. Dinner with Giles Ledger at a very exclusive country restaurant near Hungerford had been a dismal failure. Her conversational skill had been zero and eventually she had pleaded a headache and got the portly Giles to run her home early. Probably no bad thing, Emma reflected; he was far too 'keen' – more like an ardent, bungling adolescent eager for his first conquest than a thirty-two-year-old dealer in high quality antique silver and bijouterie. It was because she had got back to the cottage around ten, firmly avoiding Giles' fumbling fingers and heavy breathing, that she had caught the late-night TV news.

The reporters and interviewers had squeezed every last drop of drama from the 'Sensational Quadruple Murder at Grinling's of Bond Street' story. But they answered none of the questions screaming in Emma's mind. Emma had spent the next couple of hours trying to make contact with Catherine. There was no answer from the flat or her mobile. What did that mean? That she had to stay with Tim because he was really bad? Or dead?

Emma towelled down and brushed out her long, dark hair. 'How am I supposed to face the day?' she demanded of her reflection. 'What do I tell the staff? How much am I supposed to let on to customers?' She walked into the bedroom and clambered into the clothes that came most readily to hand – cherry-coloured trousers and a white roll-neck.

It was while she was fixing toast and coffee that the phone rang. She grabbed up the receiver.

'Emma? I haven't got you up, have I?' Catherine's voice was quite without its usual sparkle.

'No . . . no. Catherine, thank God it's you. I've been worried sick . . . How's Tim?' She asked the question cautiously, fearful of the answer.

'OK. He's going to be OK. It happened in a taxi. Perhaps the best place. The driver was fantastic. He had paramedics there within minutes. The doctor says it was only a warning attack – what he calls "a shot across the bows".'

'Oh, Catherine, I'm so glad. How's he feeling now?'

'He looks dreadful, poor dear. Wired to lots of machines and drugged up to the eyeballs, but everything seems to be working OK. I'm going back to the hospital in the middle of the morning. The doc says he'll be able to cope with visitors then.'

'Good. Give him my love. Can I come up and see him?'

'Emma, that's sweet of you, but one of us must be at Farrans. This couldn't have happened at a worse time. I'll get back just as soon as I can but right now I can't say when that'll be. That's why I wanted to go over a

few things. Have you heard about this wretched ...
with the chalice?'

'I saw it on the news last night. What . . .'

'Don't ask. It's just too awful and complicated for
words. The thing is, we bought the chalice for Wes
Cherry, as arranged, and Tim phoned him and told him.
Knowing Wes, I'll bet he went wild with excitement.
Then this appalling thing happened and the police have
taken the chalice off with all the plates and glasses and
food to run tests.'

'So we can't get the chalice to Wes?'

'That's right. He's going to be pretty mad. You know
what he's like when things don't go his way.'

'But it's not our fault.'

'Try telling him that . . . Er, look, Emma, that's exactly
what I'm asking you to do. He's flying down to Farrans
this morning to pick up the chalice. I tried to call him
last night but the answerphone was on and I didn't
want to leave a detailed message. I haven't been able
to get hold of him this morning either. I don't know
what he's heard – probably nothing; Wes and the boys
aren't really switched on to what's happening in the
real world.'

Emma thought, Thanks a bundle, but she said, 'Don't
worry about it. You've got enough on your plate. I'll
deal with Weird Wes. Hey, everything'll be OK. Lots
of people have heart attacks.' She just stopped herself
saying, and go on to lead perfectly normal lives. 'Tim's
a fighter. Give him lots of love from me when you
see him.'

She put down the receiver, gulped down the rest of
her lukewarm coffee, took another bite of butter-spread
cardboard and decided to throw the rest out for the birds.
She plunged her feet into wellington boots, grabbed up

her anorak and set off across the sodden parkland towards
the big house.

Yesterday's storms had passed, leaving grass, trees and
hedgerows washed and glistening in the low sunlight. But
the morning freshness was wasted on Emma. She swung
her legs over the stile and strode, head-down, across the
large meadow that was euphemistically referred to as the
'south lawn'. Usually she enjoyed arriving at Farrans
Court, impressive yet at the same time comfortably
reassuring in the Wiltshire hollow it had commanded
for more than five centuries. Today she did not glance
up at the crenellated medieval stone of the main building
or the Elizabethan wings whose upper windows were just
catching the September sun. She was too busy composing
the story she would tell the staff – a carefully edited
version of the truth.

As she reached the wide gravel before the arched doorway of the porch she heard the clatter of an approaching
helicopter.

CHAPTER 4

The cardiac wing was a cluster of single-bed wards around a central nucleus which served as office and lobby. Catherine nodded and smiled at the young sister behind the desk. 'Hello. I'm here to see Mr Lacy. Room Three, I believe.'

The nurse looked up from her computer console. 'It's Mrs Lacy, is it?'

'That's right.' Catherine began to move towards the glass-panelled door with the number three painted large in black on white.

The duty nurse stood up quickly. 'I'm sorry, Mrs Lacy. You can't go in just at the moment. Mr Lacy is only allowed one visitor at a time.'

Catherine frowned – puzzled, apprehensive. 'But I'm his wife. There can't be anybody else with . . .'

The sister came round the desk, well-practised reassurance irradiating her fresh features. 'Please take a seat, Mrs Lacy. It's the police. They asked to have a word with your husband as soon as he was up to it.'

'Police! Not Detective Inspector Edgerson!'

'Yes, I think that was the name.'

'Edgerson's in there pestering Tim with tomfool questions? If you want my husband to have a relapse, letting Edgerson at him is just about the quickest way to do it.' Catherine strode towards Room Three.

The nurse was too quick for her. She ran over and stood in front of the door. 'There's really no need to worry, Mrs Lacy.' She assumed her most soothing tone. 'Doctor Singh is with them. He'll make quite sure the patient is not upset. If you'll just take a seat, I'm sure the inspector will be through very . . .'

The door opened behind her and D.I. Edgerson backed out of the ward, still talking. 'I'll get a sergeant to call and take your statement as soon as these people say you're up to it. Meanwhile, if you think of anything else . . .' He turned and saw Catherine. 'Mrs Lacy. How convenient. This saves me tracking you down.'

Catherine glowered. 'You've got a nerve . . .'

'I've got a case to solve, Mrs Lacy. Quadruple murder, to be precise. I have to follow up every possible lead, and I can't afford to let the grass grow under my feet. Shall we?' He waved her towards the row of chairs along one wall. The thin, young policeman had the restlessness and the armour-cased persona of the fanatic.

Catherine stared back at the unblinking, humourless eyes. Over the centuries eyes like those had watched heretics burn and soldiers turned to shreds by enemy gunfire. 'Some other time, Inspector. I'm here to see my husband.'

'I think you'll find that the doc is just putting him to sleep.'

At that moment, a white-coated and turbaned figure emerged from Tim's ward. 'Ah, Mrs Lacy, good morning.'

'How is he, Doctor?' She turned her back on Edgerson. 'Can I see him now?'

The Sikh's smile revealed two rows of perfect teeth. 'Not at the moment, I'm afraid. I have just administered a mild sedative. Mr Lacy must have rest. That is the first priority. Perhaps in a couple of hours . . .'

'But he is all right? He hasn't had a relapse or anything?' Catherine struggled with the emotions that made her voice sound strangled.

The doctor led her to a chair and sat beside her. 'Mr Lacy is as well as can be expected. No, I think I may even say better than can be expected. He is a strong man and, apart from this one minor malfunction, he is in very good physical condition. But cardiac arrest – even mild cardiac arrest – is a serious business. If he is to recover completely – and not have a recurrence – he will have to take things very easily for a time and follow my instructions to the letter. *To the letter*, Mrs Lacy.'

Catherine forced a smile. 'I'm afraid Tim's never been very good at following instructions.'

'So I supposed, Mrs Lacy. You are just going to have to be very firm with him. An attack like this takes months to recover from fully.'

'Months!'

'Just so, Mrs Lacy. Months of medication, strict dietary control – and, above all, absence of stress.'

Catherine tried to get a mental image of Tim sitting around at Farrans, reading books and playing patience. She was unsuccessful. 'Doctor, I don't think . . .'

The bearded man smiled benignly. 'We all like to think we are indispensable, Mrs Lacy. It is perhaps good for our egos to discover that the hospital, shop, business – whatever – continues to operate without the benefit of our unique expertise.' He rose to go. 'A member of our counselling staff will discuss Mr Lacy's convalescence with you before we release him.'

'You'll be able to release him soon?'

Dr Singh shrugged. 'A couple of days. Some further tests – just to be on the safe side. Then, providing there are no complications, we shall release him into your tender care. We are only a repair garage, Mrs Lacy. We patch people up and put them back on the road. We hope that they will be driven sensibly and that we shan't see them again. But that is outside our control. Now, if you'll excuse me.' He shook hands with Catherine briefly then went out through the swing doors.

Throughout the conversation Edgerson had been hovering. Now he swooped. 'Right, Mrs Lacy, just a few questions.' He took the seat just vacated by the doctor.

Catherine glanced despairingly towards the door of Room Three. 'I can't imagine why you've been pestering Tim. For heaven's sake, he wasn't even in the building when those people were poisoned.'

'Ah well, we don't know that, do we?'

'Meaning?' Catherine glared from beneath lowered eyebrows.

'I'm still waiting for the analysis of the poison. Until it comes in I shan't know when or how it might have been administered.'

'So, you think Tim . . .'

'I didn't say that, Mrs Lacy. Your husband has been guilty of some very odd behaviour in his time, not to mention getting under my feet in an important investigation. But I don't reckon him as a mass murderer. Frankly, I've got enough suspects already – the staff of Grinling's, all the guests at the lunch, the caterers. I don't need another. What I want to know about is Mr Lacy's interest in this goblet thing that seems to be at the centre of the case. Do you think,' he glanced sheepishly down at his feet, 'there's anything in these stories about it?'

Catherine smiled despite her anxiety. 'You must be scraping the barrel if you're taking five-hundred-year-old malicious gossip seriously.'

'That's all it is then; an old story.'

Catherine stood suddenly. 'I'm going to get a coffee. If you want to come, too, I can't stop you.'

They walked to the hospital canteen and Edgerson surprised her by paying for the drinks. When they were seated at one of the plastic-topped tables, the inspector said, 'About this chalice then – what do you reckon?'

Catherine added a spoonful of sugar to her cup – a rare indulgence but today she needed the energy – and sipped the black liquid thankfully. 'The Borgia Chalice – if it is the real thing, and that's a matter of dispute as you probably know – has been examined by just about every expert in the country. They've established that there's no hidden compartment, no secret mechanism, no way of introducing poison into the contents of the cup. If you can figure out a way that six people can drink from the chalice and only four manage to drink poison you'll be solving one of the riddles of the ages.'

'Hm!' Edgerson stared mournfully at the open note-book on the table before him. 'You saw the performance yesterday. Are you sure the Santori youngsters actually drank from the Chalice? Couldn't they just have gone through the motions – not actually swallowed anything?'

'I wouldn't get in a witness box and swear it on oath but they both looked as though they were taking a good swig.' Catherine saw Edgerson's eye widen with hope and hurried on. 'But you don't really suspect the Santoris, do you?'

'I'm holding them for questioning. I haven't figured out – yet – how they did it, but they certainly had a powerful motive. As for that sidekick of theirs, the one they call O.K., he's a wrong 'un if ever I saw one. What can you tell me about them?'

'Absolutely nothing. I met them for the first time

yesterday. They struck me as nice kids who just want to put all the publicity and notoriety behind them and get on with life.'

'They must have been pretty bitter about the way their father was treated.'

'Not bitter enough to kill, I'd say. And probably not stupid enough to kill in front of all those people.'

'I wouldn't be too sure about that. Revenge is sweet. Public revenge is sweeter. I gather Mr Lacy knew old man Santori. I asked him about the children but he seemed pretty hazy.'

Catherine flared up. 'Hazy! Is it any wonder? He's had a heart attack, for God's sake! Just think how you'd feel about answering idiotic questions if you'd just had that kind of a shock.'

Edgerson also raised his voice. 'I'm sorry about your husband but he's not my main concern. I've got four bodies in the morgue of people who had more than a nasty shock. They're my prime responsibility. Now, please tell me what you can about your husband's contact with the Santoris.'

Catherine sighed. 'OK, if it'll stop you pestering him. Tim had known Gregor for some years – just as an acquaintance; they were never really friends. It must have been about four years ago that Santori asked him to install a security system. That was when Tim got to see the old man's workshop and collection. He was very impressed. Santori gave him a personal tour and Tim reckoned no one knew more about Renaissance metalwork – and all self-taught. Tim came up the hard way as well, and he's a bit of a rebel, too. I think he felt a sort of bond with Santori. He was certainly disgusted with the way the art establishment hounded him.'

'How well does he know the children?'

'Not at all. He'd never seen them till yesterday. They both live in Italy, I understand.'

'Yes, and right now they're pretty hopping mad because I won't let them go back.'

'Are you sure you're right to grill them? They don't strike me as cold-blooded killers.'

Edgerson smirked. 'Feminine intuition? Or is this the celebrated Lacy sleuthing streak showing itself? The Santoris are the only ones with motive – unless you know different. They are the only factor common to four highly respected art experts. Who else would want to bump off these particular people?'

Catherine stood up. 'That's for the police to work out, Inspector. I'm sure you'd be the first to tell me to keep my nose out of your business. But, at the risk of having my wrist slapped, I might just point out that the art world has more than its fair share of cranks. You know, the sort of demented individuals who throw acid at old master paintings? Many of them have no love of rich critics and dealers. What better opportunity could there be than yesterday's sale for making a particularly vicious protest against the establishment? All those TV cameras and reporters at Grinling's? A story that's been in the headlines on and off for a couple of years? And a situation in which, as you yourself said, there are dozens of suspects? It looks to me like a gift for a particularly twisted mind. But you're the expert. Now, if you'll excuse me, I'm going to go and see if they'll let me sit by my sick husband till he awakes.' She moved away through the rows of tables and chairs.

The oppressive heat and humidity of August lingered into September and brought the plague to Rome or, rather, created the conditions under which *Xenopsylla cheopis*, the plague-bearing rat flea, thrived. Although Brother Pietro spent some time thoughtfully exploring the streets and alleys near where Giovanni Borgia's body had been brought to the river, he was kept busy housling the sick, shriving the dying and taking comfort and food and dressings to the boarded-up hovels where doomed families were shut in with their groaning, suppurating loved ones for fear of spreading the contagion. The pope had given dispenation to his little friar to relieve him from the routine observances of his convent, so that he would be free to go about the city on his special mission. But Foscari could not bring himself to devote much mental or emotional energy to the brutal murder of one grandee when hundreds of men, women and children were dying horribly all around him. When, therefore, he came across his first real lead it was quite by chance or, as he preferred to believe, a reward for the faithful carrying out of his charitable duties.

Pietro's many friends among Rome's poor were delighted at his release. In their assorted needs they tended to send for him rather than their parish priests. Thus it was that, one wet September morning, he was called to the bedside of Sebastiano Sancia, a young man who had been injured in an accident with horses. The friar climbed the rickety staircase of the house in the Borgo San' Spirito and arrived in the room the boy rented. There was little in it apart from the bed on which he lay, inadequately covered with blankets. Water dripped from a hole in the roof and made a pool in the centre of the room.

Sebastiano tried to sit up as Pietro approached the bedside and threw back his cowl. The effort was too much for him. All he could manage was a weak smile and 'Bless you for coming, Brother.'

Pietro looked down anxiously at the matted, black hair and the glazed eyes in the sweat-streaked face. The truckle bed shook with the young man's shivering. The friar pulled aside the thin blanket but his nose had already told him what he would find. The lower part of Sebastiano's left leg was swollen, and blotched livid black and green. The smell of putrefaction was almost overwhelming. 'How did this happen?' he asked.

'Kicked by a horse in Signore Alfredi's stable. It was too spirited, only half broken.'

'You're a groom for Arturo Alfredi, the banker?' The friar wanted to keep his patient talking to impede the onset of delirium.

'Was. He threw me out after the accident. Said it was my fault. Fat pig! I was glad to go. Signore Alfredi is no good. Not like my last master.'

Pietro undid his scrip and took out the earthenware jar of soothing cream he had obtained from the friary infirmarian. 'And who was your last master, my son?'

'Cardinal Petrucci. He was kind. Good to us all.'

The gentle fingers applying the ointment to the necrotic flesh paused, but only momentarily. 'Petrucci? The one who died last year?'

'Died?' Sebastiano's body twitched agitatedly with pain or anger or both. 'Poisoned by the man he thought was his friend. The others . . .' Pietro bent close but could not distinguish the next words. '. . . not Petrucci.'

'Rest quiet, my son.' Foscari dipped a cloth in the puddle of rain water and applied it to the boy's fevered brow. Then he returned to treating the gangrenous leg. When Sebastiano's breathing had become quieter and more regular he asked, 'Who poisoned the cardinal, my son?'

'Pope . . . poisoned all three with that accursed chalice . . . everyone knows . . .'

'But they were evil men, were they not, plotting against his holiness?' Pietro began tearing strips of cloth to bind the leg.

The young man shook his head violently. 'Not Petrucci . . . I know.' Suddenly he stared intently at the friar. 'It was a secret, Brother Pietro.'

'What secret, my son?' Foscari held another compress of soaked cambric to the boy's forehead. There was no reply until he repeated the question.

'Mustn't tell anyone . . .'

'You can tell me, my son.'

The boy smiled up at him. 'Dear, good Brother Pietro . . .'

'That's right. What was this secret about Cardinal Petrucci?'

'I took the letters . . . no one would suspect a stablehand . . .'

'You took letters from your master to his holiness?'

'Mmm . . .'

Foscari looked down at the flickering lids. Soon the poor lad would be unconscious. Just as well for him. He would feel nothing when the surgeons took his leg off. That must be done as soon as possible. Fortunately, with the pope's gold in his purse, Pietro could afford Rome's best. But would the patient survive? He grasped the boy's hand firmly and offered a fervent prayer. His duty now was clear; he must prepare Sebastiano Sancia for eternity. The pope's business must await the young groom's recovery.

'Sebastiano, my son, do you hear me?'

The patient muttered something and opened his eyes.

'Do you put your trust only in Christ, the Saviour,

who died for you?' Foscari had long abandoned the paraphernalia of holy oils, invocation of saints and the other last rites prescribed by the Church. He looked anxiously at the young man for some response.

It came in a rush of sudden coherence but it was not the affirmation Pietro had hoped for. 'Every time there was a meeting in the villa at Orvieto or at the palazzo in Rome . . . Lots of them . . . all the pope's enemies . . . The cardinal gave me a letter and a special pass to get me to . . .'

'Yes, yes, my son, you can tell me this later. Now you must think . . .'

Sebastiano gripped the friar's hand tightly. 'Once, he was there, the one who wanted me to go to France . . . the murdered one . . .'

'Who? Who was there?' Pietro leaned forward to catch the word that slipped from Sebastiano's lips as nothing more than a sigh.

'Gandia.'

Wes Cherry came in like a lion and went out, if not like a lamb, at least like a softly purring big cat.

Emma watched his two-man helicopter settle on the south lawn, saw the athletic Afro-Caribbean spring down and come bounding lithely across the grass towards the house. He was incredibly tall – six foot three or thereabouts she supposed – and his black leather trousers and matching, fur-lined flying jacket made him look even bigger.

She held out her hand as he reached the gravelled drive. Instead of shaking it, the pop idol hugged her enthusiastically in an embrace that lifted her off the ground.

'Emma, hi! It is Emma, isn't it? I remember you came with Tim to suss out the mansion. Is Tim here?' He released her and stood staring up at the front of Farrans Court. 'Hey, this is cool. I love these old places. They really turn me on. I might get a new lyric out of your little mansion. Yeah! Great! Now, where's my little baby?'

Emma led the way into the house. She had no idea how she was going to break the news that would plug the flow of Wes's enthusiasm. But, then, he had the habit of setting his own itinerary. Emma shrugged and decided to go along with it. They entered the hall with its armorial glass and high, hammerbeam roof. This was the main exhibition gallery and the musician became absorbed in the autumn collection of work by young artists. Emma found his comments surprisingly perceptive. She showed her guest the smaller galleries, the seminar rooms, the restaurant and finally the business suite. At the end of half an hour Emma sensed rather than knew that there was something both childlike and yet enormously adult about Wes Cherry. She very much wanted him to like Farrans, to like her. She settled him in the business lounge and fetched coffee. When she returned she found him sprawled in one deep, leather armchair with his feet on another.

He looked up at her, suddenly serious. 'OK, Emma, what's wrong?'

'Wrong?'

'Yeah, wrong. You're not going to mess with me, are you? No Tim, no Catherine, no chalice and you giving out vibes that could shatter glass. So, what's wrong?'

Emma folded herself into a chair opposite. 'Well, quite a lot, actually. The last twenty-four hours have been pretty hellish. I guess you haven't seen the papers.'

Cherry shook his head. 'More interested in making the news than reading it.'

Emma related the previous day's sequence of events and Wes listened in concentrated silence.

When she had finished, he said, 'Hey, that's bad.'

'I'm sure the police will only want the chalice for a few days. The story will soon die down. And, of course, none of us have mentioned your involvement with the affair.'

'Hell, Emma, I wasn't talking about the chalice. I mean it's bad about Tim. What's the latest news?'

'He's had a nasty shock but I gather it's not as bad as we feared. Unfortunately, he's going to be off work for some time. And right now we need him more than ever.'

'Why?'

'I can't tell you, I'm afraid.'

'Business bad, huh?'

Emma shrugged.

'I know about these things. Me and the boys started Cool Jungle five years ago. OK we got a few early breaks but we worked shit hard. We hit the big time about three years ago. "Fever Woman" was number one for six weeks. Our first album, *Voodoo*, was a rave. Suddenly, we had it all – the cars, the glitz, the hype, the women. I was twenty-five and top of the tree. I knew I deserved to be there and I thought I could stay there. Wrong! There's not many people around ready to give you a hand up, but man, there's, sure as hell, plenty eager to give you a hand down. The trick isn't getting there; it's staying there. Man, that's lesson number one in the pop world and I guess it's the same in business.'

'And how do you do it?'

'By being the best.'

'But we *are* the best.' It was almost an anguished cry.

'OK, Emma. Then, the other thing you have to do is *mache Schau*. A Berlin promoter told us that early on. Let everyone see you're the best.' He jumped to his feet. 'A bit more hip wiggle, a bit more sex, some more top notes.' He went into a few wild bars of "Tropic Night", Cool Jungle's latest hit, swaying sinuously and suggestively across the carpet towards her and drawing the final falsetto F sharp out over what seemed impossibly long seconds.

Emma giggled. 'I don't think that's really Lacy Enterprises' style.'

Wes shrugged and sank back into his chair. 'OK, but the thing is to find your style – then flaunt it. P.R., that's the name of the game today. You can sell any crap if the marketing's right and the best ideas'll go down the pan if the marketing's wrong.'

Emma said, 'Thanks for the advice, Wes. I'm very sorry about the chalice. Is it really important for you to have it soon?'

'No sweat, kid. This could even be a lucky twist for us. We're planning to call our new album *Poison*. We figured to have the Borgia Chalice on the cover and, perhaps, work it into the video. So, if we go ahead and there's a court case running at the same time people are going to accuse us of bad taste. Now there ain't nothing sells more records than some real bad taste.'

'Well, it's good of you to see it that way. I know Tim and Catherine will be relieved. They were very upset about the police holding on to the chalice.'

'Hey, talking about the chalice.' West thrust a hand into the back pocket of his shiny trousers and pulled out a slightly crumpled slip of paper. He handed it to Emma. 'That should cover the cost plus the auctioneer's cut and Tim's commission.'

Emma stared stupefied at a cheque for £900,000. 'I don't think I can accept this, Wes. You haven't got the chalice yet. I'm sure Tim's not paid for it and won't pay for it till the police release it.'

'No sweat. That makes us all square. As soon as it's available you can get it to me.'

'Well, thanks, I'm sure . . .'

'Just one small condition.'

'Yes?'

'When you do get the chalice, Emma, I'd like for you to bring it up to Gloucestershire in person.'

Catherine returned to Wiltshire three days later, after the weekend. She had seen Tim through the crisis time and, on his insistence, had come back to Farrans to watch over the business which, he commented mournfully, was in greater need than he was. She spent the rest of Monday and half of Tuesday in Tim's office with Sally, his secretary, going through Lacy Security accounts and other files she normally did not look at. At Tuesday lunchtime she summoned a council of war in the Lacys' east-wing apartment. There were three people present besides Catherine: Emma, Sally and George Martin, Lacy Security's head of installations and Tim's right-hand man. They helped themselves to soup in the kitchen and carried their bowls through to the sitting room.

'OK,' Catherine began when everyone was settled, 'you don't need me to tell you that things are pretty black. Tim's going to be all right if he keeps strictly away from all work stress for several weeks. The doctors have read the riot act to him and so have I. You can imagine how he took it. He kept on insisting that now of all times he couldn't afford to be away.'

'What did the Major mean by that?' George, whose relationship with Tim went back to army days, always referred to his boss by his military rank – a habit that most of the others in the company had picked up.

'That's exactly what I asked him. He was very cagey but bit-by-bit the truth came out – or some of it. Lacy Security is heavily in the red. Tim's been keeping the situation pretty much to himself.'

Sally, a mid-thirties brunette, nodded. 'For the last six months he's insisted on opening all the mail himself. I wasn't supposed to tell anyone that.'

George set down his empty soup bowl on the coffee table. 'Me and the lads have noticed orders dropping off over the last year, of course, but we just put it down to the recession.'

'There's more to it than that,' Catherine said. 'Things are tight, of course. People just aren't spending as much money on extras. The profits of the gallery are down twenty per cent on last year. That just means a little less jam but it's the security side of the business we all rely on for our bread and butter. Tim believes we're being squeezed out of the market by unfair competition, even dirty tricks.'

'Saul Druckmann!' George uttered the words with contempt. 'The original one-armed bandit.'

'Yes, Tim mentioned that name. Who is he?'

'Someone who sails very close to the edge of the law – and not always on the right side. Plausible. Devious. He'd do anything to turn a dishonest buck. He had a run-in with the Major twenty years ago in Germany and he's had it in for him ever since.'

Emma handed round a plate of sandwiches. 'But how can he do any harm to Tim now?'

'He's set up one of these new cowboy security companies

promising clients miracle results and using methods that don't bear too close looking at.'

'You mean illegal?' Sally asked.

'He's probably too clever for that – at the moment – keeping just the right side of the line.' George chewed a mouthful of ham sandwich before continuing. 'Look. His operation – Artguard – works something like this. Suppose you've got a stately home full of valuable knick-knacks. You're dead scared of burglars but you don't want to pay through the nose for decent protection. You write to Lacy Security and we come along and give you a reasonable quote to make your home as secure as possible. While you're mulling it over, lo and behold, who should turn up on your doorstep out of the blue but the man from Artguard. He gives the place the once over, quotes a figure lower than ours and offers what he calls an insurance-linked guarantee that your home won't be broken into and that, if it is, Artguard will replace all stolen items.'

Sally protested. 'They can't possibly make such a commitment.'

'Oh, but they can. You see, what you don't realize is that Artguard is funded by the very crooks they're supposed to be guarding you against. The syndicates get their cut and cross you off their list of potential victims.'

'Isn't that what used to be called a protection racket?' Emma wanted to know.

'No. So far there's nothing illegal in the operation. That comes in phase two. After a year or so you receive a polite call from the nice man at Artguard who explains that, due to inflationary pressures, rising costs, etc., etc., it has become necessary to introduce an annual premium over and above the cost of the maintenance contract. If at that stage you elect not to renew your contract . . . Well, the rest I can leave to your imagination.'

Emma, leaning forward, brushed a strand of chestnut hair back from her cheek. 'But supposing one of Artguard's clients *does* get burgled – by an outfit not in on the payout?'

'Time to send in the cavalry – in this case the first brigade Mounted Sewer Rats. Broken knee-caps all round. In this country, that is. In places where they have more liberal gun laws Artguard provide armed custodians; graduates from the top penitentiaries; all licensed to kill. Perfectly respectable public institutions and private collectors find themselves actually employing criminal gangs and are, in fact, in their clutches.'

'Tim said something about Grinling's going over to Druckmann's outfit for the security on their new warehouse. Surely, that can't be true, can it? I mean, Buck House? Maybe. The Bank of England? Perhaps. But Grinling's!' Catherine fastidiously brushed crumbs from her suede skirt.

George scratched his close-cropped, iron-grey hair. 'You can see the attraction, can't you? Insurance costs are soaring. Every attempted break-in notches them up further. Then there's the twenty-first-century criminal – brawn *and* brain. As fast as we think up sophisticated security systems – laser controls, heat sensors, ultra-sonic detectors, integrated computer systems and the like – they dream up ways of getting round them. And if they can't do that they're as likely to burst in through the front door brandishing guns. Security guard nowadays is a bloody dangerous job. I know that Grinling's and other West End houses are having to pay absolutely top whack to keep staff. So when friend Druckmann comes along with a proposal that may not be absolutely Queensberry

Rules but does look effective, well it's time for the old Nelson-and-the-telescope trick.'

Catherine sighed. 'Well, in heaven's name, how can we possibly stop them?'

George grinned. 'I reckon it's time we stopped playing by the Queensberry Rules, too. Leave it to me and the boys. We'll see what we can come up with.'

'Thanks, George, that's a positive start.' Catherine stood up. 'Who'd like coffee?'

'I'll get it.' Sally gathered up plates and dishes and hurried through to the kitchen.

Catherine resumed her seat. 'But as well as that we just have to drum up new business – p.d.q.'

'*Mache Schau.*' Emma announced.

'What?'

'*Mache Schau.* It's something Wes said. It means "high profile".'

Catherine noted the way Wes Cherry was suddenly being quoted as an infallible authority. She let it pass. 'High profile means publicity and publicity costs money – which in our case we have not got.'

Again it was Emma who bounced back with a suggestion. 'I think I may be able to help there. Wes reckons his P.R. chap is a great ideas man who'll do us a good deal.'

Catherine looked doubtful. 'OK, but we have to do something quickly. The bank wants a new business plan within a month or else . . .'

George took the coffee mugs from the tray as Sally came back with it and handed them round. 'Well, everyone's behind you; you know that. I reckon you should call the whole workforce together and lay it on the line. Same as you have with us. We'll all do whatever it takes – even a cut in salary if that'll help.'

The others murmured their agreement and for several moments Catherine was too moved to respond. At last she said, 'That's absolutely terrific of all of you. Thanks.' She paused. 'And now we come to the really big problem: what are we going to do with Tim? You know what he's like. There's no way he's going to sit back and watch us trying to rescue *his* business.'

Sally perched on an arm of the sofa. 'The only way to stop him getting involved is to get him physically away from here. But how do we manage that?' She shrugged.

The internal phone buzzed on the table beside Catherine. She picked it up. 'Hello.'

'Oh, Catherine, sorry to disturb your lunch. This is Mary, front desk.'

'Hi, Mary. That's OK. Problems?'

'No. It's just that I have a couple here who've called to see you without an appointment. Their name's Santori.'

II

NO RIVALRY
WITH THE DEAD

Soderini thought to extinguish envy with time, with goodness, with his fortune and by benefiting others . . . He did not know that time cannot wait for anyone, that goodness is not enough, that fortune changes and that malice finds no gift which placates her. So . . . he came to ruin.

Niccolò Machiavelli, *The Prince*

CHAPTER 5

The journey on foot from Rome to Orvieto along the valleys of the Tiber and the Paglia took two days. Brother Pietro did not hurry. He savoured the clean, fresh country air after the foetid humours of the city. Sometimes he read as he walked, rejoicing in the freedom to study those mystics and inspired thinkers the Church forbade to hungry souls because it feared what it could not understand. Sometimes he paused to cool his feet in the river while he said one of the daily offices or prayed informally. But most of the time he thought.

There was much to think about. Not least important was his own situation. The pope had claimed that he was taking the friar into his confidence and for the sole purpose of righting an outrageous wrong. Pietro had not been wholly convinced at the time. Everyone in Rome said that Alexander was as devious as he was ruthless and that he was as ruthless as he was steeped in lust and debauchery. Pietro never paid heed to rumour; it clouded judgement and placed verdict before evidence. Yet experience now suggested that his holiness was using his 'little friar' in some as yet undisclosed intrigue. He had secretly set his pet Dominicans to interrogate Lombardi and then had deliberately concealed from his 'confidential' agent things that he knew about the Michaelmas Massacre.

Foscari neatly laid out in his mind the facts as far as

he understood them at the moment. Some of the cardinals and an undisclosed number of other malcontents had been plotting against the Spanish pope. Nothing new in that. In the treacherous mires and thickets of Italian politics every supreme pontiff had enemies and rivals. However, there were two facts which made the Borgia particularly vulnerable. His own behaviour was utterly outrageous. Nepotism and simony were the common currency of Vatican commerce but Alexander had minted new coin in unprecedented abundance. Lands, offices and favours were lavished upon supporters, family and children. Children! There was scarce a priest in Christendom who had not sired bastards but most of them were put out discreetly to nurse or brought up by relatives. Yet here was the Church's priest-in-chief with no less than six sons and daughters all paraded openly before the world; the girls married into noble houses, the boys made grandees in their own right, swaggering about Rome as though they owned the city – as in not inconsiderable measure they did. The wonder was not that someone had put an end to Giovanni's braggadocio but that he and his siblings together had not been disposed of years ago. The other fact gnawing at the foundation of the Borgia papacy was French gold. The young King Charles VIII, who believed himself destined to become a second Charlemagne – nay greater: the emperor of a reunited Christendom – hated Alexander because he opposed French ambitions in Italy and because he was manifestly unfitted to rule the Church. The king was even now planning a new invasion of the peninsula and the summoning of a general council to depose the pope. His court at Amboise was well peopled with disaffected churchmen and temporal rulers and the clusters of malcontents within papal territory were generously funded from Charles's coffers.

Orvieto had obviously been one such festering s. the body of the Papal States. Yet Alexander had be well aware of the meetings taking place at the Petrucci villa, for Cardinal Petrucci had been his own man. Why, then, had Petrucci been poisoned along with two other ecclesiastics of known disloyalty? Such indiscriminate death-dealing made no sense, whoever was responsible. And why had Alexander made no mention of his secret relationship with Petrucci? Indeed, he had dismissed the cardinal as a 'traitor' like the others. And had the Duke of Gandia really been consorting with his father's enemies?

There was one more question in Brother Pietro's bundle of mysteries and it worried him more and more the closer he drew to his destination. It was late afternoon on the second day of his journey that he had his first view of Orvieto. It was an impressive sight. Out of the flat valley plain a sheer outcrop of rock thrust itself into the air like a monster drawn in a bestiary rearing its head and scaly spine from the swamp. The town sprawled across the summit, its cathedral pointing towards heaven, the houses and palaces clustered around it. The municipality was surrounded by a wall, crumbling in places, but undergoing repair as the scaffolding and clouds of dust testified. Orvieto had once been and would be again a formidable fortress guarding the main route from the north to Rome. It would be vital for Alexander if Charles VIII attacked. It would be a major coup for the French king if the citadel were delivered into his hands. And the man responsible for Orvieto, the governor, appointed not four years since, who was even now putting the town in a good defensive state, was Cesare Borgia, Alexander's eldest son. As Pietro began the steep final ascent and listened to the clang of masons' tools he wondered whose side Cesare was on.

*   *   *

'Ginny, Tristram, what a lovely surprise!' Catherine welcomed the two young people and ushered them into her office.

Ginny, casually dressed in jeans and a cashmere sweater, explained, 'We're sorry to burst in on you unannounced like this. We were really hoping to see *Mr* Lacy but your receptionist told us that he's away today.'

'I'm afraid that the truth is that he's in hospital, Ginny.'

'Oh gosh, I'm sorry. That makes our turning up here much worse.'

'Don't give it another thought. It's been a worrying few days but Tim's on the mend now. You must have had a pretty rough time since last Thursday.'

'Yes, indeed.' Tristram looked grave. 'It's no doubt very salutary to find oneself on the wrong side of the law but it's distinctly unpleasant.'

'It was hell!' Ginny pouted. 'The policeman in charge of the case is a bully and pretty thick with it.'

'Inspector Edgerson?'

'That's right. He let slip that he knew you and Mr Lacy. I'm afraid he wasn't very complimentary.'

Catherine laughed. 'To be insulted by Edgerson is positive flattery. What did he do to you?'

'Kept bringing us in for questioning. He actually locked us up in the cells Sunday night. But, of course, he had nothing to charge us with so he had to let us go. He hated it that Tris is a lawyer and was absolutely clear about our rights.'

Catherine's golden hair caught a shaft of sunlight as she nodded emphatically. 'Yes, he has this illusion about being in complete control. He gets very upset when anything happens to call it into question.'

Ginny shrugged. 'Well, anyway, he's out of our hair now. I think it's clear even to him that he can't pin yet another crime on the wicked Santoris.'

'Are you going back to Italy?'

'You bet – on the first available flight.'

'My senior partner's getting a bit restless,' Tristram explained, 'and Ginny has quite a bit of work piling up.'

His sister nodded. 'Fat Italian tome on zoology to translate into German – boring but lucrative.'

There was an awkward silence which Catherine eventually broke. 'So what can Lacy Enterprises do for you?'

Tristram nervously adjusted his tie. 'Well, obviously nothing. It was a long shot anyway and now that we know that Mr Lacy is ill . . . It's probably best that we don't trouble you further, Mrs Lacy.'

'Catherine, please. It makes me feel terribly old when people of your age call me Mrs Lacy. Look, now that you've come all this way you might as well tell me what's on your mind. Apart from anything else, you've raised my curiosity, so you must satisfy it.'

Ginny laughed. 'Fair enough, Catherine.' Then she was suddenly serious, her dark eyes becoming pools of weariness. 'Tris and I have discussed last Thursday a great deal and the only thing that seems at all obvious about the whole wretched business is that someone's still got it in for us. You remember, just before those four experts keeled over, I said that at last we could put the Borgia Chalice business behind us. Well, that was the world's most classic example of speaking too soon, wasn't it? We're never going to be free of it until whoever did kill those people is behind bars.'

Catherine attempted reassurance. 'Oh, I'm sure you exaggerate. This sort of thing is always a nine-day wonder.'

Tristram shook his head. 'I can't agree, Mrs . . . er . . . Catherine. I think it will be one of those spectacular cases like the disappearance of Lord Lucan that crops up every time a tabloid journalist is stuck for a new story. It's going to be a skeleton in the Santori family cupboard. Right now I don't know whether it might cost me my job. My senior partner sets great store by what he calls "professional conduct in the private sphere". I doubt whether being a suspect in an unsolved case of multiple homicide comes within that category.'

'I see your point. But there's no reason why the case should run. With all the publicity the case is getting the police are going to be under a lot of pressure to get a result p.d.q.'

'And you reckon clever Inspector Edgerson is the right man to come up with all the answers?' Ginny's cynicism gave her voice a hard edge.

Tristram's appraisal was more balanced. 'To be fair, it seems to me this case would tax the best brains Scotland Yard could produce. I mean, it was obviously well planned. There were probably dozens of people who had a chance to administer the poison.'

Catherine suggested, 'The police should be able to narrow the field when they know the result of the autopsies.'

Tristram looked up sharply. 'Oh, you haven't heard. But, no, why should you? I think Edgerson only told us because he thought it might shock us into a confession.'

'Heard what?'

'They've found out what the poison was: *Clostridium botulinum*, the bacterium that produces botulism. Edgerson spared us none of the gory details. Unless treated quickly this kind of food poisoning is fatal in most cases and usually strikes two to three hours after ingestion, depending on the strength of the poison. Whoever administered it last Thursday made sure of its impact by supplying a highly concentrated dose.'

Catherine shivered. 'How horrible.'

'There's more,' Tristram added sombrely. 'The forensic squad detected traces of the toxin in the chalice.'

'But that's ridiculous. Impossible. The poison can't have been . . .'

'Exactly,' Ginny agreed. 'So what we appear to have is the perfect crime – committed in public and in a way that defies all logic. You can see what Tris means when he says this case is destined to run and run – until it's solved.' She looked shrewdly at Catherine as she spoke the last three words.

The other woman nodded. 'I think I begin to see . . .'

'It was something Edgerson let slip that made us think of Mr Lacy,' Ginny explained. 'Something about a murder that he was on the point of solving when Mr Lacy blundered in and stole his thunder.'

'Yes,' her brother added, 'and then we remembered Dad saying that your husband often helped the police with cases involving works of art. Well, you can see what we're getting at, Catherine. It just seemed to us that we had nothing to lose and, perhaps, quite a lot to gain by asking for his opinion on this case.'

Catherine shook her head. 'Even if Tim were fit – which he's not – you can imagine how Edgerson would react at Tim poking his nose in.'

'Oh gosh!' Tristram looked really concerned. 'We didn't mean we expected him to *investigate* – go around tailing suspects, interrogating witnesses, that sort of thing.'

'No,' Ginny said. 'We just wondered whether he could possibly come out to Florence for a few days and think about the murders with us. He knows some of the victims and the world they move in. We thought if we could put our heads together quietly we just might come up with some leads to give the police – anonymously if necessary. We didn't expect Mr Lacy to do any running around. We could do any of that that had to be done. We simply wanted the benefit of his experience.'

'Well, anyway,' Tristram concluded. 'That's what we thought. Of course, we can see, now, that it's quite out of the question.'

Catherine sat back and surveyed the handsome young couple with a thoughtful smile. 'Don't be too sure about that.'

On the second day of his stay in Orvieto Brother Pietro had three interesting conversations.

At mid-morning he preached in the piazza in front of the cathedral's variegated marble façade. As always, a crowd of the curious gathered to hear the new attraction, a crowd swollen by those who knew of his brush with the Inquisition. Once he had them there, Pietro had no difficulty keeping them there. He enjoyed preaching and there were few audiences of which he failed to get the measure. He knew when to make them laugh and when to cry, when to hold them with a long story and the precise moment for the dramatic denouement. He knew when to set his booming baritone reverberating from the buildings around and when to speak so softly that every man, woman and child leaned forward noiselessly for fear of missing a single word. He knew how to encourage hecklers and then isolate them from the rest of the congregation behind a glass wall of ridicule. But most of all he exulted when his hearers responded to the message that, he believed, was not his but the Holy Spirit's. On this morning a group of about twenty men and women stayed behind to hear more. One of them, a middle-aged widow called Maria, was the proprietor of a local wine shop and to her premises Brother Pietro's band of disciples repaired.

Over earthenware beakers of smooth, golden wine from neighbouring slopes the talk moved from spiritual matters to the decadence of the times. Alcohol and growing mutual confidence relaxed tongues. For much of the time Foscari sat back and allowed the conversation to run its own course, only occasionally interposing a question or statement to lever it in a more promising direction.

'What examples do we have to point out to our young people?'

'That's right. It's a waste of breath for holy friars and priests to preach about godliness when we have Cardinal Cain and his brood breaking every one of the ten commandments.'

Amid the laughter which followed Foscari asked, 'Who's Cardinal Cain?'

'Who's Cardinal Cain?' The voice registered astonishment at such a naive question. 'Why our revered governor, Cardinal Cesare Borgia, the pope's number one bastard.'

'Not to be cardinal much longer, I'll wager,' the hostess prophesied. 'There's a flagon of my best says he renounces the purple inside a twelvemonth.'

'I still don't understand why you call him Cardinal Cain,' Pietro insisted.

The reply was couched in the almost pitying tones one might use to a man beside his wits. 'Cain was Adam's firstborn. Right? And he had a younger brother, Abel. Right? And Cain killed Abel. That's what the Church teaches. Well, it's the same with the pope's sons; Cesare killed Giovanni. Everyone knows that.'

'And why does everyone say that Cesare did this terrible thing?'

Opinion was obviously divided on that score.

'Well he's always been jealous of the younger son,' Maria suggested. 'It's because he was originally the second son and so had to be a priest. Then, when his older brother died, all his lands and titles passed to Giovanni. So Giovanni could marry a rich wife and go to the wars and build up large estates while Cesare had to be content with titles and honours conferred by his father. That's why I say he'll take off the cardinal's hat very soon. He's not going to be trapped like that again.'

'I heard it was all to do with the sister, Lucrezia. Cesare found out that Giovanni had been screwing her and he thought that was his privilege as elder brother.'

'Well my cousin – who was secretary to Cardinal Petrucci – told me that it was all political.'

Foscari made a mental note of the speaker's face and name. 'What did he mean by that?'

The man tapped his nose. 'He wouldn't go into details. Said it was all hush-hush but that the pope's sons didn't see eye to eye on some very important matters.'

The trouble with gossip, Pietro reflected, as he made his way to the Franciscan convent, was that five per cent of it was usually true but one did not know which five per cent.

After the brothers' midday meal he was approached in the cloister by one of the younger members of the house, eager to hear about Pietro's travels and experiences. Like many friars professed scarcely a year, Brother Tommaso was a bundle of enthusiasms and ready judgements. He wanted to know about Foscari's first-hand experience of the Inquisition and the Dominicans who operated it. Tommaso had absorbed all the traditional Franciscan bitterness about the rival order of friars mendicant.

'Have you seen the latest impertinence from that troublemaker, Savonarola,' he asked, pulling a small, printed tract from his sleeve.

'I don't believe I have.' Pietro, of course, knew about the Florentine friar whose bold preaching had won him an immense popular support in his own city and stern denunciation everywhere else, especially in Rome. He had more than a sneaking regard for the hawk-nosed Dominican whose invective against loose public and private morals had led hundreds to change their ways. But he would not shock Tommaso by saying so. 'What does Brother Girolamo have to tell us.'

'Well,' the young man stopped his perambulation around the cloister and drew his companion to the low wall of the colonnade, 'you know how sorely tried his holiness has been.'

'He certainly doesn't take kindly to preachers who claim visions from God telling them to denounce the head of the Church.'

Tommaso scowled. 'The man is deceived and a deceiver. But he has the support and protection of the Florence signoria. So, because he couldn't discipline the wretched Dominican, his holiness magnanimously offered him a cardinal's hat.'

Pietro closed his eyes and had a clear picture of Alexander in his large padded chair, smiling benignly – a smile that concealed far more than it expressed. 'That was a mistake, of course. Savonarola could only regard it as a bribe.'

'Ingrate! Turning down the greatest honour the pope could bestow! Of course, all his holiness could do after that was excommunicate the hell-hound. Well, here is Savonarola's response to that.' Tommaso brandished the pamphlet. 'This "epistle", as he calls, it is on sale in every town and city.'

'Do we know that Savonarola, himself, published it?' Pietro asked cautiously.

The young friar, who was turning the pages in search of a passage he had marked, muttered, 'Who else?'

Foscari shrugged. 'Some over-zealous disciple, perhaps.'

Tommaso was not listening. 'Ah yes, here we are. See what you think of this: "This excommunication is invalid both in the sight of God and man, inasmuch as it is based on false reasoning and the accusations of enemies. I have always submitted to the authority of the Church but no one is bound to yield to commands which are opposed to charity and the law of God. When our superiors issue such commands they are no longer the Lord's representatives. It is not only permissible to resist commands by which the pope seeks to enforce his authority to the detriment of the Church; it is obligatory. We dare not keep silent."' Tommaso looked up, clearly scandalized. 'Where would such teaching as that lead us?'

Foscari thought the Dominican's measured argument perfectly reasonable but he said, 'Anarchy?'

'Exactly! Every man believing and doing whatever seems right to him. It would be the end of the Church. The end of the faith.'

Pietro smiled indulgently. 'Oh, I think the faith might manage to survive. It has probably encountered worse in the last fifteen hundred years.'

But two hours later, as Foscari walked the two kilometres from the town to the Villa Petrucci, he thought hard about Savonarola, and Pope Alexander – and himself. The Borgia had two ways of compelling obedience and silence – fear and bribery. The Dominican fanatic had resisted both – and would probably burn for it. Pietro had been ready to burn – or as ready as a man can ever be for so hideous a mortal end. Now he saw that he had failed the second test. His cardinal's hat had been the view from a window of the Castel Sant' Angelo. And he had accepted it. He had been caught unawares. The prospect of sudden freedom had been irresistible; the offer of confidential work for the head of the Church had been flattering. As a result here he was wandering the country, subordinating the service of the Gospel to the pope's political intrigues, indulging his own sinful curiosity.

He entered the Petrucci estate and ambled through a lemon grove where the sunlit fruit glowed like miniature lanterns amidst the foliage. Beyond it a sloping vineyard provided the setting for a long, two-storey villa with terracotta roof tiles. Before he reached the house, Foscari had made three resolutions: this would be his only special assignment for the pope, even if declining others meant a return to prison; he would keep meticulous notes of every significant interview, so that no one could accuse him of misrepresentation; and he would – very assiduously – watch his own back.

In the kitchen of the villa the servants gave Brother Pietro bread and chicken broth and gathered round to watch him eat. The steward explained that, though friars and beggars were always welcome and he had orders to make sure that food was ready at all times, they had few callers these days. In the cardinal's time there had been a daily procession of genuinely poor people and scroungers – of course, always there were scroungers – but his eminence would not allow the servants to discriminate. Some days they had all been rushed off their feet from dawn to dusk. Pietro encouraged them to talk about their late master. It seemed that he had been a model employer in every way – generous, fair-minded and approachable. Cautiously, Pietro broached the subject of the cardinal's demise. The memory still distressed and angered them. None of them had any doubt about the manner of Petrucci's death: the pope had poisoned him. And, what was worse, he had labelled their master a traitor. Mary and all the saints were their witness that no more loyal servant of the Church existed. Why, the good cardinal had been far too straightforward and simple a soul to engage in plots.

When Foscari pressed them on that point – had the holy cardinal not sometimes welcomed here men who were known enemies of the pope – they all fell silent. It was the steward who explained that his eminence had entertained a great deal. That was why he had kept a large staff here at the villa, unlike the present master and mistress, who had sent several servants away. The cardinal had made no judgements of men. All were welcome to his table. Brother Pietro wondered if he might be permitted to pay his respects to the present owners of the Villa Petrucci and the steward went to make enquiries. He returned to explain that the master was still absent but that his mistress would be happy to receive the friar.

The upper chamber into which Foscari was shown was a long room with tall, wide windows at one end facing the lowering sun across the valley. Valentina Torelli was seated with two companions before this opening using the evening light to read by. Before coming to the villa Pietro had made a point of discovering that it had passed to Petrucci's niece, Valentina who was married to Alfredo Torelli, a nobleman of modest fortune. She set aside her book at Brother Pietro's approach and greeted him very properly. He saw a woman of about eighteen whose orange-gold hair, though braided, was allowed to fall freely about the shoulders of a blue dress sewn with golden stars. A chair had already been set for him and, as he sat, he noticed that a glass of wine and a dish of sweetmeats also stood at his elbow.

'Madame, you are very gracious to unexpected guests.'

She smiled, a relaxed, girlish smile. 'My uncle used to say that the uninvited guest was the best kind because he came entirely of his own free choice.'

'I wish I'd met your uncle. Everyone who knew him speaks very highly of him.'

'"Good faith that yields to none and ways without reproach and unadorned simplicity."'

Pietro recognized the quotation with surprise. 'Ovid. I've never before met a woman schooled in the classics.'

Valentina laughed. 'Only my outward form is a woman. I was brought up in my uncle's household after my father died. And he said that, as he didn't understand women at all, he would have to bring me up as a man. That meant all the best tutors, teaching me poetry, philosophy, mathematics, music – even fencing, though I was never much good at it.'

'You have suffered a great loss.'

'Not just me; the world is the poorer for Niccolò Petrucci's death. But we must not dwell on past sorrows. Tell me about yourself, Brother Pietro. Where are you from and where have you been?'

They talked of inconsequential matters until the servants came to light the lamps. Then Valentina jumped up and said, 'Come, I will walk with you as far as the

ve the evening. I often sit in the lemon grove
Virgil and listening to all the birds pleading with
th not to go down. Sometimes I stay until there's
only me and the nightingale left.'

As they walked between the rows of vines, avoiding
the baskets already put out for the next day's pickers,
Foscari brought the subject round to the death of the
three cardinals. 'As well as being an act of the vilest
evil, it seems to have been utterly pointless.'

Valentina sighed. 'I've thought about it so much my
head aches. It's politics, of course. My uncle didn't
like politics but he thought I ought to understand it
so we sometimes had long discussions about what was
happening in the Church and in Italy.'

Foscari was suddenly very interested, hopeful. 'He
told you all about the rivalries; who was plotting against
whom?'

'Not everything, I'm sure, but enough for me to realize
how complicated it all is. Oh, look! A salamander!'

For several minutes they watched the black and yellow amphibian shuffling along the grass path. Then
Pietro ventured, 'Your uncle was a friend of the pope's,
wasn't he?'

Valentina considered the question. 'Friend? No I never
heard him use that word. In fact, I don't think he liked
either of them.'

'Either of them?'

'Borgia or della Rovere. As far as I can work it out the
trouble started at the last papal election. Rodrigo Borgia
and Giuliano della Rovere both wanted to be leader of
the Church. They bought as many of the votes of the
sacred college as they could. Cardinal Petrucci was
one of the few who could not be bribed. He didn't
like either of the main candidates but it was obvious

one of them was going to win. Originally, he gave della Rovere his support, then, after agonizing over his responsibility for several hours, he switched to the other camp. Della Rovere never forgave him. Now, as you know, he spends all his time either at the French court or with Ludovico Sforza, Duke of Milan, making as much mischief as possible and brooding on his revenge.'

'So, you think Cardinal della Rovere was somehow behind your uncle's murder?'

'He's the only man I've ever heard of who thought he had a quarrel with him. My uncle tried desperately hard to patch up the quarrel. Not just between himself and della Rovere. He could see the damage all the splits were doing to the Church: pro-French versus anti-French; pro-Borgia versus anti-Borgia; pro-della Rovere versus anti-della Rovere. That's why he held meetings here to try to bring different factions together. Oh, why is it always the peace-makers who suffer, Brother Pietro?'

'I think because they're followers of the Prince of Peace, my child.'

Valentina sighed again, a long deep sigh. 'It doesn't really matter now but something inside me won't rest until the truth about my uncle's death comes out. If it was della Rovere, why were the other two murdered – Montadini and della Chiesa? Everyone knows that they were della Rovere's biggest supporters. Oh dear, Brother Pietro, as you say, it all seems utterly pointless!'

'Utterly pointless.' The words echoed over and again through Foscari's mind as he walked back to the convent, as he shared automatically in the evening office, as he sat in his cell writing his notes with the aid of a lamp begged from the sub-prior.

Utterly pointless; a piece of blind, vicious evil? Or diabolically clever; a crime planned so as to appear that it had no plan? The question was still unresolved when Foscari closed tired eyes in sleep.

'The basic problem about this multiple killing is to try to work out whether it's the work of some psychopath with a grudge against the art establishment or whether it's a focused murder plot by a clever, if twisted, assassin.'

Tim spoke from the cushioned comfort of a BMW's deep rear seat, where he had been gingerly deposited by his host and hostess, as though he were an inadequately boxed Meissen figurine by Kändler. Other vehicles raced past as Tristram Santori took the vehicle at a sedate 110 kph along the autostrade linking Pisa and its airport with Florence. Tim was slightly amused at the way the two young people had pounced on him as he emerged from the customs' hall, Tristram grabbing his small travelling bag and Ginny linking her arm through his to lead him to the waiting car.

He had fallen in with Catherine's master plan of a trip to Tuscany 'to help out those poor Santori kids', not because he did not know what her real motive was, but because he wanted to convince her that he was at least going to go through the motions of convalescence. He owed her that. And his heart attack had given him a bad scare. To be honest, it had shaken him quite a bit though not as much as it had Catherine, their two boys and the team at Farrans. Yes, he owed it to her – to them all – to be a good patient and allow himself to be sent off for a few days' rest. Of course, it could only be a few days. With business in the state it was and Artguard using every dirty trick in the book he could not afford to be away from his desk any longer than that. Meanwhile, he would do what he could for poor old Gregor's pleasant – if over-attentive

– offspring. Not that that would be much. On the plane he had studied the file dramatically labelled 'BORGIA CHALICE CASE' in Sally's neat capitals. It was a very thin folder containing a couple of newspaper cuttings and reports by Catherine, Ginny and Tristram on all that they could remember about the auction and the lunch party.

His first impressions – and first impressions were often useful – was of a bizarre crime perpetrated by someone with a bizarre mind. This was really all he had to offer when, as they passed the Lucca junction, Ginny asked if he had reached any conclusions.

'Well, whoever was responsible has a love of theatricality and total ruthlessness, but he's also clever enough to realize that suspicion will fall on you two – not to mention clever enough to find a way of administering the poison to four different people. Now, that could be someone with a massive grudge against art critics in general or the four critics in particular or the Santori family. On the other hand it might be someone with a much more specific motive for killing all or, perhaps, just one of the victims and who realized that the Borgia Chalice legend and all the recent publicity provided a very effective smoke-screen.'

Tristram glanced at him in the rear-view mirror. 'So you don't think the poison was in the chalice. That still seems to be the line Edgerson's working on.'

Tim lifted his eyes heavenward. 'Edgerson's problem is that he doesn't know whether or not to believe your statements. You made very public and widely reported threats during the trial, so you're still his number one suspects. He's still trying to figure out how you worked the conjuring trick. You're the only ones who know categorically that you really did drink from the chalice with the others.'

'But we did,' Tristram insisted.

'Thought we might as well get a mouthful of decent champagne out of the whole business,' Ginny added.

'There you are, then. There's no way that you could have escaped a lethal dose of botulism if it had been in the chalice. So we can forget all the illusionist nonsense that seems to be fascinating the tabloid press and some of the police.'

'Then, the traces of poison in the chalice . . .'

'Were added, afterwards, Ginny, just to confuse things. They must have been.'

Tristram frowned and summarized methodically. 'So the murderer is someone who had access to the victims before the sale and to the chalice afterwards.'

Ginny groaned. 'That doesn't narrow the field down very much, does it?'

'I'm afraid not,' Tim agreed. 'But it does mean that the police should be checking the victims' movements throughout the morning meticulously. Who were they talking to? Did anyone give them sweets, cigarettes, chewing gum? Were they seen to take any medication? There are dozens of ways of administering poison quite casually and openly without attracting any attention.'

They turned off the motorway at the first Firenze intersection but instead of heading into town Tristram took the BMW, by ever-narrowing roads, into the hills to the north of the city.

After a few minutes, Tim said, 'I thought you lived in the centre.'

The siblings exchanged the briefest of glances before Ginny explained, 'We do, but our apartment is tiny and terribly noisy. Friends of ours in Rome have a weekend place up here. We have the use of it whenever they're not here. They won't want it till Christmas now, so you'll have plenty of peace and quiet. There'll be just you and your minder.'

'Minder? Nobody said anything about a minder.'

She laughed. 'Oh, you'll like O.K. Anyway, you can meet him now.'

The car had rounded one edge of a grove of poplars and come abruptly to rest before the building they screened. Tim got out and found himself in front of a villa whose appeal was nothing diminished by its peeling stucco and sun-bleached shutters. Along its entire frontage ran a veranda over which an aged vine twisted its gnarled branches. From one of the half dozen or so wicker chairs enjoying its shade a young man in black jeans and T-shirt detached himself and emerged into the sunlight.

Ginny made the introductions. 'Tim, this is O.K., your chef, chauffeur and general factotum.'

'Good to meet you, chief.' The ex-goldsmith's apprentice turned to his friends. He pulled a gold half-hunter from his pocket. 'So what kept you? It shouldn't take an hour and a half from the airport.'

The Santoris accepted the rebuke with only slightly embarrassed silence. Tim assumed they accepted their friend's role as nanny. O.K. picked up Tim's bag and with the implied command, 'Supper in twenty minutes', strode back into the house.

Two hours later, as they moved on to the veranda after the meal, Tim was forced to acknowledge that what O.K. lacked in social graces he more than made up for in culinary ability. The cuisine might best have been styled Anglo-Italian. There was a salad with pasta, chicken casseroled with apricots and a cassata of blackcurrant with a hint of vermouth.

'That really was a delicious supper, O.K. Thank you.'

'Six hundred and fifty calories each,' the young man said.

Ginny hurried to explain. 'Catherine faxed us a copy of your diet sheet a couple of days ago. O.K.'s been practising ever since.'

'I see. I'm going to be kept up to the mark, am I? No sloping off to the nearest trattoria for fettucini and a glass or two of Montecarlo?'

Tristram's face showed genuine concern. 'We promised Catherine we'd help you follow doctor's orders. She thought you might need a little bit of . . . encouragement.'

Tim smiled. 'If that meal was a typical example of your help, I'm definitely encouraged.'

They sat in the creaking wicker chairs and watched the lights come on in the valley and along the opposite hillside. Tim looked at his watch. Allowing for the time difference Catherine should be back in the flat preparing dinner for herself and the boys – unless she decided to work late, juggling the accounts, writing polite, delaying letters to pressing creditors. He decided to give it another hour before phoning.

'. . . like being on a star.'

Tim suddenly realized that Ginny was talking to him. 'Sorry. Miles away. What was that?'

'I was just saying that we're sitting here, looking at all those lights and where some of those lights are, people are looking at our lights and perhaps thinking "I wonder who lives over there". It's a bit like stars and planets and things – all isolated in space and not knowing what's happening on other stars . . . and things . . .' She tailed off, aware that the three men were looking at her with bemused smiles.

Tristram laughed. 'You must forgive my sister, Tim.

112

She gets these philosophical turns when she's forgotten to take the tablets.'

'Soulless cretin!' Ginny riposted. 'For that you don't get any more coffee.' She turned to their guest. 'Another cup for you, Tim?'

He hastily declined. He had no taste for decaf – doctor's orders or no doctor's orders.

They all went back to admiring the nocturnal view until O.K. said what they were all thinking. 'How are we going to track down this murderer then?'

'Tim thinks it's a pretty hopeless task – too many suspects.'

'That isn't quite what I said, Tris. I merely observed that the police would need to question everyone who spoke to or even saw the victims on the morning of the murder. That's plodding, meticulous routine work but it's what the police do best and it often produces results. It would be pointless for us to get involved in that and we'd make ourselves pretty unpopular if we tried. No. I think we should come at the problem from the other end.'

'Other end?' Ginny looked puzzled.

'Yes – victims rather than suspects.' Tim searched the unenlightened faces staring at him in the dim light reaching the veranda from inside the house. 'Look, as I said earlier, the key to the crime is motive.'

The young people nodded, not wholly convinced.

'We can rule out "the Revenge of the Santoris". That leaves, as I said, either a demented artist with a grudge or someone who had a good reason for wanting one or more of the victims dead. Well, for my money, we can rule out the first alternative. This crime was carefully planned by someone who had inside knowledge; someone who could approach the victims and was probably known to them.

So, some research on the victims themselves might pay dividends.'

'You mean see if they had any enemies?' Ginny asked.

'Yes, but it's more a question of finding out what sort of people they were, who they associated with, what skeletons were hidden in their cupboards, whether they'd given someone cause to hate them badly enough to kill them. If you can discover such a someone and find out that he or she was at Grinling's on the fateful morning . . . Well, then you've got yourself a real suspect.'

The Santoris looked thoughtful but said nothing.

O.K. hoisted his feet to the veranda rail. 'Sounds like pretty hard graft.'

Tim agreed. 'Make no mistake about it. It'll mean a lot of leg work, a lot of nosing around, a lot of questioning people who may not want to be questioned. You have to decide right at the outset whether it's really worth all the effort.'

The others exchanged glances. It was Ginny who spoke for them. 'Ever since Tris and I were kids we've had to live down the name Santori – at school, at college, at work, among our neighbours and our friends, and, of course, the media. When Dad died our only comfort was the thought that now we'd be left in peace. We could actually start, in our mid-twenties to discover our own identities, live our own lives. It might be possible to go shopping without people turning to stare at us and to meet people at parties who didn't say "Santori? Didn't I see something on telly last week about someone with that name?" It's been almost as bad for O.K. since he became virtually an adopted member of the family. Tim, the thought that all the gossip and suspicion and sidelong glances may never stop . . .

Well, it's just unbearable. We have to get this poisoning case settled and dealt with and out of the way if we possibly can. I don't care how much work it involves.'

Tim saw the others nod in agreement. 'If that's how you all feel, then I'll do whatever I can to help. As long as you realize that we may all put in bags of sweat and mental effort and still have nothing to show for it at the end of the day.'

'Have you got a plan of campaign for us?' Tristram asked.

'Well, there are five victims. It's just a case of researching each one in turn. That's going to mean a bit of travelling. Heinrich Segar's base was near Munich. Julia Devaraux lived in London. Saint-Yves was every dapper inch a Parisian. And Mort Bronsky, of course, hailed from New York.'

'Five?' O.K. lay back and gazed up at the dense overhanging foliage. 'You said we had to get the lowdown on five victims.'

'That's right. Don't forget the victim right at the centre of this whole sordid business. Whoever planned this crime planned it around the Borgia Chalice. That magnificent piece of craftsmanship was made an accessory to murder – just as, presumably, it was five centuries ago, either by the pope or someone who wanted to pin a triple assassination on him. We ought to find out as much as we can about it.'

'Yeah, but that's all history,' O.K. protested.

'It's history our murderer chose to make use of. I think we ought to know as much about it as he does – preferably more.'

Tristram took up the idea eagerly. 'Well, at least that information ought to be on our doorstep. If there are any records about the legend and how it started they ought to be in the Vatican Archive. I've worked there a couple of times before. I could certainly check.'

'And I could start on the German. I have to deliver a typescript to the publishers in Frankfurt as soon as I've finished it. I'll go by road and spend some time in Munich on the way back.' Ginny stood up. 'I guess we'd better be getting back into Florence. We'll come up again tomorrow evening. If there's anything you need in the meantime, Tim, just let O.K. know or call us. Our home number and Tris's office number are by the phone.'

'I'm sure I'll be fine. Thanks for everything.'

As soon as the Santoris had departed Tim phoned Catherine.

'Hi, darling.' She sounded relaxed but Tim thought that was probably an act for his benefit. 'How are you? Good flight?'

'Everything's fine. It's a lovely spot – very quiet, restful.'

'Good. What about Ginny and Tristram? Have you been able to set their minds at rest?'

'Well, we've worked out a plan of action and they've gone off all enthusiastic. They're obviously happy to be doing something. I did tell them that the chances of discovering anything really valuable are pretty remote but they seem determined to believe that I can work miracles. How are things your end?'

'Something interesting cropped up this afternoon. You know *H.S.*?'

'Not that I recall. Have I met him recently?'

'It's not a "him"; it's a magazine – *High Society*, the journal of the upwardly mobile.'

'That explains why I don't know it.'

116

'Silly! Well, anyway, their features editor phoned up wanting to know if I'd do an appreciation of Julia Devaraux for them.'

'As if you hadn't enough on your plate. Anyway, why you?'

'That was the question I asked. The girl – typical Sloane: slices of hard arrogance thick-spread with smarm – waffled about a bit but what it came down to, of course, was the connection with the Borgia Chalice. The article on Devaraux was just an excuse to run their own piece about the famous poison cup.'

'You told her to take a running jump?'

'Not in quite so many words, but yes. That deflated her more than somewhat. She obviously wasn't expecting to be turned down. She actually made a very generous offer for a thousand words. I thought of the bank manager and was almost tempted . . . But only almost. My guess is she'll try again tomorrow with a bigger deal.'

'And how are things in the office generally?'

'Oh, fine.'

'Good . . . Anything new on the Naseby contract?'

'Tim, I said things are fine. We're coping. We're dealing with things as they crop up. We're making decisions. We're developing a business strategy along the lines we discussed with you a couple of days ago. We'll make sure that Lacy Enterprises survives. Your job is to make sure that Tim Lacy survives. Now I must get on. The boys had some friends in this afternoon and the place is a tip.'

'Right. Goodnight, then.'

'Goodnight, darling. Take very special care. We all love you.'

'Thanks. You too . . . I suppose Devaraux's P.R.

people would have most of the information so it wouldn't take you too much time . . .'

'What was that, Tim?'

'Nothing, nothing. Just an idle thought. Goodnight. See you soon.'

CHAPTER 6

Tina felt nervous and embarrassed as she slipped her light raincoat off in the foyer. Her bra was a size too small and uncomfortable. But obviously effective. One of the uniformed guards at the security desk nudged his colleague and they both helped themselves to a long look as she advanced across the expanse of black marble. They saw an above-average height, nineteen-year-old girl with dark, shoulder-length hair, smiling eyes, full lips and a figure whose contours were emphasized by the white blouse and thigh-length black skirt.

She signed in, collected a pass and took the lift to the fifth floor. The next couple of minutes would be tough. She would have other women to cope with. Rapidly, she went over her script in her mind.

The receptionist gave her a professional smile. 'Can I help you?'

'I'd like to see Mr Druckmann, please.'

'Do you have an appointment?'

'No, but if you could give him this, I think he'll see me.' Tina handed the girl a long plain envelope.

'Well, I'll see but I don't hold out much hope. Mr Druckmann never sees anyone without an appointment.' She went through an interior doorway.

Tina walked with apparent nonchalant curiosity about the room. She had spotted the surveillance camera as

119

came in and was careful not to make her
obvious. She sauntered around the desk and
ntal note of the information she wanted.

ceptionist reappeared. 'Please take a seat, Ms
Meadows. Mr Druckmann's secretary will be out in just
a moment.'

'Thanks. Could I use your ladies' room while I'm
waiting?'

'Sure. Third on the right along the corridor.'

Tina went through the door that led to Artguard's
administrative centre. 'Well, here goes nothing,' she
said to herself, and strode straight down the passageway
towards the door at the far end with an assumed air of
complete assurance. She put a hand out to the handle of
Saul Druckmann's door, took a deep breath and marched
straight in.

She took two steps inside before halting. 'Oh, I'm so
sorry.' Her hand went to her mouth. 'I obviously got the
wrong door.'

Druckmann was alone. He stood up behind his desk
and surveyed the intruder, obviously liking what he saw.
'Who were you looking for, Miss . . .?'

'Tina. Tina Meadows.' She smiled a candid smile.
'Oh, you're Mr Druckmann, aren't you?' She managed
to infuse the question with a sense of awe.

'That's right.'

'Gosh, I was hoping to get to see you but I didn't mean
to burst in. I'm looking for a job.'

'Well, I have someone who handles all junior staff
appointments, Miss Meadows.'

'Yes. I sent my C.V. through to your secretary.'

'Then I'm sure you'll be hearing from us very soon.
We put all applicants through a very stringent screening
process. In a business like ours that's essential.'

'Of course. Even a go-getting, ground-breaking company like Artguard must have rules and procedures.' Tina treated the large, one-armed man to her warmest smile and wondered if she had done enough. She saw Druckmann look at his watch and thought she probably had. She half-turned. 'Well, I'm sorry to have burst in on you like this. I won't waste any more . . .'

Druckmann came around his desk. 'Well, seeing as you're here, Miss Meadows, and as I do have five minutes before my next appointment, take a seat and tell me something about yourself.'

Tina moved to the chair in front of the desk. Druckmann buzzed his secretary and asked her to bring Miss Meadows' C.V. through. Tina greatly enjoyed the scowl the immaculate, mid-twenties blonde unleashed as she came in with the letter Tina had delivered minutes before.

She waited for Druckmann to become engrossed in her impressive – and totally fictitious – C.V. but he did not give the document his full attention: he could not keep his eyes off her. She wondered if she had overdone the tight bra and deep neckline of the blouse. She did not dare to make her move till he averted his gaze for several seconds.

'You've certainly crammed a lot into a very young life,' he observed.

'Time's short, Mr Druckmann. I want to make the most of every minute. I'm on a fast track to the top. That's why I prefer the direct approach. I can't wait around looking in the sits vac columns and writing hundreds of applications. I find the pro-active approach pays off far better.'

'I'm sure you're right. What made you choose Artguard?'

'I'm only interested in innovative companies that are

expanding, Mr Druckmann. Since Artguard started, eighteen months ago, your performance has been very impressive.'

'Well, thank you, Miss Meadows. I'll look forward to explaining my business philosophy to you sometime.'

I'll bet you will, Tina thought. She watched his eyes rolling like a chameleon's as they registered and re-registered all he could see of her above the desk top. How was she going to divert his attention elsewhere in these rapidly diminishing five minutes? 'I believe Artguard is all set to become a major international force in the world of specialist security. I love travel – and art.'

'Yes, I see from your C.V . . .'

'That's not a genuine Corot is it?' She pointed to the picture on the wall behind him.

'It's clever of you to spot that, Miss Meadows.' He swivelled his chair round. 'The experts tell me it's a very good copy . . .'

Tina wasn't listening. She opened her handbag, took something out and bent swiftly below the level of the desk top. Her trembling fingers fumbled the job. The bugging device dropped to the thick carpet. She retrieved it, fixed it and in the same moment saw Druckmann's feet swing back into view.

When he turned completely she was leaning forward, elbow on the desk, peering intently at the canvas behind him. 'Would you agree with that verdict?'

'Well, I'm no expert.'

'Please, take a closer look.'

Tina walked round the desk and tried to stare knowledgeably at the painting. But she was more aware of the man who now stood behind her resting his hand lightly on her thigh. Thank the Lord the man only had one arm.

'Yes,' she said, resisting the urge to move away from him, 'very competent brushwork.'

Druckmann's hand began to move upwards. Tina glued the relaxed smile to her face. What now? A bit late to insist that she was not that kind of girl. If she suddenly went prim and coy he would very probably smell a rat. She felt his breath on her neck.

Then the intercom buzzed. Druckmann moved to the desk to flick the switch. The secretary's voice announced, 'Mr Routledge is here.'

Tina skipped round the desk and retrieved her coat and bag. 'Well, thank you so much for seeing me, Mr Druckmann. I do hope you'll give me a ring when the next suitable vacancy crops up.' She held out her hand.

He shook it firmly. 'Thank you for calling, Miss Meadows. We may well contact you. I've a feeling that you're the sort of young woman who could fit well into our operation.'

Tina forced herself to walk slowly back along the corridor and through the outer office. Only when she reached the lift did she let out her breath in a long sigh of relief.

In the café on the corner of the street she collapsed into a chair. 'Tea, Dad, hot and sweet and quick,' she gasped to the man opposite.

'How did it go, luv?' George Martin asked.

'You were right about Druckmann. Yuk! He gives me the creeps.'

'You got to his office, then?'

'Yes.'

'Great! And the bug?'

'Under his desk top.'

'Well done, Tina.' George summoned the waitress. He ordered tea and a plate of cakes. 'What did you manage to find out? Quick, while it's fresh in your mind.'

'Well, you got the layout about right from the Major's description.' She pointed to the drawing on a pad lying on the table. 'The reception area's a bit bigger, though.'

'Show me.'

Tina made alterations with a biro. 'All the doors have locks operated by access cards. I saw TV cameras here and here, at either end of the corridor, and in Druckmann's office here and here.'

'Fixed or roving?'

'Fixed. There are infra-red scanners all over the place but nothing more sophisticated that I could see.'

The food arrived. Tina gratefully gulped down her tea while George speedily disposed of two eclairs. Through a mouthful of cream and choux pastry he asked about their office systems.

'The very latest: Cyclops 94 with all the gizmos.'

'Fabulous! Kid, you're an angel!'

Tina giggled. 'I didn't feel much like an angel back there, giving a middle-aged man the come-on. And if you ever breathe a word about this to Paul I'll never speak to you again.'

'Forget Paul. Let's you and me go on the game. My management skills and your obvious . . . talent . . .'

'Dad!'

George laughed, then was suddenly serious. 'I might be looking for another job anyway if this doesn't work. It's a question of either we put Artguard out of business or they do the same to us.'

Tina got up and gave him a quick hug. 'You'll do it, Dad, and when you do I want to be around to watch that slob Druckmann squirm.' She picked up a small hold-all from under the table. 'Right now I'm going to change out of these clothes that are making me feel like toothpaste in a tube.' She moved away to the door marked 'Ladies'.

George picked up his mobile phone and punched in a number. Inside a van in a multi-storey car park two streets away another machine bleeped. The driver clicked it on.

'That you, George?'

'Yes, Steve. You should be getting something from Druckmann's office now.'

'Oh, yeah, loud and clear. Pete's already recording it.'

'Good. Make sure you don't miss anything. Since we don't know what we're listening for we can't regard anything as trivial. Is Johnny there?'

'Just popped off for some pies and a six-pack.'

'Well, when he gets back tell him that Artguard's office PC system is Cyclops 94. Tell him to get all the gen that he can on it and its immune system, then to shift his arse back to Farrans and find a way of hacking into it. His job – all our jobs – could depend on it. It won't be long before they find the bug and then they'll know we're on their tail. What they won't know is that we're inside their corporate head. OK, Steve, talk to you later.'

George closed up the mobile. 'Right, Sergeant Druckmann. If you want to fight with the gloves off, that's fine by me.'

There were moments during the next two weeks when Pietro Foscari ardently wished himself back in the entrails of the Castel Sant' Angelo or even at the stake with the flames beginning to gnaw at his legs. From his acquaintance at the wine shop he learned the name of the man who had been secretary to Cardinal Petrucci – Bartolomeo Nepi. According to his kinsman, the unemployed clerk had travelled far and long since the Michaelmas Massacre in search of an employer worthy of his services and had eventually joined a noble household in the ancient and once-great city of Genoa. With stoical resignation, the Franciscan set off in pursuit. He made his way to the coast at Civitavecchia and after a couple of days was fortunate to find a ship bound direct for Genoa. The vessel was only in port at all because its mast had split shortly after leaving Ostia and the captain had put in for repairs. This captain, a short, swarthy Corsican, was ill-tempered at the best of times and the delay made him more so. When Pietro approached him, the mariner told him to be off; there was no room on his ship for passengers or beggars. His tune soon changed, however, when the friar showed him that he could pay and pay handsomely for his passage.

They weighed anchor on the next morning's tide, much to the disapproval of the crew. Even a landsman like Foscari could see that the autumn storm which had brought the *Sant' Anna di Bastia* into port had not yet abandoned its warfare with the sea. But the captain would not wait. On the quayside at Ostia he had snapped up a consignment of pepper from a bankrupt importer. This high-profit commodity promised him ten times his usual return on a humdrum coasting voyage and he was impatient to land his cargo. The deceptively bright and tranquil dawn in which the vessel slipped its moorings yielded rapidly to a turbulent day of tumbling, grimy clouds, clashing waves and an easterly wind that set the newly spliced mast creaking ominously. Through a day and a night all on board watched anxiously the eyelets and lashings of the fully stretched sail, expecting, at any moment, to see the canvas torn from its fastenings or simply split across. A second day passed, and a third. There was no let-up in the tempest. But as long as the storm was at their back, driving them on a north-westerly course, parallel to the coast, the captain would take no action. When one of the crew pleaded with him to furl sail before it or the mast gave way, the captain struck him a blow that almost carried him over the side.

By that time Brother Pietro was taking only a passing interest in events around him. As the ship swayed, rocked and bounced from wave to wave he lay in the narrow space between cargo bales which had been allotted to him and yearned for stability in a bucking, cavorting world gone mad. He shivered, he groaned, he vomited and went on vomiting long after there was nothing left in his stomach. A dozen times an hour he prayed for deliverance. And a dozen times an hour he prepared himself for the Great Encounter.

He lost all contact with the passage of time and did not know that it was before dawn on the fourth day of the voyage that he was dragged from exhausted slumber by a cacophony of crashes, screams and shouts. Crawling out from his space in the bow he could make out nothing on the deck but a swaying jumble of writhing figures on an indistinct rolling surface. His first thought was that the vessel was filling with water. Then something cracked across his shoulders. He looked up and saw the captain, stick in hand, screaming at him above the howl of the wind. 'Don't just lie there, you useless bastard! The mast's down. Help fold the sail!'

Pietro staggered to where he could now see crewmen wrestling to detach wet, heavy canvas from tangled ropes and bits of broken spar. Somehow they managed on that dark, slippery, heaving deck to cut the sail free from all encumbrances, roll it up and wedge it against the starboard scuppers. With the emergence of half-hearted daylight there were injured men to be tended. A quick tally showed that one of the crew had been lost overboard, one had a badly fractured skull and could not survive and two were suffering from broken limbs that needed resetting. Pietro gave all his attention to the afflicted. He muttered prayers over the man who died without regaining consciousness. He found shards of broken mast and cut cords from cargo bales to make splints for the wounded. Still the *Sant' Anna* spun and wallowed in the grip of wind and wave. She was lost and powerless. The rudder was damaged, so she responded only feebly to the helm. When the growing light revealed a long stretch of ragged coastline dead ahead there was clearly no way the *Sant' Anna* could avoid being smashed upon it.

George had been right about the attitude of the Farrans workforce. Catherine had called a general meeting and explained the situation as honestly as she could. The response had been a hundred per cent support. Everyone wanted to know what they could do to help. Both in the meeting and in several half-embarrassed private messages afterwards Catherine had received sympathy, and a variety of suggestions about new ideas and personal sacrifices that individuals were prepared to make in the interests of rendering Lacy Enterprises more profitable. As soon as she had announced the leadership team's intention of meeting three times a week for review and planning, someone had suggested a working breakfast and the kitchen ladies had volunteered to come in early on a rota basis. It all seemed to be organized almost as soon as Catherine had mooted it.

At seven thirty a.m. on the third Wednesday in October, Catherine, Sally, Emma and George sat round a table at one end of the empty restaurant. George reported first on Tina's infiltration of Artguard's citadel. 'The tapes will come back here every evening and we'll go through them carefully. My guess is that Druckmann will locate the bug after a couple of days but hopefully before then we'll have picked up something incriminating.'

Catherine's green eyes narrowed in concern. 'You're sure there's no way they can trace the bugging back to us. If Artguard were able to take us to court that would just about finish us.'

George momentarily stopped shovelling cornflakes into his mouth. 'I reckon we're safe enough. There's no way Druckmann can suss out Tina's real identity. She's away from here all term time and he'd hardly think to start looking for her in South Finchley College of Art and Design. He'll suspect us right enough but he can't prove anything and even if he could I don't see him doing anything to draw Artguard to the attention of the police.'

Catherine sipped her black coffee. 'I hope you're right. It makes me uncomfortable to be on the wrong side of the law.'

'Oh, me too.' George nodded enthusiastically. He said nothing about Johnny's efforts to hack into Artguard's computer system or the plans he was working on, if all else failed, to break into Druckmann's office.

Catherine looked at Emma. 'What developments on the P.R. front?'

'I spent yesterday afternoon with Wes's experts. They agree that we ought to go for a video.'

'Won't that be expensive?'

'Well, it would certainly need to be a good, professional job but Wes says that Cool Jungle would provide a backing track for us and his regular film crew would do a couple of days shooting at little more than cost.'

'I'm not sure about this involvement with Wes Cherry and his outfit, Emma. It's very good of him to help us but I wouldn't want to think . . . Oh, hell, I sound like my own grandma . . . You're not leading the poor guy on, are you?'

Emma laughed. 'If anyone's doing the leading, it's Wes. He's certainly keen to whisk me away to his Cotswold lair. But I haven't given him any encouragement. He's got lots of women and I don't reckon to be another entry in his little black book.'

'Well, OK. I guess you know what you're doing. I just wouldn't want to feel that you were getting yourself in too deep for the sake of the firm.'

'No need to worry on that score. Now, about the video: what we roughed out was some shots of this place intercut with, say, three buildings where we've installed systems – prestigious, visually attractive places. I've already set up a meeting tomorrow with Andy Stovin, the security chief at Grinling's, and I hope to persuade him to let us film there.'

'Tim reckons Grinling's are planning to drop us in favour of Artguard,' Sally observed.

Emma reached for another piece of toast. 'All the more reason for keeping a high profile there; make them realize that Lacy's is far from being down and out.'

George collected his plate of eggs, bacon, sausage and fried bread from the hotplate. 'I'd like to be in on that meeting. I want to find out just what stories Druckmann's crowd has been spreading about us.'

The conference concluded with a long discussion on finances based on figures presented by Catherine. It was as people were closing files and George was stacking plates that Catherine added, 'Oh, I almost forgot, *H.S.* magazine has asked me to do a feature on Julia Devaraux.

I turned them down but they were persistent and I got the impression that Tim thought I should take it on.'

Emma looked puzzled. 'Why would Tim be interested?'

'Perhaps he thinks I might turn up some clues about the murder. Anyway, anything we can discover that will keep him in Florence thinking about the Borgia Chalice affair and not worrying about Lacy Enterprises is good news. It's going to mean a bit more work at this end but it's worth it. Sally, I'm afraid you're going to have to do the routine donkey work – get some bumph from Devaraux's P.R. agent, get the names of two or three close friends and colleagues I ought to talk to, make appointments. OK?'

'I think I may have found something important!' Tristram bounded with uncharacteristic ebullience into the bistro on the Piazza del Duoma where they had all agreed to meet for coffee on Wednesday morning.

'Yes, so you said on the phone.' Tim pushed aside with a grimace the glass of diet Coke which had been permitted by his minder.

Tristram yanked out a chair and seated himself at the table. 'Oh, by the way, Ginny sends her apologies. She's working flat out to finish her German book so that she can travel up to Munich and get started on Heinrich Segar.'

The waiter came over and Tristram ordered a cappuccino. Then he cleared a space on the table for a file he took from his briefcase. 'I had some business in Rome yesterday – or, rather, I arranged to have some business in Rome yesterday. I was able to spend most of the afternoon in the Vatican Archive. Fortunately, I have a friend on the staff there and I explained to him what I was looking for – saves a lot of time ploughing through catalogues. He reckoned the place to start would be papal correspondence. I requisitioned the years 1496 to 1498 and sat down at a desk to wait. When it came my heart sank. There were five massive boxes each containing dozens of letters. My Latin's pretty good – I even did some medieval Latin in my degree course – but all that cramped handwriting and the conventional abbreviations don't make it very easy. All I could do was skip through looking for references to the three cardinals we're interested in. There were a couple of letters from Petrucci but they were from quite early on and didn't seem particularly relevant. It was all pretty tedious. By the time I was getting to the end of the fourth box I was beginning to nod. And I very nearly missed it.'

He paused while his coffee arrived and he paid for it with a 5000-lire note. He opened the file and revealed a dozen or so sheets of photocopied handwriting.

Tim looked at the even lines of precisely formed letters. 'Looks like it was written by someone with a very tidy mind – a lawyer perhaps?'

Tristram smiled. 'Almost. A Franciscan friar. His name was Fra Pietro Foscari. His letter is really a long report to Alexander VI and it's headed, "Investigation into the Death of the Duke of Gandia".'

O.K., who had been staring vacantly across the square, showed sudden interest. 'Duke of Gandia?'

'Who he?' Tim asked.

The minder explained. 'One of the pope's bastards – nasty piece of work by all accounts. Got himself bumped off one dark night and nobody ever found out whodunit. It's one of the great unsolved mysteries of history. I thought everyone knew that.' He looked at Tim pityingly.

'Well, I didn't.' Tim was impressed by his companion's unsuspected erudition.

Tristram laughed. 'Don't take any notice of O.K. He's just showing off. He has a passion about the Borgias. He's read just about everything written about them in English and Italian.'

'I might go on *Mastermind* one day and take the Borgias as my special subject.' O.K. scratched his stubby chin.

Tristram took up the narrative. 'Fascinating though the Gandia murder is, it wasn't the murder I was looking for so I turned over Foscari's letter. I was just about to pick up the next when I noticed the concluding sentence. Look.' He turned to the last of the A4 sheets and pointed to some words in the last lines of the text, '"*mortes Montadinis, Petruccis et della Chiesae*" – the deaths of Montadini, Petrucci and della Chiesa.'

'So what's the connection with the murder of Gandia?' O.K. wanted to know.

Tristram grinned. 'Give me a chance. It'll take quite a time to translate this lot. All I've gathered so far is that this is a private report prepared for the pope into the death of his son and that it does trace a definite connection with the assassination of the cardinals which took place several months before.'

'Is there any reference to the chalice?' Tim was so absorbed that he drank more Coke without realizing he was doing so.

'There do appear to be some references but I can't get their meaning out of context. I'll have to put in several evenings on the manuscript.'

'That'll be fascinating.' O.K. was equally absorbed. 'Do you think it'll tell us how the gruesome deed was done?'

Tristram shrugged, lawyerly caution reasserting itself. 'Even if it does it probably won't help us to understand why the people were killed at Grinling's.'

Tim looked thoughtful. 'On the other hand it just might.'

CHAPTER 7

The *Sant' Anna* was brushed towards the shore like so much rubbish by succeeding sweeps of the waves. The storm had passed its fiercest but it was clear that the vessel would be tossed, helpless, against rock, beach or cliff face. If she got that far. Two sailors lashed to the tiller strove, with what remained of the rudder, to prevent her coming sideways on but she wallowed cumbersomely through every trough and took in more water as each crest roared over her.

The captain staggered about the deck bellowing orders and hitting out with his stick against those who did not obey. No one took any notice. Every crew member thought only of his own safety. Pietro, hampered by the weight of his saturated habit, helped the two injured men to tie themselves to the stump of the mast. Then he, too, wound a length of rope around himself and the timber upright. He stood, braced against it, peering through mist and spray towards the dark mass ahead. He made out two headlands stretching out rocky arms to grasp the *Sant' Anna* in fatal embrace.

Brother Pietro clenched his eyes shut and prayed. 'Lord, have mercy on your servant but especially on these other men. My life is yours. My death is yours. But these are not yet ready to face the judgement. If I must come before your throne today, let it be so, but give them more time.'

He opened his eyes. And stared. He closed them, rubbed them, opened them and stared again. The shoreline had come suddenly much closer. He could make out people on one of the promontories, a group of stationary men watching the stricken ship and doubtless calculating where she would strike and scatter her cargo. But Brother Pietro also saw something else.

'There!' he shrieked, looking around for the captain. He saw him clinging to the aft deck rail. Pietro grabbed the rope round his waist. He struggled to untie the wet knots. The bonds fell away and he half-staggered half-crawled to the rear of the vessel. He pulled himself up to the raised aft deck. The captain was screaming incoherently at the tiller men who were too weary to respond to his hysterical orders. Pietro grasped the captain's jerkin. 'There! Look!' He pointed. 'God has provided a way!'

The little Corsican shook Foscari's hand free, impatiently. But he did look where the friar was pointing. And immediately he recognized the offered salvation. The two pinnacles of rock standing out from the land were not the extremities of a wide bay but the sentinels of a passage between two islands. If the *Sant' Anna* could be put there and if the bottom was not too shallow she might pass into sheltered water.

The captain roused the drooping tiller men and threw his own weight also against the shaft. Pietro joined them. Bracing themselves as best they could on the slippery deck the four men wrestled with the beam which tried to swing to and fro with each battering of the waves. Every crest threw the *Sant' Anna* closer to the waiting rocks. Her response to the helm was faint and sluggish. Slowly, too slowly, the bow came round to face the channel. With only a hundred metres of open sea between ship and land it seemed they must be thrown against the rocks to port.

The four men grunted and strained with all their might to lever the vessel away from doom. Fifty metres. Twenty. The waves were splintering themselves on the jagged outcrops and roaring as they did so.

Then the *Sant' Anna* was in amongst them. With a juddering crash which sent Pietro and his companions sprawling on the deck she grazed the rock wall with her bulging side. She bounced away. Pietro gazed up at the grey-black tower and recorded clearly every outcrop and crevice of its shining surface. Once again the *Sant' Anna* was thrown towards it. But now a more powerful force controlled her destiny. The current racing between the islands gripped her and swept her forward. She twisted her way between crags and pools of whirling water and floated, at last, into a lagoon on the north of the island where the storm could no longer reach her.

Brother Pietro clung exhausted to the port rail and offered prayers of thanksgiving.

On the surface everything at Grinling's was normal. The wide foyer was filled with people buying catalogues, seeking interviews with departmental experts, ascending and descending the staircase leading to the galleries. Staff with county accents and lapel badges indicating their names – names like 'Rupert', 'Francesca', 'Electra' and 'Tarquin' – attempted to strike the mix of helpfulness and condescension considered appropriate to their role, as they dealt with enquiries. It was when Emma and George went through into the grid of corridors and offices behind the façade that they sensed the atmosphere. There was no one factor that screamed 'Crisis!' at them; it was more a combination of impressions. Junior staff walked quietly from room to room. People they passed cast anxious glances in their direction. No office doors stood open allowing inhabitants to call to one another. There was no banter. No laughter.

Andy Stovin rose to greet them as they entered the office labelled 'Security Director'. He was a thin, ginger-haired, fortyish ex-policeman. 'Emma, George, good to see you.' His forced smile gave the lie to his words of welcome.

'Good of you to give us some time, Andy,' George responded. 'I guess things are a bit difficult around here at the moment.'

Stovin raised his eyebrows. 'You can say that again. Having four people murdered on the premises is decidedly ungood for business.'

'There seem to be plenty of punters around this morning.' Emma nodded towards the door. 'Quite the usual hive of industry out there.'

'Most of them come to gawp. Grinling's has become London's number-one tourist attraction. Do you know the front desk gets dozens of enquiries every day from people who want to see the room where "it" happened. Sometimes I despair of the human race.'

'Didn't someone say no publicity is bad publicity?' Emma suggested brightly.

'Don't you believe it. Having the place swarming with the curious and the ghoulish doesn't do anything for the cash flow. Mr and Mrs Average who pop in to "have a look" aren't likely to stay and bid for a Tang pot or a Lalique vase. On the other hand, clients havering between giving millions of pounds worth of business to us or one of our rivals might decide Grinling's is no longer the discreet, staid, respectable auction house it was. We've had three major negotiations broken off since the murder.'

George shook his head. 'Hardly seems fair, does it? It's not Grinling's fault some nutter chooses this place to make his crazy protest.'

'Right enough, George, but it's all to do with image. Reputation counts for a hell of a lot in our business, especially when the market's as volatile as it is at present. There are five top international auction houses and they all happen to be based in London. We all need a throughput of big sales, prestigious sales, sales that attract the right kind of publicity. That means we're all competing like tigers in a cage for every juicy scrap that comes along.'

Emma tried to strike an optimistic note. 'This business will blow over.'

'Well, it's taking its time. According to what I hear from colleagues, the police are nowhere near an arrest and, of course, that means that the press don't leave us alone. Some of the bastards have been virtually camped out here for the last three weeks. They've cost two members of staff their jobs.'

'How?' Emma asked.

'Oh, the usual – flashing money around, trying to get "inside" stories. Two of the kids agreed to give interviews to the tabloids; "Behind the Scenes at Grinling's" – that sort of thing. The boss – Deventer – was furious. He didn't just given them their cards. He called the whole staff together in the main gallery, after work last Friday, and gave them the biggest rocket you could possibly imagine. God, was he mad! I've heard some A1 dressing downs in my years on the force but nothing compared to that performance. He made it crystal clear that if anyone else so much as thought about talking to the press they'd get a one-way ticket to cardboard city.'

139

'I thought the atmosphere in here was a bit subdued,' Emma said.

'Subdued? That's an understatement. It's going to take months for morale to recover from this bloody business. I certainly wish I'd never heard of the Borgia Chalice.'

George assumed a frown of sympathetic concern. 'You've had your share of aggro, I suppose.'

'And some. Grilled by the Yard – some bloody, wet-behind-the-ears sprog called Edgerson – and carpeted by the boss. I don't know what I was supposed to do that I didn't do. The chalice got the same treatment as every other valuable, highly portable item. Displayed in a locked and wired case. Moved by members of my staff to the strongroom the night before the sale. Laid out with all the other items in the anteroom by the porters under the supervision of my men. After the sale I, personally, took it up to the penthouse for the lunch – Mr Deventer's last-minute brainwave – and I stayed up there, just to be on the safe side.'

Emma was intrigued. 'So no one could have interfered with the chalice that morning without you or one of your security team seeing them?'

Stovin shook his head emphatically. 'Absolutely not. But I don't think anyone believes me. Certainly not Edgerson – who can believe whatever he likes for all I care – and probably not Deventer – and if he's looking for scapegoats . . . Still, enough of my problems. What can I do for you folk?'

George leaned forward confidingly. 'Well, Andy, I think our problem's much the same as yours – image. Lacy Security hasn't been going as long as Grinling's but, as you know, we've built up a reputation in our own field which is on a par with yours in the auction business. Like you we've run into a spot of bother recently which is putting a dent in our reputation.' He kept his eyes fixed on Stovin, who, he was pleased to see, was uncomfortable at the scrutiny. 'The difference between your problem and ours, Andy, is that you know the cause of yours but we don't know what – or who – is behind ours. And that,' George smiled broadly, 'is where we thought you could probably help us.'

'Me?' Stovin shrugged and tried to appear mystified.

'Someone appears to have been putting around stories about Lacy Security – financially insecure, not keeping pace with changing technology, getting slipshod, you know the sort of thing. Untrue, of course, but like your in-house murders, they do tend to shake confidence. Have you heard any of these stories?'

Stovin held the other man's gaze as he said, 'No, George.'

Martin sat back in his chair and ran a hand over his bristled head. 'Oh, hell, that makes everything even more puzzling. You see, we know that Grinling's have lost confidence in us and not invited us to tender for the new warehouse. We thought that was because of these false rumours. If we were mistaken that must mean that you're genuinely dissatisfied with our service. Now, I'd like to think that, after all these years, you'd come clean with us.' He looked up expectantly.

Stovin covered his embarrassment with bluster. 'Don't get sarky with me, George. Business is business, as you very well know.'

'You mean, some rival firm is making it worth Andy Stovin's while to cut us out.'

'That's not what I meant, and it's not true. OK, a decision was made not to invite Lacy Security to tender, but it had nothing to do with me.'

'Oh, pull the other one, Andy. It says on your door that

you're Security Director. That means you're involved in all matters of security.'

'Not this one. The order came from higher up.'

'How much higher up?'

'No, George, that's all I'm saying.'

'Oh well, I suppose we shall have to talk to Mr Deventer.'

Stovin glared. 'You do that and you drop me right in it.'

George returned the stare. 'You'll know how it feels then, won't you? Someone here has already dropped my outfit in it.'

'OK, boys, time out.' Emma intervened. 'Let's try a bit of lateral thinking. The way I see it, George, if Grinling's, for whatever reason, don't wish to avail themselves of our services for the new warehouse, well there's not a great deal we can do about it. I'm sure Andy would help us in this matter if he could but, as he says, his hands are tied, and we must accept the fact. However, I'm sure no one at Grinling's would want to deny that their past relationship with Lacy's has been highly satisfactory.' She raised an eyebrow at Stovin, who nodded warily.

'Good. You see, Andy, we're trying to overcome this image problem and one of the things we're doing is making a promotional video to show to potential clients. It will feature some of Lacy Security's many, many satisfied customers and we'd like to think that Grinling's would be happy to be involved in this little venture.' She took a file from her briefcase and laid a couple of sheets of A4 in front of Stovin. 'That will give you an outline . . .'

Andy held up a hand. 'Look, I'm not sure . . .'

'. . . of how we see the video shaping up.' Emma spent several minutes on detail, her enthusiasm and femininity chipping relentlessly away at Stovin's resistance.

She was just reaching the end of her sales pitch when the door opened.

'Andy I . . . Oh, I'm sorry. I didn't know you were busy. I'll come . . . Why, George, Emma. I didn't recognize you at first.' Corinne Noble stepped into the room to shake hands. 'How's Tim? I was devastated to hear about him. I was going to phone but . . . Well, things have been pretty bloody here, as Andy's probably told you.'

Emma stood up. 'I guess we'd all be happy to wipe the last three weeks out of our lives. Tim's OK. We've actually managed to get him away to Italy for a rest. As a matter of fact, the Santoris have taken him under their wing. So perhaps some good has come out of this awful business.'

'The Santoris? How strange.' Surprise flickered over Corinne's face.

'Why strange?' Emma asked.

'I didn't realize Tim knew them that well.'

'Oh, he doesn't . . . didn't. It's a sort of symbiotic relationship: Tim needs a rest and the Santoris think he can help them get to the bottom of this chalice business. He has something of a gift for these things. Anyway, we were just about to leave, so we'll let you two get on with Grinling's' business.'

Corinne smiled. 'Do you have to dash away? It would be so nice to have a chat. Can you manage lunch?'

George and Emma exchanged glances and George said that they'd be happy to have a quick lunch. He turned to shake hands with Stovin. 'Goodbye, Andy. You will raise that matter with Mr Deventer, won't you? We'll look forward to hearing from you.'

He and Emma withdrew and, a few minutes later,

Corinne Noble joined them by the front desk. She led them to a wine bar a couple of streets away and they settled themselves in a corner table of the cellar restaurant. After they had ordered their food Corinne asked, in more detail, about Tim and seemed genuinely relieved about his recovery. 'I'm very fond of Tim,' she explained, 'and, of course, he's been an enormous help to Grinling's over the years.'

George made no effort to conceal his scepticism. 'Right now Tim could do with some help from Grinling's and he doesn't seem to be getting it.'

Corinne was crestfallen. 'You mean the security contract for the new warehouse. God, I feel awful about that.'

'So tell us what's going on,' Emma insisted. 'Dump us if you must but surely we deserve to know why.'

Corinne looked from Emma to George and back again. 'Oh, it's so awkward. I hate divided loyalties. What can I say?'

George prompted, 'Start with Artguard and their dubious tactics.'

'You know about them – yes, of course, you would. So you realize they've got some pretty big names on their board. One of them is Lord Lochinver . . .'

'The financier . . . head of Celtic Banking and Insurance?'

'That's right, Emma. Well, he's a great friend of Adrian – Adrian Deventer.'

Emma frowned. 'Surprising. I thought your M.D. had better taste. Lochinver, or Jimmy "the Fist" McNair as he was before his peerage, is, by all accounts, the dirtiest fighter in a pretty dirty game. His record of mergers, takeovers and asset-stripping . . . Ugh!'

'I gather he does have his good side. He's also a big

client of Grinling's. He buys a lot through us to furnish his four or five homes, as well as maintaining an antiques investment portfolio.'

There was a pause in the conversation as a waitress arrived with plates of food.

George investigated the interior of his steak and kidney pie with marked suspicion. 'I suppose we can guess the rest. Lochinver is someone Grinling's can't afford to upset. He tells you that Lacy Security is on its last legs and recommends Artguard. End result? We quietly get the cold shoulder.'

Corinne played uncomfortably with her smoked salmon terrine. 'Adrian's a good M.D. – he really is. And he's a pleasant man. I think it's just that he's too conscientious. He's a hundred and one per cent involved in Grinling's and he lets business worries get on top of him. These last three weeks have put years on him.'

'Surely it wasn't that bad.' George looked up briefly from the pie which he was finding better than he had feared.

'Wasn't it just? Adrian went very public over the Borgia Chalice. He gave several press and TV interviews. He used every media outlet to plug the Santori sale even down to taking the rostrum himself and presiding over that rather fatuous charade. It was all part of a carefully planned P.R. campaign designed to heighten Grinling's profile and increase our market share. Then, just when everything was simmering nicely, the pot boiled over in a very nasty way – police and paparazzi all over the place and poor Adrian personally being made to look a first-class prat. He's desperate to see the murder investigation successfully concluded. He told me the other day that he'd reached the conclusion that the poisoning was organized by one of our rivals along the road – and I don't think he was joking.'

Emma finished her salad and pushed the plate away. 'By all accounts the police aren't making much progress.'

'No. I suppose it could go down as one of the great unsolved crimes of the century,' Corinne agreed mournfully. 'Did you say Tim was doing some investigating of his own?'

'Only in a very lackadaisical sort of way – or so we hope. It's really something to keep his mind off work. Hopefully he'll spend another two or three weeks in the Italian sunshine puzzling out the original crime, the mystery of the murdered cardinals. Who knows? He might just come up with something relevant to the poisonings at Grinling's. It wouldn't be the first time.'

'Well if he does discover anything useful by studying the Michaelmas Massacre he'd better let the police know. I reckon they'd grab at any help.' Corinne glanced at her watch. 'Heavens, look at the time. I must get back. We've had a batch of cancellations and they've thrown our winter cataloguing schedules into chaos.'

With that part-explanation, Corinne Noble said her hurried goodbyes and left.

If Emma could have seen how Tim was occupied while she and George were at Grinling's she would have heartily approved. At the moment when Corinne took her leave he was sitting with O.K. in the nave of Siena Cathedral. He gazed up at the spectacular columns of banded black and white marble supporting the dome where mosaic patterns shimmered in the reflected light from below.

'Fantastic, isn't it?' O.K. looked up from the guidebook in which he had been immersed for several minutes. 'And to think it was never finished. Did you know that, in 1339, the Sienese decided to build a whole new nave running south. That would have made it the biggest church in Christendom.'

'That's right. Unfortunately the plague killed thousands of them off, so the building was abandoned. There's a moral in that somewhere.'

O.K., who had been about to make the same point, snapped the book shut. 'Right, well, I'll bet you didn't know that Rodrigo Borgia supervised some of the decorative work here, as well as the building of the Palazzo Piccolomini overlooking the Piazza del Campo – that's where . . .'

'They have the horse races.' Tim laughed at his minder's frown. 'Sorry, O.K., but I have been here before. Not that I mind coming again,' he added hastily. 'That was a good idea. It's a wonderful city. I didn't know that business about Borgia, though. Tell me more.'

'It was before he was pope, of course. Pius II sent him up here to oversee various building works for his family, the Piccolomini. He obviously thought highly of Rodrigo's ability.'

'I get the impression you're quite a fan of Alexander VI. Do you reckon he and his family have had a raw deal from history?'

''Course they have!' The contempt in O.K.'s voice suggested that he was stating a truth that should be obvious to all. 'Stands to reason, doesn't it? Just think of all the things he's accused of – buying off Cardinal Sforza in the papal election with four mule loads of silver, having sex with his daughter, seducing Giulia Farnese when she was fifteen and he was fifty-six (having already done the same with her mother and grandmother), poisoning at least fifteen people, watching Cesare hack his chamberlain, Perroto, to pieces before his very eyes, holding regular orgies, systematically raping the daughters of Rome's leading citizens, and, at the end of all that, accidentally poisoning himself. Put that lot in a movie and it would be laughed off the screen.'

As they walked out beneath the ornate west façade into the sunlit Piazza del Duomo O.K. was still holding forth. 'You want to know why the Borgias have got a bad press? Because history is written by the victors. I read that somewhere. Don't remember where but it's true. Lots of people hated Alexander VI but his biggest enemy was Giuliano della Rovere. He hated him like poison because he was good at his job, because the cardinals voted for Borgia as pope and not della Rovere, but above all because he was different, he was Spanish. He schemed and plotted against Alexander throughout his whole papacy. He spread lies about him. He couldn't do too much to blacken the pope's name. He even brought a French army on to Italian soil. He was obsessed. When everything failed he had to wait for Alexander's death before he could become pope. But he hadn't finished with his enemy even then. Oh, no. He refused to allow masses to be said for Rodrigo Borgia's soul and he paid historians to write all that rubbish about rape, incest and multiple murder. And you know what?' O.K. reached his indignant climax as they crossed the car park where part of the biggest church in Christendom might have stood.

'What?'

'All the historians who came after just repeated what Julius's writers wrote down.'

'Julius?'

'Julius II – della Rovere. Even Edward Gibbon, who wrote *The Decline and Fall of the Roman Empire*, called Alexander VI "the Tiberias of Christian Rome".' He was talking loudly now, his voice echoing in the narrow street, and gesticulating freely. 'They always win. If they can't get you when you're alive, they'll do you after you're dead. It was the same with Gregor. For years he laughed at them. He even laughed at them when he was in prison. So they're hitting back now.'

'Just a minute.' Tim paused on a corner where two streets met, one of them little more than an alleyway between irregular medieval façades. 'You're not seriously suggesting that some sworn enemy of Gregor's bumped off four people – people who didn't like Gregor either – just to blacken the old man's memory.'

O.K. was truculent. 'Why not? Julius II did it and he was a pope.'

'Why not?' Tim resumed the walk, taking very slowly the steep, right-hand turning that would bring them up to the Piazza del Campo. 'Because I thought you wanted to get at the truth and you won't do that if your head is cluttered with prejudices.'

'You don't believe that some of those art snobs really resented Gregor, really hated him?'

'Sure I believe it. Just as I believe that there were lots of people who had it in for Rodrigo Borgia. But I don't buy all this over-simplified revisionist stuff. The Borgias *were* a bad lot. Alexander *was* a lecher, a simoniac, a ruthless politique and an arranger of convenient deaths. It's all documented, and not just by hacks paid to do a hatchet job. Probably he wasn't much worse than other contemporary rulers of Italy but we don't do truth any favours by trying to whitewash him. And we shan't begin to get at the facts about the chalice murders if we assume that dear old Gregor was squeaky clean and just the victim of a hate-crazed villain.'

O.K. maintained a sulky silence until they emerged from the warren of ancient streets on to the wide, fan-shaped piazza whose rose-coloured surface was divided into nine segments for the Council of Nine who governed the city for centuries before and after the Renaissance. They sauntered past the open-air cafés bordering the square. A few late lunchers were still in evidence but most of the tables were unoccupied. Tim suggested a rest and they sat facing the glowing terracotta of the Palazzo Pubblico.

O.K. nodded approvingly when Tim ordered iced tea and asked for the same. 'Why do you think there's a connection between the two chalice murders?'

'That's easy. Because the murderer does. Haven't you noticed how closely he's modelled his crime on the original. He hasn't just repeated the circumstances of the old legend. There's more to it than that.'

'How do you mean?'

'Well, look at the timing for example. When were the cardinals murdered? What day?'

'Well, Michaelmas apparently.'

'Which is when?'

O.K. shrugged. 'August or September, isn't it?'

'Twenty-ninth of September. And when did the Grinling's murders take place?'

'Twenty-ninth of September. Could be coincidence.'

'Of course, but there's a limit to the number of coincidences that are credible. The more we know about the original atrocity the more the Grinling's incident looks like a copy-cat crime. Let's have another look at Tristram's notes.'

O.K. opened his guidebook and took out the two pages of neat typing that Tristram had brought out to the villa the previous evening. They were the beginning of his translation of the Foscari report. 'Do you want me to read it from the top?'

'Well you can cut out the flowery address, all that business about the writer humbly presenting his respects to the most pious and holy, etc., etc. Get to the meat.'

'Right, this is where the important bit starts. "Having been instructed by your holiness to explore a possible link between the lamentable death of the Duke of Gandia and the incident men call the Michaelmas Massacre . . ." He doesn't say why he thinks there's a link. "My first task was to examine the chalice which was allegedly used to administer poison to Cardinals della Chiesa, Petrucci and Montadini. With your holiness's permission I took it to Signore Barci, the goldsmith who resides in the Piazza Campo dei Fiori, next to the Palazzo Orsini. He submitted it to the closest scrutiny and confirmed what your holiness told me." Pity he doesn't spell that out,' O.K. commented.

'Yes, but there's not much doubt about it, is there? The pope wanted Foscari to be convinced that the famous chalice had no secret compartment for concealing poison. If there was anything wrong with it Alexander would hardly have let someone go wandering around Rome, showing it to people.'

O.K. grinned triumphantly. 'Well, at least that proves that the Borgia Chalice is genuine. It's a crying shame we didn't have this evidence years ago.'

Tim shook his head. 'We mustn't run before we can walk. It doesn't prove that our chalice is *the* Borgia Chalice. What it does suggest is that there never was a poison cup.'

'The whole story is just another of the lies spread about by the Borgias' enemies.'

'That's right. And that gives us another point of comparison between the two crimes. In both cases the chalice is a red herring. For my money, what happened back in 1496 was that someone murdered the cardinals, probably in the Vatican, and then deliberately put about the story of the chalice. Foscari virtually says as much, doesn't he?'

O.K. referred to the translation again. '"Having concluded, therefore, that some person, as yet unknown, murdered their eminences and compounded their impiety by seeking to cast suspicion on your holiness, I made it my business to discover, if at all possible, any person who might have strong cause to wish the death of all or any of their eminences. Early in my enquiries I discovered that Cardinal Petrucci was, unlike the two others, a friend of your holiness – a fact your holiness had not seen fit to reveal to me. I decided, therefore, to begin my investigation among those who had been intimates of the said Cardinal Petrucci. Accordingly, I made my way to Orvieto . . ." He goes on to talk about his meeting with Petrucci's niece.'

'Who painted a picture of her uncle as someone already overdue for canonization. I wonder if our Franciscan friend had reason to question that evaluation later. We'll have to wait for further instalments of Tristram's serial. But don't let's miss the important points in what we have got.'

'There's nothing else in this.' O.K. put the two sheets down on the table with the guidebook acting as a paperweight.

'On the contrary, there's something very intriguing here.' Tim took the translation and pointed to two lines of text. 'Doesn't that ring bells with you?'

The young man frowned in concentration but after several seconds shook his head. 'I don't see . . .'

Tim stood abruptly. 'Well, you can puzzle it out while we continue our tour. Now, are you ready for the splendours of the Palazzo Piccolomini?'

CHAPTER 8

The island upon which Brother Pietro had been cast was Elba. He lost no time in getting ashore and many were the thanksgivings he offered as he knelt on the beach and dug his fingers into the dry gravel above the water line. He obtained lodging at a small Augustinian cloister whose members ministered to the needs of the rough Elbans who mined and smelted iron ore along the east coast. He spent two fruitless hours the next day arguing with the captain of the *Sant' Anna*. Pietro demanded a refund of his passage money since he had not been conveyed to Genoa as agreed. This was angrily brushed aside and, though Pietro persisted for a while, he eventually abandoned what was obviously a waste of time and energy. The one offer the captain did make was the one above all other that the friar was determined to decline. The Corsican said he was welcome to wait until the *Sant' Anna* put to sea again and resume his voyage. As Pietro made clear to the captain, he would not set foot aboard that unseaworthy barrel even if the fiends of hell were at his back. After three days rest, during which all hint of menace drained away from the sea and sky, he boarded one of the many small boats plying between Azzurro and Piombino on the mainland. Continuing the journey on foot along the Via Aurelia was tedious but at least the hills and valleys did not move.

He began making enquiries for Bartolomeo Nepi as soon as he reached La Spezia, the first town of importance in Genoan territory. No one knew the name but many people suggested noble Ligurian families with whom the clerk might have taken service. Several of them kept establishments in Genoa, as the friar realized on his second day in the spacious harbour city of bustling wharves, wide paved streets and magnificent public and private buildings. His first and most hopeful call was at the Palazzo della Rovere. The cardinal's family was native to Genoa and it seemed likely that Nepi might have made use of his connections to gain employment with one of Italy's most prestigious households. Pietro discovered that Giuliano's uncle was the current head of the family and it was in the hope of learning something from one of the nobleman's servants that he approached the imposing square building flanking the church of San' Matteo on the Piazza Doria.

But as he drew near, his expectations dwindled. Every shutter of the house was firmly closed. Nevertheless, Pietro climbed the steps to the main door and hammered on the panelled oak. His blows echoed around the space inside. He tried again and was on the point of turning away when he detected a faint shuffling within. It was followed by the sound of bolts being drawn and locks turned. The massive timber opened inwards. In the gap stood a creature more hideous than Foscari had ever seen outside a travelling show where such unfortunates were displayed for gain. It was small and draped in loose, drab garments. Straight, grey-yellow hair escaped from beneath an ill-fitting linen cap. The features were brown and crazed like a poorly fired pot. The nose was large and the mouth beneath disfigured by a hairlip. Only the eyes – dark, alert and glistening – displayed the existence of a soul that might be fully human, rational, even lovely. As to the sex of this being, Pietro could make no informed guess, until it spoke in a high, cracked timbre.

'Well?'

Pietro made the sign of the cross. '*Pax tecum*, my daughter. Are any of Signore della Rovere's kinsmen within?'

'Everyone's away except Old Dort, Mad Dort.' She began to close the door.

'A moment, my child.' Foscari thrust a sandalled foot into the gap. 'I seek a man who serves the signore – Bartolomeo Nepi.'

'There's none here except Old Dort, Mad Dort.' The crone slammed the door on his foot with a force that made Pietro wince. He jumped back and immediately the portal crashed shut. Limping slightly, the friar descended to the stone-flagged street. He was disappointed but also thoughtful. For he was convinced that, in the few seconds the door had stood open, something or someone had moved amidst the gloom within.

Three hours later he arrived back at the local head-quarters of his order, having made four more fruitless visits. A message awaited his return. It was upon good-quality paper and fastened with wax but unsealed. The wording was brief: 'Come to the Palazzo della Rovere after Vespers.'

Pietro had to call upon every spiritual discipline he had learned to focus his mind on the devotional book which he read, throughout the afternoon, standing at a desk in the library. He joined with his brothers for the evening worship and struggled to keep his mind on the chanted prayers which slipped easily from his lips. Afterwards, he had an argument with the sub-prior who declined to open the door and let him leave. The hour after

Vespers, he insisted, must be devoted to quiet study and private devotion, followed by sleep. Pietro was obliged to produce the pope's letter before he could escape. He hurried through the evening streets, worried that the delay might have put off his elusive quarry.

The house looked exactly as it had in the morning save that the long shadows streaking its even brickwork made it seem even more devoid of life. Pietro mounted the steps and knocked sharply. This time the door opened immediately and was thrown wide. The old châtelaine stood before him holding a lamp in one hand. She made a grotesque, exaggerated curtsey, turned wordlessly and led the way across a wide, marbled hall. Pietro followed her through a succession of well-furnished rooms, leading one off another. It was as they passed through a door giving on to what was, as far as he could see in the dim light, an area of kitchens and storerooms that the friar's keen ears picked up a sound behind him. His half-turn was too late.

Strong arms gripped his. There were two assailants but Foscari could only see their dim outlines and hear their rapid, excited breathing.

'Stop! What do you mean by this?' Pietro struggled. The fingers only bit into his arms more deeply. His hands were pulled back behind him and a cord was tied around his wrists.

'Keep walking,' a voice said. 'Follow the crone.'

Pietro stumbled after the old woman through another doorway. He saw her standing in the middle of a small room beside an open trapdoor. Stone steps descended into what was obviously a wine cellar.

'Down you go,' the voice ordered and Foscari felt a fist in the small of his back. He looked about desperately. There was no escape. Reluctantly, he felt his way down the shadow-soaked steps. There were ten, then a level floor. As he reached it, the trapdoor slammed shut and he was plunged into utter blackness.

'What's her star sign?'

'I beg your pardon?' Sally wondered if she had heard properly.

'It's a perfectly straightforward question, young lady. What is Mrs Lacy's star sign? I need to know that before I can process her request.'

Sally thought quickly and said the first thing that came into her head. 'Virgo.'

'You're quite sure?'

'Absolutely.'

'Phone me back in five minutes.' The line went dead.

Sally's probing into Julia Devaraux's background had resulted in the predictable handout biography from her P.R. company, a bundle of cuttings culled by a professional researcher in the National Press Archive – and the phone number of Julia's only known relative, an aunt by the name of Maud Benedict. It was the request for an interview with Miss Benedict which resulted in the bizarre exchange.

Sally gave the old lady a good five minutes before dialling again the outer London number. 'Hello, Miss Benedict, this is Mrs Lacy's secretary again . . .'

'Yes, yes, of course. Now, see here, it will have to be tomorrow, Saturday, four o'clock, tea. That's the only propitious time for weeks.'

'Just a moment while I check . . .'

'You will need the address. It's Briony, Ashlar Hill, Hampstead. There are only half a dozen houses. She'll find it if she has any wits at all.' Once again the brittle voice was replaced by the steady brrr of an empty line.

'She sounds absolutely batty,' Sally explained to Catherine a few minutes later. 'Shall I call back and cancel?'

Catherine sighed and pushed her chair away from the desk, scattered with bank statements and bills. 'No, I'd better go through with it. Anyway, it'll give me a break from all these figures. If I don't get out for a few hours, I'll only spend the whole weekend trying to square the circle.'

There was a tap at the door and George walked in. He was smiling. 'I thought you could use some good news.'

Catherine looked up. 'That's for sure.'

'I've just gone through the second post. This was in it.' He handed her a sheet of crisp notepaper.

Catherine saw Grinling's' embossed logo and beneath it a few succinct lines of text.

Dear George,

Further to our conversation of yesterday, I have pleasure in inviting Lacy Security to submit a tender for security installations at the new Grinling's warehouse in Loin of Beef Yard.

I enclose details of the building and Grinling's' requirements. Please telephone for an appointment to visit the property.

Yours sincerely
Andrew Stovin
Security Director, Grinling's

'What did you say to him, George?' She looked at her colleague wide-eyed.

'I wish I knew. As far as I could tell, Artguard had the whole contract sewn up. Of course, they may still have. This could be just going through the motions so that we can't complain we've not been given a chance.'

'Still, it's a step in the right direction, and there haven't been too many of them lately. Thanks for showing me, George. Have a good weekend.'

'It'll be a busy one. I'll be listening to half a dozen tapes with Johnny and Steve. Druckmann still hasn't rumbled us. There must be something in those hours of phone calls and private chats that'll incriminate him in some way. Perhaps I'll have some more good news come Monday morning. Cheerio.'

The next afternoon Catherine discovered Briony, Ashlar Hill, Hampstead to be a sprawling, turn-of-the-century house behind high hedges. The gardens had once been carefully laid out. The edges of herbaceous borders could still be made out despite the encroaching lawns. Roses stretched their blooms bravely on overgrown stems amidst the upreaching grasp of weeds and unclipped shrubs. A wide porch with stained-glass windows guarded an imposing front door. Catherine yanked on an iron bell-pull and heard a distant jangling response. Holding only a file and a miniature tape-recorder she waited in half-amused expectation for she knew not what.

The door was opened by a plainly dressed woman in her mid-fifties, who informed Catherine that 'Madam' was awaiting her in the library. She led the way to one of four rooms giving off a wide, panelled hall. She tapped on the door, opened it to allow the guest to enter and closed the door quietly behind her.

Catherine found herself in what she immediately recognized as organized chaos. There were books everywhere; not just in their proper places on the shelves filling three sides of the long room, but on every flat surface – the medium grand piano by the French windows, the large, double-sided mahogany desk at the other end of the room, the armchairs and sofas, the low tables, the wood and metal grilles concealing the central-heating radiators; there were even islands of the things scattered over the three large Persian rugs covering the parquet floor. Where there were no books there were papers – magazines, newspapers and bundles of typescript – and where there were not papers there were photographs, most of them in expensive silver frames.

'Sit down if you can find somewhere but please don't move anything.' The disembodied voice seemed to come from beyond the piano. As Catherine perched on a narrow space at one end of a leather chesterfield the voice's owner stood up from where she had been crouched. 'Got it!' Maud Benedict announced triumphantly waving a small volume in eighteenth-century embossed leather binding. 'Damned thing's been hiding from me for days. Typical of Rousseau, I suppose.' She advanced to the centre of the room, keeping carefully to the sea lanes. 'You're Mrs Lacy and you've come to ask me all about the little monster.' Statement, not question.

Catherine saw a woman she guessed to be a well-preserved octogenarian. She wore a floor-length woollen burnouse with wide sleeves decorated all over in a jagged, geometrical pattern. Her white hair was frizzy and stood out, bush-like, from her head. She carefully removed a pile of yellowing newspapers from the piano stool and sat, erect, staring at her guest with an appraising, shameless scrutiny.

Catherine was determined not to be intimidated. '"Little monster" suggests that you weren't on very good terms with your niece, Miss Benedict.'

'When I use the word "monster" I simply repeat what seems to be the prevailing view of those who knew Julia well. For my part, I haven't seen her in years. Since she left this house to make a career for herself she's been back to see me three times and not at all during the last decade. She never even came to Oscar's funeral. Family ties never meant much to that miss. Not like Greg. He often popped round.'

'Greg?'

'Gregor Santori, you know, the goldsmith, the one who was always getting himself in the news.'

'You knew Gregor Santori?'

'Well, of course I did. He could hardly grow up under this roof without my knowing him.'

'Gregor Santori grew up here?'

'Yes.' Maud Benedict smiled with mischievous triumph, enjoying her bombshell. 'You don't know, then?'

'Know what, Miss Benedict?'

'That Julia and Gregor were virtually step-brother and sister.'

Foscari's first priority was to establish the size and shape of his prison. From the foot of the steps he shuffled along a wall on his left with his back to the stonework so that his fingers could feel it. At the same time he measured it by making sideways strides. Three such steps brought him to a corner. After a further six and a half, the wall turned away from him. He traced out a space which was something between a large niche and a small annexe. Within it his feet encountered a pile of straw. He knelt down until he could smell it and feel it upon his cheek. It was dry and fresh. His captor intended him to sleep, then. That suggested that Pietro's stay was destined to be a long one. He felt more outraged than afraid at the prospect.

Standing again with his back to the wall, he returned to the corner where the stonework made a sharp right angle. Sharp indeed. Foscari began to rub his bonds up and down against the edge. He had no means of knowing how long the task took him. Not the slightest sound from the outside world penetrated the silence of his oubliette. He knew only that when the cord round his wrist did finally snap he was very tired. Thankfully, he sank on to the straw and, with his cowl over his head and his feet drawn up within his habit, he slept.

At the first scraping of the trapdoor's bolt he was fully awake. When, seconds later, dim light caused him to clench his eyelids he was on his feet. He held his hands behind his back, wrapped the cord loosely around them, and let his wide sleeves fall so as to cover the bonds.

'You there, come out!' The order was shouted by a man who stood halfway up the steps holding a lantern aloft and peering into the darkness. As soon as he saw Pietro come forward he retreated to the upper level. 'Come on, up here!'

Pietro noted that the brusque commands contrasted with a nervous quaver in the voice. The captor knew more of fear than his prisoner. The friar felt reassured. He made his way up the steps, stumbling once or twice for effect. The man motioned him through several doorways and followed a couple of metres behind. He set down the lamp. Thin slivers of light showing through the shutters told Pietro that it was now full day. Within the house they provided just enough illumination for furniture to stand out as grey-black blocks against the lesser gloom.

'Sit down in that chair,' the voice ordered and Foscari eased himself into a cushioned seat over which a rug had been thrown. His companion took up position between this and the covered windows so that he was only visible in outline. The Franciscan strained his ears for any other noise in the house. He could detect nothing and assumed that he and his captor were alone.

Before the other man could speak, Foscari took the initiative. 'Signore Nepi, all this is quite unnecessary.'

'Who are you spying for?' The words came as a nervous gasp.

'If I were a spy, Signore Nepi, I would hardly go around asking for you quite openly.'

'Who sent you? You come from Rome. You must be a Vatican cur.'

'If you know where I come from it must be you have been doing some spying.'

'I had a message to say a friar from Rome was snooping. That's all.'

'My mission is a very simple one.' Foscari spoke soothingly, attempting to put Nepi at his ease. 'I am enquiring into the death of your old master, Cardinal Petrucci.'

'And what should I know of that?'

'You were closer to his eminence than most men. You would surely know if he had any enemies.'

'All men have enemies.'

'But most men don't get poisoned by them.'

There was a pause before the voice from the shadows said, 'That was the pope. Everyone knows it.'

'What everyone knows may not be true.'

'Well, that's all I know.'

'My son, guilty secrets are dangerous things to keep. Like mad dogs they are apt to bite the hand that feeds them.'

'I know nothing!' the other man shouted.

'Then what do you fear, my son? Why do you waylay helpless friars who can do you no harm? And why do you live here in the shadows?'

'I don't live here!' Nepi seemed stung into a response. 'I'm with Signore della Rovere. He's on his estate at Pontedecimo. He gave me leave to find out why some Roman friar has been looking for me.'

Fra Pietro guessed that was a lie but he did not challenge the man. He continued to speak in a low calming voice. 'I imagine you enjoy a position of considerable trust. You enjoy your master's complete confidence. And you certainly wouldn't want to put that position in jeopardy.'

'That's right.'

'You were also privy to your previous employer's inner thoughts and secrets, I'm sure.'

'Of course.'

The semi-darkness helped Foscari to concentrate on every hesitant change of timbre and pitch in Nepi's voice. Once again he knew the man was lying. He decided to try out the theory he had developed during the long dusty or muddy days on the road. 'It would never have entered the head of an honourable man like yourself to betray your employer's secrets, would it?'

'Certainly not.'

'Just as I thought. But after the death of his eminence . . . Well, naturally the situation would be different. Nothing can harm the cardinal now and – being the generous and understanding man that he was – he would not begrudge you making the best possible use of any information that you have. Information that would be useful to Cardinal della Rovere, the Duke of Milan and others of their party. My son, it is very gratifying to see how well you have been rewarded.'

166

Nepi growled. 'It's time to return you to your chamber, Brother.'

Foscari made no move. 'How long am I to enjoy Signore della Rovere's hospitality here?'

'Until it's decided what to do with you. The crone who looks after this place will see to your wants till then. She's simple but not easily tricked. Come on, up you get!'

Foscari made as if to rise from the deep chair, then fell back. 'It's difficult with my hands trussed like this. You'll have to help me.'

Nepi stepped forward and took his captive by the arm. Pietro sprang from the chair and in the same movement grabbed Nepi by his jerkin. The other man cried out as the friar swung him off his feet. The next instant he landed face down on the floor, all the breath knocked out of him, unable to utter a sound.

Foscari knelt on Nepi's back and gripped his arms in his strong hands. 'I must decline your gracious invitation. You see, I find the company of traitors unpleasant.'

The prisoner squirmed and Pietro jabbed his knees more firmly into the small of his back. 'Lie still, son of Judas, I've not finished with you.' He took the cord which was still loosely fastened round his left wrist and bound his prisoner's hands with it.

Nepi, meanwhile, gulped in enough air to be able to vent his anger. 'Don't call me Judas, friar. I betray no one.'

Foscari laughed, deliberately goading.

'It's true. If you're looking for faithless traitors, journey to hell and seek out the son who betrayed his father.'

Pietro stood up. 'Stay exactly where you are.'

'What are you going to do with me?' Nepi muttered.

'Nothing at all. Your hands are not tightly bound. You

will be able to free yourself in a few minutes. By then, I shall be gone.' He stepped across to the doorway, where he turned back. '*Pax tecum*, my son, and remember what I said about guilty secrets.'

Nepi struggled to his knees. 'Take care, friar,' he called out, not altogether in anger. 'If you heed my advice you'll go far from this territory. Disappear. You don't understand the danger you're in.'

The warning was still echoing round Fra Pietro's head as he stood blinking in the harsh sunlight on the steps of the Palazzo della Rovere.

Catherine stared in speechless amazement at her hostess. Was this eccentric but apparently highly intelligent woman fantasizing or being deliberately mischievous?

Maud Benedict hugely enjoyed her guest's discomfort. 'You are now thinking,' she announced, 'that this silly old biddy has flipped her lid. Well, she hasn't. She has simply decided that there is no need to maintain a secret that has already been kept for far too long just to humour a vain, snobbish woman. You're free to make whatever use you wish of the information – not that I imagine anyone's really interested in it.'

'Er . . . thank you.' Catherine could think of nothing else to say.

'I can see you're still gobsmacked.' Miss Benedict relished the modern idiom. 'I suppose I'd better start at the beginning.' She pointed to the tape-recorder. 'You can switch your machine on if you like.'

She turned to the piano and picked up an old sepia family group in a heavily embossed frame. Two young children were posed with their parents in front of the very house in which Catherine was sitting. The woman was holding a baby on her lap. It all looked very nineteen-twenties.

'My father, Sir Aynsley Benedict, my mother, my elder brother, Oscar, me and baby Giles,' the old lady explained. 'My mother died the year after this was taken – tuberculosis. Pity, she was a wonderful artist. I'll show you some of her watercolours if you're interested. The three of us grew up here with our father, who made his money in publishing. Got his baronetcy for churning out government propaganda in World War I. We were brought up by governesses and tutors and things but we learned more from our parents' friends. They were brilliant, witty outrageous people: artists, writers, theatre people, wits and raconteurs – outer circles of the Bloomsbury Set, I suppose. The house was always full of these frightfully clever people. It was an extraordinary atmosphere to grow up in. We never wanted to be anywhere else, so we never were anywhere else. Oscar went into the firm but spent most of his time writing poetry. I went to various lectures at London University. Never bothered with degrees – just did my own research and published.' She waved a vague hand towards one of the bookshelves. 'Astrolatry – star worship in layman's language.'

At that moment the nameless woman appeared in the doorway. She said nothing, but Miss Benedict jumped up. 'Ah, tea in the conservatory.' She led the way to a plant-filled room running the length of the house. There among the exotic ferns and rubber plants a wicker table had been laid with floral-patterned Coalport and silver-handled knives and cake forks. Over smoked salmon sandwiches, seed cake and vanilla slices Maud Benedict continued the family chronicle.

'In 1939 the boys went off to war, of course, and in

1943 our father died. I was involved . . .' She interrupted herself with a gesture of impatience. 'You don't want to hear about my war. The important thing is that Giles came back with a wife – and a ready-made family. More tea?' She poured lapsang suchong from a brown earthenware teapot that sat incongruously among the exquisite, hand-painted porcelain. 'Never found anything that makes a better brew than old Brown Bess,' she explained.

Catherine squeezed lemon into her cup and declined a second slice of cake. 'Was Giles' bride someone he met abroad?'

'Yes, it was all desperately romantic. Beatrice Devaraux was studying art in Rome when the war broke out. I expect she could have got back if she'd really wanted to but she didn't want to. She was a free spirit and she was involved with one of her tutors, a man called Antonio Santori. He was married and sometime early on in the war his wife produced a son.'

'Gregor?'

'Yes, dear Greg. Well, Antonio was called up and disappeared somewhere in the Western Desert. Then, in 1943, his widow was killed in an American bombing raid. The end of it all was that Beatrice was left looking after little Gregor. She had a pretty rough time until the Allies marched in. That was when Giles met her and took pity on her. He helped her to establish her British nationality and got her repatriated.'

'What about Gregor?'

'Beatrice passed him off as her son and no one asked any questions. One thing led to another, of course, and she and Giles were married three months after V.E. Day. Julia was born in 1946.'

'And you all lived together here?'

'Yes. It was wonderful having the house full again

after the silent, empty years of the war. Having the children here kept us all young. They were good years. We had a great deal of fun.' She chuckled. 'I especially remember the Christmases. We had our own traditions. A Briony Christmas was quite unlike anybody else's. It was an endless charade. We all had to make up and play various spontaneously imagined parts over the three days. I remember Greg – he must have been about ten at the time – prowling round in an oversized deerstalker with one of Giles' pipes in his mouth peering at everyone through a magnifying glass – Sherlock Holmes, you see. Some roles became traditional. There was the Christmas fairy – a fat ungainly creature called Cous-cous. She had a top-hatted sidekick named Snarl. It was they who distributed the presents in the small hours of Christmas morning. Santa Claus was far too old hat for us!'

'It sounds idyllic. What went wrong?'

'We all grew up . . . At least, we all grew older. "Up" and "older" are not necessarily the same. The root of the problem between Julia and Greg was that Beatrice always favoured the boy. Julia was her own child but somehow there was never the same bond between them as there was between Beatrice and her ex-lover's son.'

'Sounds like a recipe for disaster.'

'Yes, it was. When they were old enough Beatrice explained to the children the exact details of Greg's parentage and from that point on Julia regarded Greg as the cuckoo in the nest. She had always thought of him as her half-brother but now, well, he wasn't really even a step-brother. He was a non-person, an intruder, an outsider who had no right to be there.'

'So what happened?' Catherine asked, fascinated.

'Nothing dramatic. Just a steady build-up of hatred on Julia's side which made life miserable for all of us. At thirteen she was packed off to boarding school. Not long after that Greg went to art college. In 1963 Giles and Beatrice were killed in a stupid car crash. After that Julia cut her links with Briony. As soon as she was eighteen she adopted her mother's maiden name. She went to Oxford, did very well and cultivated the intellectual élite. Her family could only be an embarrassment to her and she certainly avoided anything that could connect her with Greg, especially when he began making a name for himself.' Maud Benedict sat back in her chair. 'And that's about the end of the story.'

Catherine clicked the tape-recorder's 'off' button. 'Thank you very much for telling me all that. It puts Julia Devaraux's career in a very new light.'

'Unhappy child.' The old woman nodded reflectively. 'She developed many talents but never the talent for love. It was partly our fault, but mortals can't fight the influence of the celestial realm. Sagittarians have a propensity for enmity.'

Catherine was struck by a sudden thought. 'Do Gregor's children know about this relationship?'

'Tristram and Ginny? Delightful youngsters. I've named them as my joint heirs. I decided that when that stupid fraud case came up. They've had a terribly raw deal. I wanted to do what I could to make amends. They'll get whatever is left of the Benedict fortune. The business was sold up years ago when Oscar died but there'll be Briony and some investments. I wrote and told Julia a couple of years ago, just so there would be no misunderstanding.' She chuckled. 'That had a most gratifying effect. Angry letters from her solicitors saying that she would contest the will and the estate was rightfully hers and what right had I got to leave everything to the offspring of that odious little Italian, and so on. Sorry, I'm rambling. Did

Ginny and Tristram know? I don't think so. Greg and I had a tacit agreement never to mention Julia in their presence and I certainly don't have any photographs of her on display. I keep the few I have got in a drawer. I'll show them to you. You might like one for your article.'

They returned to the library and Miss Benedict produced a folder from her desk. Catherine turned over the loose photographs, one at a time. She paused at one which seemed very recent. She took it to the window to see it more clearly. 'I've seen that woman. Who is she?' Maud Benedict donned reading glasses and peered at the small print of Julia and a blonde young woman against a background of trees and mown lawns.

'Goodness, I'd forgotten about that. It was a couple of years ago. I bumped into Julia in St James's Park. She was with a friend. Embarrassment all round, of course, but Julia had the manners to introduce us and this friend . . . No I don't remember her name . . . she insisted on taking photographs. She was an effervescent, highly strung creature. As I recall, they were involved in a joint business venture. A small gallery, I think. *Anyway*, she snapped Julia and me smirking hypocritically at each other, then asked me to take a photo of the two of them. A couple of weeks later she sent me a copy.'

Catherine's brow creased in concentration. 'I'm sure I've seen her recently.' She slipped the photograph into her folder. 'Miss Benedict, you've been very kind, but I mustn't take up any more of your time.'

'Time is the one thing I have plenty of, my dear.' For the first time the mask slipped and Catherine saw a lonely old woman, the last of her tribe, with only her memories and her abstruse researches to give her meaning.

Maud Benedict picked up a small brass bell and rang

it. Immediately the silent companion appeared to escort Catherine to the front door.

Throughout the drive home Catherine could not get the puzzle of the unnamed blonde out of her mind. She had definitely seen the woman, or someone incredibly like her, and not long ago. For some reason a telephone also floated into her memory. It was not until she turned off the M4 on to the Hungerford road that the mist cleared. The tall blonde woman had been taking telephone bids at the Santori sale. She was on the staff of Grinling's.

CHAPTER 9

'Thus it was that, in pursuance of my mission for your holiness and at no small risk to my own life, I reached Genoa. After exhaustive enquiries I located, in interesting circumstances, Bartolomeo Nepi, who was sometime secretary to the late Cardinal Petrucci. This Nepi is now attached to the household of Allesandro della Rovere. My enquiries into the political situation there indicated that all the country under the sway of Ludovico Sforza is united in opposition to your holiness. Everyone believes a second French invasion is only a matter of time.

'Your holiness will realize that I was interested to know why a close servant of your holiness's friend should now be in the pay of your holiness's enemies. I questioned the man closely and reached the following conclusions:

i   Nepi was not party to the secret correspondence between Cardinal Petrucci and yourself but I believe that he discovered or suspected that his eminence was keeping your holiness informed of the activities of the conspirators.
ii This information and other confidential matters the scoundrel hastened to turn to advantage to help him gain employment with Cardinal della Rovere or his associates.
iii I regret to have to inform your holiness that Nepi

175

made certain allegations concerning the Duke of Gandia.

'At this stage of my enquiries the connection between the assassinations of Michaelmas 1496 and the murder of the Duke of Gandia eight and a half months later was far from clear. If they were all in league against your holiness – Cardinal Petrucci excepted – the only discernible political motive was that of thwarting their plans. This would suggest that the perpetrator of the crimes was someone who believed himself to be acting in your holiness's interests.

'In my endeavours to confirm or negate this suspicion I resolved to discover what I could about the activities of Cardinals Montadini and della Chiesa.'

Tristram dropped the latest instalment of his translation on to his lap. 'Does that get us any further?' He looked from Tim to O.K. and back again. It was a warm Sunday afternoon and they were sitting in garden chairs on the lawn outside the villa.

Tim rubbed a finger along the bridge of his nose, eyes closed in concentration. 'I'd like to have met this friar. I understand the way his mind works. You can almost hear the ideas buzzing around in his head but he's not going to commit them to paper till he's got proof. I reckon the clue is in what Foscari doesn't say, or doesn't say yet. He's pushing the theory of a multiple political murder as far as he can and he's coming to the conclusion that it won't move any further. If three people were killed because they were the pope's enemies, either he ordered the murders or he knew who did.'

'In which case,' O.K. chipped in, 'he wouldn't have sent this friar to find out the truth.'

'Exactly. But if it wasn't the pope it can hardly have

been della Rovere. He's not going to bump off important members of his own faction.'

Tristram shook his head dubiously. 'Political allies have been known to fall out.'

'True, but I think in this case there was too much at stake. Della Rovere and Sforza and Charles VIII are in top-level talks, planning a massive military intervention. They want as much support as possible. They've got some of the princes and several of the cardinals on their side. You've read up the Borgias, O.K. What was the situation in 1496?'

'Yeah, certainly lots of these top people were fed up with Alexander and his brood. They could see he had plans to expand the papal states and probably put his sons in charge of what would become a hereditary Borgia state.'

'Right, so della Rovere is organizing plots inside and outside Italy. He's even weaned one of the Borgia brats away from his father. Then, just as the plans are coming together, three of his top lieutenants are murdered.'

'But Petrucci was a traitor,' Tristram insisted.

'Della Rovere didn't know that – not as far as Foscari could find out. So, whichever way you look at it, these murders weren't political. That means they were personal. So instead of having to find a reason for the Michaelmas Massacre, a reason for the extermination of three men, all we're looking for is a strong enough motive for murdering one of them. Someone wanted one of the cardinals dead and he was quite prepared to kill the others as well. That would muddy the waters.'

'People would assume it was political assassination,' O.K. added.

'Yes, whereas the murderer had no interest whatsoever in the political repercussions. Foscari could see that.

That's why, having failed to find a motive for the murder of Petrucci, he went on to probe the two others.'

Tristram looked uncertain. 'And you really think there's a parallel with the Grinling's murders?'

'I'm sure the first thing we have to do is stop looking for some motive that encompasses the death of all four victims.'

Inside the house the phone rang. Tim stood up. 'That's probably Catherine.' He went indoors, lifted the receiver and heard his wife's voice.

'Hello, darling. How are you?'

'Fine, and you?'

'Missing you but glad you're not here. Are you getting lots of rest?'

'Oh, sure. O.K.'s promised that, if I'm very good, I can take a few steps with my zimmer tomorrow.'

'You poor old thing. I guess you're feeling a bit frustrated.'

'Not at all – I'm feeling a hell of a lot frustrated. What is going on back there? Come on, just give me a résumé.'

'Well, the bad news is that we've all discovered that you're not indispensable.'

'Thanks for that boost to my ego. What's the good news? Is there any?'

'Plenty. For starters, Grinling's have invited us to tender for the new warehouse.' Catherine gave a censored report on the meeting with Stovin, the plans for the promotional video and some encouraging contacts she had had with clients. Before Tim could quiz her in detail she hurried on to ask, 'How are you getting on with the Michaelmas Massacre?'

'The what?'

'The Michaelmas Massacre. Last time we spoke you

said Tristram had found a document about it and was going to start translating it.'

'Yes, it's fascinating.' Tim gave his wife the gist of Foscari's report. 'I'm getting a definite feel about this business. I'm convinced the answer – if there is an answer – will only come from probing the lives of the victims. Ginny went to Germany a couple of days ago. She's going to see what she can find out about Segar.'

'Well, I had a fascinating conversation yesterday with a remarkable old lady called Maud Benedict.'

'Never heard of her.'

'She's Julia Devaraux's aunt. Now, get this, buster . . .' Catherine paused for effect. 'Julia and Gregor were brought up together – virtually as brother and sister . . . I take it from your lack of response that you're impressed with my sleuthing.'

'I'm stunned.'

'Well, there's more. Listen to this.' She gave Tim a potted version of the relationship between the two children who had grown up and grown apart at Briony. Then she went on to the odd business of the woman in the photograph.

'Intriguing. Can you follow up on that?'

'Yes. I'll pop into Grinling's next time I'm in town . . . Tim? . . . Tim are you there?'

'Sorry, I was just thinking about that other business. It's a bit worrying.'

Tim was still brooding over Catherine's report when he returned to the garden a few minutes later. Two things were disturbing him about the conversation with his wife. He decided to tackle one of them head on. He sat down and gazed intently at the young lawyer. 'Tristram, is there something you haven't told me? Something important? Something about Julia Devaraux and your father?'

Tristram stared uncomfortably at his feet but made no reply.

'Come on, spill it. Unless you can deliver a pretty convincing explanation you and Ginny have an excellent motive for murder.'

At that moment Ginny was standing on the steps of an impressive Bavarian *schloss* fifteen kilometres west of Munich. She had not intended to call. She had taken the Sunday afternoon drive out from the city simply from curiosity, to see where Heinrich Segar lived. But she had been so overwhelmed by the prospect of Elberhof that she decided to pluck up courage and call unannounced on the scholar's widow. The palace-castle was not large, nor was it façaded with Baroque exuberance like other south German stately residences, but it was a compact architectural masterpiece created by an amalgam of historical styles. Through the wrought-iron gates Ginny saw a straight gravel drive leading to a bridge across a moat. Beyond, round turrets with conical roofs flanked a range of medieval solidity. At right angles, and perfectly complementing the older construction, an elegant, multi-windowed, eighteenth-century building fronted the drive. Ginny gazed admiringly at Elberhof for several minutes. Obviously the Segars had money as well as taste. On a sudden impulse, she got out of the car and pressed the intercom button. She bent to the grille, prepared to explain her unannounced arrival, but there was a click beside her and the heavy gates began to swing open.

Ginny had prepared her alias very carefully. She was Giulia Amati, a freelance editor working for various European publishing houses. A fax typed on the headed notepaper of Schröder-Neumarkt Verlag of Frankfurt had announced that publisher's intention of producing a commemorative volume of essays by Heinrich Segar. It was to be prefaced by an extended biographical note. This letter had gone to the Director of the Augsburg College of Art and Technology, where Segar had headed the Department of Renaissance Studies, asking for assistance in compiling an appreciation of the late Herr Doktor. Ginny had followed up with a phone call and enjoyed a pleasant conversation with Professor von Götz, who had invited her to call at the college on Monday to meet some of Segar's colleagues and students. A visit to Elberhof, though not part of the plan, suddenly seemed to make excellent sense.

As the door opened Ginny's first impression was of a wide smile of welcome that faded rapidly to a fown of disappointment and surprise.

'Oh . . . I was expecting . . . Sorry, can I help you?' The speaker was an elegant, grey-blonde woman in, Ginny judged, her early fifties, though an expensive sweater, tailored trousers and impeccable make-up took ten years off her age.

'Frau Segar? My name's Giulia Amati. I do apologize for calling unannounced. I represent Schröder-Neumarkt Verlag of Frankfurt.' Ginny explained about the fictitious book. 'I was on my way to Augsburg and it suddenly occurred to me that I really ought to come and explain the project to you,' she concluded.

'I see . . . then you'd better come in.'

Ginny noticed that Mrs Segar looked anxiously down the drive before she closed the door. But interest in her hostess's behaviour was instantly replaced by admiration for her surroundings. The hall was panelled in bleached oak. On an expanse of wall to the left three Sienese school religious paintings, individually lit, glowed with gold and enamel-like colours. On a plinth in the adjacent corner stood a fifteenth-century polychromed statue of the Madonna and Child. The shorter wall facing these splendours was reserved for a French ivory triptych displaying the Crucifixion, the Resurrection and the Dormitian of the Virgin. Ginny guessed that it must be fourteenth, perhaps even thirteenth century. But what dominated the room from its position beneath the sweep of the staircase, striking an almost incongruous contrast with its other treasures, was a mounted Renaissance figure in gleaming, damascened Nürnberg armour, massive sword held triumphantly aloft.

'Shall we?'

Ginny was aware that she was standing still in the middle of the hall and that Mrs Segar was waiting patiently by an open door. 'I'm sorry. I was stunned by your beautiful things.'

The older woman shrugged. 'My husband was a compulsive collector. Everything he admired he had to have.'

Ginny noted the slight edge of bitterness to the widow's voice as she followed her into a green and gold salon whose coordinated decor and delicate, graceful furnishings radiated the very atmosphere of the Enlightenment. Here, Ginny quickly noted, was the celebrated Segar collection of Renaissance bronzes. Her gaze moved rapidly from one precious item to another. Figurines from several of the leading Italian, German and French masters standing on console tables, side tables, inlaid commodes and bonheurs-du-jour glowed in the afternoon light from tall windows. Ginny remembered her father telling her about this amazing assemblage of pieces he had never seen and knew that he would never see, thanks to Segar's hostility.

'Your husband will be greatly missed,' she ventured, as she seated herself carefully on a Louis XVI sofa. 'So much knowledge; so much experience.'

'Thank you, Miss Amati.' The smile was a little forced. 'But I hope you haven't come to ask me about any of these things. I'm a total ignoramus. My husband told me nothing about his treasures. I wasn't even allowed to handle them.' She ran a finger down the flank of a sixteenth-century Italian cupid on the table beside her, as though in open defiance of Heinrich Segar's ghost.

'Our book will, we hope, be a permanent record of his contribution to Renaissance scholarship.' Ginny floundered for words. She realized that in her impulsiveness she had not prepared any questions. What should she try to find out? 'I wondered if there were any papers here that might be of interest – unpublished essays, articles in obscure magazines, that sort of thing.'

Frau Segar shook her head. 'My husband did all his work at his office. He kept nothing here. The person you should speak to is Maria Heuss, his assistant. She was . . . invaluable to him, went everywhere with him, organized his research, typed his lecture notes.'

'Yes, I gather she's the key person, I'm due to meet her tomorrow morning. So you never travelled with Doctor Segar?'

'Seldom. Although I was with him in London when he was killed. I went along strictly for the shopping, you understand.'

'It must have been a terrible shock for you. Such a ghastly and pointless crime.'

There was a buzzing noise. In response Mrs Segar crossed to a concealed panel by the door, opened it and picked up a handset. 'It's you. Good.' She pressed a button, returned the telephone to its rest and returned to her seat.

Ginny stood up. 'You have someone else coming to see you. I'll be getting along.'

'Oh, please don't rush.' The other woman jumped to her feet. 'Look, I've just remembered that there might be some papers in my husband's desk that would be of interest to you. I haven't had time to go through it yet.' There was the sound of a car arriving and coming to a standstill in front of the house. 'Do sit down. I'll fetch them for you.' The ungrieving widow stepped quickly across the room.

Ginny heard the front door open and a brief *sotto-voce* conversation. Another door opened and closed and then there was silence. It was five minutes before Mrs Segar returned, carrying a folder.

'Sorry to have been so long. It took me ages to find the study key. My husband always kept it locked and I had to go through his pockets. This was all I could find. It seems to be a catalogue of articles he wrote. Perhaps it will be a useful check list for you.'

'Thank you very much. May I return it to you in a couple of days?'

'Oh, I shouldn't bother. It's of no interest to me. Well, if that's all I can do for you . . .' The hostess who, minutes before, had urged Ginny to stay, now seemed anxious to see her off the premises. Seconds later they were shaking hands at the front door. As soon as Ginny turned to descend the steps the painted timber crashed shut behind her.

On the gravel beside her car there now stood a very new, very bright yellow Porsche. Ginny cast her eyes over it admiringly. She looked inside at the gleaming black leather and the elegant fittings and jealously ogled the fashionable and very expensive pigskin travelling bag on the passenger seat. With a sigh, Ginny walked across to her own modest vehicle.

*   *   *

After two weeks, Foscari was coming to the conclusion that he had drawn a blank in Ferrara. He had travelled to the city of the Este dukes because Sebastiano Montadini had been bishop there for fifteen years. During that time many people had known him. Several had memories and stories they were prepared to share with the Franciscan. Yet they did not amount to much. They told of a conscientious administrator who ran his diocese efficiently; of a disciplinarian who attempted to raise the moral and intellectual tone of his clergy; of a scholar who was patron to artists and enjoyed the company of poets and writers; of a man of personal piety who followed a strict daily régime himself and encouraged his household to do the same. Yet all these aspects of Montadini's life seemed to Foscari to be so many veils, concealing the man himself. Of the cardinal's thoughts and feelings, convictions and ideas, friends and enemies, hopes and fears he could discover nothing. Certainly, there was no intimation of why this exemplary ecclesiastic should have been plotting against the vicar of Christ.

Brother Pietro enjoyed his days in Ferrara. There was certainly much to see in the city that Duke Ercole was turning into Italy's most modern and prestigious ducal capital, the envy of other rulers. It was ten years since Pietro had last been there and he was amazed to see the changes that had been made by Ercole d'Este's army of builders, masons, architects, sculptors, carpenters, tilers and painters. Part of the old wall, embracing what was already a sizeable, if cramped, metropolis, had been demolished so that a whole new area, the Addizione Erculea, as large again as the original city, could be added. Within the new fortifications, patrolled by a much enlarged ducal guard, straight streets were marked out by ropes and pegs. Many churches and palazzos were already being built. Wealthy merchants were staking their claims in the locales designated as new trading centres and laying out the gardens and groves that would surround their residences. Ercole and his architect, Biagio Rossetti, had not forgotten the ordinary Ferrarese. Development was strictly controlled and included piazzas and parks where the duke's subjects could take their leisure.

Foscari did not enjoy unlimited freedom for sightseeing. He had to attend the regular worship of his order in their convent alongside what had been the city wall and was now a wide thoroughfare. And there were daily works of charity to be performed. His superiors welcomed an addition to the Franciscan ranks. The city's growing population created ever-increasing pastoral demands. Pietro was, therefore, given many opportunities for preaching. On most days he devoted two morning hours to this activity in a variety of locations – churches, piazzas, cemeteries and cloisters – throughout the city.

It was after three days that he noticed a small knot of people – usually three men and a woman – who attended all his sermons. They stood on the outside of the crowd but always listened intently and seemed to discuss his message among themselves. Other people came and went while Fra Pietro preached. Some lingered to ask questions. But this group always stayed the course and hurried away as soon as he had finished. Once when he attempted to speak with them they scattered like startled birds. Pietro was curious and a little anxious. It was a favourite trick of the Inquisition to plant seemingly ordinary people in a congregation to check on a preacher's orthodoxy. Once a man was marked by them they watched him carefully, sending news of his movements along their own particular grapevine, so that their agents in distant places were forewarned and ready to pounce at the slightest suspicion of heresy. Foscari was particularly careful to guard his tongue and not to express any of his more radical views, but every morning he half-expected to encounter a delegation of little grim-faced black friars at his preaching venue.

It was after his fourteenth sermon, which he delivered in the Piazza Nuova, the centrepiece of Rossetti's grand schema for the Addizione Erculea, that Pietro realized he was being followed. He had geared his address to the workmen on the various building sites of the city extension. He had taken for his theme 'Christ the Rock and True Foundation'. At one point he had been unable to resist a jibe at the Carthusian monks whose vastly enlarged and luxurious premises were clearly visible under construction across the debris-scattered open space to the north. 'Our Lord had nowhere to lay his head,' Brother Pietro reminded his audience. 'Some of his followers,' and he waved a hand towards San Cristofor alla Certosa, 'don't seem to have that problem. They sleep cosily. They fill their bellies amply. They live in palaces while God's children go homeless and must beg for crusts.' The words were mild in comparison with those that had landed him in the Castel Sant' Angelo but, though they drew a cheer from his congregation, he wished he had not uttered them. It was as he strode along the Via Palestro, towards the city centre, that Foscari sensed a presence behind him. He stopped to watch some workers removing the scaffolding from the newly completed marble façade of an impressive palazzo. From the corner of his eye he saw one of the men who had so assiduously attended his sermons.

The stranger faltered in his stride, momentarily paused,

then appeared to change his mind. He came up to Pietro and greeted him with a half-smile. 'Good day to you, Brother. You preach truth.'

'Good day, my son. I like to think so.'

'Shall we talk as we walk?' The stranger, who was tall and sharp-featured and wore a merchant's fur-trimmed gown, took Pietro familiarly by the arm.

'And what are we to talk of, my son?'

'Why, the things of God, Brother. What else should Christian men discuss?'

'And with whom have I the honour of debating the divine mysteries?'

'Paolo Alviano, a brother in Christ. You are nervous about me, of course. We all have to be careful in these evil days. But you have nothing to fear from me. I, too, belong to the Third Age.'

'Not all who use the words of the Brotherhood are brothers,' Foscari responded cautiously.

'I don't expect you to accept me without question, especially after what you have suffered at the hands of Antichrist – oh yes, we know about your trial by the Inquisition. But we of the Truth must fellowship together. Come tonight and you shall find yourself among brothers and sisters in the Truth.'

'Tonight? Where? When? I am not sure . . .'

'I will be outside your convent after Vespers.' Before Foscari could question him further, the tall man turned along a side street and strode quickly away.

Brother Pietro was in two minds about keeping the suggested appointment. If Alviano really was a believer in the Third Age, the final stage of divine revelation which should usher in the Second Coming, well and good. His underground movement should be encouraged. But there were many bizarre sects around which rejected the testimony of Scripture and threw up false messiahs. Yet, for all his reservations, Foscari did emerge on to the Via San Francesco as darkness seeped into the narrow street.

There was a flash of light from a closed lantern on the opposite corner and the friar crossed towards it. Alviano gripped his arm in enthusiastic greeting and propelled him with quick steps. They passed the cathedral, going in the direction of the castle, but then his guide directed him through a labyrinth of lanes and alleyways and Foscari lost all sense of his whereabouts. The journey ended when they descended a flight of steps and Alviano tapped on a low door. It was opened a crack. The tall man identified himself and he and Foscari entered a cellar well lit by lamps hanging from ceiling beams.

About twenty people were already gathered, men and women. Most of them were artisans but there were two priests present and three or four others who, like Alviano, were men of some substance. Pietro was introduced as 'a brother from the very lair of Antichrist who has suffered much for the Truth and who will be able to tell us about our brothers and sisters in Rome.'

Then the proceedings began. A Scripture reading was announced. Some of the company took out small well-worn copies of the New Testament in Italian. One of the women read a passage from *Revelation*, after which Alviano expounded it at some length, showing how Pope Alexander was the scarlet woman, the mother of whores, riding on the beast and gorging himself on the blood of the faithful. Foscari looked around at the eager faces accentuated by the lamplight. They were totally immersed in Alviano's words, nodding as he made his points and occasionally calling out 'Yes' or 'Amen'. Foscari had attended such conventicles before but seldom had encountered such complete commitment and concentration.

After the sermon the brothers and sisters took part in a breaking of bread. The service was conducted in the vernacular and bore little relation to the Latin mass. The communicants passed the bread and wine round among themselves and no priest pronounced words of consecration over them. As the formal part of the proceedings came to an end there was an atmosphere of excited, yet solemn conspiracy; the fellowship of those who share a forbidden secret. Pietro was asked to give an account of his suffering before the Inquisition and the fate of others in Rome who refused to bow the knee to Antichrist. Foscari asked how long the Brotherhood had been meeting in Ferrara. 'Five years,' somebody replied. 'But things are more difficult now, since this new bishop came. He has his informers everywhere,' another added.

'Then the old bishop – Montadini – was more lenient?' Pietro asked.

Alviano faced him across the table that had been the makeshift altar. 'Brother Sebastiano was one of us. That's why the scarlet woman murdered him.'

190

CHAPTER 10

Tristram stared across the valley, as though expecting some inspiration to emerge from the distant haze. 'I suppose Aunt Maud's been talking.'

'Never mind where the information came from,' Tim responded indignantly. 'What's all this about a family feud between Julia Devaraux and the Santoris?'

The young lawyer struggled to channel his feelings into calm, considered language. He failed. 'That woman was a monster!' The words exploded like a cork from a bottle. Others gushed out behind them. 'She had a capacity for hatred such as I've never seen. From childhood she loathed my father. They were cooped up together in that house in Hampstead and she just fed on her animosity. It started with childish bitchiness – telling tales to her parents, tearing up his books, that sort of thing – and got worse. She was a vicious little vixen. As soon as they could escape from an impossible situation, she and my father left the Hampstead house and had nothing more to do with each other. Except, of course, that she continued her vendetta whenever she had an opportunity. At one time she even tried to get him deported as an unregistered alien. Fortunately, by then my father had obtained naturalization papers.'

'He told you all this?'

'Oh, not for years. We had no clue that there was any

connection between him and the Devaraux woman until about the time the trial started. Aunt Maud decided she wanted to remember us in her will.'

'I gather she made you and Ginny her sole beneficiaries.'

Tristram nodded. 'That was the last straw for Julia. She went berserk and wrote us the vilest letter you could imagine. It came as a total surprise to us. That was when our father had to let us in on the secret.'

'So Julia Devaraux was planning to come between you and a substantial inheritance?'

Tristram shrugged. 'There was nothing she could really do. If Aunt Maud made a proper will – as I'm sure she must have done – Julia had no legal claim on the Benedict estate. Giles Benedict, Julia's father, was already dead when Sir Oscar died and he left everything to Maud, his closest surviving relative. It's up to her to do whatever she wants with it.'

Tim persisted. 'But Julia could kick up a stink when the time came – set the lawyers arguing for months, even years?'

'Well, I suppose . . . But . . .'

'If I were in your position I'd be pretty angry at that prospect. Here's this woman who's ruined your father doing everything in her power to make life unbearable for you and Ginny. In your place I'd be thinking, "Is this wretched business never going to end? Are we going to be haunted by it for the rest of our lives? How can we get this bloody woman off our backs?" And I might come up with an answer.'

'Tim, you can't believe that!' It was an anguished shout.

'It doesn't matter what I believe. Right now Edgerson's scrabbling round for anything that will link you two more firmly to the murder. Why the hell didn't you come clean with him about the will?'

'Basically, for the very reason you've just stated. The police want to pin the crime on us. If Edgerson had known about the family feud he'd have found some way of keeping us in England. As it is, he'd need some solid evidence before he could extradite us. Anyway, he's not going to find out anything, is he? No one knows about the will except us and Aunt Maud.'

'And the family lawyers, and the Devaraux lawyers, and anyone else Julia may have grumbled to, anyone who half-knows the truth and decides to spill it to the press – and Catherine!' Tim almost shouted his exasperation. 'Can't you see what a mess you've got her into? She's been given information that may be relevant to a criminal prosecution. What's she supposed to do with it – pass it to the police and make more trouble for you and Ginny, or sit on it, which is an offence for which she could go to jail?'

'But all this stuff about feuds and wills is irrelevant.'

'I imagine D.I. Edgerson would say that he's the best judge of that. Right now, Catherine doesn't realize the implications of what she's been told. I'm going to have to get back to her and tell her what to do. Any ideas?'

Tristram looked miserable. 'I suppose you want us to come clean to the police.'

Tim lay back in his chair, eyes closed. 'I don't know. I just don't know. We could sit tight and hope no one else leaks the story. We could come clean and try to persuade Edgerson that it isn't important. It's your decision. You're going to have to have a serious talk with Ginny about it. One problem is that if Edgerson chases after this particular hare he's going to stop concentrating on other aspects of the case that are vital. Catherine's come up with another lead.' He explained about the photograph and the woman at Grinling's.

Tristram clutched at the straw eagerly. 'That sounds really important – a breakthrough.'

'Don't raise your hopes. We must see what happens when Catherine follows it up. Till then I suggest we lay this other business on ice.' He stood up. 'I'm going to call Catherine back and put her in the picture.'

Augsburg's College of Art and Technology is behind the Dom and housed in an imposing eighteenth-century building which was once the town house of a branch of the Fugger banking family. Ginny parked her car in the lea of the squat Romanesque-Gothic cathedral and had to run through the college's grassed courtyard as a heavy shower swept over the town. Professor von Götz received her immediately and was effusive in his courtesy and enthusiasm for her publishing project. The death of Dr Segar had been a tragedy of immeasurable proportions and, of course, he and his colleagues would contribute in any way over the publication of a fitting memorial volume. For the first time Ginny's conscience gave her a tweak. What was this earnest academic going to feel when he realized there was no commemorative collection of essays? Oh well, no time to worry about that now. After a few minutes of polite general conversation the professor indicated that Maria Heuss, Dr Segar's assistant, was eagerly awaiting her. He escorted her to an office along the corridor.

Any image Ginny had formed of Maria Heuss as a serious, bespectacled student who lived for her studies evaporated quickly. The woman who welcomed her with a smile and a firm handshake was slim and stylishly dressed, and her perfume was expensive. Intelligent grey eyes looked out from a well-sculpted face and her hair was black and lustrous with expertly applied grey highlights. 'Come and sit down. Coffee?' She poured the beverage from a cafetière in a corner of the room. 'I gather you plan to do a special edition of some of Heinrich's articles. How many do you want?'

'Probably a dozen or so depending on length. We thought a mix of his more important scholarly contributions and a few lesser-known papers would give the best overall impression of his work.'

'That sounds a good scheme.' Maria sat behind her desk and opened a folder. 'I've prepared a list . . .'

Ginny opened her briefcase. 'Actually, Mrs Segar has already given me a list. I called on her yesterday.' She produced the two sheets of A4 the academic's widow had provided.

Maria raised an eyebrow. 'Really? That's surprising. He kept his home life and his work in very separate compartments. May I see?' She perused the lines of type. 'Oh no, these are not articles. They are the names of individual works.' She read some of the items. '*Crucifixion* by Niccolò dell' Arca; *Hercules* – a copy of a lost Verrocchio, *c*.1540; *Moses and Aaron*, workshop of Jean Goujon.' She continued surveying the list in puzzled silence for some seconds. Then she looked up with sudden understanding. 'Ah, I think I know what these are – they're works Heinrich helped to identify or authenticate.'

Ginny smiled. 'Thank you. I wasn't sure Mrs Segar had got it right. Those letters in the right-hand column mystified me. Do you know what they mean?'

Maria looked closely at the marks beside each entry. The dell' Arca piece was accompanied by '\ XXOL', the Verrocchio copy was marked 'B MOLL', the French relief carvings had the note 'B KXXO'. She shook her head. 'It looks like some kind of secret code. I'm afraid it means nothing to me.'

'Mrs Segar suggested that you were privy to all the late doctor's secrets.'

The words were spoken lightly but Fraulein Heuss chose to take them seriously. 'I thought I was. I suppose that goes to show how little we really understand those we think we know well.'

'You must have been very close to Doctor Segar?'

'We worked together for six years, but I'd known him before that. He was my tutor when I was studying for my degree.'

'And he picked you out as a star pupil?'

'Something like that.'

'What was he like to work with?'

'Inspirational.' The academic looked across the desk with expressionless eyes.

'Can you expand on that? I'm sorry if I'm waking painful memories. It's just that I have to do this appreciation of Doctor Segar and . . .'

'I quite understand, Miss Amati.' Maria smiled a faint, bemused sort of smile. 'What can I tell you? He was immensely knowledgeable – that goes without saying. But he had a *feel* for fine and beautiful things. He instinctively knew if something was genuine. He made some amazing finds in quite unexpected places.' She pointed to a framed photograph on the wall showing the marble bust of a youth with exquisite locks of curling hair. 'That Bernini was lying in the corner of a monumental mason's yard in Bologna covered in brick dust. And of course you know the story of him spotting a Michelangelo drawing in Christie's when he was only a student. The other side of the coin is that he was quite ruthless in exposing fakes.'

'Mrs Segar tells me he was something of a compulsive collector. There are certainly some wonderful things at his house.'

'So I believe.'

'You mean you haven't seen his collection?'

'As I said, he kept home and work strictly separate.'

'But surely you, as his personal assistant . . .'

Maria Heuss simply shook her head by way of response.

Ginny frowned thoughtfully. 'Then, I seem to be getting a picture of a very secretive sort of man, someone who enjoyed his possessions in an almost . . . well, miserly sort of way.'

'Heinrich was a very private person. He never let anyone get very close to him.' Maria paused. 'Look, I wouldn't want you to misinterpret that. He wasn't a cold fish, far from it. His lectures were highly entertaining. You can meet some of his students; I'm sure they'll agree with that.'

'But?' Ginny prompted.

'Well, I suppose what you could say is that he was in love with art and that his sculptures, paintings and drawings met all his emotional needs. Anyway.' Her change of tone indicated that that particular subject was closed. 'As I say, this is a complete list of his published articles. Would it help if I marked the more significant ones? Some were of quite seminal importance – changed our thinking abut a number of leading Renaissance artists.'

'Thank you. That would be helpful.'

Maria ran her eye quickly down the titles and ticked seven or eight of them. 'There, I think your anthology must include these. We have them here, of course. Let me know if you'd like anything photocopied. Otherwise, I think the best thing you can do is talk with some of his students. I've checked on who's in today and asked a couple of them to meet you in the common room. Shall we?' She stood up and ushered Ginny out of the office.

A few paces down the corridor Ginny stopped. 'Oh, I think you forgot to give me back the list – the one Mrs Segar let me have.'

Maria Heuss looked surprised. 'Did I? Are you sure? I'll check while you're chatting with the others.'

The two young people Ginny met moments later were introduced as Ingrid and Hans, third-year students, majoring in Renaissance studies. The three of them sat down in well-used armchairs in a corner of the common room and Ginny asked her questions. The youngsters spoke with enthusiasm about Heinrich Segar as a lecturer and supervisor of studies and with horror about his sudden death. But Ginny learned little from them. She was about to take her leave when Maria Heuss came into the common room.

She held out the missing list. 'I'm sorry, Miss Amati. You were quite right. It had got under some other papers. Are you leaving?'

'Yes. Thank you so much for your help – all of you.' Ginny shook hands with the others. 'I'll let you know, Miss Heuss, as soon as we've decided on the contents of the book.'

'I'd like to see what you write about Heinrich before it goes for publication. Would that be possible?' Maria asked.

'Yes. I don't see any problem about that. You obviously knew him better than anyone – except, of course, his wife.'

Maria responded with a slightly quizzical glance but only said, 'I'll show you the way out.'

Ginny was walking across the courtyard when she heard footsteps on the gravel path behind her.

'Hello, may I join you?' It was Hans, a spindly, tousle-haired young man who walked with a gangling, slightly uncoordinated gait. 'I'm just going for lunch. Do you want some?'

'Well, I . . .'

'I don't think you heard everything back there that you should have done.'

'Meaning?'

'This way.' He turned right out of the college grounds and plunged into a narrow, meandering street that led down to the town centre.

They had only gone a few paces when he stopped. 'Odd.'

'What's odd?'

'Maria Heuss usually parks her brand-new Porsche in the staff car park – very prominently where everyone can see it.' He nodded to the row of vehicles on the other side of the street.

Among them was a bright yellow sports car. Ginny stepped quickly across the road and peered inside. On the passenger seat was an elegant pigskin travelling bag.

George Martin had interesting information for Monday morning's meeting. He put a tape-recorder in the middle of the breakfast table. 'We've been listening very carefully to all the stuff our bug's come up with. Most of it's useless, of course – routine office chat. My guess is that Druckmann e-mails anything that's particularly sensitive. What wouldn't I give to get into his computer files.'

'Any chance?' Emma asked through a yawn.

George shook his head. 'Not so far. Johnny's been working at it night and day. But Artguard's using the most up-to-date software. It's got all sorts of anti-hacking devices. The foolproof system is yet to be invented but every new one that comes out gets harder to crack.'

'But you've managed to get something on tape?' Lines of weariness showed through Catherine's carefully applied make-up.

'Yes. What we've got is bits and pieces of telephone conversations. We've been over them time and time again and put together a compilation tape. The bugger is you can only hear one end of the conversations. Still, I reckon there's some very revealing stuff here. See what you think.' He pressed a button and they all heard Druckmann's deep voice over the background hiss.

'Jim, hello . . .'

('We reckon this is a call from Jimmy McNair, Lord Lochinver,' George explained.)

'You have? From Adrian? What's bugging him now?

'Really? Well, I'll say this for them: they don't give up easily. When Lacy had his heart attack I thought that would finish them off.

'Adrian panics unnecessarily but if he wants to cover himself by cutting them in on the tendering that's no skin off my nose. We all know who's going to win the contract.

'Yes, Jimmy.

'Yes, I realize that, but . . .

'I know. Our budget's tight, too, but it can't take much longer. And as soon as Lacy Security's in the bag we can start to clean up. The place in Wiltshire alone must be worth a couple of million. Then there are all their contracts. That'll give us plenty of cash to pick off the remaining smaller operators.

'Yes, Jimmy, I appreciate that but you can tell our friends not to worry. Another couple of weeks – three at most – and Lacy's will drop into our hands like an overripe plum.

'Of course you can. Trust me, Jimmy.

'Goodbye . . . and, hey, enjoy the pro-am golf tournament on Sunday.'

George switched the machine off. The four people round the table had been listening intently, eating and drinking suspended. The silence continued for several more seconds.

It was Emma who broke it. 'Bastard!'

George smiled. 'I'll second that.'

Catherine helped herself to coffee. 'So what Lochinver and his cronies are aiming at is a monopoly of the security business. My God, but that's sinister.'

'It makes a lot of commercial sense,' Emma acknowledged grudgingly. 'Security's a fast-growing business in these uncertain times. There aren't many industries that cover the whole range from major contracts for government installations to fitting burglar alarms on the homes of Joe Public.'

'And what happens when all that business is controlled by organized crime?' George began attacking his usual breakfast fry-up.

Sally protested. 'That's a bit far-fetched, surely, George.'

He shook his head. 'You've got too trusting a nature, Sally. You don't know Druckmann like I do. He's in with some of the top criminal brass in the country.'

'Can we prove that?' Catherine asked.

'Listen to this next bit. This call came in on Friday, a couple of hours after the conversation with Jimmy the Fist.' George re-started the tape.

'Trevor, hi!' This time there was a nervous edge to Druckmann's self-assurance.

'Yes, I've already had a word with him.

'I really don't think there's any need to worry, Trev . . .

'We only need to wait . . .

'I don't think that's necessary . . .

'Of course, you do, Trev. I don't want to dictate . . .'

George said, 'There was a long pause at this point. "Trev" must have been holding forth at some length. I've cut to Druckmann's reaction.'

'OK, if that's the way you want it. Do whatever you like about Hartnell. I don't need to know . . .

'Yes, of course I can, Trev. I'll have to go through the files and get back to you on that one. A public gallery would be best . . . More media coverage . . . I'll call you within the hour. Goodbye.' The listeners heard the phone replaced on its rest. Then Druckmann muttered, 'Paranoid ape!'

George left the tape running. Druckmann's voice returned. 'Hello, Saul Druckmann here. Put me through to Mr Shand, please. He's expecting my call . . . Trev, hi, Saul. I've got that information you wanted. I reckon Grove's Gallery, Mount Street is your best bet. Three rooms full of modern art. Two security guards. Lacy's updated their system a couple of years ago. It'll be a doddle for a couple of men with shooters and there's a quick getaway into Park Lane. If you really think it's necessary . . .

'No, Trev, no way. You know best . . .

'OK . . . Yes. As soon as you've hit Grove's I'll lean more heavily on the Lacy woman. I'll personally enjoy watching her squirm. The only pity is that her old man's out of the country recuperating. I'd love to turn the knife in his back.

'Right, Trev. Cheers!'

George switched off the machine. He looked around at the others. 'That's it.'

'George, you've done a marvellous job,' Catherine said.

He shrugged. 'Team effort, Catherine. The annoying thing is that we can't use it directly. We can scarcely admit to the police that we've been illegally bugging commercial premises. And anyway the tape wouldn't be admissible evidence in court.'

Sally asked, 'Do we know anything about this Trevor Shand?'

George nodded emphatically. 'Oh, yeah. We know lots. None of it good. The Shand Brothers, Trevor and Frankie, are the nearest thing Britain's got to a national Mafia. They operate from south of the river and they're into all the usual syndicate activity – drugs, prostitution, protection, extortion, art theft, gambling. They've got various legit fronts – a couple of West End clubs, a chain of gyms and sports centres, a health farm and a haulage company. Frankie's the brains of the outfit – Harvard Business School degree no less. Trevor provides the muscle. It's a nasty combination but at least we know who we're up against.' George cleaned his plate. 'Any toast?'

Sally stood up. 'I'll get some more.' She paused on her way to the kitchen. 'Surely we can do something to stop this awful raid on Grove's Gallery. Poor Alison Grove – she's such a gentle soul. I can't bear to think of thugs breaking in and waving guns at her.'

'Don't worry,' George said firmly. 'I've already done something to put a stop to that caper. I reckoned an anonymous tip-off to the police would do the trick, so I left a message for our old friend D. I. Edgerson. I thought he could do with a break.'

Catherine smiled. 'Nice thought. Pity he won't know where the information came from. That would really annoy him.' She paused. 'I thought there were some encouraging things in what we've just heard. Druckmann is obviously under pressure from his bosses.'

Emma agreed. 'They're looking for quick results. I'll bet Lochinver and Shand have both been pouring money into Artguard and now they're beginning to demand some returns.'

'That's how I see it, too.' George reached for a slice of toast from the rack Sally put on the table.

'Then everything we can do to stall them will pile the pressure on,' Emma said. 'How long do you reckon Druckmann can survive if he doesn't deliver the goods?'

George shrugged. 'He's got involved with ruthless men who won't hesitate to pull the plug if they think it's necessary.'

Catherine sighed. 'So it's going to be a struggle for survival – Artguard and Lacy's sitting it out to see who cracks first?'

George demurred. 'I reckon our time bombs should speed things up a bit. If we can abort this raid on Grove's that'll set the cat among the pigeons. Our Trev will want to know where the leak came from. Then when Druckmann discovers the bug under his desk he'll guess the answer. That'll put him into a panic.'

Emma's face lit up. 'Yes, of course, he'll be terrified that the Shands find out. We've got him!'

Catherine was cautious. 'It's far from over yet. Let's just say we've dealt ourselves an ace. We've got to think carefully how and when we play it. Anyway, well done, George. You've given us a chance that we certainly didn't have before. Now, can we move on to other things? I have a meeting with the accountants this afternoon and while I'm in town I want to follow up this mystery woman at Grinling's. Emma, what's on your agenda?'

'I've got a couple of definite filming locations for the video and I'm going up to Wes's place to discuss script with his P.R. people.'

'Oh, so it's "come into my parlour" time, is it?'

Emma laughed a little self-consciously. 'No, nothing like that, Catherine. It's strictly business.'

An hour later, as she drove her bright red Honda northwards on quiet roads bright with autumn sunshine, she was still asking herself whether her confident assurance was true and, if it was, whether she wanted it to be true. She switched on the radio. BBC2. A reggae number bounced and jangled its way out of the speakers. She turned the sound down and concentrated on her own thoughts. She was twenty-six – an age when, as her mother never tired of pointing out, an attractive young woman should be thinking seriously about settling down. Emma giggled. What would that epitome of middle England think about a black pop star as a partner for her daughter? More importantly, what did Emma think about the prospect? Wes was great fun. And he was keen. Hardly a day passed without him phoning, supposedly to discuss plans for the Lacy Security video. He was rolling in money and enjoyed spending it. It would be silly to pretend that did not matter. If things did not work out at Farrans and she lost all her capital . . . Well, Wes would certainly be a well-filled cushion to fall back on. But immediately she caught herself thinking that Emma reacted vigorously. Of course Lacy Security was not going to fail! Not if she had anything to do with it! She cared about it passionately. Could she give it up for a life of globe-trotting as the 'other half' of a famous man?

The thudding of the music became intrusive. Emma switched channels to Classic FM. The hourly news report was on. '. . . Graham Hartnell. The police are treating the incident as suspicious and are questioning Doctor Hartnell's fellow workers and recent visitors to the laboratory.' Hartnell? Why was that name important? Where had she heard it before? Recently. Very recently. Memory returned with a rush. Druckmann had mentioned that name or one very like it in his conversation with the mobster Trevor Shand. Emma struggled to recall his words. 'Do what you want to with Hartnell. I don't want to know about it.' Something like that. Was there a connection or was there just a coincidence in the names? She told herself to listen out for the next bulletin. Yet, when it came, she was so absorbed in watching the road and thinking her own thoughts that she nearly missed it. It was the name that cut through her other preoccupations.

'. . . only victim was Doctor Graham Hartnell, head of one of the laboratory's research teams. Doctor Hartnell was carrying out experiments related to food poisoning with the aid of a grant from the Camrose-Pargiter meat and confectionery conglomerate. Colleagues expressed surprise that Doctor Hartnell was in the laboratory late on Sunday evening. One of them told reporters of her shocked reaction. She said that it would be impossible to imagine a more dedicated scientist than Graham Hartnell. Neighbours reported seeing two men prowling in the grounds before the fire and police are treating the incident as suspicious. They are questioning Doctor Hartnell's fellow workers and recent visitors to the laboratory.'

'Brother Sebastiano had a vision,' Alviano explained. 'An angel instructed him to seek out the Brotherhood and protect us from those placed in the Church by Satan to prevent the truth being known. He found us and, after much prayer, as you can imagine, we embraced him. He attended several of our meetings, in disguise, of course, and sat meekly under the instruction of the Spirit.'

Foscari puzzled over what he was being told. A prince of the Church a secret member of an underground heretical sect? 'It must have been difficult for him to avoid discovery?'

'Yes. The local Inquisitors began to be suspicious when he denounced them for cruelty and harassing poor people without cause. Brother Sebastiano saved four of our number from being investigated. He was surely God's shield for the faithful and we thought he was to have been God's sword against the Antichrist.'

'I'm not sure I understand what you mean.' Pietro looked around the circle of faces. Their features, accentuated by the lamplight, resembled so many intense, staring gargoyles.

'We had revelations,' one of the women explained. 'Sister Elsbeth has revelations. It is her gift. She told our brother that he was the Lord's weapon against the scarlet woman.'

'To do what?'

'To remove her and her brood from the earth.'

Foscari felt his head spinning. It was oppressively warm in the cellar. The mingled smell of lamp smoke and human sweat was overpowering. The friar had to force his mind to work coherently. 'Are you saying that his eminence . . . That Brother Sebastiano was planning to kill the pope?'

'Aye!' several voices replied. 'And his children – the children of Satan. They are an abomination. Their sins cry to heaven for punishment. Blasphemers! Whores! Murderers! Blasphemers . . . Murderers . . . Murderers . . .'

The cries echoed, though whether around the walls or

inside his brain Pietro could not tell. He stood up. He moved towards the door. He felt himself swaying.

'Whores . . . Blasphemers . . . Blasphemers . . . Murderers.'

The dimly lit room spiralled. Pietro felt himself held by strong hands as he collapsed.

When he opened his eyes Foscari felt cooler. He was lying on a hard surface. Someone – one of the women – was pressing a damp cloth to his forehead. A breeze caressed his face and he could see the stars. But between him and the heavens there was a ring of people, looking down at him and keeping up a murmuring chant. Pietro realized he was being prayed over.

He struggled into a sitting position. 'I'm sorry.' He turned to the woman kneeling beside him. 'Thank you, sister, I am better now.'

'It was a devil sent by the prince of devils,' she assured him, 'but we have driven him hence.' She helped him to his feet.

Foscari looked round and realized he was in a moonlit inner courtyard. 'Thank you, my brothers,' he muttered. 'Your prayers have prevailed. I must return now.'

Alviano stepped forward and took him by the arm. 'I will see you to your convent.'

Twenty minutes later Pietro lay down thankfully on the truckle bed in his cell. He crossed himself and uttered a quick Paternoster before closing his eyes. But the sleep that came was infested by hideous demons with leathern wings, scaly bodies, hairy limbs and leering, bulge-eyed, blotchy features.

Daylight and the singing of Prime cleared his head. He spent the morning study time sitting in the cloister, thinking. The extraordinary revelation of the previous night had illuminated much that he had already discovered –

or rather not discovered – about Montadini. It was now clear why the cardinal's life resembled a chained book in a college library that one could not take into the daylight for closer scrutiny. Or perhaps it was better to think of it as a coded volume. Now that Foscari had the key he felt that he would be able to decipher the inner reality of a man gripped by a holy, secret, terrible zeal.

It was the prior who helped him. Fra Niccolò had entrée to the ducal court. He was a scholar who had studied in Pisa and Paris and was greatly respected by Ercole d'Este. Frequently he was summoned to the castle to debate issues of theology and philosophy before the duke with members of his entourage and visiting intellectuals.

Fra Niccolò came upon Foscari sitting by the cloister fountain encased in thought. 'Well, my son, are you enjoying your stay in Ferrara?'

Startled, Pietro opened his eyes and jumped to his feet. 'I'm sorry, Father. I was . . .'

'Thinking deep and holy thoughts?' The old man smiled. 'That is as it should be.' He seated himself on the fountain's rim.

They spoke of many things. The prior spent several minutes praising Ercole d'Este – his piety, his concern for the people, his vision for the city, his love of scholarship, music, poetry and art.

'What is his attitude towards the holy father?' Pietro asked lightly.

'Obedience sustained with difficulty would, I suppose, be the most concise answer to that question. He reveres the office but has little reason to respect its current holder. A few years ago the pope formed an alliance with Venice to cheat him out of the Polesine, that vast tract of fertile land between here and the Po.'

'Has the duke joined with his holiness's enemies?'

'He tries to keep out of politics as far as possible but I think he would not be unhappy to see the Borgia unseated.'

'Did you know his eminence Cardinal Montadini well, Father?'

'I have heard of your interest in our late bishop, Brother Pietro. The cardinal's death was a great blow to us all here. He was a just and fearless pastor, dedicated to restoring the purity of the Church. But he was a man with few intimates. I suppose Father Leonello knew him better than most.'

'Father Leonello?'

'The duke's chaplain. Would you like to meet him?'

'Very much, Father.'

'I will invite him to supper this evening and allow you to spend some time with him afterwards.'

The man Foscari met a few hours later was a rotund priest with such a profound love of the ancient authors that he was forever quoting them.

> '"No threatening tyrant can command
> The man of just and iron will,
> And citizens in vain demand
> His base assent to deeds of ill"

Those lines of Horace often come to my mind when I remember dear Sebastiano. The man was a saint and the world has a short way with saints.'

They were perambulating the cloister in the cool of the evening and the chaplain, though unused to frugal Franciscan fare, had not been put in a bad humour by the maslin bread, bacon broth and salt herring set before him in the refectory.

'May I enquire why you are interested cardinal?' he asked.

Foscari, who had anticipated the question, rep reflect upon the suffering and death of holy m is a valuable spiritual exercise, is it not? I wonder who killed Sebastiano Montadini and why.'

Father Leonello paused and gazed quizzically at his companion. 'But everyone knows the answer to that: he was silenced by the pope who was tired of his persistent criticisms. It was a monstrous act yet one which defines the spirit of the age: *"crimine ab uno disce omnes"*; "from a single crime one can understand the nation", as Virgil says.'

Pietro stared across the atrium at the conventual buildings. Most of the russet brickwork was dulled by the encroaching dusk but a narrow band of the top storey glowed in the rays of the setting sun as though painted with red gold. 'I have heard the story, of course, and yet I wonder if that was the alpha and omega of the affair. Some say that the cardinal was not content with criticism; that he was in league with the holy father's enemies.'

As they resumed their slow walk Father Leonello was silent for several moments. When he spoke it was in a quiet, half-musing tone. 'I recall him once saying that no man could call himself a Christian who knew the truth and failed to act upon it. It was, I suppose, about eighteen months ago. There were six of us sitting in the duke's garden discussing the use and abuse of power. Sebastiano had brought along a friend from the Sforza court at Milan. This fellow, no mean scholar, was very indignant about Vatican corruption – as one might expect from that quarter. He reminded us that, in the early days of the Church, Basilides of Alexandria had been branded a heretic for teaching, "the perpetration of any

211

voluptuous act is a matter of indifference". Was there anything to choose, he asked, between such ancient Gnostics and the man who now occupied the chair of St Peter? We all agreed that Rome has become the moral latrine of Christendom. That was when Sebastiano quietly challenged us to match deeds to words. If the pope was a heretic – or worse – should he be suffered to remain in office? There was an unusual intenseness, an excitement about him as he spoke. Just for a moment I thought I saw a gleam in his eye such as I have seen only once before. But, perhaps . . .' Father Leonello faded back into silence.

After waiting several moments for the priest to amplify his comments, Brother Pietro prompted, 'Where did you see such an expression before?'

'On the face of a fanatic burning at the stake.' Another long silence followed before he added, 'Perhaps Plato was right: "Rather the madness of God than the sobriety of men."'

CHAPTER 11

Ginny walked down into the centre of Augsburg struggling to keep pace with the long strides of her companion. They fetched up at an outdoor café, protected by a canvas awning from the rain which threatened to return, in a small square close by the imposing town hall with its twin onion-shaped domes. When Hans had ordered beefburgers and beers Ginny asked, 'What did you mean about my not having heard everything I ought to hear?'

The student stared at a nearby fountain and avoided meeting her eye. 'That rather depends on what the information is worth.'

Ginny laughed. 'Hey, I work for an academic publisher, not a sensationalist newspaper.'

Hans shook his head. 'I don't think so.'

Ginny felt a spasm of anxiety in her stomach. 'Whatever do you mean?' she bluffed.

'An old schoolfriend of mine works for Schröder-Neumarkt Verlag. I phoned him. He hasn't heard of Giulia Amati.'

'That's not surprising. I'm a freelance. I don't go into the office very often.'

'No, you're not. He checked.'

Ginny thought hard. She decided it was best not to respond to the young man's allegation. 'If you were suspicious of me why didn't you tell the professor?'

'Preferred to cut myself in on the action. There are odd things going on – people getting bumped off, people lying, people hiding secrets, people being dead nervous about a publisher's editor turning up to ask questions – only you're not really a publisher's editor – people getting suddenly rich. With all that happening I reckon there must be some money in it somewhere for me. I mean, it must be worth something for me not to phone a certain publisher's office in Frankfurt.'

Ginny scowled at him. 'Do you make a serious hobby of blackmail?'

Their food arrived at this point and it was some moments before Hans replied. 'I'm just a poor art student struggling to get myself through college. Who you are I don't know and I don't really care. If you're investigating Segar and the others I'm sure you've got your reasons. I'm prepared to help you – tell you things nobody else will tell you. But you've got to help me, too. That's not blackmail; it's just good business.' He bit into his beefburger. 'These are good.'

Ginny was at a loss. 'What am I supposed to do now? Write you a cheque? Ask you what your terms are?'

The young man smiled. 'Well, this is the city of the famous Fuggers. You mustn't be surprised if we're all on the make.' He was suddenly serious. 'Maria and the beautiful Frau Segar are certainly doing very well out of old Heinrich's death. Something very odd is going on. When the prof told us you were coming he got all Segar's students together and told us that you were only interested in the doctor's work and that on no account were we to repeat common-room gossip. Now that makes me very curious. So if you're here to prise up a few stones I'd like to help – as well as taking a good look at what's crawling around underneath.'

214

'Well, Hans, at least you're honest. I'll be equally straight with you. I'm trying to find out all I can about Heinrich Segar's death. If there's anything you can tell me which might throw light on it, I'll make sure you are adequately rewarded. At this stage I can't promise anything more specific.'

The student thought while he took a long pull at his Pils. 'OK, I suppose someone has to trust someone. Well, the first thing you ought to know is that Maria Heuss was more than Heinrich's assistant.'

'They were lovers?'

Hans sneered. 'I doubt little Maria knows the meaning of the word "love" and probably Heinrich didn't either.'

'So?' Ginny spoke through a mouthful of beefburger.

'Well, we'd best go back a few years. Maria was a bright student – very bright. Heinrich admired her mind – as well as the body it came wrapped in. He offered her a deal: she could become his assistant and he'd supervise her doctorate work free of charge.'

'Sounds like a good career move for Maria.'

'Yes and no. She got the prestige of being Heinrich's assistant. Going everywhere with him. Meeting all the right people.'

'But?'

'But she was cheated out of a major scholarly coup. She came across and correctly identified a group of drawings by Agostino Carracci which linked him with some frescoes in Rome that had been unattributed before. It was one of those discoveries that crops up once in a scholar's lifetime – if then. It would have been a brilliant thesis and would have made her name. The trouble was, Maria threatened to outshine her teacher and Heinrich couldn't allow that.'

215

'What did he do; tell her that her attribution was wrong?'

'No, something much simpler. He plagiarized her work. Took all her research and published it in his own book on the Carraccis, which is now a standard text.'

'God! I'd be furious if that happened to me.'

'Yes, I'm sure Maria was.'

'Why didn't she expose Segar?'

'Two reasons: it would be her word against his and Heinrich persuaded her that if she stuck with him he would make her career.'

'And she believed him?'

'Ah, I wonder. Was she lured to the master's desk and bed by the prospect of advancement or was she just biding her time? Heinrich had conned her into trusting him. Perhaps she decided that two can play at that game. The more he relied on her, the more power she had.'

'Was she that devious?'

Hans shrugged. 'You can never tell what Maria is thinking. I believe she has a split personality. One day the dowdy research assistant, keeping meekly in the background. The next wearing designer clothes as though she's been doing it all her life and flashing around in sports cars.'

'Yes, I wondered about the Porsche.'

'It appeared about a week ago and Maria made sure everyone saw it.'

'How could she afford it?'

'She said a distant relative had died and left her a big legacy.' Hans' tone intimated the amount of salt that should be taken with that claim.

'Talking about money, the Segars were obviously well-heeled. You've seen Elberhof?'

216

'Only from the outside. People say it's packed with good things.'

'It is, believe me. Where did all the funds come from? Obviously not from his job at the college and lecture tours and articles in obscure magazines.'

'I assume he married money.' Hans pushed his empty glass away. He sat back staring up at the canvas awning on which rain had once more begun to rattle. 'Herr Doktor Heinrich Segar certainly had it all – a brilliant mind, a good-looking wife and a mistress, a *schloss* stuffed with beautiful things, international acclaim. Yes, he had it all.'

'I take it you didn't care for him very much.'

The young man looked shocked. 'You couldn't be more wrong. I admired him enormously. He had a real insight, a real understanding of art and artists. He could spot promising students and he was always ready with help and encouragement. I owed him a lot. And I hope the British police get the bastard who killed him.'

'So do I,' Ginny agreed. 'So do I.'

'Catherine, have you come to see me? I shall be devastated if you say no.'

Adrian Deventer had emerged from a taxi outside Grinling's just as Catherine arrived. She stopped to gaze into a Bond Street shop window, waited a couple of minutes to give him plenty of time to get to his office and then entered the auction house. She spotted the managing director immediately, standing at the foot of the staircase in conversation with two staff members and turned abruptly to examine the display of catalogues. She was not quick enough. The effusive Deventer advanced upon her, hand outstretched. He was dressed in what

Catherine thought of as 'Seventies Art Establishment' style – well-cut suit over a lavender shirt and a floral bow-tie, his velvet-collared topcoat draped round his shoulders.

'Hello Adrian, just back from one of your client lunches?' Catherine glanced up at the Blitz Clock which announced the time as six minutes to four.

'Now, you mustn't make fun of me. In these times we have to drum up business wherever we can at whatever sacrifice – these middle-of-the-day meals play havoc with the digestion.' He grasped Catherine's arm and steered her towards the stairs. 'You really couldn't have appeared at a better moment. We've just hung our contemporary art sale. Do come and look. I particularly want to pick your brains.'

Seeing no obvious escape, Catherine allowed herself to be escorted to the Long Room, where her guide pointed out various of the canvases lining the walls.

'As you can see, we're selling three Maitlands. Now, my spies tell me he's doing rather well in America at the moment.'

'Yes, he's enjoying a resurgence of interest, especially on the west coast.'

Deventer beamed. 'That's exactly what I wanted to hear; what I knew you could tell me. We've contacted all the collectors and institutions we can think of but you're much closer to the market. You know who's starting to buy, who's enlarging a collection, who's diversifying investment. I'm sure you can give us some names we might have missed. And over here,' he continued before Catherine had time to respond, 'is a positively splendid Sarah Giles. Now, wouldn't you say that's absolutely one of her finest pieces? We really ought to be able to attract some of the top dealers and collectors with that.'

The tour continued for half an hour. Catherine enjoyed the pictures and endured the commentary. When a gap opened in the one-way conversational traffic she entered it quickly. 'I believe we have to thank you for the invitation to tender for the new warehouse.'

Deventer held a hand to his heart and looked doleful. 'My dear girl, I was mortified when I heard about that stupid oversight. You can be sure that as soon as I did hear I kicked a couple of backsides very smartly.'

'Well thank you, Adrian. It's good to know that Lacy Security still enjoys your confidence.'

'Never doubt it for a moment. Now, tell me, how is Tim? Recuperating in Italy, I believe.'

'You're well informed.'

'Well, naturally I'm concerned. Especially since you were both involved in that tiresome business of the chalice. We still can't get it back from the police, by the way. My secretary has a standing instruction to pester them every day. But they insist that it's material evidence. Heaven knows why. It should be obvious to an idiot that Santori's wretched goblet has nothing to do with the deaths.'

'Yet, it seems the poison must have been administered here somehow.'

'I refuse to believe it. All four unfortunate victims arrived separately. And after the sale I had to send out to round up them and their wives and appendages for the lunch. They simply were never all together except for the few minutes of Santori's ridiculous and tasteless little piece of theatre.'

'I guess that's why the police are sticking to their theory that the poison must have been administered in the chalice.'

Deventer clapped a hand to his head histrionically. 'My

219

God, I wish I'd never agreed to that demonstration.' He lowered his voice and bent his head close to Catherine's. 'Between you and me – and there aren't many I'd admit this to – that appalling business has cost Grinling's millions. We'll ride it out, of course, but it'll take a year or more to recover our market share.'

It was some minutes more before Catherine was able to detach herself from her garrulous host. Promising faithfully to provide him with a list of current enthusiastic buyers of contemporary art, she eventually slipped away and went in search of Corinne Noble.

The head of Grinling's Medieval and Renaissance European Paintings department was absorbed in a discussion in her outer office with two junior colleagues. They were looking at a large painting of the Nativity in glowing, yet smoky, colours. Corinne beckoned her friend over, 'Catherine, come and give us your opinion. We need a fresh eye.'

'Early Renaissance is hardly my period.' Catherine crossed the room and surveyed the picture with its warm browns, reds and ochres emerging from mysterious shadows. 'A little bit two-dimensional?' she ventured.

'By the same hand as these, do you think?' Corinne handed her a couple of large colour reproductions of similar religious scenes.

Catherine looked at them carefully. 'It's terribly difficult comparing originals and prints but I reckon the figure work is more self-assured in these.'

'But our painting could be an early work by the same hand?'

'Yeah, I guess . . . but, as I say, this sort of stuff is out of my league.'

'My gut feeling is that this is a Garofalo – *circa* 1500, before he came in contact with Raphael and Michelangelo.

I've seen his work in Ferrara and Bologna. I'd love to be able to attribute it instead of putting it in the catalogue as "Ferrarese School". Anyway, enough of my problems. What can I do for you?' She waved Catherine towards her office and called over her shoulder. 'Be an angel, Imogen, and fetch us some tea.'

Catherine took a seat by the window with its view over West London roofs. 'I don't want to take up your time, Corinne. Just a simple question really. Can you tell who the younger person in this picture is?' She took Maud Benedict's photo from her handbag and handed it over.

Corinne studied it under her desk light. She looked puzzled. 'Isn't that Julia Devaraux?'

'Yes, but it's the other woman I'm interested in. Do you know her?'

'No, I don't think so.' She frowned. 'Should I?'

'She reminds me strongly of someone who works here. I must be mistaken.'

'Here?' Corinne scanned the photograph again, head on one side. 'Yes, I suppose there is some resemblance . . . But I'm not sure. May I ask what this is about?'

Catherine remembered Tim's warning to say nothing about the Devaraux-Benedict-Santori connection. 'Oh, it's just a long shot. *H.S.* magazine have asked me to do a piece on the late, not-very-lamented, Julia. In my researches I came across this picture and it reminded me of someone here and as whoever this is was obviously a friend of Julia's I thought . . . Ah, well, another dead end.' She held out her hand for the picture.

Corinne's face lit up suddenly. 'Georgina! I'll bet that's who you're thinking of. Georgina . . . What *is* her other name? Something double-barrelled . . .' She closed her eyes. 'Georgina . . . Georgina Harding-Beck. Got it! She works in Client Accounts. Would you like me to see if I can raise her for you?'

'Would you mind? I shan't take up much of her time. The chances are I've got it wrong anyway.'

'No problem.' Corinne put through an internal call and had a brief conversation. 'There, that's fixed. She'll be waiting for you. Her office is on the ground floor. Turn right out of the lift and go to the end of the corridor.'

Imogen came in with tea and Catherine stayed to make small talk while she drank it. She mentioned her conversation with Deventer. 'He seems pretty highly strung, right now.'

Corinne raised her eyes heavenward. 'He's like a badly packed box of dynamite. This chalice business has really got to him. No one goes anywhere near him if they can help it. We're all walking round on tip-toe for fear of causing explosions. To be honest, Catherine, I think he's heading for a breakdown.'

Catherine remembered the comments she had heard Druckmann make on George's tape: 'Adrian panics unnecessarily'. Small wonder, she thought. Who would not be nervous with business associates like Druckmann and Jimmy the Fist? She wondered, not for the first time, whether the boss of Grinling's realized he had links with the Shand brothers. She said, 'This is obviously a very worrying time for him.'

Minutes later she set down her empty mug, said good-bye to Corinne and went in search of Georgina Harding-Beck. She found her in an open-plan office where five people were working at computer terminals. The young woman who stood up to shake hands wore spectacles and had her fair hair drawn back and tied behind. She looked very different from when Catherine had seen her last, without glasses and with loose hair. However, the resemblance was still there.

'Mrs Lacy.' Georgina smiled pleasantly. 'It was you who bought the Borgia Chalice wasn't it? If you're worried about the sale you don't need to be. The transaction still stands, though of course we won't be able to finalize it until . . .'

'No, that wasn't why I wanted to have a brief word. It's just that I wondered whether you could help me solve a little mystery.' Catherine produced the photograph. 'Can you, by any chance, tell me anything about this?'

She was totally unprepared for what happened next.

Georgina's eyes opened wide in horror. She uttered something between a yelp and a screech. She stepped backwards, fell over her chair and lay prone on the office floor.

The internal decor of Whorton Grange was something that the woolmaster who built it in the 1720s would have been unable to imagine in his most garish nightmares. He would, however, have been at one with the entrepreneurial spirit of the twentieth-century owner. Wes and the three instrumentalists who made up Cool Jungle had turned most of the domestic offices into a fully equipped sound studio. The well-proportioned reception rooms which had once quietly asserted the power of new money now did the same thing more demonstratively. Wes Cherry had given the designer he had brought from New York two specifications: he wanted plenty of colour and he wanted to project the band's image. The result was an outrageous combination of lurid drapes, sumptuous *nouveau decadence* upholstery, bizarre frescoes, laser-show effects and framed stills from Cool Jungle videos. As well as the obligatory indoor pool and gym, Whorton Grange boasted a private cinema, a ballroom equipped with state-of-the-art disco quadraphonic sound and a TV wall, and a bowling alley in the old stable block. It was one of the most photographed homes in Europe. Scarcely a month passed without a fashion periodical, pop magazine, colour supplement or 'modern living' glossy somewhere in the world running a feature on it and its celebrated proprietor. That, of course, was the purpose for which it existed. As Emma was shown round by her enthusiastic host she wondered what it was like living in an advertising hoarding.

After the tour they settled in a sitting room whose walls offered *trompe l'œil* vistas of a strange world inhabited by a menagerie of monsters and mythical beasts. Then two people arrived from the band's P.R. company – a man called Mike who introduced himself as 'concept engineer' and Penny who gloried in the title 'audio-visual coordinator'. For two hours they engineered and coordinated. Emma produced photographs and other details of the locations Lacy Security wanted to use. Wes played the backing track Cool Jungle had decided to donate. The meeting went well and, around midday, Mike and Penny left, promising to fax their 'project costings' to Farrans in a day or two.

Emma also made to leave but Wes protested. 'Hell no, you can't rush off just when I've got you here.'

'Is this "come into my parlour" time?' Emma gave him a quizzical look.

He laughed a deep-bellied laugh. 'No, just an invitation to lunch. Come on, I've got a surprise for you.'

He took her by the hand and led her through French windows, across a terrace and over a long lawn that sloped to a lake. At one end of the watercourse stood a small folly in the form of a circular Greek temple. Wes went up the steps, opened wide glass doors and ushered Emma inside. The room in which she found herself was quite unlike all the others at Whorton Grange. Light entered through a glass dome into a chamber panelled in limed oak. Four framed old drawings maintained the mood of restrained decorum. A circular dining table covered with a crisp lilac cloth was laid for two with elegant china and silver.

Wes whisked out a chair and made an elaborate bow. 'Would madam care to be seated?'

Emma laughed as she took her place at the table. 'You're full of surprises, Wes.'

The black man beamed. 'You like? I knew you would. I knew this was more your style. You've got class.'

'What's that supposed to mean?'

He looked down at her, for once awkward and searching for words. 'When I saw you at Farrans Court . . .' he began, then broke off. 'Oh shit! Let's eat.'

From a fridge he produced plates of garnished smoked salmon, and a bottle of Bâtard-Montrachet.

For some while they ate and drank in silence. Wes made no attempt to explain his thoughts and Emma was disinclined to spoil the moment. She was grappling with various emotions. The experience was idyllic. Part of her wanted to relax and enjoy the secrecy and romance of it all. Yet relax was the one thing she could not do. She looked across the table with its central spray of roses, through the glass doors to sunlit autumn woods reflected in the lake. There could hardly be a more perfect setting for a tryst – if that was what it was. She glanced at the man who had touchingly taken such trouble to make this a special occasion and who was nervous about its success. She hoped her reaction would not disappoint him but she did not know what he wanted. Nor did she know what she wanted him to want. Worst of all, try as she might she was unable to give Wes all her attention. The morning had produced so many disturbing revelations which she could not understand or interrelate that her mind was whirring like a baffled computer.

Eventually, Wes asked anxiously, 'Food OK?'

She gave him her warmest smile. 'Absolutely marvellous. Do you do this sort of thing often?'

'What, with a woman?' He seemed shocked at the suggestion. 'Hell no. This is where I come to be alone. I . . .' He seemed on the point of sharing a confidence, but stopped. 'Some of my best lyrics have come to me here. Now,' he jumped up. 'I hope you're still hungry.' He cleared the plates and from a heated hostess trolley produced beef Wellington, mixed vegetables and Cumberland sauce.

Emma laughed. 'I'll bet your millions of fans would be surprised if they could see you now – Wildman Wes, playing the quiet, attentive, philosophical host.'

'Yeah, well, what the public sees is an act, isn't it? There aren't many people who know the real Wes Cherry. Come to that, I don't know the real Emma Kerr. What I can see is a self-assured, Oxbridge-educated woman but what's behind the front? Most of the time we play-act, don't we – put on masks so that people will see what we want them to see?'

Masks, masks hiding the truth . . . Emma's imagination drifted. Into her mind came the face of Adrian Deventer. She had only seen him a couple of times at close quarters and had found him, then, knowledgeable, witty and brimming over with old-world charm. In other words, he had completely matched the public image of one of the most liked and respected figures in the international art world. Yet was the reality a man who was in the pockets of organized crime? He was associated in some way with people who thought nothing of killing. There could be no doubt that the Hartnell whose name had cropped up in Druckmann's conversation with Trevor Shand was the scientist who had died in a suspicious fire last night. He had been an expert in food poisoning. And the Grinling's four had died of botulism. Did that mean that the refined and slightly precious Adrian Deventer . . . The thought seemed too bizarre to entertain . . . Yet if anyone had the opportunity . . . 'Sorry, Wes, what was that. I was miles away.' She was suddenly aware that her host was both talking and looking at her very intently.

He sat back hurt, embarrassed. 'You didn't hear what I was saying?'

Damn! Emma pinched her leg beneath the table. She had spoiled things. Could she repair the damage? 'Wes, I *am* sorry. I was just enjoying the view; it's so beautiful. What were you saying?'

'Hey man, forget it. No sweat. Eat up. It'll get cold.'

They completed the meal talking inconsequentialities, drifting like sailing ships in a flat calm unable to make closer contact. Afterwards, they walked back across the lawn. Emma collected her papers and Wes accompanied her to her car. The awkward goodbye moment arrived.

Emma said, 'Thank you for a lovely lunch – and for all you're doing for us.' She held out her hand.

Wes grasped it. He pulled her into his arms. Lifted her off the ground. Kissed her with a sudden, rough tenderness. Released her. Turned and strode into the house.

Most of the return journey Emma drove automatically, body and mind fizzing. Somehow the car found its way through Burford and Lechlade without the driver being conscious of directing its route. But as she neared the

Swindon bypass she took herself in hand. 'Emma Kerr, you are not a lovesick, seventeen-year-old schoolgirl. You have other things to think about than Mr Wesley Cherry.'

She drove into the centre of town, made for the mainline station, parked and walked into the foyer. On the newstand she found, as she had hoped, that the evening papers were already in. She bought one, took it back to the car and searched it eagerly. Nothing on the front page. It was on page two that Hartnell's death merited a couple of column inches. At last she was able to fill in the vital details.

The fire brigade and police had been called on Sunday night to a blaze at the Leonard Everett Institute, Grantchester, a commercially funded laboratory affiliated to the University of Cambridge. The fire had been brought under control quite quickly but, inside, the body of a young man, later identified as Dr Graham Hartnell, had been discovered. Colleagues could not explain why the scientist had been in his office on a Sunday evening. The police were interested in tracing two men seen earlier in the laboratory grounds. The possibility that animal-rights activists might be responsible had not been ruled out although the institute carried out few experiments involving live animals. The Leonard Everett Institute undertook chemical and biological research for major pharmaceutical companies and food manufacturers. It was believed that Dr Hartnell had been working on methods of treating botulism, the most virulent form of food poisoning.

Emma dropped the paper on the passenger seat. It simply could not be a coincidence. So Trevor Shand's hirelings had killed Hartnell and Hartnell was an expert on the virus that had killed four people at Grinling's and

Adrian Deventer was involved with Shand – or, at least with Lochinver, who was certainly involved with Shand. But why on earth would a London crime boss want to dispose of four art experts, and in such a spectacular way? Emma sat pushing the pieces of the puzzle around for several minutes. None of them seemed to fit. She decided to do two things: get this latest information to Tim and contact Geoffrey – a Cambridge friend who just happened to be a research chemist.

She saw a traffic warden approaching and remembered in the nick of time that she was on a yellow line. As she slipped the engine into gear her eyes fell on the newspaper's back page, stop-press column. She just had time to register the headline. 'Police foil West End gallery raid.'

The cart trundled and bounced its way along narrow Apennine tracks on its way to the goldsmiths' city of Arezzo. The driver on his box swayed easily with the rhythm. Beside him, Brother Pietro felt the jolt and jarr of every rut and pothole. The imprint of the rough wooden seat grooved his buttocks and he grasped tightly the rope securing the wine casks stacked behind him. The friar had made most of the long journey south from Ferrara on foot but had been glad to beg occasional lifts even on transport as precarious as this haulier's waggon. He was relieved to be embarking on the last stage of his investigation of the Michelmas Massacre. In the della Chiesa estates sprawled over the southern slope of the hills between Bibbiena and Gubbiano he hoped to learn about the third victim of that atrocity, even though, as casual informants told him, he would discover little from the late cardinal's kinsmen and tenants.

The trouble, they said, was war. A territorial feud lasting as far back as anyone could remember had flared up with unprecedented violence in the last two years and the country for several kilometres around Arezzo was in a parlous state. Businessmen like this haulier chose the less frequented routes in order to avoid encountering troops of foraging and marauding soldiers. Yet Pietro travelled hopefully. If God favoured his quest he would be able to pick up those scraps of information he needed to complete the story of violence, deception and ruthlessness forming in his mind. He would certainly pray for that at La Verna. Good Franciscan that he was, Brother Pietro could not pass this way without stopping at the monastery established by the founder of the order; the hallowed place where St Francis had received the holy stigmata. Pietro had been once before to the little convent built on an outcrop shaped, legend insisted, by an earthquake at the very moment that Christ died upon the cross. The friar was looking forward to a few days' peaceful prayer and meditation. He yearned to resolve his papal mission in such a way that Alexander would completely relieve him of any further obligation and allow him to pursue his own spiritual journey unhampered by worldly concerns.

But Fra Pietro did not get to La Verna.

The cart was lumbering its way through a thickly forested region when a group of horsemen appeared on the track ahead. Two facts were immediately apparent: they were soldiers and they were in a hurry. They galloped onwards, helmets and part-armour glinting in the sunlight that slanted through the trees. The waggoner urgently tugged at the reins trying to make room. But there was no room. Tree stems and boulders lined a path that was little wider than the ruts into which the cartwheels were clamped.

The advancing horsemen skittered to a halt.

'Get that contraption out of the way!' The captain who roared the order was a large man with a red matted beard. Over his breastplate he wore a surcoat in the della Chiesa colours of purple and white.

'Signore, there is nowhere,' the carter whined. 'I cannot pull off the track and there is no space to turn.'

'That's your problem,' the soldier shouted. 'If you don't move, my men will move you.'

The carter jumped down. He grabbed his horse's noseband and pushed him closer to the wall of timber and rock. The beast threw his head up, protesting loudly as his shoulders met rough, unyielding tree bark.

Foscari stood up. 'Captain, what you demand is impossible. If you and your men could just retreat until we all come to a passing place . . .'

'Hold your tongue, friar. I've no time for insolence and obstruction. There's a garrison of sick and wounded men in the valley waiting for reinforcements.'

'Then surely . . .'

Pietro's attempts at reason were brushed aside. The captain turned to face his troop of thirty or forty mounted men. 'Right, six of you, get this buffoon out of the way.'

Some of the soldiers dismounted. While the haulier gibbered ineffective protest, one of them slashed the horse's traces with his sword, then gave the animal a smart slap across the rump. Freed from its burden the creature leaped forward and the mounted soldiers made way for it to canter down the track. The six men now transferred their attention to the cart. Lining up along one side they set their shoulders to the wheels. Foscari jumped down as the vehicle started to sway. He watched helpless as the soldiers heaved rhythmically and finally toppled the waggon over low boulders. Woodwork splintered. Casks broke free from their fastenings. Wine splashed everywhere and ran in purple rivulets along the ruts.

The captain gave the order to remount and spurred his horse forward. After a few paces he stopped. He turned in the saddle. 'You, friar, have you any skills as a physician?'

'I have no special training but I often tend the sick. However . . .'

The leader was not listening. 'You might be useful. Agnani, bring him.'

Before Pietro could make even a token protest, one of the soldiers came alongside, reached down, grabbed the rough habit and pulled. Pietro gripped the saddle with one hand and lifted his skirts with the other as he was hoisted astride the horse's crupper.

The troop rode for half an hour, mostly along downhill forest tracks and emerged, at last, on to level fields bordering the main road to Arezzo. Foscari found himself looking on a desolate landscape of flattened crops, uprooted vines and gutted farm buildings. A couple of kilometres along the road the party came to a walled village. Gaps in the defensive ring had been filled roughly with layers of new stone and brick. When they passed through the gateway Pietro noted first that the houses and cottages seemed to have escaped the ravages of the outlying areas and secondly that the place was inhabited almost entirely by soldiery. The village had obviously been commandeered by a section of the della Chiesa private army. The captain ordered his men to dismount and quarter their horses. Foscari edged his way to the back of the group, hoping that he might have been forgotten. Then he heard the bushy-bearded man bellow, 'Where's that confounded little friar?' Hands pushed him into the captain's presence. 'Oh, there you are. Agnani, Scoppio will look after your horse. Find out where they've put the wounded and take the holy man there.' He turned away, no longer interested in the abducted friar.

Pietro was conducted to a long barn on the village's perimeter. Half of it was still stacked with grain which Pietro assumed must have been commandeered by the garrison from farther afield since this year's crop had not been garnered locally. The remaining space had been spread with straw and sacks on which lay about thirty sick and injured soldiers. Moving among them were a priest and two female camp followers. Pietro introduced himself to the priest and was warmly welcomed.

Father Jacopo, the gaunt, black-haired cleric, was weary and despondent. 'There's little we can do for most of them because we have no simples, no leeches, no balms. I even have to beg cloth for binding up open sores. You'll find oil and wine in those jars over there, and there are a handful of sharp knives for removing fragments from wounds.'

'Have we anything to cauterize the wounds?' Pietro asked.

'We boil some of the oil and I add a little treacle to help it adhere but we're running out of that.'

'Any egg yolk for salves?'

'Out of the question, I'm afraid. All food items are commandeered for the fit troops. What our physicking comes down to is preparing men for the next world while the women try to maintain their interest in this one.'

Foscari laboured all day and well into the night doing what he could for a succession of groaning, frightened men, many of them little more than boys. As fast as patients left to resume duties or, more usually, were carried out for burial, others came in to take their places.

As he talked with them about their experiences, Brother Pietro pieced together what was happening on the battle front. In 1496 the della Chiesas had made important gains and consolidated what they considered to be their hereditary lands. But, in the 1497 campaign season, their enemies, the Montefalcos, had hired a condottiere who brought troops from papal territory. For months the della Chiesas had been fighting desperately, not only to cling on to their recent gains, but also to defend their principal strongholds. Three fortified villages and small towns were currently under siege and the clan chiefs were desperately pressing all their tenantry into armed service. Foscari held the hands of trembling child soldiers who wept and cried out at the memory of horrors they had witnessed; truculent young men who died breathing revenge against those who had burned their homes and violated their sisters; weary old men who had buried their sons and, in any case, no longer had farms or vineyards to leave them.

By the moonless hours the rush in the makeshift hospital had subsided. One of the women brought bread and cheese from the soldiers' kitchen. When they had fed those of the sick capable of eating, the medical team sat on sacks of grain to take their own frugal meal together. Shared experience and tiredness broke down the usual barriers separating men and women, religious and lay. Everyone talked freely. Maria, the older of the women, was large and in her forties. She was here, she said, to help her kinsmen and neighbours to kill as many Montefalcos as possible. She had lost three sons in the fighting and revenge was the only passion which now gave her life meaning. Since she could not bear arms, she devoted herself to patching up the menfolk who could continue the struggle. Anna was a slender, doleful-eyed seventeen-year-old whose face was already lined with grief. She had last seen her husband when he was snatched from the bridal bed and a sword thrust into his hand. She knew not whether he was alive or dead and anxiously scanned the face of every moaning combatant carried into the barn.

Father Jacopo leaned against a broad oak post and closed his eyes. 'We must pray God to send the winter rains soon this year. That is all that will put a temporary halt to this madness.'

Maria would have none of such defeatist talk. 'I pray him to send us Duke Sforza's mercenaries from Milan.'

'What do you know of such things, my child?' the priest asked.

'I know what I hear the officers talking about. Duke Sforza promised aid months ago and still has not backed his word. Would that the cardinal were alive. No one dared trick him or play him false.'

Foscari pricked up his ears. 'Cardinal della Chiesa was a man of moral and spiritual stature who commanded respect?'

Maria laughed, a coarse, rasping laugh. 'His eminence was a soldier. Any respect he had lay in his sword. He got his red hat for providing soldiers for the last pope.'

'To the common people these matters seem very simple,' Father Jacopo explained to Pietro.

Maria was not to be so lightly dismissed. 'Do you deny our cardinal spent more time on his horse than on his knees – and God bless him for it, I say. Prayers don't stop your crops being burned or your sons killed.'

Anna intervened quietly. 'I don't think we should talk like that. I'm sure his eminence was a holy man.'

'Quite right, my child.' The priest was relieved to

find one member of his flock whose faith had not been undermined by cynicism. 'We must pray all the more earnestly, and seek the aid of the Blessed Virgin in times of hardship.'

Pietro, who did not want the conversation to end in vague homily, interrupted. 'It is true, though, is it, that the cardinal was his holiness's ally?'

The priest nodded. 'Certainly, he *was*.'

'What happened to change things?'

'I'll tell you what happened . . .' Maria's tirade was cut off at source by an impatient gesture from Father Jacopo.

He took up the explanation, choosing his words carefully. 'His eminence felt disappointed at the degree of support he obtained from his holiness.'

'Della Chiesa helped the pope with troops when he wanted them but the pope didn't hurry to the cardinal's aid when he needed military support to defend his own lands?'

'That is substantially correct, Brother, as I understand the situation.'

'And that obliged his eminence to seek aid from the Duke of Milan and others of the pope's enemies?'

The priest shrugged. 'I know nothing of politics, Brother, and I don't approve of gossip . . . However,' he hurried on as Maria tried to leap back into the conversation, 'I understand that Duke Ludovico Sforza and Cardinal della Rovere made certain overtures to his eminence.'

'Were these things not kept secret?'

'Not by his eminence. He hoped to use the interest of the Sforza party to press the pope into providing support. His holiness sent the Duke of Gandia to Arezzo for preliminary talks with the cardinal. Then his eminence was summoned to the Vatican to conclude an agreement with the pope.'

'Yes,' Maria crowed, refusing to be silenced any longer. 'And we all know what happened then, don't we?'

CHAPTER 12

Tuesday evening at the villa was hectic.

Tristram and Ginny both arrived for dinner but were more interested in reporting excitedly on their various discoveries than in the food O.K. had laboured long to prepare. As he tried to set dishes, plates and glasses down on the kitchen table he found himself competing for space with files, notebooks and sheets of paper the others insisted on scattering over its surface.

Both Santoris eagerly started describing the results of their researches until Tim stopped them. 'Hang on, let's take one at a time. Tris, what's the latest on the Foscari saga?'

Tristram passed round two photocopied sheets of typing. 'Well, as I was saying, I've now got up to the point where he's gone to Ferrara to check on Montadini. It seems the chap was a religious nutter.' He talked them through Foscari's account of his movements in Ferrara. 'You'll notice there are infuriating gaps in his report. He simply refuses to name names. Like here, where he says "I met a group of people who were intimates of his eminence". Who were they? How reliable?'

Tim smiled. 'It's not really very surprising, is it? Modern journalists call it "protecting their sources". What these people revealed was dynamite. If Alexander had discovered their identity they'd all have ended up in the torture chambers of the Inquisition.'

'So, how was the minestrone?' O.K. looked round at the others who were distractedly finishing their soup.

They all muttered their appreciation.

O.K. stood up. 'Give us your bowls then. God, I don't know why I bother. I could've got it out of a packet for all you lot care.' He shuffled across to the sink and dropped the crockery into it with a pointedly loud clatter.

'So, it looks as though Montadini was in league with della Rovere and Co. and that he was all psyched up to assassinate the pope.'

'Which gave Alexander a pretty convincing reason to move in first,' Ginny commented. 'It doesn't get us any further, does it? If Montadini was the intended victim the only person with a motive was the pope. So, perhaps everyone was right all along: the Borgias *were* responsible for the Michaelmas Massacre.'

'Only if they knew about Montadini's plans.'

'The pope must have had his spies.'

'Possibly, Ginny, but we don't know that. As far as we can tell the only people who realized that Montadini saw himself as the angel of death were these mysterious "intimates" in Ferrara and his contacts at the Sforza court.'

'Agreed,' Ginny persisted. 'But they wouldn't want to stop him.'

Tim nodded. 'Perhaps not. All I'm saying is that we shouldn't cloud our minds by assuming things for which we have no evidence.'

'Well, anyway, all this is irrelevant.' Ginny rested her elbows on the table and looked triumphantly around at her companions. 'I've solved the crime. I know who our murderers were.'

With the aid of shorthand notes, she described her

meetings at Elberhof and in Augsburg. When she came to the end of her account she dropped her notepad. 'And that all left me with three questions. One: where did Segar get all his money from? It sure as hell didn't come from lecturing, writing academic books and authenticating works of art. Two: why did Segar's widow and his assistant both insist they had little contact with each other when in fact Maria had spent Sunday night at Elberhof? Three: how come Maria is suddenly in the money and can splash out on expensive cars and designer luggage?'

Tristram looked up. 'And your answers, sister dear?'

Ginny ignored the sarcasm. 'It's obvious when you think about it: the two women got together to plan Segar's murder. They had motive in plenty. First of all there's the money. The stuff in that house is fabulous. I only went into a couple of rooms but the paintings and sculptures I saw were worth tens of thousands . . . no, hundreds of thousands. Assuming Segar had treasures like that all over Elberhof, you're looking at millions. Quite enough to kill for, even when the proceeds are split two ways. Pretty obviously, Maria has already laid her hands on some of the Segar money. But I don't think that was the main motive. What Maria and Mrs Segar were really out for was revenge. Heinrich had treated them both atrociously for years. He was blatantly unfaithful to his wife and showed her no affection at all. He stole his assistant's work and then bribed her with the prospect of professional advancement into saying nothing about it *and* into becoming his mistress. The man was a monster. I'd cheerfully have murdered him.'

Tim smiled encouragingly. 'That's all very interesting but we need more than motive to prove homicide.'

Ginny was quite undaunted. 'They also had opportunity. Both the women were in London on the day of the murder. Maria accompanied Heinrich on virtually all his travels. Mrs Segar almost never. But on this occasion she did. That has to be significant. It was a heaven-sent opportunity. You see, they couldn't bump the insufferable doctor off in Augsburg without becoming the prime suspects. The police would immediately ask who stood to benefit from the crime and the answer would be staring them in the face.'

'So they did the deed in London and killed the other three victims to throw the detectives off the scent.' Tristram completed Ginny's scenario.

'How?'

Brother and sister looked at Tim as he uttered the monosyllable.

'It's a great theory and I don't want to pour cold water on it. What I have difficulty with is seeing how it was done. Poison was somehow administered to four different people and we're all agreed it wasn't put into the chalice.'

Ginny frowned. 'The same objection applies whoever did it.'

'Agreed, but it's even more of a problem with your suspects. They didn't know the layout of Grinling's. As far as we can tell they didn't know any of the other victims.'

'When we were talking about Segar's bizarre death, Maria did mention that she had met the American. She said her boss had warned her to have nothing to do with Bronsky because the man was a charlatan.'

'Even if Maria knew the others by sight, it still doesn't get round the central problem that she wasn't familiar enough with them to go up to them and offer them something to eat or drink. Then there's the other difficulty about how she or her accomplice could have got hold of the poison. *Clostridium botulinum* is a bacterium. It has to be grown. You can't buy it in garden shops like weedkiller or steal it out of a chemist's poison cupboard. So where did Fraulein Heuss or Frau Segar obtain it?'

'Hey, I didn't say my theory was all neatly buttoned up. But, anyway, that's not a real problem. Surely the beauty of this kind of poison is that anyone can produce it. It grows in rotten meat, doesn't it? So either of them could have cultivated it without anyone knowing.'

Tim shook his head dubiously. 'I'm not sure about that. My guess is that you'd need some sort of training. But let that pass. Have you thought how the poison could have been administered? Or when?'

Ginny shook her head.

'Timings are vital. The murderer had to know how long the toxin would take to work,' Tim mused.

O.K. stood at the head of the table, crouched over a dish of osso bucco. 'More anyone? White arsenic.'

Three pairs of eyes gazed up at him in bewilderment.

'White arsenic. Cantarella – a compound of arsenic oxide.'

Tristram said what they were all thinking. 'O.K., what are you talking about?'

'Obvious, isn't it? Cantarella is the poison the Borgias are supposed to have used. The main ingredient was white arsenic and it was mixed with other substances to make it soluble in wine. By varying the strength they could control the time it took to take effect. Everyone knows that. Now, do you want any more veal or do I chuck it in the bin?'

Intimidated, the other three asked for seconds.

'Would it work the same way with botulism?' Ginny asked.

At that moment the telephone rang. O.K. answered, then held out the receiver to Tim. 'Catherine.'

'Hello, darling, how are things at Farrans?'

'Great, just great. Now, listen. Emma's on the extension and we've got a lot to tell you. Is this a good time?'

'Yes, no problem. Fire away.'

'Right. Well, first I must tell you about George. He's the hero of the hour.' She described the bugging of Druckmann's office and the tapes that linked Artguard, Lord Lochinver, the Shand Brothers and Adrian Deventer. She told Tim about the plot to raid Grove's Gallery. 'George sent Edgerson an anonymous tip-off about that and for once Edgerson managed to get things right. He staked out Mount Street and yesterday morning when three of Trevor Shand's armed thugs turned up he bagged the lot. They won't talk, of course, Shand's lawyers will make sure of that, but they'll go down for a stretch and that won't please our Trev. He'll be looking for the leak in his organization and I guess he may trace it to Druckmann . . .'

'That's wonderful, darling. Buy George a drink for me. I don't suppose this will get Artguard off our backs for good and all but it'll give them something else to think about.'

'Sure.' Catherine was hurrying along. 'There's more. Emma thinks she's tracked down the source of the poison.'

Emma took up the story. She described the reference to Hartnell on the tape and the attack on the Grantchester laboratory. 'The newspaper report said that Doctor Hartnell was researching food poisoning. So I got on to a friend of mine in Cambridge who's in the same line. He knew this Hartnell chap quite well and confirmed that he was doing some pretty important work on botulism.'

'Botulism!'

'Yes, interesting eh? But get this: Hartnell had money problems – gambling debts my friend thought.'

'Which would explain how he got into Shand's clutches.'

'Exactly.'

'So what do you think? Did Shand get hold of a batch of toxin for Deventer to administer?'

Catherine replied, 'I can't see Adrian as a poisoner. He grabbed me for a long chat yesterday. He's all broken up by the killings and the bad publicity. You know how hard he's worked establishing Grinling's reputation.'

'So there's still a missing link in the chain from Shand to the murders?'

'I guess so. Unless its Georgina Harding-Beck.'

'Who?'

'The girl in the photograph I told you about. Well, I was right about her. She does work at Grinling's. I tracked her down yesterday. When I showed her the snapshot she freaked out . . . Fainted clear away.'

'So what did you find out from her?'

'Nothing, I'm afraid. She was still in shock when she came round. All her colleagues were glaring at me, wondering what I'd done to their friend. So I couldn't push it any further, but she's sure as hell sitting on some guilty secret. I'll try again in a day or two but I guess she may well refuse to see me.'

'Well, her silence will be eloquent in itself. You've all done incredibly well. Now, how about . . .?'

Catherine headed off his probing about the business. 'We thought we'd found some pieces for your jig-saw puzzle. They might interlock with whatever you've found out about the Michaelmas Massacre. Does any of this help?'

'I'll have to push some of the pieces around to see if they fit. Anyway, the rest has done me a power of good. I'll be back fighting fit in a couple of days.'

'No way!' Catherine's voice was sharp. 'Look, I could do with a break myself. I thought I might come out for the weekend.'

Tim argued but, with two determined females at the other end of the line and three young people round the table all glaring at him, he had to give in.

He said goodbye and put the phone down thoughtfully. The others eagerly pressed him for the latest news from England. Before he answered, Tim turned to O.K. 'You've read just about all there is to read on the Borgias. Do any of the books refer, by name, to the Michaelmas Massacre?'

Wednesday at Farrans Court was a day of ups and downs. The breakfast meeting did not finish till nine o'clock and its three participants left with lists of jobs to add to their routine workloads. Emma had several clients and potential clients to contact but in an interval when she was not using the phone a call came through from Wes Cherry.

'Emma, hi!' He sounded his usual breezy self. 'Look, do you want me to apologize?'

'What for, Wes?'

'For Monday.'

'Monday? No, it was lovely. The meeting was useful and I enjoyed seeing your house and the lunch was . . .'

'Hell, man! You know what I mean.'

Emma paused and concentrated on getting the right inflection into her voice. 'I enjoyed that, too, Wes.'

She held the receiver from her ear as the pop star whooped at the other end of the line. 'Hey, really? That's great. Can we take it from there, then, when I get back?'

'Get back from where?'

'Oh, shit, didn't I tell you? I guess I never got round to it. The band's off tomorrow on a European tour – Amsterdam first, Paris on Saturday, then Berlin and so on. We'll be away three weeks.'

'Well, have a great time, Wes. We'll catch up with each other when you get back.' Emma was aware that she felt resentment and she was annoyed with herself.

'Hey, why don't you come along?'

Emma laughed. 'Don't be silly, Wes. You know I can't.'

'No sweat, kid. A woman's gotta do what a woman's gotta do. I'll call you in three weeks – if not before.'

For the next twenty minutes Emma tried to concentrate on her work – and failed. At last she walked through to Catherine's office.

'Emma, you must be psychic.' Catherine looked up from her desk. 'You're just the person I wanted to see. Park yourself.'

Emma perched on the arm of a leather chair. 'What's cropped up?'

'Tim's just been on the phone. He's really been bitten by this Borgia Chalice bug.'

'Our plan has worked, then?'

'Yeah, perhaps too well. He's starting to come back with things he wants us to find out.'

'Has he forgotten we're busting a gut to pull an ailing business back to life?'

'I doubt it but if he has I'm sure not going to remind him, even if it means somehow finding time for some extra work.'

'What does he want us to do?'

'He was hoping you could get back on to your chemist friend and ask him some more questions. He gave me a list.' Catherine waved a sheet torn from her notepad.

Emma took it and quickly scanned it. 'No problem. Anything else?'

Catherine frowned. 'He says that if we're to do a proper job of investigating this crime we have to probe the lives of all the victims. He wants me to follow up my leads on Julia Devaraux while he takes a closer look at Heinrich Segar. That still leaves Patrice Saint-Yves and Mort Bronsky. Darned if I can see how anyone here can go dashing off to Paris and New York right now.' She sighed. 'Anyway, that's my problem. Now, what was it you wanted to see me about?'

'Oh, yes, what was it?' Emma seemed suddenly preoccupied. 'I remember. How much time do you think we've got – realistically?'

'To get the business back on its feet?'

'Yes.'

'Well, Wes Cherry's cheque was an enormous help and has kept the bank happy but we daren't draw against it in case anything goes wrong with the purchase of the chalice and we have to give Wes his money back. What we have, as I explained the other morning, is a breathing space. If we can spike Druckmann's guns and get the orders flowing again – with the help of the video and the other promotional ideas we've worked out – and if we all work flat out twenty-five hours a day, then we should be able to offer our creditors a better-looking sales projection for next year. How long to persuade everyone that Lacy Enterprises is fighting back? Well, I guess the next six to eight weeks are crucial.'

'Make or break?'

'Being realistic – yes.'

'Thanks.' Emma stood up and walked slowly to the door. She turned. 'I suppose I could spend the weekend in Paris if that would help.'

As the door closed the phone rang. Catherine picked it up and heard Sally say, 'I've got Georgina Harding-Beck on the line.' She made the connection and Catherine said, 'Ms Harding-Beck, good morning. I do apologize for what happened the other day. I had no idea . . .'

'That's perfectly all right, Mrs Lacy. The fault was mine. It was stupid of me to react so hysterically. It was just the sudden shock of seeing that photograph of my sister.'

'Your sister? But I thought . . .'

'You thought it was a picture of me. You're not the first to make that mistake. Marianne was a couple of years older than me. We were quite similar, I suppose, although our colouring was different. A few months ago I dyed my hair blonde. I wasn't thinking about Marianne but the first time I looked in a mirror I got quite a shock. It was almost as though I'd brought her back to life. Anyway, what was it you wanted to know?'

Catherine read between the lines of Georgina's explanation and proceeded very cautiously. 'I'm doing an article on Julia Devaraux. It's for *H.S.* magazine. I came across that snapshot, thought I recognized you and that if you were a friend of Julia's you might be able to tell me something about her.'

There was a pause. Then Georgina said, 'There's an awful lot I could tell you about Julia Devaraux but I'm afraid most of it wouldn't be printable.'

'I understand. She seemed to have quite a talent for getting up people's noses.'

'There's rather more to it than that. She killed my sister.'

Stunned by the uncompromising statement, Catherine did not know how to respond. 'I'm sorry. I've obviously trampled on a private grief. I . . .'

'It's all right, Mrs Lacy. It even helps to talk about it sometimes. It's a sad story but a short one. If you want to hear it, it will only take a couple of minutes.'

'Well, if you really don't mind. Shall we talk later? It must be a bit difficult for you in the office . . .'

'Oh, I'm not at Grinling's. Adrian – Mr Deventer – insisted I took a couple of days off. So, if you have the time now . . .'

'Yes, certainly.'

'Marianne was very gifted. She was an innovative artist and technically brilliant. But she didn't get the lucky breaks everyone needs to make a start, so she earned her living working in galleries. She was in Spence's of Jermyn Street for three years. That was where she met Julia Devaraux. Julia was a friend of Tom Spence – until she savaged one of his exhibitions. That led to a falling out and Tom said some very true and very damning things about Julia in a very public place. Well, she was the sort of person who was very good at dishing out insults and criticism but not very good at taking them. She was determined to get even and one of the ways she chose was to steal Marianne away from the gallery. She persuaded her that she could run her own show. Marianne was very flattered at being taken up by the great Julia Devaraux.'

'So she went into business for herself?'

'Yes, she put in what little capital she had and Julia contributed a lot more. They opened up a few doors away from Spence's and the idea was that Julia would find promising unknowns and show them in DHB – that was what they called the gallery.'

'Now that you mention the name, I do remember it. As I recall it didn't last very long.'

'Seven months.' Georgina's bitterness came very clearly down the phone line. 'That was all it took for Julia to get tired of the venture. She neglected it. Poor Marianne had to start looking round for decent artists to exhibit. DHB never got into a profit situation and Julia, naturally, blamed Marianne. She got very depressed. When Julia insisted on closing down Marianne was faced with losing everything. One day she walked to Green Park station and threw herself under a Piccadilly-line train.'

'Georgina, I'm so sorry. If I'd known any of this I would never have come pestering you with that photograph.'

'Please don't blame yourself. It's all history anyway. Now that nemesis has caught up with Julia Devaraux I hope my sister will rest more easy.'

'I can imagine you feel that justice has been done now.'

There was a long sigh at the other end of the line. 'It was a terrible business and whoever was responsible must be really sick. I feel terribly sorry about the others but I'm afraid my pity doesn't extend to Julia Devaraux. She had it coming to her.'

Catherine mused for some time after putting the phone down. If anyone had motive and opportunity for killing one of the 'Grinling's Four', as the tabloid press had dubbed them, it was Georgina. And she had reacted very dramatically to the photograph. Simply the shock of seeing her sister's picture? Or guilty conscience? Then again, she had been very frank on the phone. She could have refused to speak to Catherine but, in fact, she had taken the initiative. Yet had she any real alternative? She would guess that Catherine could find out from other sources about Julia and Marianne. Silence might be taken as evidence that she had something to hide. One should certainly keep an open mind about Georgina Harding-Beck.

Catherine put the Grinling's business from her mind and settled to a couple of hours' paperwork. It was interrupted at last by Sally who slipped into the office closing the door behind her.

To Catherine's enquiring glance she responded, 'You're not going to like this. Detective Inspector Edgerson is here.'

Catherine groaned. 'What on earth does he want?' When the angular policeman stalked in in his usual I'm-in-charge-here manner, she said, 'Good morning, Inspector, you haven't come all this way just to see me, have you?'

Uninvited, Edgerson dropped into an armchair. 'Yes and no, Mrs Lacy. Yes and no.' He stared at her in what she supposed was meant to be an intimidatory manner.

'Are you going to elaborate or are we playing guessing games?'

Edgerson replied flatly, either ignoring or not noticing the sarcasm. 'I was hoping to have a word with Mr Lacy but I gather he's away . . .'

'Recuperating.'

'With the Santori kids.' He managed to make it sound like an accusation. 'However, as it happens, I do have a bone to pick with you, Mrs Lacy.'

'What am I supposed to have done?'

'I gather you've been upsetting one of my witnesses.'

'Do you mean Georgina Harding-Beck?'

Edgerson nodded. 'Some of the people at Grinling's are pretty indignant about your interrogation of her. May I ask exactly what it was you were talking to her about?'

'For a start, Inspector, I didn't interrogate her. I showed her a photograph and she fainted.'

'What photograph?'

Catherine reached across her desk for a file and extracted the snapshot of Julia and Marianne. She handed it to Edgerson, who frowned.

'This is . . .'

'Julia Devaraux and Marianne Harding-Beck, Georgina's sister.'

'If you knew there was a connection between this Grinling's woman and the deceased why didn't you report it to me?'

'Oh really!' Catherine gasped her exasperation. 'Is everyone who knew Julia Devaraux a suspect? Last time we met you told me that you had too many possible culprits without looking for more.'

Edgerson refused to be diverted. 'So what is all this business about the Harding-Beck woman?'

'Good grief, Inspector, why don't you ask her? You don't need to come all the way out here to question me about her.'

He smiled a cynical smile. 'Humour me. Do you have some suspicions about this woman?'

Suddenly, Catherine realized what the inspector's visit was all about. He was clutching at straws. He had been nearly a month on the case and he was no nearer making an arrest than he had been at the beginning. 'It isn't for me to have suspicions, is it, Inspector? All I can tell you is that Georgina knew Julia Devaraux and had no cause to love her. If you want any more detail you'll have to ask her.'

'Oh, I shall. I certainly shall. She has some explaining to do. I simply wanted to check what you'd found out before I tackled her.'

'What do you mean, she has some explaining to do?'

'Miss Harding-Beck had a unique opportunity to poison the victims.'

'How so?'

'After the sale, Devaraux, Bronsky, Segar and Saint-Yves were dispersed in various parts of the building. Mr Deventer sent out to collect them together for the lunch. The person he despatched to do it was Georgina Harding-Beck. Like a dog rounding up sheep, she got them all in a ground-floor office and then took them up to the penthouse for lunch. So you see, I want to find out all I can about her before I bring her in for questioning.'

Catherine wondered how Edgerson had stumbled on the truth and whether it accounted for Georgina's behaviour. If she had discovered the inspector's interest in her that would explain why she had been so anxious to account to Catherine for her reaction to seeing the photograph. When Edgerson questioned her about her connection with Julia she could say, 'I've made no secret of it. I even told Mrs Lacy all about it.' She said, 'So Georgina was the only person to be alone with the four victims?'

'Not absolutely alone. Another Grinling's employee – a Ms Noble – was there part of the time. Segar had a couple of women with him – his wife and his assistant and Saint-Yves was accompanied by his boyfriend but I can't imagine any of them having reason for multiple homicide.'

'So you think that Georgina offered them something to eat or drink while they were waiting?'

'That's my guess. The other witnesses will be able to confirm it.'

'But you still can't prove that she administered poison.'

'Not without a confession. That's why I need every scrap of evidence before I interview her. So, what can you tell me?'

Not until the weather turned sour in late November was Foscari released from the della Chiesa garrison. No peace was concluded; no truce agreed; no territorial realignment proposed or accepted. Everything remained to be contended for next season. Fighting simply dwindled as heavy rain turned tracks into horse-impeding quags and slackened crossbow strings. The Montefalcos' mercenaries went home despite the protests of their paymasters. Stalemate sieges were abandoned. Cautiously, little-by-little, peasants returned to their ravaged homes from the forest encampments where they had eked out a fragile existence throughout the summer. The della Chiesa forces were allowed to disperse. The field hospital over which Father Jacopo had presided was closed and Brother Pietro was allowed to continue his journeying. He took the road south; the road which led back to Rome.

It was a slow progress. Most days it rained and the little friar spent hours huddled in barns or wayside chapels or enjoying the hospitality of simple folk who counted it a privilege to share their frugal fare with a religious. Pietro did not resent the enforced leisure. It was good to have more time to think.

To think of two matters whose urgency increased with every kilometre that took him closer to the Vatican. Could he present to Pope Alexander a report that would satisfy him? Could he do that and yet avoid incurring the wrath of dangerous and powerful men? As Foscari sorted and re-arranged the scraps of information his quest had uncovered, glimpses of truth tantalized him – deductions and conjectures, painstaking considerations of minutiae and wild leaps of imagination. Foscari felt like the sculptors he had sometimes watched releasing saints and biblical characters from stony imprisonment. He, too, chipped away the marble flakes of irrelevance and lies. The difference, of course, was that the artist knew the torso and the visage that lay within the block while he could only fumble his way towards the truth. And truth was the imperative. Truth was the goal on which he had to fix his eye. Nothing easier than to confess to his holiness that he had been unable to penetrate the mysteries of the Michaelmas Massacre and the death of his son. But that would be to violate truth. To violate God – for all truth met in Him.

Pietro's weeks at the garrison had brought him scraps and fragments of overheard conversations and murmured confidences. He now had a clear image in his mind of della Chiesa. The cardinal, as the second son of a family of the lesser nobility, had been set upon an ecclesiastical career. The strategic position of his family's territory had meant that promotion had been rapid. He was only twenty-three when he was raised to the purple. He had become the effective leader of his clan when his elder brother fell beside his wits. He grew up headstrong, impatient and choleric. He was also cunning. He knew how important he was to the pope and to the pope's enemies. The intense Borgia-della Rovere rivalry provided him with a golden opportunity to sell his services to the higher bidder. Father Jacopo's charitable portrait of a churchman basically loyal to the holy father did not bear close scrutiny. When Charles VIII had sought passage through della Chiesa lands on his southward march in 1494 the cardinal had received a considerable gift of French gold not to impede the invader's progress. When a second incursion was being planned by the powerful Valois-Sforza-della Rovere triumvirate there was every prospect of further material advantage.

And della Chiesa needed to exploit every opportunity, for his local rivalry with the Montefalcos could only end in the ultimate defeat of one side or the other. Alexander had had no alternative but to try to outbid the opposition and Foscari was convinced that della Chiesa had consistently raised the price of his support. Hence the Duke of Gandia's embassies to Arezzo and the cardinal's fateful summons to Rome.

Who, then, stood to gain from della Chiesa's death? That tragedy had left legal ownership of the family's estates in the hands of a twelve-year-old boy, the son of the cardinal's mad brother. The only adults left to act on his behalf were two elderly great uncles. It was their ineffectual handling of the private war which had resulted in the severe reverses of the last few months. That and Borgia gold. Alexander had found the Montefalcos much easier to deal with. It was money from the deep Vatican coffers that had paid the wages of efficient mercenaries. Della Chiesa had been a politique whose removal had thrown an effective barrier across the main approach road to Rome.

Montadini's death, similarly, could only be seen as advantageous to the pope. The zealous churchman's opposition to Borgia corruption was well known. He, too, had been in league with the della Rovere faction and it may have been they who had put him up to assassinating Alexander. Certainly they had encouraged that deranged plan. Had the pope got wind of it? If he had, it would have been absolutely in keeping with his character to strike first.

So, of the three victims of the Michaelmas Massacre the pope had good reason for removing two. That left Petrucci and he stubbornly refused to fit the pattern. The cardinal from Orvieto had been Alexander's man. He had been privy to anti-Borgia plots and had revealed them to the holy father. His death could only be a blow to the pope. Yet it was the pope who had summoned Petrucci to the Vatican, along with the others, in September 1496 and they had all been partakers of the same poison, however it had been administered.

If Alexander was not the instigator of the murders – as he insisted – who else stood to gain? Certainly, della Rovere and his associates would have wanted Petrucci out of the way if they had come to suspect his duplicity. But they could have had no reason for killing the others. Della Chiesa and his valuable lands were in their pocket. As for Montadini, even if he never carried out his 'divine' mission to rid the world of the papal Antichrist his constant complaints about Borgia corruption were vital propaganda for the pope's enemies.

Then there was the Duke of Gandia. Where did he fit in to this sordid schema of secrecy and deceit? He had appeared in Orvieto and in Arezzo, though not, as far as Foscari had been able to discover, in Ferrara. Who had he been representing, his father or his father's enemies? Bartolomeo Nepi had been in no doubt about the answer to that question. A son turned against a doting and over-indulgent father.

Yet, if the young ingrate was in league with the della Rovere faction that made his murder even more puzzling. His co-conspirators would not want to lose someone who was close to the pope and was privy to his most secret thoughts. Foscari's earliest theory linking all the deaths had been one involving revenge. Alexander and Cesare had left Rome shortly after sharing a loving-cup with the cardinals. The pope had said so and Foscari had checked the statement. But the Duke of Gandia had been left behind. Therefore, he had the opportunity to administer the poison. If someone close to one of the victims had found out they might well have taken upon themselves the divine prerogative of vengeance. But now the friar was less happy with this hypothesis. Once again the difficulty was motive. For whom had Gandia been acting? There was no common link between the victims which might justify killing them all. Perhaps, after all, there was no connection between the Michaelmas Massacre and the hacking down of the pope's son. Perhaps there was truth in the gossip about fraternal jealousy. Fra Pietro knew, with a growing and unwelcome certainty, that back in Rome he would have to examine stealthily the activities of Cesare Borgia. These were the realities and half-perceived truths that Foscari's inner eye saw as he looked upon the various facets of the sculpture his mind was trying to fashion. Frustratingly, he felt sure that one or two more blows of the chisel would reveal the whole design. But where to apply its blade? That was the question. The answer came from a wholly unexpected source and, he never for a moment doubted, in answer to prayer.

CHAPTER 13

On Friday afternoon Emma and Catherine set out together for Heathrow in Catherine's car, one to catch the four-fifteen flight to Pisa; the other to depart at five for Paris.

They had just reached the motorway when the mobile phone buzzed.

Catherine said, 'Take that, will you, Emma?'

Emma unclipped the handset. 'Hello. Oh, hi, Sally. Problems already? Oh him! Hang on, I'll ask Catherine.' She turned to the driver. 'Saul Druckmann's been trying to get hold of you. He says he needs to speak to you urgently. Sally wants to know if she should give him the mobile number.'

Catherine pulled a face. 'This is where he tries to lean on "the Lacy woman". Tell Sally to call him back with the number in about five minutes. That'll give us time to collect our thoughts.'

Emma relayed the message and put the receiver back. 'What line do you think he's going to take?'

'I expect he'll bluff – say he can't leave his offer open much longer, that sort of thing.'

'So, we tell him to get lost. That's what Tim would do.'

'Yeah, I guess.'

'He doesn't know we know he's running out of time and that his associates are getting impatient.'

'Not to mention that little business at the Grove Gallery and Shand's probable connection with the Grinling's killings.' She eased the Ford out into the fast lane and overtook a column of traffic.

'Perhaps we ought to let him know what we know. That should stop him in his tracks.'

'Not yet, Emma, not while George is still hoping to collect some more incriminating information. My God, when I think of what Druckmann and his crooked friends are up to it makes my blood boil. I want to see that lot put away, for a long time. For that we're going to need evidence the police can act on. I don't want Druckmann to guess that we're on to him. So, for the time being, it's got to be bluff and counter-bluff. We're the bravely defiant outfit determined to go down fighting rather than yield.'

Emma wondered if that description was not uncomfortably close to the truth but she said nothing.

The phone buzzed again and Catherine took it.

'Hello.'

'Catherine? Saul here – Saul Druckmann.'

'Good afternoon, Mr Druckmann.'

'Oh please, not so formal. I do have your interests at heart.'

'That's not what Tim says.'

'How is Tim? I was so sorry to hear he was poorly.'

'He's still recuperating – abroad.'

'That's a pity. We were in the middle of some delicate negotiations and I'm very anxious to bring them to a satisfactory conclusion.'

'The way I heard it, Mr Druckmann, Tim told you "No Deal", loud and clear.'

'Tim was agitated when we last met and obviously ill. Look, I really do want him to understand our position. I'm sure when he does . . .'

'It'll make no difference, Mr Druckmann.'

'Catherine, let me appeal to you. Tim is sick. He needs rest; needs to get away from business stress. Wouldn't you like to see him able to retire now while he still has several years of active life ahead? If he carries on trying to rescue Lacy Security against all the odds . . . Well, next time he might not be so lucky.'

'My husband isn't ready for the slippers and pipe routine just yet.'

There was a pause, during which Catherine could almost hear Druckmann calculating his next move. At last he said. 'Could you give him a message for me? Tell him we're prepared to increase our offer – substantially – providing, of course, we have an agreement in principle within the next few days.'

'What does "substantial" mean, Mr Druckmann?'

'What I have in mind is rather complex, Catherine. Could you pop in to the office and let me explain properly?'

'I don't think . . .'

'*Please*, Catherine, you can't make up your minds until you know exactly what we're offering.'

Catherine sighed. 'Oh, very well. I can be in London on Monday morning but I don't want to spend very long there.'

'What I have in mind will only take a few minutes. Shall we say nine thirty?'

'O.K., nine thirty.'

'Thank you, Catherine. I'll look forward to it. Goodbye till then.'

'Smarmy creep!' Catherine slammed the receiver back into its housing. 'Did you get all that.'

Emma nodded. 'Yes. Do you think you were wise to agree to see him?'

'Why not? It'll string him along a bit longer. What we need most, right now, is time.'

Emma agreed. 'Too right. Still,' she added brightly, 'at least we're getting away for the weekend. The break will do us both good.'

'Yes. Have some fun in Paris. Don't spend all your time trying to track down Saint-Yves' associates.'

'I'll try.' Emma smiled to herself. She said nothing about the phone conversation she had had with Wes, the ticket he had sent her for the concert, or the arrangement to meet up in his dressing room after the show and make a night of it.

'I'm certainly looking forward to seeing Tim. I do hope this rest . . .' The phone sounded again. 'Oh, for heaven's sake, what now?' She picked up the receiver. 'Hello.'

'Catherine, Sally again. Sorry about this. Everyone seems to be after you this afternoon. Now it's Inspector Edgerson. Do you want to speak to him?'

Catherine groaned. 'Oh, no. Tell him you can't raise me. Ask him to phone Monday afternoon. I'll be back, then – hopefully with a bit more energy.'

'Will do. Have a great weekend. Give Tim my love.'

''Bye, Sally.' Catherine put her foot down on a stretch of empty road and did not even consider what 'Edgy' Edgerson might have to say.

It was a little after ten a.m. the following day when Emma emerged from the Courcelles metro station, strolled along the rue de Courcelles, turned into the avenue Van Dyck towards the Parc de Monceau and discovered the apartment block where Patrice Saint-Yves had once resided. She approved the location in a chic part of the eighth arrondissement. The large street doors were open and she slipped through into the courtyard. She was hoping to find a garrulous concierge who might gossip about her late resident's habits and friends but the woman who came to the door on the right-hand side of the entrance did not look like the chatting kind. Emma's mention of 'Monsieur Saint-Yves' brought forth a torrent of indignant French.

Emma picked out a few phrases. 'It is not proper! . . . I do not permit . . . All these people and that *THING* . . . Tell them I want that *THING* out or I call the police!'

She was about to slam the door when Emma asked. 'Where can I find . . .'

'*Sept bis!*' The wood crashed and shuddered in its frame.

Emma found the appropriate staircase and began to climb. As she neared the first-floor landing she became conscious of a strange, low chanting sound. The door of *sept bis* was ajar and the mantra of unaccompanied voices was coming from inside. Cautiously, Emma pushed the heavy oak. She found herself in a small hallway.

The quavering music was louder now. It filled the confined space and resonated with the few pieces of exquisite furniture. It was accompanied by the sickly, aromatic odour of incense. Both were emanating from an inner doorway, whose portal also stood part open. Emma hesitated. She was overwhelmed with a sense of something sinister, decadent. Whatever was happening in the room facing her touched a switch deep in her psyche which lit warning signs – 'Beware', 'Unwholesome', 'Unholy'. She took a backward step and put a hand out to the door behind her. Then rationalism and curiosity took over. 'Pull yourself together, girl! You haven't come this far to turn and run.' She raised her head and stepped firmly forward.

The room was large and darkened. The only light came from seven tall candles on stands, arranged around a draped catafalque in the centre. As her eyes accustomed themselves to the smoke-laden gloom, Emma saw three circles of chairs facing in towards the covered table and realized that the thing upon it was an open coffin. The pungent aroma was overpowering. The unintelligible chant continued its own monotonous, mesmeric rhythm. Emma felt herself swaying to the thrumming beat. She put out a hand to steady herself and almost knocked over a stand just inside the door. On it was a large bronze bowl containing a scattering of white tablets. Emma almost leaped away from their implications. Some chairs in the outer circle were empty and she collapsed on to one of them.

There was something enervating about the aroma and the music which she was determined not to submit to. She tried to make sense of the repetitive chant. There were no French words that she recognized. She concentrated on the dozen or so phrases being intoned over and over while trying to resist their seduction to somnolence. At last she realized that the chant was Latin performed with a Gallic accent. The neighbour on her right leaned across the empty chair between them holding out a goblet. Emma vaguely realized that it was being passed around the congregation and that she was expected to drink. She raised the chased silver bowl to her lips. The dark wine was sweet, heavy, fragrant. She allowed it to touch her lips and tongue but did not drink. Since there was no one on her left, she passed the cup back to the young man who had handed it to her. He shook his head. He motioned to her to finish the vessel's contents. Heart thudding, Emma stared down into the goblet. It was about a third full. Did she imagine a faltering in the chant and dozens of eyes fixed upon her? She clenched her lids shut, tilted the cup and allowed the lukewarm wine to slip down her throat.

A young man with shoulder-length fair hair mounted the dais. He wore a purple robe embroidered in gold. As he raised his hands aloft the singing stopped. After a pause he began an oration in mellifluent French. 'Brothers, sisters, Dionysians, we praise the One who frees our spirits from earthly toils and raises us to the courts of perfect beauty . . .'

Emma closed her eyes against the stinging smoke and dazzling candle flames. She abandoned the effort of concentration. The voice droned on and her head throbbed. With a shake she forced herself into wakefulness. The official was now scattering flowers into the coffin. He was saying something about 'our priest who has gone before us'. Emma gazed around the circle to see if anyone was paying attention to the speaker. A few were. Others were lolling in their seats, lips smiling, eyes closed or fixed upon some distant vision of ecstasy. Some, mostly men, were fondling each other and kissing. Emma shook her head. Somewhere amidst the swirling mists within a sign flashed: 'Get away! Get away! Get away!' She tried to respond. She willed lethargic limbs into action. She half-rose from the chair.

Then a pandemonium of harsh sounds and urgent movements broke into the room. Men shouted. Chairs were overturned. Someone pulled back heavy curtains and filled the room with blinding light. A hand gripped her arm fiercely and pulled her to her feet. Emma looked around. Others were being similarly handled. Struggling men and women were being pushed towards the door by uniformed policemen.

Subsequent events were confused and incomplete, like scenes viewed on a flickering television screen whose pictures kept slipping. Emma was aware of being hurried to a van and loaded in with other people; of a swaying, lurching journey; of being sick, though where she did not know; of being confronted with incomprehensible questions; of being bundled unceremoniously into a narrow room; of a metallic door clanging loud enough to raise the dead.

When the effects of the drug wore off she was conscious of an iron band of pain squeezing her temples though her mind was otherwise clear. She was lying on a bench and three more people were in the same cell – a middle-aged woman and two men, one of whom was the blond youth who had presided at the ceremony. The other was a few years older and prematurely bald.

Emma sat up. The others looked at her suspiciously.

'Huh! Sleeping beauty wakes,' the woman scoffed.

'Who are you?' the fair-haired man demanded. 'We don't know you. Did you bring the flics?'

'No. It must have been the concierge. She threatened to send for the police. I wanted to warn you but I couldn't interrupt the ceremony.' Emma was improvising wildly.

'Who are you, then?' The high priest, who was still wearing his robe, wanted to know.

'My name's Emma Kerr.' She reverted to the story she had worked out in the plane on the way over as the one most likely to allay the suspicions of Saint-Yves' friends if she were fortunate enough to find any. 'I'm a student of Renaissance art and I've been travelling around Europe and America to meet the leading experts.'

The door opened and a shirtsleeved policeman looked in. 'Bernadette Mansard, come on. Your turn.'

'About time too. What do you mean by keeping innocent people locked up for hours?' The woman hurried out.

'Officer,' Emma called out, 'I want to talk to . . .'

The door slammed shut again.

'You're wasting your breath,' the older man said. 'They'll get around to you when they're good and ready.'

'What are they holding us for?'

The others laughed. 'Listen to Little Miss Innocent,' the bald man scoffed.

His companion stood in the middle of the cell and raised his arms in a theatrical gesture. The full sleeves of his purple robe hung down like silken wings. Emma gazed at his sardonic features and found herself mesmerized by eyes dilated either by drugs or fanaticism. 'You want to know what the guardians of drab mediocrity have against us? Then I'll tell you. They don't like the Dionysians because we're different. We dare. We reach for a higher realm. We tread the golden paths of truth and beauty. We see things, know things, paint things, draw things, write things that mere crawling mortals know nothing about. The flics,' he invested the word with total contempt, 'see no further than their noses. A few little tablets, some packets of white powder and they think they know what the Dionysians are about. My God, if they even suspected . . .' He ended in a high-pitched laugh.

The other man frowned a warning. 'Careful, Master, we know nothing about this woman.'

'Very true. Well, Emma Kerr, you were telling us about yourself.'

'There's not much more to tell. When I was in New York a few weeks ago someone told me I must look up Patrice Saint-Yves. That's why I came to his apartment today.'

'And who was this person in New York who told you to look up Patrice?'

'He's a top dealer and connoisseur – Mort Bronsky.'

'Bronsky!' The young man spat the name. 'Philistine! Patrice wanted nothing to do with him or his schemes. Were you sent to persuade him?'

'Persuade him what?'

The 'Master' ignored the question. 'Well, you were too late. Patrice has gone to the golden land, where all the masters of the ages live. We were celebrating his release today, as soon as the officials released his remains.'

'Patrice was one of the Dionysians?'

'He was our master, our priest. He wore these very robes until a few weeks ago. And do you know what happened then?'

The bald man jumped up from the bench. 'Master, have a care!'

The other waved him to silence. 'Why should she not know? She can prove nothing. The police can prove nothing.' He advanced until he was standing over Emma, arms once more spread out. She looked steadily into eyes that gleamed madness. 'Shall we let you into our little secret? Very well. It was I who sent the master on his last journey. That's the way of the Dionysians; the new priest releases the old.'

Emma fell back on to the bench. 'You mean you killed him?'

He laughed. '"Killed"? Yes that's the word mortal insects use; those who have no concept of time and eternity; those who have never walked with the gods.'

Emma trembled. Was this insanity or hideously insane reality? 'But how . . .?'

'Oh, very cleverly. Very cleverly, indeed, you may be sure. These things have to be masked from the ignorant. Each master, when his time has come, is released by his successor and he is the only one who knows about "how".'

The door opened again. 'Bernard Marais!' the officer commanded. With a melodramatic swirl of his purple robe, the Master of the Cult of Dionysus made his exit.

Emma slumped back against the wall with a sigh of relief. The blond man had taken a foetid atmosphere with him. The air in the cell was somehow cleaner for his departure. But what was she to make of his crazed outpouring and of the events of the morning? There was nothing new, she reflected, in the bizarre union of decadence and art, in the conviction that the true artist walked with the gods and was above the constraints governing 'mere mortals'. She thought of the nineteenth-century aesthetes, the voluptuary Wilde and the brilliantly bizarre Beardsley – men who lived out Walter Pater's ideal of 'burning with a hard gem-like flame' and sacrificing all that convention holds true and holy in order to maintain the ecstasy of creation. She remembered Shelley, the atheistic libertine, Coleridge and Van Gogh, whose wild imaginations were released by drugs and alcohol. Oh yes, the followers of Dionysus (or Bacchus as the Romans renamed him) had hundreds of antecedents. It was not difficult to imagine people obsessed with beauty, like Saint-Yves and his circle, seeking to break free from the mundane, everyday world and the drab fellow citizens who, unaccountably, seemed satisfied with it. But murder? Had the master despatched his predecessor? And had he covered his tracks by wantonly slaying three others and all in a foreign capital? Was that what he meant by his cleverness?

Half an hour passed in silence. Emma's cellmate was not disposed to make conversation. Then he was fetched for interrogation and she was left alone. She had no idea of the time. Her watch had been confiscated along with her other belongings. When the door was once more unlocked she was called out and led through a large vestibule. A clock on the wall registered five thirty-five p.m. Emma was relieved. She still had just under two hours to make the concert. The police would not keep her very long. She could tell them little.

She was shown into a room where two officers, one of them female, already sat at a table. She was motioned to a seat opposite and the interrogation began. She confirmed her identity and her arrival in Paris the previous evening – both facts they could check because they had her passport and her airline ticket. The rapid-fire questions came from both interviewers and Emma was given no chance to organize her thoughts.

'Why were you at the apartment of the late Patrice Saint-Yves this morning?'

'I wanted to see if I could find out something about his death.' Useless to lie to the police.

'You are employed by Scotland Yard?'

'No.'

'You are, perhaps, a private investigator?'

'No, I . . .'

'Then why were you concerning yourself with a criminal investigation?'

'I just thought I might be able to find out something helpful to the police.'

'Really, Miss Kerr, you must think we French flics are very stupid.'

'Not at all. What I . . .'

'The truth is that you came to make contact with a group of drug users with a view to opening up a fresh market.'

'Certainly not! That's a preposterous suggestion!'

'We shall see. You will be strip-searched at the conclusion of this interview.'

'That's outrageous! You have no right . . .'

'We have every right, Miss Kerr. We suspect you of handling illegal substances and associating with known pushers and users.'

'That's nonsense. I work for a reputable English company.'

'Lacy Enterprises?' The policeman looked at a letter taken from Emma's handbag.

'That's right. My colleagues there will vouch for me.'

'And who are they?'

'Mr and Mrs Lacy – Tim and Catherine.'

'And we can contact them at this address – Farrans Court, near Marlborough, Wilts?'

'Yes . . . er . . . no. Not at the moment. They're in Italy. I'm afraid I don't have their address.'

'You obviously all travel a great deal. How do you transport your drugs?'

'We don't deal in drugs.' Emma rubbed her perspiring hands on her skirt. She felt the tremor in her legs. 'Look, you've got everything all wrong.'

The man shrugged. With a long finger he probed Emma's personal effects which lay scattered on the table. He picked up a slip of green paper. 'This is a ticket for a concert tonight being given by Cool Jungle.'

Emma saw a slightly open door and rushed towards it. 'Yes. The lead singer Wes Cherry is a friend of mine. He'll . . .' Immediately she recognized her mistake.

'You are a personal friend of the pop star. You move in the party world of pop musicians and groupies? A very lucrative market.'

'No! Yes! You've got me confused.'

'We will be at this concert this evening in force, Miss Kerr. And do you know what we will find? Young people in possession of every kind of drug from pot to heroin and cocaine. We will find gibbering junkies with arms pock-marked with syringe scars. If we're lucky we will find some pushers. But you won't be among them because we've already got you here.'

'But I'm not carrying drugs!' Emma screamed her fear and frustration. 'You can't hold me!'

The policeman stood up. 'My colleague and another woman officer will now carry out a thorough search and you will then be returned to the cells.'

'No! Please stop! Listen to me. I'm not trying to conceal anything from you. I don't know anything about those other people you found me with this morning. I've never seen them before. Ask them. They'll tell you they don't know me.'

He resumed his seat. 'Oh, I don't think we'd be in a hurry to believe anything they told us. Since you pretend to know nothing about the Dionysians, as they call themselves, let me enlighten you. They're a bunch of junkies and queers. Some of them are prominent in the Paris artworld but most of them are inadequate hangers-on. That makes them a target for narcotics dealers. And narcotics lead to other crimes because users need cash to feed their habit and because syndicate bosses are always looking for ways to launder money. So people in the late Monsieur Saint-Yves' little coterie are into forgery, art theft, the false-attributions racket and just about any fraud you can think of. The irony is that Saint-Yves himself, as far as we know, was clean – perhaps too clean for his own good. Of course, he was a depraved old quean. He picked up most of his young men at life classes in the art schools. That's where he met Marais, the golden-haired wonder – as nasty a piece of work as you'd ever wish to meet. That particular affair ran for a couple of years. The boy was taken into the avenue Van Dyck apartment and had absolutely everything – clothes, jewellery, sports cars, foreign holidays. He became a fixture in Saint-Yves' silly little Dionysian set-up. But Marais got bored and he got greedy. He started dealing in a pretty big way, although we've never caught him – yet. It was the drugs that came between him and his indulgent provider. A few months back there was a falling out. Marais was thrown out of his Garden of Eden. But he had made himself indispensable to the Dionysians and he hit back by trying to oust Saint-Yves from his little kingdom. Some say he tried to make it up with Saint-Yves recently and went with him to London. Others say he hated his ex-lover like poison. Given time I reckon he'd have done the old queer in. Only someone else got there first, didn't they?' He stood up again. 'That's the sort of people you're mixed up with, Miss Kerr. But then, I expect you know that. Now I'll leave you to the tender mercies of my colleagues.'

Half an hour later Emma was glad to get back to the privacy of a prison cell. She was in a state of shock. Humiliated, browbeaten and accused of the most abhorrent crimes, she was totally disorientated. For a long time all she could do was sit on the hard bed, hugging her knees to her chest and shivering. She did not touch the food that was brought to her. For hours she could not sleep. When she did drop into unconsciousness it was only to wake frequently with trembling limbs and sweat standing out on her forehead.

The night passed and half the morning. At ten fifteen, twenty-four hours after she had walked into the apartment on avenue Van Dyck, Emma was released. There was no ceremony. A duty officer returned her belongings, advised her to make sure she caught the evening plane on which she was booked and bade her good day. She stood dazed on the steps of the *poste de police* staring up

275

and down the quiet Sunday-morning street. All she knew was that she wanted comforting, needed a friendly face, even more a friendly shoulder to cry on. She found a cab and was driven to the theatre where Wes's concert had been held. It was all shut up but she did find an open, untenanted stage door. She walked through to the foyer and eventually tracked down a young man in an adjacent office who turned out to be the assistant manager.

Emma explained that she was trying to locate Cool Jungle. Did he happen to know which hotel they were staying in? The young man was in no mood to be co-operative. He was still fuming about the previous night's police raid. He scowled at Emma and told her that he could not reveal confidential information. Emma explained that she was a friend of Wes Cherry and that it was vital she spoke with him. The assistant manager regretted that it was strictly against the establishment's policy to divulge the addresses of performers. With tears in her eyes Emma implored him. She had missed an appointment with Mr Cherry and needed to explain why. The man shrugged and opened the front door for her. He watched her walk dejectedly down the street. 'The lengths some of these fans will go to,' he thought.

CHAPTER 14

O.K. pulled out all the stops in honour of Catherine's visit. Tactfully, he left Tim and his wife to their own devices on Friday evening. He spent the time on advanced preparations for an elaborate dinner the following night. On Saturday he assumed the role of chauffeur-guide on a trip to Rome. He was eager to show his guests the Vatican's Borgia Apartments and the Lacys were curious to see the rooms where Alexander VI had enjoyed the company of his children, plotted with his closest advisers and fatally entertained three cardinals in September 1496.

'They're smaller than I imagined,' Catherine observed, as the trio passed from the Sala della Sibille into the Sala del Credo whose frescoed figures seemed to overpower the human beings proceeding through the rooms on a tourist conveyor belt. 'Of course it doesn't help having them cluttered up with this stuff.' She waved a hand at the display of largely indifferent modern religious art.

O.K. hung back, dividing his attention between the guidebook and the architectural and artistic details to which it directed the reader's attention. 'Yeah, it's a pity we can't see them exactly as they were when Rodrigo Borgia had them decorated. All these paintings would have been fresh at the time of the Michaelmas Massacre. Pinturicchio and his pupil, Antonio da Viterbo, finished them a couple of years earlier. Like I said before, Rodrigo was an important supporter of the arts. Did you know he was Copernicus's first patron?'

Tim laughed. 'O.K. is determined to make us think well of the most notorious pope in history.'

'No one's wholly bad,' he responded seriously.

They made their leisurely way into the third chamber whose walls gleamed with gold and glistened with bright enamel-like colour.

'This was Alexander's study,' O.K. announced.

Tim looked around the room and its almost oppressive frescoes illustrating the patron deities of the sciences and the liberal arts. 'So this is where Rodrigo Borgia talked with Brother Pietro Foscari and hired him as a Renaissance P.I.?'

O.K. considered the question. 'Could be. But Alexander did spend part of his time in his suite in the Castel Sant' Angelo. He was paranoid about security and had another set of luxurious quarters made inside the fort.'

'No.' Tim insisted, 'I think it was here. This room has a closed-in, secret atmosphere. I can just imagine the two of them, in here alone, sizing each other up. The pope's probably sitting in some large, well-stuffed chair looking imposing. The little friar standing in front of him, fidgeting and uncomfortable. Yet it's Alexander who's really at a disadvantage. If he's ever going to find out about the death of his son he has to trust this insignificant but clever Brother Pietro. The difficulty is Alexander trusts no one. He has enemies everywhere. There's no one he can be honest and open with. Not even Brother Pietro.'

Tim was now walking back and forth, engrossed in his reconstruction. Tourists ambling through the sala eyed him curiously. He paid no attention. 'I'd love to have been a fly on the wall at that conversation. O.K., do you remember, in Siena, I pointed out to you an interesting sentence in Foscari's report?'

'Yeah, it was something about Alexander not having told him that Petrucci was a friend. I didn't see the point. I still don't.'

'Look, Alexander is desperate to avenge his son's death. It turns out there may be a connection with the Michaelmas Massacre.' He broke off and turned to Catherine. 'Remind me to check with you about that later. Now, where was I? Yes, the connection between Gandia's murder and the deaths of the cardinals. Alexander says to his P.I., "All right, you have my permission to look into all these killings." But he doesn't go on to say, "Oh, by the way, Petrucci wasn't a traitor; he was a friend of mine, a political ally." That would have saved time. Brother Pietro had to find it out for himself. Why the reticence?'

Tim looked from O.K. to Catherine and back again. Their faces were blank.

'Because the investigation was moving into the political arena. It was beginning to uncover facts that he wanted to keep secret. One thing's always bothered me about this relationship.' He waved a hand around the room, now clearly occupied in his imagination with the tall Borgia pope and a diminutive brown-habited Franciscan. 'With all the resources at his disposal, why did Alexander employ an obscure friar to work in secret? Didn't he start a full-scale murder enquiry immediately after his son's death and then suddenly call it off?'

O.K. nodded. 'Yes, people at the time said that all the evidence pointed at Cesare and that's why the pope put the lid on the investigation.'

'But now we know he continued it secretly and that

to his own detective he refused to provide sensitive information.'

Catherine took Tim's arm and steered him through to the next room. 'So where's all this leading?'

'Straight to the world of cover-ups and whitewashes and closed files and vulnerable reputations and sleaze and duplicity "in the public interest" and professional assassins.'

'That has a modern ring,' Catherine said.

Tim smiled grimly. 'People don't change, especially people in power.'

In the Sala dei Santi they paused before Pinturicchio's extraordinarily exotic *St Catherine of Alexandria Before the Emperor Maximilian.*

'Isn't that supposed to be Lucrezia Borgia?' Catherine pointed to the figure of the saint, a young woman with flowing fair hair.

O.K. consulted his book. 'Yeah. Not a bad looker.'

'And I suppose you're going to tell us that she wasn't as black as she's been painted.'

''Course she wasn't, Catherine. Poisonings by the score? Incest with her father and her brothers? I don't buy it. She was nothing more than a political pawn, poor kid.' O.K. surveyed the picture, head on one side. 'I reckon you can see resignation and sadness in that face. She was married and unmarried by Alexander whenever his pattern of alliances changed. Her first marriage was annulled on the grounds that her husband couldn't do the bizz. That was a load of codswallop. Her second husband was hacked to bits right here in the Vatican. Lucrezia was heartbroken by that. She didn't really get any peace till Alexander died.'

'She no longer had any political significance,' Tim observed.

'Right. She lived as Duchess of Ferrara, had seven kids and died at the age of thirty-nine.'

'Men!' Catherine muttered and strode through the doorway into the Sala dei Misteri della Fede.

They admired the frescoes illustrating the main events of the New Testament and came to a halt before the depiction of the Resurrection.

'That must be the old reprobate himself.' Tim pointed to the bald man kneeling in adoration and wearing a sumptuous bejewelled cope.

Catherine surveyed the fat features and beak-like nose seen in profile. 'Piety doesn't become him.'

Tim agreed. 'He reminds me of a government minister at one of those religious functions they have to attend – memorial services and such like – kneeling in a suitable attitude of fervent prayer and not believing a word of it.'

'They reckon the Roman soldier standing just over there is Cesare and the other young man nearby is Giovanni, the Duke of Gandia.' O.K. turned a page of the guidebook and read aloud. '"In this remarkable portrayal of the pope and his two sons the family likeness can be clearly seen. History suggests that Cesare inherited his father's forceful and ruthless personality, while Giovanni became heir to Rodrigo's voluptuousness and sensuality." The trouble with paintings is you can read whatever you want into them.'

'Not if they're good paintings,' Catherine mused. 'But these aren't all that good. Those figures are just two handsome young men. If they are the pope's sons you can't tell much about them.'

'Cain and Abel?' Tim asked.

Catherine shrugged. 'Who knows?' She looked around. 'What was this room used for?'

'"Thought to have been Alexander's private dining room,"' O.K. read out.

'So this is where the cardinals were poisoned?'

'We don't know that, darling,' Tim said. 'It may have been here that they shared the Borgias' loving-cup but we know that didn't kill them. I sure as hell would like to know how it was done. I wonder if Foscari found out?'

They completed their tour of the apartment, emerged into a damp, grey autumn city and went in search of lunch.

As they strolled across the vastness of St Peter's Square, Catherine said, 'What was it you wanted to ask me about the Michaelmas Massacre?'

'I want to know why you call it that.'

'What an odd question. That's simply what it's called, isn't it?'

'Well, no. That's the point. O.K.'s done some research. He's gone through several of his books and he's searched his memory. He can't find any reference to the murder of the cardinals as the Michaelmas Massacre.'

'But that's silly. We've always called it . . .'

O.K. shook his head. 'No, Catherine, I never came across the expression till Tris found it in that document from the Vatican Archives.'

Tim added, 'And there's not much that O.K. doesn't know about the Borgias.'

Catherine was insistent. 'Then you must have told me about it.'

'I don't think so. I was surprised when you mentioned the Michaelmas Massacre on the phone.'

'But if I didn't hear it from you . . .?'

'Exactly. You must have heard it directly or indirectly from someone else who has read Foscari's manuscript.'

Catherine tightened the scarf covering her blonde hair. 'That's a bit far-fetched, Tim.'

He shrugged. 'I'm open to other theories. Can you remember where you first heard the phrase?'

'That's kinda hard. I've had a lot on my mind recently.'

Tim gave his wife a quick hug. 'Of course. Forget I asked. Look, darling, I hate to see you coping all on your own. It's time I came back. I'm fine now. Never felt better.'

Catherine gripped his arm tight. 'No way, buster. You've got an appointment with the doc next Friday. After that, we'll see. Anyway, who says I'm coping on my own? Everyone back at Farrans has been magnificent. In fact, it could be that your being away for a bit is the best thing that could have happened to the business. It's made people more self-reliant. Decisions have gotten made at a lower level. We're all sharing the load. You'll see quite a difference when you do come back. And, anyway, you can't come back until you've solved the Grinling's murders. I didn't tell you, did I, that Edgerson's got a new suspect. He's hot on the track of Georgina Harding-Beck.'

'And you reckon he's got it wrong again?'

Catherine pursed her lips. 'I don't know. She certainly had opportunity and motive. But . . .' As they ambled slowly down the broad via della Conciliazione Catherine described what she knew, what she guessed and what she suspected about Georgina Harding-Beck.

That evening they were joined at the villa by Ginny and Tristram. O.K. served a sumptuous but calorie-conscious meal in the dining room on a table laid with china and glass brought up from the Santoris' flat for the occasion. By unspoken agreement no one mentioned the Grinling's case or the Michaelmas Massacre until after dinner. It was when they were all sitting round a log fire and the coffee cups were being refilled that Tim brought the subject up.

'With Catherine here, I thought this would be a good opportunity to go over everything and see whether what we've discovered makes any sense. Tris, have you finished Foscari's report?'

'Almost.' The young lawyer handed round copies of his latest effort at translation. 'No deductions yet. This friar was a very methodical man. He just went around talking to people and compiling evidence bit by bit. He must have had a pretty dull life.'

Ginny giggled. 'He sounds like a lawyer.'

Tristram pulled a face and went on. 'I've got to the point where he's learned all he can about the three murdered cardinals. As you can see, della Chiesa was a bit of a political schemer, playing the pope off against his enemies for his own private advantage . . .'

There was silence for several minutes while they all read Tristram's notes. Ginny looked up with a bemused frown. 'He doesn't seem to be getting anywhere.'

Tim shook his head. 'I wouldn't say that. Tris is right. Foscari is being very thorough. He's establishing beyond any shadow of doubt that there is no obvious link between the three victims. There was no interested party who would be advantaged by all three deaths.'

'Then the triple murder was a way of confusing the issue. The murderer has one victim in view, so he kills three. A sort of smoke-screen. That's what you suggested at the beginning.' Tristram got up and put two more logs on the fire.

'I suggested that might be a possibility. Now I think we can exclude it – or, rather, I think Foscari is coming round to excluding it. Even in those bloody days poisoning *three* important people at one fell swoop was a bit much. The stakes had to be pretty high for that sort of drastic action. Foscari realized that there were big political issues involved. I'll bet he went back to Rome with more than a few butterflies in his stomach. If he was successful he would be exposing the plans of very dangerous men who would not hesitate to silence him. If he cried off, Alexander's displeasure might prove just as fatal.'

'And you still reckon all this is relevant to our murders?' O.K. sounded dubious.

'Oh, yes. More than ever. I'm now sure that somebody else read this document in the Vatican Archive.'

'And planned a copycat killing?' Catherine asked.

'I don't suppose it was as simple as that. I think the Michaelmas Massacre gave our killer the general idea. He – or she – realized that five hundred years ago someone pulled off a bizarre and very successful triple murder, *and* that what had worked in 1496 could work again.'

Catherine was not convinced. 'You're asking us to swallow a pretty big coincidence.'

Tim sat forward in his chair, a look of triumph on his face. 'Not at all. Think about it for a moment. The Borgia Chalice has been in the news on and off for nearly four years. In that time how many people have been exploring its history? Dozens; scores probably. Is it so surprising that one of them should have found the document that Tris stumbled across on his first visit to the archive? Now what would any historian or art historian do if he made a nice little coup like that about something very much in the public eye?'

'Publish,' Ginny said.

'Exactly! Can't you just see it? *"Fresh Light on the*

Borgia Chalice". It would cause quite a stir in a specialist journal. It would earn more as a colour-supplement feature. It might even merit a TV programme. So our researcher would have to have a pretty good reason for keeping the story under wraps. That means that he or she was playing for bigger stakes.'

Ginny looked crestfallen. 'Does that mean you don't buy my theory about Segar's womenfolk ganging up on him?'

'And you're letting Georgina off the hook,' Catherine added.

Tim held his hands up. 'Not necessarily. I agree that all those people had opportunity, especially . . . Catherine, did Emma manage to get the information I wanted from her chemist friend?'

'Oh yes. Sorry I forgot.' She rummaged in her handbag and handed an envelope to her husband.

Tim read the enclosed note quickly and thumped his fist on the edge of the chair. 'Yes! I knew there had to be something wrong about the timings. It came to me the other day when O.K. was telling us about cantarella.' He explained for Catherine's benefit. 'Cantarella was the Borgias' favourite poison – basically arsenic oxide. It was tasteless and soluble so it could be administered in different strengths according to how long a gap they wanted before it took effect. Now, listen to this: "In its natural form the toxin produced by *Clostridium botulinum* bacteria appears in inadequately cooked or preserved meat, fish, vegetables and dairy products. Ingestion of affected food may produce symptoms after anything from three to twenty-four hours, depending on various factors. However, under laboratory conditions filtrates of extreme toxicity can be produced. Some countries are even believed to have contemplated use of this poison in biological warfare. If ingested in a liquid and in some strength, symptoms would certainly manifest themselves in a short space of time. Rapid action of the toxin would also result if it were ingested on an empty stomach. It is very unusual for death – almost invariably from respiratory paralysis – to be quick. However, laboratory experiments with animals suggest that, if concentration of the toxin is sufficiently high, it can act rapidly upon the nervous system."' Tim looked round the circle of faces. 'So now we know how and when the Grinling's Four were poisoned.'

The others looked blank. O.K. spoke for them. 'Is this where someone says, "What do you mean, Holmes?" and you reply "But it's elementary, my dear Watson"?'

Tim ignored the taunt. 'Look, the sale began at ten. No one could have got at the victims before then. We discount the poison being in the chalice. The sale must have ended around twelve thirty and afterwards the victims were wandering about the salerooms, chatting to various cronies. Now, what time did the deaths occur?'

Catherine reflected. 'The lunch started just after one o'clock. I guess it was about an hour later that Julia and Saint-Yves collapsed, almost simultaneously. Someone sent for an ambulance and while we were still waiting Segar keeled over. That'd be another ten minutes or so. Bronsky was the last one to feel the effects. The paramedics were already there by then. I suppose the time would have been around two twenty-five.'

'So that narrows down the time the poison can have been administered to between twelve thirty and one p.m. And it must have happened when the four victims were collected together for the party.'

Catherine groaned her disappointment. 'Is that it? You give us this big build-up and then announce something that even Edgerson has cottoned on to. He's worked out when the four were poisoned. That's why he's now got his sights fixed on Georgina.'

'But he's guessing and we know. He's worked out the only time before the lunch that the victims were all together. What he hasn't got is the scientific evidence that will tell him that the toxin was served in a drink of some sort. And what he also doesn't know is where the toxin, almost certainly, came from.'

'But he knows enough to pull Georgina in and charge her,' Catherine objected.

'He doesn't know enough to ask her the right question.'

'Which is?' Tristram asked.

'Does she have a working knowledge of medieval Latin? Don't lose sight of the fact that our murderer modelled the crime on the Michaelmas Massacre.'

Catherine wrinkled her nose. 'I've been thinking about that. I've remembered when I first heard the term. It was Emma who mentioned it after she and George had been up to Grinling's.'

'To see Andy Stovin?'

'Yes.'

'Was he the only person they spoke to there?'

'I think they had a chat with Corinne. Apart from that . . .' She stopped, eyes and mouth open wide. 'Tim, you don't think . . .'

'Head of the Medieval and Renaissance Paintings department? Frequent visitor to Italy? I bet she has more than a nodding acquaintance with medieval Latin.'

Catherine shook her head. 'Corinne Noble, a quadruple poisoner? It's ridiculous.'

'Were you with her all the time after I left on the day of the murders?'

'No . . . She said I could stay in her office if I wanted because she had things to do in other parts of the building. I had a pleasant hour or so browsing through her books till she collected me to go to the penthouse.' She glared at her husband. 'OK, smartypants, so it looks bad for her. I still don't believe she had anything to do with the murder.'

Ginny intervened. 'There's someone else who qualifies: Maria Heuss. She's a Renaissance scholar. She must read medieval languages. *And* she was in the room where the four were poisoned.'

Tim rubbed a finger along the bridge of his nose. 'Right, we can't rule Maria out. So, we've got Maria, Georgina and Corinne – and for all we know there were others in that room who also qualify. What I can't figure out is what it's all about. This isn't a *crime passionel* about jealousy or revenge. It's premeditated; meticulously planned. There has to be a big reason and I mean "big". Something that involves the Shand brothers and a burning laboratory and some scheme, some plot, some criminal activity that calls for ruthless multi-murder. Oh, I wish I knew who else had seen Foscari's letter.'

'Is that all you want?' Tristram spoke from the depths of an ancient armchair. 'I can find that out for you – I think.'

Tim turned to him, eyes gleaming. 'You can?'

'Probably. At the archive you have to fill in requisition slips for old books and manuscripts. They keep them and put the information on a database – for their own statistics, I suppose. If I get my friend in a right mood I might be able to persuade him to tell me who else has accessed the Borgia correspondence for 1497.'

'Great!' Tim jumped up excitedly. 'Can you get on to

...ay? If I'm right, that could give us the

...mi, some eighty kilometres short of Rome, Foscari fell in with a small group of pilgrims, and though they travelled slowly he was glad to be of their company for a few hours. They travelled slowly because some of them were on foot and showing signs of exhaustion. These were penitents, compelled to undertake the rigours of rough roads over mountains and through forests in sunshine, rain and snow with the minimum of clothing, concerned only to stay alive long enough to reach the Eternal City, pray at the prescribed sites and receive there their certificates of absolution. Through sufferings inflicted on the body they would purge their souls of sin and escape the everlasting fires of hell. Those who were not burdened with the penances imposed by priest or church court and thus able to make better provision for the journey rode on horse or donkey or travelled in a waggon, often going on ahead to arrange food or hospitality for their fellow pilgrims. Such parties were common on all the main roads into Rome, though less so at this time of year.

'They that go much on pilgrimage are seldom thereby made perfect and holy.' So Thomas à Kempis had written and Brother Pietro heartily endorsed the mystic's judgement. In his sermons he often indignantly exposed clergy who charged people to gaze on or touch relics of the saints in jewelled boxes, and put about stories of fake healings and fraudulent 'weeping' or 'bleeding' statues to attract visitors and donations. He inveighed against the trade in pardons and indulgences; the turning of shrines into market stalls for the sale of leaden badges, 'holy' water, tawdry images and other gew-gaws by which the unscrupulous battened on the gullible in the name of religion. Above all, he was indignant with a Church which encouraged people to believe that God would be pleased with them if they neglected their families to go gadding off to distant holy places; that devotion lay in prostrating themselves before carved and painted images rather than patiently pursuing the tasks in life to which God had called them; that salvation could be bought with offerings at altars already laden with gold and gems rather than with alms given to the poor.

As much as he resented an ecclesiastical institution which preyed on the fear and guilt of simple people, Brother Pietro had compassion on those whose holy impulses impelled them to make pilgrimages. So, for several kilometres, he slowed his own advance to the pace of men and women who limped and staggered with fervent determination towards Rome.

Thus he met Giles de Bec, Sieur d'Evranche. He would never have recognized the wretched figure in a tattered, coarse woollen gown as a Norman landholder of ancient family. The man, who could have been no more than thirty-five, hobbled along, supported on one side by a sturdy servant and on the other by a crutch fashioned from an ash pole. His lower legs were heavily bandaged and the cloths were stained with red-brown streaks of dried blood. Every step was painful for him. He could scarcely bear to set each foot to the ground. Pietro understood immediately: he had seen many barefoot penitents, compelled, in expiation for some grave sin, to tread the pilgrim routes without boots. Many succumbed to infected sores long before reaching their destination.

It was de Bec who hailed Fra Pietro when he had been with the party for only a few minutes. 'You, friar, will you walk with me?'

Pietro fell back to dawdle beside the stricken man. 'I compliment you on your Latin, my son. Did you study in the schools? Paris, perhaps, for I think by your accent you are French?'

'My brother and I were both educated at the local abbey school. We had excellent teachers. But what of that!' He shook his head distractedly. 'You must hear my confession.' Despite the man's weakness and the frailty of his voice he carried an accustomed air of command.

It was not an authority Pietro was prepared to submit to without question. 'And why *must* I, my son.'

'It is a condition of my penance. I must be absolved by every priest I meet on my journey. You are a priest, are you not, Father?' Anxiety showed in the man's eyes.

'I seek no title but "Brother", since all men are equal in the sight of God, but I have been ordained and I will hear your confession.'

'Fifteen years ago I married the daughter of a neighbour and friend of my family. Her name was Alys. I was nineteen and she was thirteen.' In a level monotone de Bec launched into a story that frequent repetition had robbed of drama and pathos. 'It was a good marriage – advantageous, you understand. Yet she was beautiful and dutiful and I loved her. We were content. After the death of my father I became the lord of fair lands and Alys bore me three sons who, by God's grace, survived infancy. My brother, Edmond, was made Bishop of Evranche which delighted us both, for we were always very close. I had every reason to render daily thanks to God – and I did. Three years ago I had to make a journey of several days to the south. A relative had died, leaving me an estate which had been neglected for a long time. It took me many weeks to set everything in order, but at last, very thankfully, I returned home – to the arms of my *loving* wife.' De Bec's voice had become strained and his breath laboured.

Pietro suggested a few moments' rest. Between them, he and the servant lowered the pain-racked nobleman on to a rock beneath a wayside crucifix.

The man refused a drink of water. He was eager to hurry on with his narrative. 'As I was dismounting my chaplain came to me with grave news: during my absence Alys had defiled my bed with no less than two other men. People were gossiping about it locally, he said, and waiting to see what I would do. I demanded the names of the culprits. He knew only one of them – a groom from my own stable. I confronted Alys with her adulteries, but she denied everything and, despite my anger, I could not bring myself to beat the truth from her. It was, of course, beneath me to deal directly with my groom. I simply sent some of my men to make sure that he never seduced a woman again.'

'You had him killed?' Foscari asked quietly.

'It was my right – or so I thought in my stupid pride.' He hesitated and Pietro knew he was coming to the difficult part of his story. 'Thinking little of it, I confessed to my chaplain. He explained that what I had done, or caused to be done, was a mortal sin and he imposed this penance. I was astounded, shocked, angry. I struck him. Then I went to see my brother. I supposed that he would readily absolve me. Yet it was he who made me see that my priest was right. No man has the right to usurp God's power of life and death – "Vengeance is mine; I will repay, says the Lord." With tears in his eyes he pronounced the ban of holy Church until I had walked barefoot to Rome, visited the holy places and obtained absolution from every priest I met upon the way.'

Pietro took the man's hands in his own, observing

how the once-smooth skin was grimed and calloused. 'That is a terrible story my son. A vile and evil thing has been done.'

The hands trembled and watery eyes looked imploringly into Pietro's. 'I know it, Father, and I repent – truly and bitterly. I beg you, for the sake of my immortal soul, to add your absolution to the others merciful priests have given me along the way.'

But Foscari was not thinking of the assassination this man had authorized and it was almost absently that he signed de Bec with the cross and pronounced the formal declaration of God's forgiveness.

Later, when they were all lodged for the night in an indifferent wayside inn, he went to the loft over the stables in search of the nobleman's servant. They sat, by the light of a lamp, in a corner on hay that smelled mustily sweet.

'You look after your master well,' Pietro observed.

'He is a good master.' The tall, thick-set man had few words and those he did have were heavy with Norman dialect. Pietro, whose French had been learned in Paris in student days, found him not easy to understand.

'You must see that he gets home safely,' the friar urged. 'He has suffered a great wrong.'

The servant stared at him, eyes wide with astonishment. 'You know?'

'I can smell fish when they are under my nose. The groom who was killed. You must have known him well.'

'Well enough to know him innocent.' He maintained a long silence before elaboration. 'A ladies' man, yes, but he knew his place.'

'And the Sieur de Bec's chaplain?'

The tall man spat emphatically.

'He hates your master?'

'He desires my master's wife.'

'And has seduced her?'

'She is a good woman – trusting.'

'Why didn't she tell the Sieur on his return?' But even as Foscari posed the question he knew the answer. The chaplain had got his story in first, filling de Bec's mind with the smoke of jealousy, so that he was incapable of seeing the truth.

'When I told my master what people said about his priest he cursed me for an evil-minded gossip and ordered me to be whipped.'

'You're a good, loyal man.' More loyal than de Bec deserves, Foscari thought, but did not say so. 'Do you know anything of my Lord of Evranche?'

'Only what men say. He keeps great state. He has built a fine, new house and lives more like a king than a bishop.'

Pietro struggled to contain his anger. Betrayal. De Bec's was a common enough story. Yet it was particularly vile because it depended for its success on the good, open, trusting nature of the victim. If this ingenuous nobleman had possessed a thimbleful of honest scepticism he would have seen through the plot hatched in his absence, a plot designed to result in the death of the Sieur de Bec in a distant land, leaving a widow and her young children in the clutches of ruthless and grasping men. At length he gave a series of clear, insistent instructions. 'My son, it is vital you bring your master safe home. I can do little to help you here, but when you reach Rome ask for me at the Franciscan convent. I will tend his feet with excellent ointments. Then you must buy the best horses. I know a dealer you can trust. Before you leave I will give you a letter for your master. If he reads it carefully and ponders it on his journey he may avoid being manoeuvred into encompassing his own destruction and the destruction of his house.'

At his evening prayers Fra Pietro besought heaven's protection on the Sieur de Bec. It was later, as he lay on the rickety truckle bed which was no hardship to someone whose mattress had frequently been hard earth or unyielding stone, that he meditated further on how the gullible can be manipulated by the unscrupulous, how men's spectral fears can be invested with flesh and blood. And that was when he saw clearly the connection between the poisoning of three cardinals and the death by stabbing of the pope's son.

III

IN VINO VERITAS

Fortune is a woman, and it is necessary, if you wish to keep her under, to beat her and knock her about.

Niccolò Machiavelli, *The Prince*

CHAPTER 15

Emma was in no mood to be shouted at by George the first thing on Monday morning. Arriving home the previous evening after a tedious bus, train and taxi journey from Heathrow had been a dismal anticlimax to a ghastly weekend. She wanted company; people to talk to; friends and colleagues who would be sympathetic as she recounted her ordeal. But there was no one at the house and her cottage was cold and empty. She tried to relax in a bath but spent the time mentally composing furious letters to the head of the Paris Sureté, the Ministre de l'Intérieur, the French press and *The Times*. She watched an old American film on TV. She idly turned the pages of a favourite book. Nothing worked. Eventually she went to bed – and spent the next three hours wrestling with rebellious pillows and a recalcitrant duvet. It was not to be wondered at that she came to Monday's breakfast meeting with nerves and emotions stretched to snapping point.

Thankfully she sipped head-clearing black coffee.

'Catherine's late this morning,' George observed as he prepared to attack his fry-up.

'Oh, sorry, I forgot to mention it.' Emma massaged her throbbing temple. 'She won't be here this morning. She's got an appointment in London with Saul Druckmann.'

That was when George shouted, 'What?' He dropped his knife and fork with a clatter and glared at Emma.

She stared back. 'Do you have to make that noise, George?'

He took no notice. 'When was this fixed up?'

'What does it matter?' Emma found George a pain when he was being macho and assertive.

'It matters! When was it?'

'OK. OK! Don't get in a state. It was Friday afternoon. Catherine took a call from Druckmann on the mobile when we were on the way to the airport. She thought . . .'

'Sally.' George turned to the secretary. 'Get hold of Catherine, now. I assume she's at the London flat. Tell her on no account to keep her appointment with Druckmann.'

Sally got up and was hurrying towards the door of the restaurant when Emma said, 'Hang on a minute. What's going on? Anyway, Catherine isn't at the flat. She changed her ticket. She's coming back on the first morning flight.'

'Damn! Damn! Damn!' George jumped up. 'What time's she supposed to be meeting Druckmann?'

'Nine thirty.'

George looked at his watch. 'Eight twenty-three. Sally, try the mobile. She should be still on her way into London.'

Sally hurried out.

'We have to contact her,' George insisted. 'There's no way we can get there in time.'

'George, what on earth's the matter?' Emma realized something was really wrong.

He sank back on to his chair and began a tattoo with his fingers on the table top. 'It's a trap; that's what's the matter. Druckmann must have rumbled the bug sometime on Thursday. After that there's much less on the tape and it's all routine office stuff. He must have removed the device whenever he needed secrecy.'

'How can you be sure? Perhaps . . .'

'I wasn't sure till a couple of minutes ago. We've been over Friday's tapes thoroughly. There's no record of a conversation with Catherine.'

Emma stared at him, her mind grappling with the implications.

'But that doesn't necessarily . . . Druckmann wouldn't . . .'

'I hope to God you're right but we can't just sit around waiting to find out.' George pushed away his untasted breakfast. At that moment Sally ran back in, out of breath from having run all the way from her office. She shook her head. 'No reply!'

George took over. 'Right, here's what we do: Emma you stay in command here.' He reverted in the crisis to military thinking and vocabulary. 'Try and contact Catherine. Keep trying the flat and the car. Phone Artguard. If they put you on to her we'll all be able to breathe again. If they deny that she's there . . . Well we'll face that when we come to it. Keep in regular telephone contact with me.'

'Where will you be?' Emma was suddenly glad that someone else was taking a positive lead.

'I'm going to round up the lads and head for London. I want to be in the area in strength, and mobile.' He stood up and strode to the door. 'Saul Druckmann is not going to do anything to Catherine . . . And if he does . . .' He went out but immediately re-opened the door. 'Not a word to the Major – leastways not yet.'

'I'm sure he's wrong.' Sally looked anxiously at Emma for confirmation.

'Yes. You know George. He likes to make a drama

out of a crisis. Still . . .' She stood up. 'Better do as he says.'

Back in her office she phoned the Lacy's London flat. There was no reply. She rang the mobile, with the same result. She repeated the call every few minutes. At nine thirty-two she dialled the number of Artguard. She got straight through to Druckmann's secretary.

'May I have a word with Mr Druckmann, please.'

'Mr Druckmann is not in the office today.' The voice was like broken glass.

'Well, actually, I am trying to trace Mrs Lacy. She has an appointment with Mr Druckmann about now.'

'Mr Druckmann has no appointments today. He is out on company business.'

Lying cow, Emma thought. She said, 'I'm sure there must be some mistake. Can you tell me if Mrs Lacy has called at the office?'

'Any mistake must be at your end. We have no callers in the office this morning. Goodbye.'

Emma replaced the receiver and stared at it for several seconds. She felt her stomach tighten and her tongue go dry in her mouth. George was right. She called him on his mobile and reported with a quavery voice.

The ex-sergeant responded briskly and briefly. 'OK, sit tight and don't do anything until you hear from me. Say nothing to nobody.'

'Not even the police.'

''Specially the police. I don't want them queering our pitch.'

'George!' Emma gasped, alarmed. 'What are you going to do?'

'I don't think you want to know. I'll be in touch. 'Bye!'

Sit tight! All very well for George to say 'Sit tight!'

What were you supposed to do when one of your colleagues was recovering from a heart attack, another had
been kidnapped or worse and a third was probably on the
point of breaking the law?

When the phone buzzed, she jumped.

'Hello.'

'Emma, hi! How was Paris?' Tim sounded very bright
and relaxed.

'Oh . . . er . . . Tim, how nice to hear your voice.' She
tried to keep the strain out of her own. Unsuccessfully.

'What's up, Emma. Have I interrupted something?'

'No, not at all. Not fully awake yet, that's all.' She
attempted a light laugh.

'Sounds as though Paris was enjoyable. I wanted to
call you before Catherine gets back and before you get
embroiled in the day's work. Did you find out anything
over the weekend?'

'Find out anything?' Emma's mind was a sudden blank.

'About Saint-Yves. That was what you went for, wasn't
it?'

'Saint-Yves . . . yes . . . yes.' She struggled to clear
her immediate worries from her mind and focus on the
bizarre events of Saturday.

'Emma, are you sure there's nothing wrong? You
sound distracted.'

'No, I'm fine, really. Now, Saint-Yves. Well, I presume you knew he was homosexual.'

'No one could fail to know. He positively flaunted it.'

'Right. Well, he was in with a very weird bunch.
They call themselves Dionysians. They're mostly from
the Paris artworld and pretty heavily into drugs. They're
probably also dabbling in art fraud – false attributions,
fakes: you know the sort of thing. I actually blundered
in on some sort of pagan funeral rite they were holding.

303

One of them, Bernard Marais, was Saint-Yves' lover but they split up recently.' She forced her mind to reassemble details. 'Split up . . . yes . . . probably over drugs. It seems Saint-Yves was agin that sort of thing. Anyway, this Marais character actually claimed that he'd killed Patrice Saint-Yves.'

'I'd forgotten that he was in London, too. Did he say how he'd done it?'

'He didn't elaborate. He just boasted about it. I suspect it was no more than that – a boast, a wish-fulfilment. As I said, he's an oddball, a total nutter. He was probably cashing in on Saint-Yves' death to gain some self-importance.'

'Strange, though.' Tim sounded thoughtful. 'So that was all you got, was it?'

'Yes, I'm afraid so . . . No, wait, though. There was something else, something Marais mentioned *en passant*. What was it exactly? It was about Mort Bronsky. He said that Saint-Yves didn't like him and wanted nothing to do with his schemes.'

'Schemes?'

'He didn't say any more – except that he suspected Bronsky had sent me as his agent.'

'It sounds as though you had an extraordinary weekend.'

'You can say that again.'

'Well, thanks for going to all that trouble. I appreciate it.'

'I don't think I found out anything useful.'

'Oh, I wouldn't say that. Every detail helps to build up the picture.'

'Are you making any progress in clearing the Santoris? Though it seems Edgerson has gone off them as his main suspects.'

'I think I'm beginning to make sense of it. What I am sure is that it's nastier and bigger than we thought. Anyway, Catherine will fill you in on developments here when she gets back. I'd better go now. Take care, Emma. See you soon.'

After she had put the phone down Emma spent several minutes thinking about Tim – how much in love he was with his wife, how happy and complete they were together, they and the boys. If anything happened to Catherine it would break him completely. Of that she felt absolutely sure.

'This one's interesting.'

Emma was suddenly aware that Sally was standing beside her with a sheet of paper in her hand. 'I'm sorry. I was miles away. What did you say?'

'I said I've just been going through the weekend faxes and there's one here that's rather interesting. It's from Inspector Edgerson.'

Dear Mrs Lacy,

   I tried to reach you by telephone but you were unobtainable. I thought you would like to know that the Grinling's case is solved, especially as you played a part in fingering the murderer.

   After our chat the other day I obtained the address of Miss Harding-Beck and called there on Thursday. There was no answer and my men eventually had to force an entry. We discovered Miss Harding-Beck dead, poisoned. She had left a message on her PC screen explaining everything. She deliberately gave the victims poisoned champagne. It was all about a personal vendetta she had against Dr Devaraux. I suspect you knew about that. She hoped the other three deaths would cover up the murder of her intended victim. She was obviously a nasty, callous young woman. I am glad we did not have to bring her to trial. Her lawyers would probably have claimed diminished responsibility.

Anyway, thank you for your help. I hope Mr Lacy is soon fully recovered.

D.I. Edgerson

Emma handed the fax back. 'That's that, then. Have you got Tim's number in Italy? I ought to let him know.'

But when Emma phoned the villa fifteen minutes later there was no reply.

Tim hung up and strolled into the kitchen. He wandered around O.K.'s impeccably tidy kingdom. Every pot and pan, dish and jug was clean and in its allotted space. There was not so much as a breakfast mug or spoon to be washed up. Not even the smallest contribution was left for him to make towards the smooth running of the little household. During his first days in the villa he had been able to cope with the frustration. His body had clearly signalled its need of rest and his mind had acquiesced. But now? Catherine's visit had raked up the coals of anxiety about the business – especially as she refused to discuss events at Farrans.

From outside the back door came the rhythmic sound of his minder chopping wood. Tim opened a window and called out 'Coffee, O.K.?' The noise of steady labour paused long enough for the young man to reply, 'We're plumb out of milk. I'd thought we'd go into Florence as soon as I've finished this. We can have a drink in a café while we're shopping.'

Tim closed the window and stood facing the empty

room. Shopping! Coffee in a Florentine bar! Perhaps another visit to the Uffizi! And this afternoon one more of O.K.'s special treats – a trip to Arezzo to see the cathedral's amazing Renaissance stained glass! He stifled a scream. There was no prospect of his succumbing to another heart attack but the possibility of death from boredom and inactivity was certainly on the cards. He wandered over to the fridge. One of the bottles of Colli Albani they had bought in Rome was in the shelf on the door and only half empty. Last night he had been permitted one glass which he had sipped with miserly appreciation while watching the others guzzle a couple of bottles between them. He grabbed a tumbler from the dresser, filled it with the lemon-coloured liquid and carried it guiltily to the sitting room.

He dropped on to the sofa and took a mouthful of the soft, fruity wine. It was good – a symbol of the fullness of life he had been forced to abstain from. He had been virtuous, he reflected, a model invalid. But now the discipline of self-denial was becoming unbearably hard. He picked up the 'Borgia Chalice Case' folder. It was now well filled with the notes contributed by Catherine and the Santoris as well as his own jottings and musings. He took a clean sheet of paper and wrote down the information Emma had given him. As she said, it did not amount to much. But was there anything there, any scrap that would help identify the big design, the complex motive Tim was now searching for?

The phone rang. He grabbed it up and heard Tristram's voice.

'Good morning, Tim. I've got that information you wanted.'

'From the Vatican Archive?'

'Yes. I don't know whether you'll be able to make any sense of it. I can't.'

'Fire away.'

'Well, they keep requisition information on the database for about a year so that they can extract what they need for their statistics. During this year, apart from myself, only two other researchers have accessed those particular files of the Borgia correspondence. One was a professor from Heidelberg. I don't suppose you want his name.'

'Probably not. Who was the other?'

'The print-out reads, according to my contact, "15–18 March, M. Bronsky, New York".'

'Interesting.'

'It seems to invalidate your theory about identifying the killer. Bronsky would hardly have planned to poison himself.'

Tim was thoughtful, excited. 'We've certainly got to do some rethinking. Thanks, Tris. That's very useful. Must dash now. O.K. wants to go shopping.'

Before he dropped the receiver Tim had made a decision. He went out to O.K., who was busy stacking the split logs. 'Do you mind if we go into town straight away? I want to get some letters in the post.'

He went up to his room and slipped one or two items into his briefcase. Back in the sitting room he added the folder. When he went outside O.K. was waiting with the car.

Twenty minutes later they parked beneath the Mercato Centrale and climbed to the ground floor of the vast building where shoppers bustled around the poultry, meat, fish and cheese stalls.

Suddenly Tim stopped. 'I've left my briefcase in the car,' he explained. 'Give me the keys, would you? I'll see you back here in a few minutes.' He returned to the door leading to the underground car park.

By the time O.K. started anxiously checking his watch, Tim had begun his drive to Pisa airport.

'Fra Pietro! Fra Pietro!'

Foscari was walking through the narrow streets of the Borgo the day after his return to Rome when he heard his name called. Turning, he saw Sebastiano Sancia waving from a doorway. He made his way towards the young man he had last seen prone and unconscious while a surgeon sawed his leg off below the knee. Sebastiano came towards him, forcing a way through the crowd of women, children and tradesmen, and Pietro was delighted to see the comparative ease with which he moved on his new wooden limb. The two men embraced warmly.

'You are well now, my son?'

'Thanks to you, Brother Pietro.'

'You know what I must say to that, Sebastiano: render thanks to God and not his mere instrument.'

'I do, I do – daily. And I also render thanks for my good friend, Brother Pietro. Have you been away? I looked for you as soon as I was able to walk.'

They strolled towards the river engaging in happy small talk. Eventually, sensing that his companion was finding the exertion of moving his artificial leg tiring, Pietro paused by the Ponte Sant' Angelo. Both men leaned against the parapet watching a deep-laden barge moving downstream.

Tentatively, Foscari broached the subject of principal interest to him. 'Do you remember, my son, last time we talked together back in the summer you were telling me how you carried messages for your master the cardinal – secret messages?'

Sebastiano's face ceased to smile. His eyes glanced to and fro at the people passing across the bridge – priests, soldiers, liveried servants, carters and merchants. 'I remember very little about that time. I was sick. My head was stuffed with wool.' He laughed nervously.

Pietro frowned. 'You remember the poor friar who tended your wound yet you have no recollection of what we talked about?'

'I was delirious. I probably gabbled all sorts of nonsense.'

Foscari gripped the other man's arm tightly. 'Just now you were overwhelmed with gratitude for my meagre medical talents. Do you now repay them with lies?'

Sebastiano registered genuine misery. 'Then, I thought I was dying,' he muttered.

'And you feared – rightly – facing Christ the judge with a terrible secret on your conscience?'

The young man nodded.

'And is your case so different now? No man knows the hour of his death. Next week all Christian men rejoice at the birth of the Saviour. Yet neither you nor I can say for certain that we shall be here to share in the celebration. In Rome men die violently every day, struck down by robbers, jealous rivals, mindless drunkards, angry enemies – some assassinated for no reason at all.' He stared out over the turgid water. 'They say that this year alone no less than twenty-seven bodies have been hauled out of the Tiber. Now I have a particular interest in one of those bodies. You know who I mean, don't you, my son?'

Again, Sebastiano inclined his head by way of an answer.

'So what can you tell me about the Duke of Gandia, of his visit to Orvieto and what happened afterwards?'

The other man looked at Foscari imploringly. 'Brother, I am afraid.'

'And who is it that you fear more than God?' Pausing and receiving no reply, Pietro went on. 'It is Cesare Borgia, is it not?'

Sebastiano's eyes opened wide. 'You know?'

'Most things. I only need certain scraps of information and I shall complete my understanding of . . . a certain matter. You need not fear to tell me. Nothing you say will reach Cardinal Borgia or his agents.'

The young man was trembling, uncertain. 'You swear it?'

Brother Pietro smiled reassuringly. 'I did not play some small part in saving your life just to offer you on a dish to a godless assassin.'

They resumed their walk across the bridge and Sebastiano Sancia told Fra Pietro what he knew, what he conjectured and what friends claimed to have seen. Nothing came as a surprise to the friar. Except the depths of depravity to which the human spirit can sink: despite all the evils he had seen in his journey through the world, the little friar never lost the grace to be shocked by that.

He made his way back to the convent with a burden of despair pressing down on his shoulders and a more immediate concern squeezing his mind: how to bring the truth to light, if possible without forfeiting his life in the process.

Catherine collected her car at Heathrow and drove into London. The Monday-morning traffic was stacked up all the way to the Chiswick flyover so she parked the car near Turnham Green Station and finished her journey by tube. When the District Line train pulled in she took the last seat in the end carriage and checked her watch. Eight thirty-five. She was in good time. She gave her mind to the forthcoming interview. She had already decided how she intended to handle Saul Druckmann. Since time was vital to both Lacy Enterprises and Artguard, the appropriate strategy was still to hang on as long as possible and see who cracked first. The way things were going she was really beginning to believe that it would not be Lacy's. Druckmann was in the hands of powerful and impatient associates who would not hesitate to pull the plug once they decided that Artguard was a liability. Jimmy 'the Fist' McNair was not renowned for charitableness when it came to money-losing operations. And Trevor Shand was not going to be in the best of moods after the Mount Street fiasco and the arrest of his men. Druckmann's heavyweight backers might well conclude that there were other ways of cornering the business-security market. For all Druckmann's self-assured, aggressive manner, he was a worried man – and had every reason to be so. The fact that Catherine knew her adversary's weakness put her in a strong position and she intended to make the most of it. So, she would be polite and give every appearance of listening seriously to Druckmann's revised proposal. She would get him to spell it out in detail, then go away to 'consider' it. Over the next few days she would respond evasively to his urgent telephone calls and eventually reject his offer. If that did not, by itself, do the trick it would give George and the boys more time to turn up something damaging about Druckmann and his associates and devise some way of feeding it (perhaps anonymously) to the police.

When she arrived at the Artguard office she had to wait

several seconds after pressing the bell. Then a smartly dressed, sharp-featured young woman appeared on the other side of the glass door and let her in.

'Mrs Lacy?' the secretary enquired. 'Please come with me. Mr Druckmann is expecting you.'

She led the way through the outer office, which Catherine noticed was untenanted. At the far end of a corridor they turned right into the secretary's room.

'Please sit down.' The young blonde waved Catherine to a chair. 'Mr Druckmann won't be long. He's just taking an international call. Can I get you something? Coffee? Lemon tea?' She switched on a professional smile.

'Coffee would be great. Milk, no sugar, please.'

The secretary went into an adjoining office and returned moments later with a steaming china cup on a saucer. The coffee was good, a distinct improvement on the anonymous liquid Catherine had drunk on the plane three hours before. She looked around the well-appointed office. Artguard, it seemed, pampered their staff. Not only was the furniture new, comfortable and well designed, but the decor was tasteful and on the wall behind the desk were a pair of mid-nineteenth-century English watercolours, depicting peasants and children in idealized landscapes. The detail was exquisite and could only be from one master's brush. Catherine reflected that there could not be many firms who ennobled the offices of junior staff with Birket Foster originals.

The particular member of staff in question showed no inclination for conversation. She rattled away at her computer keyboard and seemed absorbed in her work. Apart from that there was no sound. In fact, Catherine realized, the place was surprisingly silent. It now occurred to her that there was something odd about her situation. Since her arrival on Artguard premises she had neither heard nor seen any employee except the woman who was ensconced behind her computer terminal and totally ignoring her.

'Where are all your . . .' She struggled to find the word. 'Staff?'

The secretary scarcely looked up. 'We work a flexi-system. Many of them prefer to arrive later and stay on in the evening.'

Catherine was now feeling very warm. The central heating must be on full belt, she thought. She tried to loosen her topcoat. Her hands felt strangely heavy. Only with difficulty could she raise them and then her fingers refused to grasp the buttons. Now her vision became blurred. She tried to focus her eyes on the Victorian watercolours and there were four of them. The secretary spoke into an intercom but Catherine could not unscramble the words. She opened her mouth to call out but no sound came. She slumped in her chair, semi-paralysed.

Then she was aware that someone else had come into the room. A man. Druckmann. He was talking to the secretary. They came across to her and lifted her from the chair. Her knees twisted under her but her legs had not lost all their strength. Half-supported by her captors, Catherine stumbled from the room on a journey she did not want to make but had no power to prevent. They left the offices. Entered a lift. Emerged in a basement car park. A large, black car was immediately in front of them. Catherine was bundled on to the back seat. She lay down and thankfully yielded to the soft leather. She wanted to do nothing but relax. She no longer cared what was happening to her or where she was being taken.

CHAPTER 16

Tim Lacy found aeroplane travel conducive to clear thought – daytime travel, that is. Night flights he loathed: it was impossible either to sleep or to be mentally alert enough for work. Flying during normal waking hours was another matter. Cocooned at thirty thousand feet from all distractions and disturbances and pampered by cabin staff, he felt able to concentrate as in few other environments. It was on the flight to New York that the accumulated information about the Grinling's murders, which had resembled the wild jumble of meaningless black notes on an orchestral score, at last began to yield a tune.

After slipping away from Florence like a guilty, truant schoolboy, Tim had driven to Pisa from where he phoned Tristram with directions for finding the car. All he had told the anxious lawyer was that he was going away for a few days and that he would be in touch by the end of the week. He had booked to New York via Paris and his plane was due to touch down at fifteen forty-five local time. First he read Foscari's report (or as much as he had) as a continuous document. Then he went carefully through the rest of the accumulated evidence in his dossier. He meticulously unpicked the theories, half-theories and suspicions he and others had knitted together, examined each skein

carefully and then began experimenting with new patterns.

Somewhere over mid-Atlantic, lunch having been
cleared away and the handful of other first-class passengers settled to snoozing or watching their personal TV
screens, Tim listed all the relevant and possibly relevant
details in chronological order, beginning with the suicide
of Marianne Harding-Beck, running up to 29 September
(he arranged the events of that day in timed sequence) and
ending with Bernard Marais' boast of having murdered
Saint-Yves. He looked at his summary appreciatively. It
made sense of almost everything. Only two or three scraps
of paper refused to be fitted in and Tim decided that they
could be regarded as irrelevant. He could now see how the
Grinling's murder had been done and by whom. Only two
things were lacking – motive and proof. There still had
to be a big enough reason for the callous striking down
of four people – five including Hartnell. Tim wished he
had had the final pages of Foscari's report in his file to
ponder. He felt a real bond with the friar who had tramped
the hills and valleys of north Italy five hundred years ago
in a relentless search for truth. And he knew with a faith
amounting to certainty that the Franciscan's conclusions
about the Michaelmas Massacre had a real bearing on
a crime committed half a millennium later. But it was
one thing to create intricate fan traceries of hypothesis
– complete, balanced and aesthetically satisfying – and
quite another to build a case likely to interest the Crown
Prosecution Service.

Having exhausted all other ideas, Tim idly picked
up one of the 'irrelevant' pages. It was the list Ginny
had brought from Elberhof, the one Maria Heuss had
surreptitiously made a copy of. Tim read it reasonably
easily; he had picked up a smattering of German during

his army tours of duty. He looked at the letters beside each item. They reminded him of the code antique dealers wrote on price labels and in their ledgers so that they could read them instantly while potential customers and rivals could not. It was simply a case of substituting a letter for a figure. If Segar's notes worked on the same principle then it should be fairly easy to make sense of them. The most common letter in the list was X. In rounded numbers the most frequent was O. So, let X = O. L cropped up fairly often, particularly at the end of a sequence, so might be 5. By trial and error he arrived at a set of equivalents that worked for the whole list. Thus an unattributed Florentine bronze horse carried a figure of 0045 and the Verrocchio copy 2955. This was presumably Segar's shorthand either for the values he had placed on the items he had identified or the prices they had subsequently realized. Disappointed that the puzzle had not provided more mental stimulus, Tim slipped the sheet back into its folder, dropped that on to the empty seat beside him, reclined his own seat, and closed his eyes.

In accord with a long personal tradition, Tim took a taxi from JFK to the St Regis Hotel on Fifth Avenue. After booking in and having a quick shower he decided to get straight down to business. Bronsky-Stein Inc. was only three blocks away and within a few minutes Tim was pushing open the door and entering the perfumed warmth of the late Mort's emporium. It had lost none of its air of plush opulence. The silk-lined walls were punctuated with a dozen or so paintings – altarpieces and classical subjects dating from *c.* 1450 to 1600. Island stands scattered over the deep carpet carried subtly lit treasures of the same period – bronzes, polychromed wooden figures, crucifixes, and glass-cased jewellery and plate.

From the back of this gleaming Aladdin's cave, a little man with crinkly, black hair advanced, arms wide. 'Tim Lacy, as I live and breathe! What a surprise! Why didn't you phone?' Harry Stein clasped his old friend in an effusive embrace.

'Hello, Harry. I would have let you know but it was a last-minute decision. How's things? It was terrible about Mort. You must have been devastated.'

The dapper dealer raised his shoulders in a shrug which expressed sorrow, perplexity, resignation and a range of other emotions besides. 'So many letters and phone calls and telegrams, you wouldn't believe. A man should die to find out how popular he is?' He shook his head. 'Anyway, come and have a drink to his memory.' He led the way to an alcove at the rear of the showroom where a desk and chairs were discreetly arranged so as not to intrude on the display.

Tim relaxed into an armchair while his host opened a cupboard to find a bottle and glasses. 'How are you managing single-handed?'

Harry pulled a long face. 'It's hard, Tim, hard. You don't plan for these things. With hindsight I guess we should have taken a younger person in years ago, trained him, taught him . . . But where can you find the kids nowadays with a real feel for beauty, craftsmanship, antiquity? Anyway, we should have tried.' Lovingly, Harry poured cinnamon-coloured liquid into brandy glasses from a dark bottle whose stained and torn label proclaimed its age. 'Always good to drink with another armagnac man, Tim. It's the mark of a true connoisseur. To Mort.'

Both men raised their goblets and drank in silence.

'You made a great team, Harry,' Tim said. 'With Mort travelling, finding neglected masterpieces in unlikely places and you making the contacts and keeping your finger on the pulse of the market. A partnership like that is very rare.'

'It was a long time building.' Stein sighed. 'Thirty years. The swinging sixties, that's when we began – two arrogant young men, opening a shop the wrong side of the river and never doubting for a moment that we could hit the big time.'

For half an hour they reminisced and Tim exercised great restraint in not allowing Harry to refill his glass.

At last Tim asked, 'Did Mort have any enemies?'

Harry nodded enthusiastically. 'Was Mort Bronsky successful? Have you ever met a successful man without enemies?'

'I don't recall meeting any who've been driven to murder by envy.'

'Ah yes, a bad business.'

'And you've no idea . . .?'

Stein shook his head. 'If I had, my guesses would have been passed to your police long ago. From what I hear it was a pointless killing; the work of some psycho son of a bitch.'

'Maybe. . . . Mort was very interested in the Borgia Chalice, wasn't he?'

Harry threw up his hands. 'That thing!' he growled. 'Mort was obsessed with it. About many things he's intrigued – sculptures, carvings, paintings even, though that's more my line than his. Always he has to find out everything there is to know. If a piece has a good story or can be linked to some important person or event . . . Well that can put hundreds of dollars on the price – thousands even. But about this chalice he's a man possessed. He chases all over the world looking for evidence that will prove it's a fake. He writes articles for several magazines about it.'

'Yes, I know. Did he tell you about the evidence he found in Rome?'

Stein's sallow features creased into a frown. 'No. It can't have been important. He told me anything important.'

'Odd.'

'So, what's odd?'

'Last March Mort discovered something in the Vatican Archive that would go a long way towards suggesting that the Borgia Chalice is genuine. Yet he seems to have kept it very much to himself. Can you think why?'

Harry shrugged. 'Business.'

'How do you mean?'

'Something's sold as a fake. You know it's genuine. You buy it at a low price. You produce evidence that, in fact, it's from the hands of this or that master. You sell at a handsome profit. It's done all the time. I don't need to tell you that, Tim.'

'But Mort didn't buy the Borgia Chalice.'

'The price was too high. There was too much publicity. As a result it made almost as much as the genuine article would have done. Say, I've got an idea!' Harry abruptly changed his tone of voice and the subject. 'You doing anything tonight?'

Tim shook his head.

'OK, you're coming with me to the Met. Gala banquet. I took a table and one of my ten guests just let me down.'

The prestigious events in aid of charity or museum funds which were held at the Metropolitan Museum of Art were legendary. The great and the good came from all over the world to see and be seen, paying anything from $500 to $1500 a head for the privilege. For that outlay they got to eat and drink in one of the museum's

exotic showpiece galleries – an Egyptian temple trans-
ported stone by stone from Aswan, a similarly acquired
French monastic cloister or the European sculpture salon
designed by one of the most avant-garde international
architects.

Tim shook his head. 'Sounds tempting, Harry, but I'm
not really into banquets right now. Strict diet. Heart.' He
tapped his chest.

'Yeah? Me too – and half the people there tonight.
We're all either stressed or overweight these days. You
need a low-cholesterol meal? I'll fix it.'

'There's also the problem that I'm travelling light this
trip. I don't have a D.J. with me.'

'No problem.' Stein brushed aside the objection. 'Here's
what you do. You go to Arnie's on 43rd and 6th. You
mention my name and you tell him you need a tux for
the evening. Arnie will see you right. You'd better go
now. Arnie gets kinda touchy if people go in to hire stuff
near closing time.'

Tim found himself being hustled from the shop with
the promise that Harry would collect him from the hotel
at seven.

It was precisely on the hour that the little dealer and his
wife walked into the famous King Cole bar featuring the
murals created for the original St Regis hotel at the turn
of the century. Feeling miserably virtuous Tim sipped
orange juice as the three of them enjoyed a leisurely
drink before leaving for the museum.

Rebecca Stein was a diminutive woman. Her straw-
coloured dress and hennaed hair made her look like a
walking vesta match and the flashing diamonds suggested
that she had just been struck. She quizzed Tim about
the European beau monde. ('I-just-love-to-travel-but-
Harry's-such-a-stick-in-the-mud-he-says-if-it's-any

- good - it'll - come - to - New - York - sooner - or - later - and
-if-it-isn't-why-bother-going-looking-for-it.')

In response to Tim's enquiry she explained the purpose
of the evening's event. 'The Chairman's Council of the
Met is honouring Rose and Irving Lettlinger.' She looked
at Tim as though the name ought to mean something and
elaborated, with an air of surprise, when she encountered
his blank look. 'You know Lettlinger's Diners and Cock-
a-Doodle-Do chicken houses. They're the fastest thing in
fast food after McDonald's. Rose, as I'm sure you know,
is first cousin to the president.'

'The Lettlingers, I presume, are important patrons of
the museum.'

'Are you kidding? They've donated half their collection of Renaissance art to the Met and paid for a new
annexe to house it. It was opened just a couple of weeks
ago. It's gorgeous! You'll see it tonight. We're having
drinks in the Lettlinger Suite before the banquet.'

Tim turned to his host. 'Sounds as though Rose and
Irving are people after your own heart, Harry.'

'Oh, they *are*!' Mrs Stein confirmed. 'Why, Harry and
Mort sold them a number of pieces and put them on to
others, didn't you, honey? That's why we just had to be
there tonight.'

'It's about time we made a move.' Rebecca's husband grabbed his chance to slip into the conversational
current.

They made the short journey to the museum in the
Steins' chauffeur-driven Cadillac. At the reception Tim
drifted away from his host and hostess. He spoke to two
or three people he knew but spent much of the pre-dinner
hour wandering, fruit juice in hand, around the Lettlinger
collection which most of his fellow guests seemed too
preoccupied with each other to notice. The quality of

the items was universally high. With such generous and stylish benefactions it was no wonder that the Lettlingers deserved the flattery of this evening's event in their honour.

He was admiring the crispness of a pair of bronze reliefs when a voice behind him said, 'Stunning, aren't they?'

Tim turned to see a man of high colour with sandy hair and moustache. 'Irving Lettlinger,' the man said. 'Good to see someone here who shares my passion. You like the Goujons?'

'Magnificent,' Tim acknowledged.

'Finest sixteenth-century work ever produced in France.'

'Is that where you bought it?'

'No. It turned up in England a couple of years back. Say, you're English, aren't you?'

Tim introduced himself. 'You must have travelled a great deal to amass this collection.'

The multi-millionaire shook his head. 'It's mostly done through agents. It was the late, great Mort Bronsky – God rest his soul – who tracked these beauties down for me.'

'I knew him well. A terrible loss to the artworld.'

'You can say that again. He was a real help to me. If it wasn't for men like Mort there would be few really big private collectors.'

'Because you rely on their expertise?'

'No one likes to be made a fool of, especially rich men in the public eye. Me, I buy enthusiastically but I buy carefully. I know my limitations. There's no way I can accumulate the expertise guys like Mort built up over many years. So I buy their knowledge, their research, their "nose" for what is "right".'

They wandered around discussing various of Irving

Lettlinger's treasures. At last they came to the item that had pride of place in the gallery. From a tall plinth a nude male figure with long hair, wielding a club and wearing a loose animal skin glowered down on the élite of New York society. The sheer, rippling power in the limbs and torso was emphasized by the burnished, tawny patina.

'My Verrocchio,' Lettlinger announced with pride. 'There's quite a story behind this baby. My spies in London told me that something interesting had turned up in a mansion in Ireland. The estate had passed into the hands of a young man whose only interest was in selling up as quickly as possible. It was just a matter of time before the discovery was trumpeted to the world. I got Mort to go over and have a look. He phoned back to say that the *Hercules* was definitely genuine. Now, I had implicit trust in Mort's judgement . . . BUT . . .'

'Let me guess: you were worried that once you bought the statue and went public with it, other experts would turn up and say it was a fake or a copy.'

'You got it. We'd negotiated a price of close on $3 million. If the Verrocchio was right it was a fantastic bargain but I wasn't about to become known as the man who spent three mill on a copy.'

Tim said quietly, 'So you hired Heinrich Segar.'

'Pretty smart.' Lettlinger's gaze indicated a new respect for this quiet limey.

'Not really; not if you know the way those two hated each other and took every opportunity to rubbish each other's reputations.'

The millionaire nodded. 'Bronsky and Segar hardly ever agreed on anything, but Mort was so sure of his ground that he reckoned Segar wouldn't dare cast doubt on such an important discovery – not even to spite him.'

'And that's how it turned out?'

'Yep, and here it is, an exciting addition to the Verrocchio canon and now the world and his wife can come and see it. That gives me a pretty good feeling.'

Moments later Lettlinger was swooped on by a trio of Manhattan matriarchs who bore him off in the direction of 'someone you just *have* to meet.' Tim was left staring up into the frowning face of the classical hero. 'So that's it!' He muttered the words but felt like shouting them.

The rest of the evening was torment for Tim. He had to make conversation and listen to speeches when all he wanted to do was get back to the St Regis, take out the Grinling's murders' file, check one or two things; make sure he'd got it right. The adrenalin flowing through his system told him that he had but he needed to make sure.

It was gone midnight when he finally regained his hotel room. The first thing he did was phone Tristram. A sleepy voice uttered an accusatory 'Who's that?'

'Tris, it's Tim . . .'

'Tim! Where are you? Do you know what time it is?'

After riding the storm of the young Italian's reproaches and apologizing for getting him out of bed at six a.m., Tim asked, 'Have you managed to finish the Foscari report?'

'Yes. I was going to show you last night.' He still sounded sore.

'Can you get to a fax?'

'A fax! What now? We don't have one here.'

'But can you get to one? I really do need to see that translation a.s.a.p.'

'I could go into the office, I suppose.'

'Would you mind, Tris? I wouldn't ask, but I think I can put the whole thing together right now with the help of our friend, Brother Pietro. I can prove who murdered the Grinling's Four and why – and I can establish that the chalice is probably genuine.'

'Really?' Young Santori's mood changed. 'That's fabulous! Are you sure?'

'Ninety per cent. Now can you fax that report to me if I give you the number?'

'Sure, I'll go right away.'

One reason Tim liked the St Regis was the business equipment that came as standard in all the rooms – including a fax. While he waited he took out Segar's list. Yes, there it was – '*Hercules* a copy of a lost Verrocchio, *c.* 1540: 2955'. That must be $2,955,000. Half an hour later the fax machine buzzed into life and pages of text issued from its clattering interior.

Tim grabbed them up and read them through rapidly. Then he kissed them. 'Little friar, I love you!'

He put a call through on the BA twenty-four-hour line and booked a mid-morning fight to London.

'Well, little friar, I'd given you up for dead.' Pope Alexander was dining alone in his apartment, attended by two servants. With a wave he now dismissed them.

'I'm sure your holiness was aware of my movements.'

'You think the pope has no better things to do than spy on heretical Franciscans?' He beckoned Foscari to the table but did not invite him to sit. 'Come and make your report.'

Pietro gazed at the burly seated figure wiping greasy fingers on a napkin and up at the same man's painted effigy kneeling in prayer on the wall behind. Appearance and reality. Truth and falsehood. Openness and duplicity. Honesty and deliberate illusion. Those were the issues that lay at the heart of the vile sequence of events that had reached a climax in this room fifteen months ago. He looked around the table and tried to picture della Chiesa, Petrucci and Montadini seated on the chairs before him together with Alexander, Cesare and Giovanni. Of that group only two were now alive.

'Well, little friar, are you going to stand there all day?' The pope glared at him and Foscari read anxiety – perhaps fear – as well as anger in the large blotchy features. 'I paid you to find out the truth for me. Have you done it?'

'You remember, your holiness, that I did tell you that you might not welcome the truth when I had discovered it?'

'I shan't know until you tell me, shall I?'

Foscari had spent several hours in prayer preparing for this interview, and now, though his heartbeat was so loud and rapid that he thought the pope must be able to hear it, his mind seemed to be floating above any turbulence like a hawk hanging in the peaceful air and observing the scene with piercing clarity. He leaned forward, pulled a chair from the table and seated himself opposite the Vicar of Christ.

Alexander's thick eyebrows met in an angry frown. He opened his mouth to curse the friar's arrogance, then thought better of it. Instead, he swept aside the silver dish with the remains of his meal still on it, and folded his arms on the table. 'To the point, Brother! To the point!'

Pietro closed his eyes and brought his palms together prayer-like before his lips. 'I met a man upon the road, a pilgrim, who had a sad tale to tell of treachery, and deceit and love repaid with villainy.'

Alexander's fist crashed down on the table setting salvers and dishes rattling. 'I don't want to hear your stories! Tell me the truth – plain and uncoloured!'

'Forgive me, your holiness, but didn't Our Lord choose

to tell stories to convey truth? I think you may understand better what I have to report if you allow me to do it in my own way.'

The pope sat back in his padded chair. 'Very well, but if this turns into a sermon . . .' He left the threat unuttered.

'This man was tricked by his spiritual adviser and by his own brother – men to whom he had shown nothing but kindness and generosity. He was made to believe that his wife had cuckolded him. He was goaded into committing a terrible sin. But far more terrible was the sin of those who drove him deliberately, pitilessly to his own destruction. Now, from this living parable I learned two truths: a trusting or a foolish man is easily duped, and the road from love to hate is short. Then, I saw that both these truths applied to your holiness's son, the Duke of Gandia. For him, too, affection had become soured so that he easily became a prey to the machinations of evil men.'

'Name them!' Alexander stared at him with such a haunted intensity that Pietro felt stirrings of pity for him.

The friar stood up. 'I have prepared a full report for your holiness and, by your leave, I will bring it you this evening after Vespers.'

The pope, too, jumped to his feet. 'Why haven't you brought it now?'

'I wanted to lessen the shock. I wanted to prepare your holiness for bad tidings. May I ask your holiness to ponder what I have said and permit me to return this evening and make everything plain?'

Borgia was far from happy about this. He was not accustomed to being dictated to – especially by independent-minded friars whose respect for the head of the Church was no more than skin deep. There was something about Brother Pietro that he found unnerving. Holy men could be so self-assured, so arrogant! He knew that the little Franciscan would not agree to any other arrangement so he did not demean himself with point-less bluster. As Foscari withdrew, the pope simply comforted himself with the thought that when this business was over something would have to be done about his over-intelligent agent.

Pietro, leaving the Vatican complex by a postern gate, was in no doubt about his position. 'Well,' he thought, as he made his way to an important assignation, 'that has set the fuse burning. Now to take precautions about the explosion.'

It was ten twenty-three when George and three members of his team arrived at the multi-storey car park near the Artguard offices. They had gone over the simple plan several times in detail. Johnny set off immediately. He walked into the vestibule of Artguard's block and stood for a few moments in front of the board listing the names of the companies in the building. He shook his head, as though not finding what he was looking for, and left.

'Rogers and Dibley, Insurance Brokers, seventh floor,' he reported when he rejoined the others on the pavement at the rear of the building. 'That's the best bet. They must get lots of callers.'

George straightened his tie. Unusually for him, he was dressed in a grey suit and carried a briefcase. 'Right. This should take no more than four minutes. Be ready.' He walked briskly round to the front of the block, entered and went up to the security desk. 'Rogers and Dibley,' he announced. The guard gave no more than a glance at the businessman before him. He pushed across the register and George wrote the name 'P.J. Kemp' in the visitors column, 'Seaforth Assurance' under the heading of 'Company' and 'Rogers and Dibley' under 'Visiting'. He added the time and date. 'Floor seven, sir,' the guard said, handing over a pass. George clipped the square of plastic to his breast pocket and walked over to the lifts. He rode to the seventh floor, stepped out and waited till his car had been summoned to another floor. He pressed the call button and when another lift arrived he entered and pressed the bottom button. The doors opened on to the basement car park. Knowing that access from the car park would be code controlled, George left his briefcase across the entrance so that the doors would not close. He ran to the grille guarding the garage exit to the street. He pressed the button to release it and his companions joined him at the double. They all took the lift to the fifth floor.

While the others remained in the lift, again blocking the door to prevent movement, George stepped across to Artguard's outer door and rang the bell. After a pause Druckmann's secretary appeared on the other side of the glass. She scrutinized George and, through the intercom, asked his business. George had not expected to be challenged and had to think quickly. 'Message from Mr Shand,' he announced to the grille on the wall. There was a click as the door was released. George stepped inside and held the door open. His co-conspirators ran in after him.

The blonde, who had turned away, spun round. 'What on earth . . .!'

That was as far as she got before strong arms pinioned her and a scarf was pulled tight across her mouth. George pushed her into a chair and nodded to the others. They ran through the inner door, into the corridor, and began checking the offices.

Seconds later Steve reported. 'The place is deserted. It's like the *Marie Celeste* through there.'

'Damn!' George grimaced. 'That means we need some answers – and bloody quick, too. Pete, you keep watch out here. Johnny find a console and start on the computer. We'll see what helpful information this young lady can provide.'

George and Steve took the secretary to one of the empty offices and sat her in a chair. George looked at her carefully. He read scalding fury in her eyes and little trace of fear. He decided that she was probably going to be difficult. 'I'm sorry we had to do that, Miss. We don't intend you any harm. Me and my friends just want some information and we want it fast. We're now going to remove the gag and ask you some questions. If you make a noise or refuse to cooperate you'll be gagged again, tied up and shoved in a cupboard out of the way while we get our information by other means. Is that clear?'

She scowled but nodded. Steve unknotted the scarf.

'You've got a bloody nerve, criminal louts! I'm going to remember your faces and give full descriptions to the police.' The woman jumped to her feet only to be pushed down again by Steve's hand on her shoulder.

George admired her spirit. There could not be many women, he reckoned, who facing possible assault, rape and murder by four strong men would stand up to them like this. 'Well, Miss, to tell you the truth, I thought of going to the police when Mr Druckmann kidnapped a friend of ours. Then I decided that direct action would probably bring quicker results.'

'I don't know what . . .'

331

'Just answer my questions, please, Miss. We don'
have time for speeches. Now where are all your staf
this morning?'

Slight hesitation. 'They're all at a meeting. They'll be
back very soon.'

George read the calculation in her eyes. 'If you lie to
me, you'll make life difficult for me and very unpleasan
for yourself. Let me rephrase the question. Has M
Druckmann given the staff the day off?'

The woman nodded.

'And you are?'

'Mr Druckmann's assistant.'

'Earlier this morning Mrs Catherine Lacy came here
to meet Mr Druckmann. What happened?'

'Sod off!' The blonde's truculence returned.

'Let's try that one again, shall we? Where did Druckmann
take Mrs Lacy?' George's impassivity could be quite
menacing.

'I'm not saying anything.'

George shrugged. 'OK. Steve, tie her up. She can do
her explaining to the police.'

The woman laughed. 'You're threatening *me* with the
police? You're the ones . . .'

'Accessory to abduction is a very serious offence, Miss
Of course, if we're talking about accessory to murder
then that ups the ante quite a bit.'

'Murder!' She showed alarm for the first time. 'M
Druckmann isn't . . .' She stopped.

'Then if Mr Druckmann isn't going to murder ou
friend what is he going to do?'

The secretary stared back, sullen and silent for severa
seconds. Then she muttered, 'He said he needed a bar
gaining counter. That's all I know.'

'Where has he taken her?'

'I don't know!' she yelled. 'You can do what you like to me. I can't tell you any more.'

George continued evenly. 'You're doing very well so far, Miss. Very helpful. I'm sure you can help us the last little bit of the way. Now, if Druckmann left here with Mrs Lacy I'm damned sure she didn't go willingly. So what happened to her? Did some of Shand's thugs manhandle her?'

'Shand!' She jumped as though someone had stuck a needle in her. 'My God, he's got nothing to do with this. If he knew about it . . .' She clammed up abruptly.

George nodded. 'So that lets Shand out of the frame and you right back in it. I really think you should cooperate, don't you? Now, where has he taken her?'

'I don't know! He went off with her in his car. He didn't say where he was going.' It was halfway between a shout and a wail and George thought it was probably true.

'Where does he live? What other premises has he got?'

The woman shook her head.

'Don't mess me about!' For the first time George let his anger show. 'Every minute you waste increases Mrs Lacy's danger. And if anything happens to her you'd better pray the police get to you before we do.'

'OK! OK! He's got a terraced house in Kensington – forty-three Langthorne Gardens.'

'Steve, get Johnny to check that on the personnel records in the database.' When the other man had gone out George said to the woman. 'Sorry to seem so untrusting but I'm sure you'd like to see us haring off to W8 so I'm just verifying.'

Steve was back within a couple of minutes. He nodded. 'She's right.'

George smiled. 'Good. How's Johnny getting on?'

'He seems happy.'

'Right, then we'd better move. Help me to truss up this young lady, would you? You'll find some twine in my briefcase.'

The secretary jumped up. 'You said . . .'

'I said I'd lock you in a cupboard if you didn't cooperate.' He held her in a chair while Steve tied her hands behind her. 'Since you've been a good girl I'm not going to do that. But I'm not going to gamble on your having a sudden change of heart and phoning your boss to warn him. I reckon a resourceful girl like you could probably get out of these bonds in a couple of hours.' He lashed her ankles to the chair legs. 'By that time I hope we'll have tracked down your esteemed employer and found out what he's done to Mrs Lacy. Whatever it is, he's in deep trouble.' He checked the knots and finally replaced the gag. 'So, as I see it, you ought to be able to free yourself by lunchtime. You can then go running to Mr Druckmann. Or you can set the police on to us. Or, like the Arabs in the desert, you can fold up your tent and steal away. In your position I know what I'd do.'

George and Steve hurried out. They collected the others in the reception area and moved quickly to the lift. George went out through the front door, handing in his pass at the desk. His colleagues left via the car park. They ran back to the van and jumped in. Steve revved the engine.

George threw a London street guide to Pete. 'Get us to Langthorne Gardens, Kensington. Quickest route. And pray we're in time.'

334

CHAPTER 17

The city's streets were dark but still busy when Fra Pietro Foscari set out from the Franciscan convent and made his way to the Vatican in a light rain which grew steadily heavier. He deliberately did not choose the most direct route which lay, via a serpentine course of narrow lanes and alleys, to the Ponte Sant' Angelo. He kept to the wide piazzas and the main thoroughfares where mounted riders, pack animals and carts manoeuvred in the wide rutted streets, and lamps hanging in house windows, shops and stalls laid slabs of faint light across the puddles and glistening cobbles.

The hood pulled well over the friar's head shut out most of the evening sounds. He certainly made no effort to listen for the following footsteps. He had no need to; he knew they were there. He simply kept well to the centre of the roadways, maintaining a steady, unhurried pace and returning the greetings of men and women who hailed him as he passed. By the time he reached the long, straight Via Recta, which Sixtus IV had broadened for the benefit of pilgrim crowds fifteen years before, the town was becoming quieter. The rain had driven indoors the revellers, the gossips and the tradesmen who stayed open to catch the last of the day's spenders. The pursuers were closer now. Pietro could feel them. He could sense their growing anxiety. They must find an opportunity to strike before the bridge. Once he was over the Ponte Sant' Angelo their chance might be lost. The Borgo teemed with life at all hours, even on such a foul night as this, and Brother Pietro was a much-loved figure with its people. An assassin striking there would be lucky to escape a lynching.

Foscari braced himself. He must give them their opportunity. Instead of continuing to the end of the street where it debouched into the Canale di Ponte, so called because of its frequent floods, he turned suddenly right, along a narrow lane which led at an angle to the Piazza di Ponte Sant' Angelo and thus to the bridge itself. It was like a black tunnel. Most of the windows overlooking it were fast shuttered and little light spilled into the street. As he advanced he counted his paces. He had reached nineteen when he heard the running steps behind.

He hurried forward to where the broken shutter of a house on the left allowed a yellow gleam to escape and splash on to the grimy stucco opposite. Pietro pressed his back against the wall and turned to face his attackers.

He could make out no details. But he could see two small, thin figures, their heads covered in soft caps, their cloaks drawn well around them in a way which left their right hands free. Those hands now held drawn swords.

'Stand away,' Foscari called, with a voice he tried unsuccessfully to stop shaking. 'Do not commit so foul a sin.'

'Rot in hell for it, shall we, friar?' One of them laughed. 'I reckon we'll take our chance on that.'

'What can you possibly gain from attacking me?' Foscari reasoned. 'I carry no money.'

'You have something we want – a paper. Hand it over.' The other villain had a remarkably high voice. Pietro judged that he was little more than a boy.

The two men closed on him, blades pointing directly at his chest.

'Best hand it over, friar.'

'We'll take it anyway.'

Pietro made one last attempt to deter them. 'Please, for your own sakes, do not attempt something you will regret.'

'Oh, we shan't regret it,' the older man bragged.

'Think again!' The words came from the darkness behind the assassins.

Pietro could not see his friends. But he heard the crack and thud of their cudgels falling on the heads of his attackers. Without even a groan they slumped to the sodden roadway.

Pietro stepped over the prone bodies and embraced the three Bovis brothers who ran a cooper's business in the Borgo. 'Thank you. Thank you, friends. That was expertly done.'

A gruff voice responded. 'No need for thanks. We can't let anything happen to our Brother Pietro.'

'It was a pity they didn't put up more of a fight,' another voice added. 'Come, Brother, we'll see you safe across the bridge in case there's any more vermin abroad tonight.'

Foscari felt his arms gripped by powerful hands which almost carried him along the street.

Fifteen minutes later, when he was ushered into the pope's warm study, well lit by lamps in wall sconces and a myriad candles in silver holders, Foscari noted well the expressions of the two men who were present. Alexander's smile was one of relief. The younger man, whom the friar had never seen at close quarters until this moment, tried to appear impassive but could not stop the cloud of anger which passed over his face. They were seated beside the fire and the pope beckoned Pietro to take the stool which stood between them.

'Your timing, for once, is excellent, little friar. Cardinal Borgia, here, had just made a wager with me that you would not come. He was of the opinion that you had fled. I told him I knew my little friar better.'

'His eminence doubtless had good reason for suspecting that I would not be here. The streets are becoming dangerous places at night, even for poor Franciscans.' Foscari shrewdly explored the features of Cesare Borgia. It was easy to see why people, especially women, thought him the most handsome man in Rome. His face was long and his mouth turned up disdainfully beneath an aquiline nose. His hazel eyes glimmered with reflected firelight and his long, auburn hair fell nonchalantly round his shoulders. But Pietro looked for other signs. He saw the arrogance etched into the face by years in which privilege had not been tempered by wisdom. He noted the cruelty which was the flower following the bud of an over-indulged childhood.

'So, Brother, what have you to tell us?' Alexander's wide smile twitched at the corners.

Pietro reflected that if the pope wanted certain matters kept dark he should not have sent an intelligent and determined man forth with a lamp. He took a deep breath. 'Here is the report I promised your holiness.' From his wide sleeve he produced a folded and sealed letter.

'So have you solved the mysteries that all our best agents have failed to uncover or have you just thrown together some vague ideas in the hope of satisfying his holiness?' Cesare sneered.

'Don't mock my friar, Cesare. He has a remarkable reputation as a man of independent mind. Sometimes it gets him into trouble, sometimes he forgets his place, but he is always worth listening to.' To Foscari he said, 'I will read this later but tell us now the gist of it.'

'As your holiness commands. The story begins with an indulgent father and an indulged son. The boy grew up with riches and servants. If he wanted a new toy, a new friend and, later, lands, titles, mistresses, he had only to ask and his father would provide them. Who shall blame him for assuming that it was his inalienable birthright to enjoy power over men and every luxury the human heart can crave? Who will be surprised that such a young man could never be satisfied and that no matter how much he had, he always wanted more? And who, with any understanding of human frailty, will be bemused that this man, so far from revering his beneficent father, should grow to despise him? By the time Giovanni Borgia reached manhood he was grasping, calculating and uncontrollable.'

Alexander scowled and opened his mouth to protest but Pietro hurried on.

'With respect, your holiness, I did warn that my discoveries might prove painful. Believe me, I do not enjoy opening the eyes of a father blinded by love but if you truly wish to know how your son came by his death I must do so.'

Foscari took up his narrative. 'As I said, Giovanni was shrewd in the calculation of his own best interests. He understood full well that papal bounty was not an eternal spring. When he looked to the future he realized that he needed to find other providers. It was thus that he fell in with your holiness's most dedicated enemies. It is no secret that Cardinal della Rovere intends to be the next pope and that he hopes with the aid of French troops and gold to unseat your holiness.'

Cesare scoffed. 'Let della Rovere and Sforza do their worst. They will find us more than a match for them.'

Pietro shrugged. 'Such political judgements are beyond my capabilities. What is clear is that Giovanni was easily duped by these men. Because he wanted to be convinced that he would have an honoured and powerful place in the new régime he allowed della Rovere's messengers to convince him. He began meeting in secret with those who were plotting your holiness's overthrow – men like della Chiesa, Montadini and Petrucci. What, of course, he did not know was that Petrucci was loyal to the head of the Church, and was keeping your holiness well informed of the enemy's plans. What a shock it must have been when you discovered that your own son . . .'

'It was a moment of youthful madness!' Alexander protested. 'He was tricked, seduced for a while – but only for a while.'

'You confronted him and, no doubt, he wept tears of penitence.'

'Yes.'

'So, travellers tell us, does the crocodile weep as he devours his prey. Giovanni lost no time in reporting to della Rovere that there was a traitor in the camp.'

'I don't believe it.'

'Tell me, your holiness, did you and Giovanni hatch a plot of your own? Did you decide that he would stay in your enemy's councils and report back to you?'

Alexander nodded.

'As I thought. He was now trusted by both sides. Vain and foolish as he was, he believed he could ride two horses simultaneously. And that brings us to the Michaelmas Massacre.'

Cesare, who had been gazing into the fire, looked up

sharply. 'You think you know who really murdered the cardinals?'

'Oh yes.' Foscari nodded solemnly.

'Who?'

'Why, all of you. Your holiness, your eminence, della Rovere, Duke Sforza – even King Charles VIII, for I imagine he assented to it.'

'What lunacy is this!'

'I told you, Father, the man's a fool!'

The Borgias spluttered their protests but Fra Pietro sat placidly, gazing straight ahead, hands clasped within the sleeves of his habit. 'It was your holiness who first raised questions in my mind. You were desperate to know about the assassination of the Duke of Gandia and offered me every assistance. Yet when I suggested that that tragedy was linked to the poisoning of the cardinals you were less enthusiastic. Only reluctantly did you sanction my enquiries and you kept certain information from me. So I wondered what it was that you didn't want me to find out. Of course, your great secret was that you ordered the Michaelmas Massacre.'

'Have a care, little friar.' Alexander glared.

But Pietro hurried on. 'The ironical truth is that della Rovere also ordered the Michaelmas Massacre.'

His listeners stared in disbelief.

'It is puzzling, isn't it? It puzzled me for weeks. Neither side wanted all three men dead. You had good reason to be rid of della Chiesa, who had thrown in his lot with the enemy, and of Montadini, whose murderous schemes you now knew about. But Petrucci deserved no death at your hands. As for della Rovere and his confederates, once Petrucci had been betrayed to them they certainly sought vengeance on him. They might conceivably have decided that Montadini was too unstable an ally. But della

Chiesa's lands were very valuable to them. Then, at last, I realized that the Duke of Gandia was the key to the mystery. It was he who was the agent, the willing dupe. I suspect it was the della Rovere faction who suggested that he poison Petrucci and Montadini. He could not do that without revealing that he was still in the pay of the pope's enemies. But if, at the same time, he proposed to the pope to get rid of Montadini and della Chiesa he would be proving his adherence to both sides. If, "by accident", three men took the poison instead of two that could be passed off as "unfortunate".'

Cesare jumped to his feet. 'Father, do we have to listen to any more of this? Let me give this man the thrashing he deserves.'

'Please sit down, Cesare. I am intrigued. So, Brother Pietro, how, in your theory, did my son carry out this triple murder?'

'He conveyed your holiness's summons to the victims, declaring that you suspected them of treason and that they had better hurry to make their peace. Their eminences were only too anxious to assert their loyalty and you accepted their protestations. You took wine with them from a common cup to signify your continuing confidence.'

Cesare blurted out, 'Are we back to that nonsense about the jewelled chalice?'

'No, the wine served on that occasion was pure and wholesome.'

'Well, then?'

'Your excellency and his holiness left soon afterwards for Viterbo. The three cardinals stayed to concelebrate a mass in the pope's private chapel. Giovanni attended that mass and put the poison in the communion chalice.'

'But then other people would have been killed also,' Cesare protested.

'Not if the three cardinals were the only clergy present. The congregation would have received bread alone. Only the celebrants drank the wine. A slow-acting poison had been chosen, so it was hours later that the victims died. By then no one could say how they had come by the poison.' He watched the Borgias carefully as he asked, 'That was the plan, wasn't it?'

Father and son exchanged glances but neither responded. After a long silence Alexander said, 'You still haven't told me who killed my Giovanni.'

Foscari gazed at the crackling logs. 'A man who has been duped is his own worst enemy. He finds it hard to accept that someone has made a fool of him. When the truth presses in upon the fragile house of his self-delusion he grabs every argument he can lay his hands on to barricade the doors and windows. That only makes the eventual disillusionment more bitter. The della Rovere faction had been using the Duke of Gandia all along. The Michaelmas Massacre had been planned to serve two purposes – to silence the traitor in their midst and to blacken further the name of the Borgias. Within days of the triple murder they had begun to spread the story of the Judas chalice – the beautiful goblet which concealed venom within its chased and bejewelled stem. It is a colourful story, the sort of story people easily believe and readily pass on. And it presented the pope and his two sons to the world as evil men so far sunk in depravity that they would stop at nothing to gain and maintain power. It was a calumny that worked remarkably well.

'Yet it took Giovanni several months to accept that he had been thoroughly deceived. He had been employed as a siege cannon against the citadel of his own family. And

343

now that he had served his purpose his new friends had lost interest in him. There were to be no rich rewards, no promises of future wealth and position. He was like a child whose favourite toy has been taken away and, like a child, he threw a tantrum. In March he borrowed money from Alfredi the banker for a visit to France.'

Alexander shook his head vigorously. 'No. In March he went for me on an embassy to Naples.'

'Was it a successful embassy, your holiness?'

'It had to be aborted. King Frederigo was away in Aragon.'

'The Duke of Gandia was, then, unable to bring back formal despatches from Naples.'

The pope nodded. 'That is so.'

'Your holiness, he was never there. I have it on good authority that he obtained not only money but that he also secretly "borrowed" members of his banker's household. He took with him a very small entourage – men he hired especially for the journey.'

'Who told you this tale?' Cesare demanded.

'Informants I trust and whose identity I have vowed to protect. Giovanni rode swiftly to the French court and spoke there with della Rovere face-to-face. What passed between them I do not know, but by all accounts the Duke of Gandia returned well pleased with his mission. His associates were less happy. To them Giovanni Borgia was now an embarrassment. He had no more value and he could not be trusted. They would have to make new arrangements to gain access to the Vatican's inner courts. Or perhaps they had already made such arrangements.' Pietro glanced at Cesare who was, once more, staring into the fire's red depths.

'Instructions were sent to agents in Rome. Then it was merely a question of waiting for a suitable opportunity.

THE BORGIA CHALICE

They almost waited too long. On the fifteenth of June
Giovanni Borgia and his brother – your eminence – were
to leave for Naples. On the mission which, according to
Giovanni's story, had had to be aborted earlier. However,
on the evening before their departure their mother gave a
party for them in Trastevere. To that festive event came
a man in a mask who, as your holiness knows, later led
the Duke of Gandia to some "meeting" somewhere on
the other side of the river.'

'Who was he?' Alexander leaned forward in eager
attention.

'His name is of little importance. He was only a messenger. The mask, which made him seem so mysterious,
was worn because someone at Vannozza dei Catanei's
soirée might conceivably have recognized him as one of
della Rovere's servants.'

'Then it was della Rovere! I knew it! That hellhound
will pay dearly for this.' Anger and relief were released
in the pope's shout.

Foscari continued in an even tone. 'The Duke of
Gandia said goodnight to his brother and others of the
party at the Tiber Island bridge and rode in the direction
of the Jewish quarter. Where did he go? Where was
the assignation? His body was thrown into the river on
the other side of the Capitoline Hill. Even at dead of
night assassins would not make a long journey with a
murdered man. When your holiness first laid this burden
upon me I spent several hours walking the streets trying to
decide the most likely location for this crime. I reasoned
that it would be close to the Ponte Sant' Angelo and
in some house to which the victim would willingly
go. I found myself returning time and again to the
Via Recta, that noble thoroughfare laid out by Pope
Sixtus IV, who was, of course, Francesco della Rovere,

the uncle of the cardinal, your holiness's enemy. And that pope built his own splendid palazzo on the Via Recta. It has a rear entrance in the narrow lane which runs beside the Hospital of San Girolamo to the river bank at the point where the body was committed to the Tiber.'

When Foscari came to the end of his summary, Alexander stretched out a ringed hand and clapped him on the shoulder. 'You have done well, Brother Pietro. You have more than justified my confidence in you and you shall have a reward. What do you say, Cesare, shall we make our little friar a bishop?'

The cardinal's morose expression did not soften. 'How many heretical bishops has the Church room for?'

'I don't think one more will make much difference,' his father replied, now in a thoroughly good humour.

Foscari stood up. 'My reward is to continue to serve God and his Church. Do I have your holiness's leave to depart?'

Alexander held out his hand for Pietro to kiss. 'Yes, go now. In a few days you will receive news of your new appointment.'

Pietro bowed himself from the room. Minutes later he stood outside in the unlit street. As his eyes grew accustomed to the dark he heard a whistle from the shadows opposite. Hurrying across, he found Sebastiano Sancia with one hand holding the bridle of a small horse while stroking its muzzle with the other.

'Here she is, Brother, as I promised. She's a quiet ride but you'll find she has a good turn of speed if you need it.'

'Thank you, my son. This is very good of you.'

Sebastiano helped the friar into the saddle. 'We're not going to let "them",' he jerked his head towards the

Vatican wall, 'do anything to our Brother Pietro. Off you go now, Brother, and God speed you.'

Foscari gathered up the reins and pressed his heels to the mare's flanks. 'God bless you, my son, and your friends. Give them my thanks. One day I shall hope to return and thank them personally.'

He steered his mount over the bridge and turned it left along the far bank. He reached the Via Flaminia. To the soldiers guarding the city gate he showed the pope's letter. A glance at the seal with its embossed Borgia bull was sufficient for them to unbolt the heavy timber portal and wave him through. Pietro rode out via the suburbs into the open country. Veils of cloud wafted about a half-moon but there was enough light for the horse to pick her way over the ruts and potholes.

Fra Pietro offered prayers of thanksgiving for his escape. He thought of the two men he had left in the claustrophobic atmosphere of the papal apartments and wondered whether Alexander would read his report before his son left. Some time in the next few hours the pope would peruse the carefully composed prose, and then . . .? Pietro felt sadness for both father and son but the truth was that they deserved each other. He recalled the final paragraph of his report. It had been composed so carefully and passed through so many revisions that he could remember it word for word.

Two interconnected problems remained to be resolved: the nature of the Duke of Gandia's death and the identity of the man on the white horse. The vicious wounds inflicted on your son were not, in my view, consistent with a political assassination. Giovanni had been savagely hacked to death and that pointed incontrovertibly to a crime of passion. This murder was inspired by anger, hatred, vengeance or jealousy. There are not many men in Rome who boast such a magnificent animal as the one described by the boatman who witnessed the disposal of the body. My enquiries among horse copers and grooms and other experts in this particular market enabled me to narrow the possibilities to three wealthy citizens. Two had no obvious connections with the Duke of Gandia. My suspicions about the third were confirmed by a rumour circulating among some of the horse fraternity that on the morrow of the murder Cardinal Borgia's head groom had to remove streaks of dried blood from the flanks of his eminence's favourite white gelding. I concluded that, after his return to the Vatican from Trastevere, his eminence changed his clothes and his horse and rode out again, unobserved, to meet his brother's captors by pre-arrangement. What concealed jealousies may have erupted thereafter, what relationships may exist between his eminence and your holiness's enemies, it is not for me to say. Your holiness asked me to ascertain the facts about the deaths of Montadini, Petrucci and della Chiesa and this I have done, with the help of God and my own poor talents.

I remain your holiness's servant to command.

Fra Pietro Foscari

The friar rode through the muted landscape knowing neither where he went nor what the future might hold.

Steve parked the van a couple of streets away from Langthorne Gardens. George sent him and Pete to find a way into the back garden, while he and Johnny went to the front. There was no elaborateness about the plan: it was a simple matter of using the element of surprise – charge whoever opened the front door and prevent his escape at the back. But when, having checked via their communicator that their accomplices had taken up their places, George and Johnny rang the bell there was no reply.

'He must have taken her somewhere else.' The younger man shook his head gloomily.

George frowned, holding back the disappointment and mounting anxiety. 'Well, this place is all we've got. We have to check it out.' He stepped back down the short path and surveyed the front of the house. Three floors plus an attic. High on the wall over the front door was a red alarm box. 'That's the first priority, Johnny, get your tools and the ladder from the van and put it out of action.' He spoke into the walkie-talkie. 'Steve, meet Johnny at the van. Simple alarm-disabling job. Pete had better stay put. Can you see anything from where you are?'

Pete's voice replied. 'All shut up tight this side and the ground-floor windows are curtained.'

'Well, hang on. I'll call you as soon as we've dealt with the alarm. Then you can get to work on the back door.'

It took the two experts twelve minutes to disable the alarm. During that time only one of the few passers-by questioned what they were doing. An elderly lady walking her dog stopped to challenge them. Steve pointed to the flash on the sleeve of his blouson jacket. 'Security firm, ma'am. Come to sort out the gremlins in the system. Don't want it going off by accident in the middle of the night, do we?' That seemed to allay her suspicions and she pottered on her way.

349

Johnny came down the ladder. 'Criminal, really criminal. This Druckmann character is the head of a security outfit and he relies on an antiquated system like this.'

George gave Pete the go-ahead and within two minutes Pete was holding open the front door.

'Pity we're honest,' he said, smiling. 'We could make a fortune if we went over to the other side of the tracks.'

'Cut the cackle!' George shoved the others inside and closed the door. 'Right, you two start at the top and work down. Me and Steve will start in the basement and come up.'

It was Pete who found Catherine. Only one room, a second-floor bedroom, was locked and it took a matter of seconds for him to open it. He saw Catherine immediately. She was bound and gagged and lying on the bed. Pete called the others, then rushed over and began to loosen the cords.

Catherine sat up slowly, staring in disbelief at her rescuers. 'How did you guys . . .? Oh God, I feel awful . . . I've never been so terrified . . . That Druckmann's a vicious creep . . . Never been so terrified . . .' A sudden shiver spasmed through her.

George sat on the bed and put an arm round her. She clung to him, face into his shoulder. Then the sobs began. He motioned to Johnny. 'First-aid box. Brandy.'

By the time the young man had returned from the van Catherine was, with an effort, getting over her shock. She gratefully swallowed a mouthful of spirit from the bottle. 'I'm sorry, George. I didn't mean to go to pieces all over you.'

'You had every right after what you've been through.' He produced a handkerchief.

Catherine dabbed at her eyes. 'I must look a frightful sight.'

'Nothing to what Druckmann's going to look like when we've finished with him. Just what is his game?'

Catherine stood up. She took a few unsteady paces across the room and stared at her reflection in the dressing-table mirror. 'God, how awful.' She prodded at her fair hair. 'Can anybody see my purse?'

After a fruitless search, Johnny was despatched to the ground-floor rooms to see if he could locate Catherine's handbag.

'Druckmann,' George prompted gently. 'Where's he gone? What was he going to do with you?'

'He said he would keep me here till Tim came to his senses over the business. And there was something else. What was it?' She shook her head, trying to dislodge the swarm of bees which seemed to have taken up residence there. 'He was hopping mad about something. Oh yes!' She turned suddenly. 'George, he's found the bug. That's got him really worried. He wanted to know if we'd planted it. Or whether it was someone else – someone called . . . What was the name?'

'Shand?'

'That's it! Shand. Of course, you know about him, don't you? Druckmann's terrified of him.'

'I'll bet. So he's worried friend Trev might have been checking up on him. What did you tell him?'

'I didn't tell him anything. I didn't know. I couldn't remember. I still don't remember properly. Oh God, do you think I'll ever unscramble my brains?'

''Course you will, Catherine. The bastard's drugged you. It'll wear off.'

'That's right. He said he'd come back when I'd recovered from the dope. He said I'd have to answer his questions then, or else.'

Johnny returned, swinging a small, leather handbag

351

from one hand. 'Found it in the kitchen with all the contents emptied out. I don't suppose I've put everything back properly.'

'We'll leave you to tidy up, Catherine.'

'You're not going away?' She turned with alarm.

''Course not. But if Sergeant Druckmann is coming back we must be sure we have a reception committee ready.'

George organized his forces. The ladder was put back in the van. Johnny was set to keep watch from a first-floor front window. Pete explored the fridge and cooked up a very respectable lunch. Catherine felt much better after the food and was able to enter into the plans that were made around the kitchen table. It was she who volunteered to go back to the room where she had been held captive.

George was on watch soon after three thirty when Druckmann appeared on foot around the opposite corner and crossed the road, unbuttoning his topcoat and feeling into a trouser pocket for his keys. 'OK. Places everyone!' George ordered.

Catherine sat on the edge of the bed. Her gag and bonds had been replaced, though only loosely. Over the thumping of her own heart she heard Druckmann's heavy tread upon the stair. Then a key turned in the lock.

Druckmann stood in the doorway, sneering. 'Ah, feeling better, are we? Ready to cooperate, I hope.' He went to the window, drew the curtains across, then he switched on the light. He went over to the bed and made the mistake of standing in front of his prisoner, legs spread wide. He stared down at Catherine's drooping head. 'Now, let's resume our unfinished business.'

'Yes, let's!' With all her strength she brought her feet up into his crotch.

Druckmann gasped and staggered back, bent double. 'Bitch!' he muttered.

He took several deep gulps of air and was about to lunge forward when the four men came through the doorway behind him. Steve and Johnny pinned his arm while George helped Catherine out of her fastenings.

'Now, Mrs Lacy,' he said, 'have you anything you'd like to say to this gentleman?'

Catherine stepped forward. With careful and deliberate aim she swung her open right hand against his left cheek. Then, for good measure, she gave the other side of his face the advantage of her backhand.

Druckmann stood sullen and silent. Pete tied his good arm to his side. Then they led him downstairs and dumped him in a sitting-room chair. The others seated themselves comfortably.

'End of the road, Sergeant,' George observed.

'What do you mean?' Druckmann tried truculence. 'It'll take more than you to get the better of me, Sergeant Martin.'

'Oh, it's not me who's going to do for you. I can't be bothered. But I reckon Trevor and Frankie won't be too pleased with today's episode – or with the tape I'm about to send them.'

Druckmann's eyes widened with fear. 'It *was* you, then?'

'Yes, it was. And we've got enough on you and the Shands to keep the boys in blue busy for quite a time.'

The one-armed man crumpled completely. 'Look, it wasn't me! I was under pressure from the Shands and Lochinver. He controlled the purse strings. He gave the orders. He . . .'

'Not interested, Druckmann,' George cut in. 'All me and my friends want is you and Artguard out of business and out of our hair. I reckon your chums will be falling over themselves to close you down when they know what we've got on them.'

Druckmann drooped. 'They'll kill me.'

'Very probably,' George agreed amiably.

'Don't do it, George. Please don't do it,' Druckmann implored.

'Why shouldn't we? You were going to sink Lacy's without trace, weren't you?'

Druckmann shrugged. 'Business, George. Business.'

'Well, that's exactly how I see it. No hard feelings, Saul old chap. This is just business . . . However.'

'Yes?' Druckmann looked up sharply, sensing a gleam of hope.

'However,' George continued. 'What we are prepared to do is offer you forty-eight hours' grace. That should give you time to put some distance between you and your colleagues. How does that sound?'

'I suppose it's the best I can expect.'

'It is. On Wednesday afternoon we'll be sending identical packages by special courier to Trevor Shand, Lord Lochinver and a certain police inspector we know. Where you are then is up to you.'

Druckmann made no response.

'I take it that means you accept our generous offer.' George stood up. 'In which case there's nothing more for us to do but wish you good day and thank you for your hospitality.'

He led the way from the room and out into the darkening evening.

Tim phoned Harry Stein from the airport to thank him for his generous hospitality. And to fire some questions at him. Harry, who had a photographic memory for every piece that had ever passed through Bronsky-Stein's since he and his partner had been dealing in top-of-the-range merchandise, provided instant facts and figures. They confirmed everything Tim suspected. He spent an hour of the return flight going through Segar's list, doing some sums and coming up with an impressive total. Then he took a couple of sheets of clean paper and wrote an account of the Grinling's murders from the killer's point of view. It was not complete but it was convincing.

At the Westminster flat he turned in early. First thing Wednesday morning he phoned Catherine. The receiver almost scorched his hand.

'And just where the hell have you been, buster?' There was an unusual tightness in Catherine's voice.

'I presume the Santoris have sneaked on me.'

'I called last night to tell you something about the Grinling's business. Ginny said you'd taken off without a word of explanation. Really, Tim, after all they've done for you, that was . . .'

'I know, I know, very inconsiderate. I'll give them a buzz later and apologize. What was it you wanted to tell me?'

'No, Tim, you can't just brush it aside. I've been worried . . . Not knowing where you were . . . Imagining all sorts of things that might have happened.' Her voice trembled uncharacteristically.

It was Tim's turn to be alarmed. 'Hey, there's something wrong your end, isn't there?'

'Of course not. Everything's fine.' Catherine made an effort to sound bright. The last thing she was going to tell her husband was that she had been drugged and tied up and that she had had periodic bouts of the trembles ever since her release.

'You're sure? Well, I'm sorry about haring off without telling anyone but I suddenly saw a way of wrapping up the Grinling's business. And I was right.'

'You're a bit late.'

'What do you mean?'

'That's what I wanted to tell you. Edgerson wrapped up the case last week, or so he thinks. Georgina Harding Beck committed suicide and left a note confessing to the murders.'

'Damn! Damn! Damn! I never thought . . . Poor kid God, that makes me angry!'

'You don't buy it?'

'You sound a bit doubtful yourself. What's the problem?'

'Probably nothing. I haven't had time to think it through.'

'Try it out on me.'

'Well, Edgerson faxed the office over the weekend He obviously wanted to crow about solving the case - although "solving" is scarcely the word for it: it's all fallen into his lap. He just gave the bare bones in his fax, so I called him yesterday to see if I could pump some more info out of him.'

'And?'

'And he said that in her confession Georgina described how she killed her victims. She took the bottle of champagne that had been opened for Santori's charade, put poison in it and served it up to the experts as they were waiting to go up to the lunch.'

'And you and I know that that's not true.'

'Exactly.'

'Did you tell Edgerson?'

'No . . . I guess I wasn't thinking straight at the time.'

'Probably just as well. He wouldn't thank you for unwrapping his neatly tied-up case.'

'So what happens now?'

'Can you meet me at the flat tomorrow morning?'

'Sure. I'm coming to town anyway – Emma and me both. The P.R. company are doing some filming at Grinling's for the promo video. I thought I ought to sit in and make sure they get things right.'

'Deventer's actually agreed to help us out?'

'Oh, yeah. He doesn't have much choice in view of Artguard's collapse.'

'What did you say?'

'Druckmann is history and Artguard with him.'

'That's amazing. Tell me more!'

'No.' Catherine managed a light laugh. 'Just for giving me a scare I'm going to hold out on you. Right now I have a business to run. See you tomorrow, darling. 'Bye.'

The filming at Grinling's, next day, went well. The team spent half an hour in the Long Room during a sixties memorabilia sale obtaining actuality footage for the voice-over to be fitted in the studio. Then they descended to the basement, where Andy Stovin took them on a tour of the in-house storage facilities and talked about the importance of security. After a lunch break they went to Deventer's spacious top-floor office for a brief interview. While the lighting technician was arranging lamps and the cameraman was setting up his rig and adjusting focus, the producer went over his questions with the head of Grinling's. At last all was ready and Deventer, important and imposing behind his wide partners' desk, did his piece, responding to the out-of-shot producer's queries and probings. After a couple of small retakes, the producer was happy. 'Thanks very much, Mr Deventer,' he enthused. 'That was great.'

'Well done, Adrian.' There was the sound of light applause from the doorway.

Deventer, squinting against the strong lights, peered in the direction of the newcomers. 'Catherine, Tim, how lovely to see you.' He stood up. Searching for a route through all the TV paraphernalia, the Lacys came over to the desk and reached across to shake Adrian's hand.

'Don't move,' Tim said. 'We just looked in to say thank you for doing all this for us. We really appreciate it.' He and Catherine sat down in front of the desk.

The producer put his clipboard away in a briefcase. 'Thanks again, Mr Deventer. That really was good. We're just off for a quick cuppa. Will it be all right if we leave our gear here for a few minutes?'

Deventer nodded imperiously as the three-man team withdrew. He turned to Tim. 'I really am delighted to see you again. How do you feel?'

'Fighting fit, thank you, Adrian. I've been wonderfully looked after. How are things here? Are you managing to put the Borgia Chalice business behind you?'

'I hope so. Dear God, I hope so.' Deventer passed a weary hand across his brow. 'We had all the reporters around again at the beginning of the week, when the police released news about the Harding-Beck woman. But hopefully it will all simmer down now. You'll be able to collect the wretched chalice for your principal and Grinling's can slip back into a comfortable rut.'

Catherine nodded sympathetically. 'It's been an awful business for you – and a terrible shock to have one of your own people owning up to such an atrocity. She must have been demented. Did you know her well?'

Deventer shrugged. 'One tries to establish a rapport with all one's staff but it isn't really possible. Ms Harding-Beck had been with us some time and worked very efficiently. I'm sure it would have been brought to my attention if she had shown any signs of mental instability – depression, that sort of thing.'

'I wonder where she got the poison,' Tim mused.

Deventer looked up sharply. 'I beg your pardon.'

'*Botulinus* toxin – it's not exactly easy to come by.'

Adrian's reply was nonchalant. 'I expect the police will sort out all the details.'

Catherine said innocently, 'While you were away, Tim, there was an incident somewhere near Cambridge. Fire at a laboratory. Research scientist killed. He was working on something to do with botulism. Isn't that an odd coincidence?'

Tim appeared to dismiss the comment. 'I'm sure D.I. Edgerson will follow that up in his usual thorough way. A great one for detail is our "Edgy".'

Catherine agreed. 'Yes, a positive martinet when it comes to tying up all the loose ends, is our zealous inspector. I'll bet even now he's worrying about the inconsistency in Georgina's story.'

Tim nodded. 'You mean about the champagne? Yes, I wonder why she lied about that in her confession. Odd thing to do, if you're making a clean breast of everything.'

Deventer had been following the exchange without a great show of interest but now he said, 'What on earth are you two on about?'

Catherine smiled. 'It's just one of those niggling details that tends to worry Edgerson. When we told him about it he was very bothered.'

'About what?' Deventer tried unsuccessfully to stop his voice rising in pitch.

'Well,' Catherine explained, 'Georgina claimed that she put the toxin in the opened bottle of champagne that had been used in the little enactment with the Borgia Chalice. That wasn't true. Tim and I had already drunk the remains of that.'

'What! You can't have!' For the first time Deventer looked disconcerted.

'Oh, but we did.' Tim stood up and walked to the door. He opened it and Corinne Noble stepped into the room.

Deventer jumped to his feet. 'Just a minute. What's going on?'

Tim said, 'I call it getting at the truth. Corinne, could you confirm that you took the half-empty bottle of Krug from the passage outside the Long Gallery while the sale was still going on and that we three shared it in your office.'

Corinne looked uncomfortable. 'I'm sorry, Adrian, but that's the truth. When Georgina served poisoned wine to your experts before the lunch it must have come from an identical bottle that had been prepared beforehand.'

Deventer waved a hand dismissively. 'Well, you can't expect a crazy woman like that to act logically or tell the truth. She was so deranged that she didn't know what the truth was.'

Catherine said, 'She told Corinne something that's been worrying her sick ever since, isn't that so, Corinne?'

The other subsided on to a chair by the door. She looked down at the hands clasped in her lap. 'Adrian, please clear this up. Please tell me there's a perfectly innocuous explanation. I went into the room where Georgina was entertaining the experts and their guests. She told me that you had sent her to round them all up, offer them the rest of the Krug but to make sure that only the four experts drank it. I didn't understand at the time. I thought Georgina must have got it wrong. Then, after that awful lunch party and the four of them keeling over . . . I simply didn't know what to think.'

'You didn't tell the police?' Tim asked.

'No. I suppose I should have . . . but . . . I wanted to talk to you about it, Adrian, but you were going about like a bear with a sore head. Eventually I spoke to Georgina. She was scared stiff. She'd put two and two together and didn't know whether or not she was guilty of murder. She thought the police were sure to find out from the others in the room, the ones who'd come with Segar and Saint-Yves. But they'd gone back to Europe. In the end we decided to say nothing.'

Catherine turned towards her. 'That explains the reaction I got when I came showing a photograph of Marianne Harding-Beck and Julia Devaraux. The likeness with Georgina is very striking but you, apparently, couldn't see it. You were working out whether to point me in Georgina's direction or not.'

Corinne nodded miserably. 'Knowing you, I guessed you'd find out sooner or later so I phoned her. But there wasn't time to warn her properly.'

'Which is why she fainted when I showed her the snapshot.'

Deventer intervened. 'I don't know what all this is about but you should have come to me straightaway, Corinne. I could have set your mind at rest immediately. That woman's story about me was obviously a pack of lies.'

Corinne gave a deep sigh. 'Really, Adrian? Oh, I'm so glad.'

'Of course, my dear. What reason could I possibly have for sabotaging Grinling's? You know the disastrous effect that episode has had on business.'

'That's right,' Corinne agreed. 'I couldn't make head

or tail of Georgina's story. I mean why on earth woul
you want to murder four perfectly respectable art his
torians?'

'Why would anybody want to murder four perfectl
respectable art historians – especially Georgina Harding
Beck?' Tim looked around quizzically.

'To avenge her sister,' Deventer said quickly.

Tim looked at him sharply. 'So you knew about that?
thought you said you'd had very little acquaintance witl
the woman.'

'It was common knowledge around the building.'

'Was it?' Tim asked. 'Corinne, did you know abou
Georgina's sister, Marianne, being driven to suicide b
Julia Devaraux?'

Corinne's eyes opened wide. 'No. I've never heard tha
she had a sister . . . But I suppose if that was the case
then she certainly had a motive.'

Tim shook his head firmly. 'No. I don't buy it. T
work out an elaborate, cold-blooded plan for killing thre
innocent people along with Julia? It's too complicate
for a mad person and too callous for anyone who's sane
There has to be a more intelligent reason for this quad
ruple murder. Motive lies at the heart of this gruesom
business; motive and a fifteenth-century Italian friar.'

Portentously, Adrian Deventer looked at his watch
'Well, my dears, fascinating though all this is, I'm goin
to have to call a halt to our little *tête-á-tête*. I have t
see . . .'

'I think you should listen to this, Adrian. I want you t
hear it before I go to Scotland Yard with it.' Tim spok
firmly and Deventer sank back in his chair.

'Let's start with a riddle,' Tim began. 'When is
masterpiece not a masterpiece? Answer: when enougl
experts can be found to say that it isn't. We all knov

that an item may or may not have intrinsic worth but that what decides its value is its authenticity and what decides its authenticity is scholarly opinion. This whole sordid business began with disagreements about the Borgia Chalice. Everyone accepted it was a magnificent example of the goldsmith's art but was it a modern fake, a piece of Renaissance work, or *the* Borgia Chalice, made for Alexander VI? Upon the answers to those questions depended its market price. Authentication – that's what has been at the centre of this affair all the time.

'In the international artworld the authenticator is a person of immense influence and potential wealth, the one who can make and destroy fortunes. A nod or a wink from the "acknowledged expert" and today's masterpiece becomes tomorrow's worthless copy – and vice versa. That's why the authentication racket is one of the oldest in the book. Now, of the four people who were so very publicly murdered here in September two, possible three, were involved in the mother and father of all authentication rackets. I have documentary evidence that it was in operation for at least three years. During those years it brought its operators millions. And the lynch-pin of this highly lucrative enterprise was the Managing Director of Grinling's, London – Adrian Deventer.'

'No!' Corinne stared in disbelief.

Adrian smiled. 'You are quite right to reject this nonsense, my dear. I'm afraid our poor friend's recent illness has affected his brain.'

'You could be right,' Tim acknowledged. 'But you know what you're supposed to do with madmen, don't you? Humour them. So, let me tell you a bit more about Deventer Deceptions Unlimited. Who better placed to supervise such a racket than the head of one of the world's leading auction houses? Every day hundreds of requests for valuation come into this building – little old ladies bringing their treasures carefully wrapped in flannel; executors writing for advice about the disposal of houses full of *objects d'art* of whose value they are totally ignorant; dealers with unwise purchases on their hands; distressed gentlefolk working their way through the family heirlooms; suburban hopefuls who've picked up something in a car boot sale that looks just like a valuable antique they saw on TV last Sunday; and hundreds of people who, for a variety of reasons, need to dispose of items anonymously. Then, in the other side of the balance are all those wealthy clients who repose their trust in Grinling's long and distinguished record – museums, individual collectors, corporations with megafunds to invest.'

Corinne protested. 'Are you suggesting we put items in the rooms with fake attributions? If so, you can forget it. We do a huge amount of research in order to get our cataloguing right. Our reputation depends on it. We'd be crazy to risk that.'

'Indeed you would,' Tim agreed. 'That's not how the racket works. Let me give you an example. Three years ago Grinling's were contracted to sell the contents of a once stately home in County Limerick. It had been occupied for years and years by a recluse and when he died, leaving everything to a distant relative, no one had been inside the house for ages. Preliminary reports suggested that it was full of good things – sufficiently good for Adrian Deventer to go over in person to investigate. The most exciting find was what appeared to be a Renaissance bronze statue. Adrian summoned Mort Bronsky to come and vet it. Verdict: the bronze was an early and very competent copy of a Verrocchio *Hercules*, which disappeared sometime in the eighteenth century. It was valuable but not nearly as valuable as the original. Bronsky knew an American collector who would pay the earth to have his own authenticated Verrocchio. So, the scam went into operation. While Bronsky reported an exciting discovery to his American client, Adrian persuaded the owner of the advantages of disposing of the statue privately and quietly. The buyer very wisely sought a second opinion. He called in the world's leading expert in Renaissance sculpture – Heinrich Segar. Segar had the added advantage of being a very public adversary of Mort Bronsky. The two had indulged in several slanging matches through the pages of leading arts magazines. If Segar backed up Bronsky's verdict then the Verrocchio must be right. And, of course, he did. Result? The statue went to the USA for $2,955,000, out of which Messrs Bronsky, Segar *and* Deventer all took substantial cuts.' Tim smiled at the man across the desk. 'How's the madman doing, Adrian?'

Deventer attempted a laugh. 'I can find only two flaws in that intriguing narrative. There was, of course, nothing underhand about the transaction. It is any auctioneer's first responsibility to give his clients the best possible advice. In this instance there were distinct advantages in arranging a private sale. As for the Verrocchio, it most certainly is genuine.'

Tim took two folded sheets of paper from an inside pocket. 'Not according to Doctor Segar's private inventory. He described it as, and I quote, "*Hercules* – a copy of a lost Verrocchio, *c*. 1540". This is a list of all the works that Segar vetted for the Deventer consortium, together with the prices those works fetched and a note of the deals (marked with a "B") in which he had to share the commission with Bronsky. It ties up with information I discovered in New York.'

Corinne was now looking very worried. 'But if Segar and Bronsky were at daggers drawn, how . . .'

Tim shook his head. 'That was all a front. The last thing they wanted was for anyone to suspect that they were in cahoots. So they put on that, rather overdone, charade.'

Deventer dabbed his forehead with a florid pocket handkerchief. 'It's time to bring your charade to an end, Tim. I've made allowances for the stress you've been under recently but, really, this is an appalling way to repay my support for your business.' He waved a hand at the television equipment.

'I won't presume on your patience much longer, Adrian. I'm just getting to the interesting bit. The question arises, with such an ideal money-spinner, why on earth bring it to an abrupt end? Why kill the geese that lay the golden eggs? The answer is that the operation was getting out of control and that a desperate situation called for a desperate remedy.'

Deventer held up a hand to stop the narrative. He leaned froward across the desk. 'Corinne, my dear, it seems that I shall either have to hear Mr Lacy out or throw him out and I abhor violence. However, there's no reason why your time should be wasted by this tiresome business. Why don't you run along? Perhaps you could take Catherine with you. I'm sure there are some interesting things downstairs that she'd like to see.'

The ladies stood up. Catherine looked quizzically at Tim but he nodded and smiled.

After they had departed Deventer's attitude changed drastically. 'All right, Tim, you've made your point. I won't insult your intelligence by denying everything but I want you to understand my position. Then I think you'll realize that there's no object to be served by going to the police. They've got their murderer. The case is finished as far as they're concerned. The authentication racket, as you call it, is wound up. I'm no compulsive murderer. The public has nothing fear from me. Can't we just leave it at that?'

Tim looked closely at the detached, ageing pillar of the art establishment. Apart from the film of perspiration on his forehead he seemed quite unmoved. He might have been suggesting the cancellation of an overdue debt rather than the cloaking of five murders. Perhaps, having spent a lifetime pricing things, he had lost the human knack of attaching value to things – and people. Tim wanted to scream at the suave insensitivity that was Adrian Deventer. Instead he said quietly, 'Yes, I should like to try to understand.'

'They were getting greedy and reckless. Segar had expensive tastes. I saw his private collection once, in his *schloss* near Munich. Remarkable, quite remarkable. He went on adding to it, compulsively, and only the finest works by the best masters. As for Bronsky, the whole thing was a game to him. He enjoyed fooling people, taking risks, sailing close to the wind. I told everyone we'd had a good run and now it was time to stop.'

'How many people were in the scheme?'

'Eleven altogether, covering various categories of art and antiques. Some were more involved than others. Most of them agreed with me. Not Segar and Bronsky. They wanted to expand. Bronsky tried to interest that odious little Frenchman, Saint-Yves. He came to see me in a positive storm of self-righteousness. I managed to pacify him somehow. Then I discovered that Bronsky was working on Julia Devaraux. That bloody woman would have been the end. She was utterly unstable. I didn't know how much Bronsky had told her. What I did know was that she might well take it into her head to blow the gaffe. So you see, Tim, we'd all arrived at a critical point. Someone had to do something. You do see that, don't you?'

'How did you get involved with the Shand brothers?'

Deventer smiled wryly. 'My word, you have done your homework thoroughly. A certain very wealthy client of Grinling's is a business associate of the Shands. I knew nothing of this connection. In fact, I'd never even heard of them.'

'I assume we're talking about Lord Lochinver?'

'Yes, a remarkable businessman and an enthusiastic collector but the sort of client Grinling's can very well do without. He put some items through the rooms on behalf of the Shands and it turned out that they were of dubious provenance.'

'Stolen?'

'Stolen or smuggled from eastern Europe and Asia. If ever the truth had come out there would have been a dreadful scandal. As it was, I was compromised. Lochinver introduced me to the Shands – an encounter such as I hope never to repeat – and they made me what is called an offer I couldn't refuse: for a retainer I would handle whatever fine art transactions they proposed or they would see to it that I was exposed as a handler of stolen goods. It followed, of course, that Grinling's had to deal with the Shands' friends in other areas of business. That's why we had to turn our backs on Lacy Security in favour of Artguard, which is part owned by the Shands. So, there I was between the devil and the deep blue sea. Bronsky and Segar on one side, the Shands on the other. Trapped. What was I to do? How could I possibly escape?'

'And then a fifteenth-century Franciscan friar gave you the answer.'

Deventer's thin lips stretched into a smile. 'I take it you have read Foscari's letter. Fascinating story, isn't it? Mort Bronsky gave me a copy back in the spring. He had taken a great interest in the Borgia Chalice during Santori's trial. So, as it happened, had Segar, Saint-Yves and Devaraux. They had all decided – quite honestly, I believe – that it was a fake. Early this year Santori's executors approached Grinling's to handle the sale of the old boy's collection. When Bronsky discovered that letter in the Vatican Archives he thought up another of his money-making schemes. We would sell the chalice unattributed and, in effect, buy it in by using an overseas proxy. Then Bronsky would publish the Foscari letter with a blare of trumpets, claiming that it went a long way towards establishing the authenticity of the chalice. Amidst all the renewed interest we could sell it on at a much inflated figure. It was ironical that when it actually came to it, Tim, your client pushed the price up to a ridiculous level and forced Bronsky's man out of the bidding.'

'And it was the Foscari letter that suggested to you that you could get rid of all your problems at one go. There were elements of the Michaelmas Massacre that you could copy: three people poisoned who had little in common, so that there was no apparent motive; someone duped into actually administering the toxin; the deed timed so that the instigators could be far away; and over it all the confusing fog of the poisoned chalice story. I think you brooded over that five-hundred-year-old crime until you became obsessed by it.'

'I prefer to think that Fortune presented me with a golden opportunity and I was a big enough man to grab it. I was sure I was right when all the little details began to fall into place. Tom Spence is a friend of mine.

So I knew all about Julia Devaraux's relationship with Marianne Harding-Beck. If the police ever got on to the fair Georgina she would be seen to have an excellent motive.'

'And if she told them that you had provided her with the poisoned champagne you would deny it stoutly, knowing that the police were unlikely to take her word against yours.'

'Exactly. But I honestly didn't believe it would come to that. The trace of bacillus surreptitiously introduced into the chalice should have kept the police concentrating on that as the means of administration.'

'So why did you have to kill Georgina?'

'But that was entirely your fault, Tim – yours and Catherine's. You were showing too much interest in the girl.'

'No, Adrian. You can't pass the buck to us. What happened was that Fortune turned her back on you. Corinne had already treated us to the remains of the Krug so we knew there was a hole in Georgina's confession. There's no reason for anyone to lie in a suicide note. Ergo, it wasn't a suicide note. Ergo, Georgina was murdered. Ergo, her story of having obtained the poisoned wine from you had to be true. Fortune also came over to the side of the angels when she led us to Foscari's report. It was he and only he who used the expression "Michaelmas Massacre". Yet Corinne had picked up the same term from someone here at Grinling's; someone so immersed in the story that he didn't realize the mistake he was making. That could only be the poisoner. And talking about poison, how did you get hold of the toxin?'

'That was easy, as well. I told Trevor Shand part of the story about Bronsky. I said he was becoming a problem and that I thought I could deal with him if Shand could let me have something to put in a drink. Shand, it seems, had this research chemist chap in his pocket and had used botulism poisoning to get rid of other embarrassments.'

'The advantage of using this kind of toxin is that it can be made to simulate accidental death by food poisoning. No wonder Hartnell panicked when he realized the way it had been employed openly and blatantly. And it was also putting you more securely in Shand's clutches.'

Deventer looked at him with a smile of manic superiority. 'You don't see it, do you? You're looking at the icing and missing the cake. My little Michaelmas Massacre wasn't just about getting rid of some troublesome associates. It also freed me from the toils of organized crime. Shand wasn't interested in me; it was Grinling's he wanted – a prestigious, international auction house to be a cover for some of his activities. So, the way to shake him off was for Grinling's reputation to suffer such a severe blow that it might never recover. And that's just what has happened. Business has been very badly hit in the last few weeks. If I manage things carefully it will continue to decline to the point where Shand's leeches can find no more blood to suck. Then they'll drop off. So you see, my dear Tim –' He sat back, calm and self-assured – 'there's absolutely nothing to be gained from taking this matter any further. I really am more sinned against than sinning. I let other people take advantage of me. As a result Grinling's got tangled up with some very unsavoury characters. But I've managed to sort everything out. I estimate it will take a couple of years to get the firm out of the doldrums and, as soon as I've done that, I shall retire. On the other hand, if I were arrested now . . . Well, I don't see how Grinling's could survive such a blow, do you, Tim? You wouldn't want to watch this cornerstone of the London art market crumble, now, would you?'

Tim stood up. He stared down at the amoral creature that was Adrian Deventer. 'You really beggar belief. Do you honestly think that you can turn me and Catherine and Corinne and the Santoris into accessories to multiple murder? I took an interest in this business to clear Ginny and Tris and their father's memory of monstrous and vile suspicions. I could only do that by discovering the truth. It's taken a lot of hard work but I've succeeded – with help from several people; decent people who believe in such old-fashioned ideas as right and wrong. I'm not about to turn my back on them, or on the truth, or on the shades of five foully murdered victims for the sake of your reputation or even Grinling's. You're going to pay for your crimes, Adrian.' He turned and strode to the door.

'Oh, I don't think so, Tim. After all, it's your word against mine and who would believe such a bizarre tale? If you persisted I might be obliged to take you to court for libel.'

Tim turned in the doorway. 'Adrian, you're not thorough enough or astute enough to be a successful criminal. You should have checked what had happened to the opened bottle of Krug. You shouldn't have gone around talking about the Michaelmas Massacre. And if you wanted to keep our conversation secret—' He pointed at the device still clipped to Deventer's immaculate pinstriped lapel. 'You shouldn't have talked into an open microphone.'

The following Monday morning Farrans Court was *en fête*. The entire staff gathered in the restaurant. They had much to celebrate. Everyone applauded Tim's return. Catherine was able to report that, with the collapse of

Artguard, orders and enquiries were pouring into the Lacy Security office. Tim made a brief speech thanking everyone for their good wishes during his illness and recuperation and congratulating them on their combined efforts, not only to keep the business going, but to pull it back from the brink of disaster. Then, he had champagne brought out and toasted the future. Just when the formalities seemed to be over a voice called out from somewhere at the back of the room, 'I've got another toast – Major Tim Lacy, the great detective!' Amidst general laughter glasses were tilted again. Someone else called out 'Can we see the Borgia Chalice, Major?'

After a hurried consultation, Sally was sent off to fetch the cup from the safe in Tim's office. It had finally been released by the police on Friday, following Deventer's being charged on five counts of murder. Tim and Catherine had driven back with it straightaway, anxious to get it safely under lock and key until it could be conveyed to its new owner. There was a cheer as Sally returned waving it above her head. 'Fancy having a drink out of it, Major?' one of George's lads asked. 'I don't think my wife would let me,' Tim called back. 'She says it might be bad for my health.' Then someone wanted to take a photograph of the Lacys with the chalice. After that Emma and George were brought in to have their pictures taken. All in all, a ceremony intended to take about fifteen minutes ran for over half an hour.

When everyone had drifted back to their respective duties Tim, Catherine and Emma were left sitting round a table with the chalice between them.

Catherine picked it up and turned it round in her hands so that the light caught its rough-cut gems and brilliant enamels. 'Do you know, I've gone off it. Now I don't actually like it very much.'

Tim smiled. 'It is a bit O.T.T., isn't it? Still, Wes likes it and that's all that matters.'

'I guess there are some who have cause to be thankful for it,' Catherine mused.

'Oh, who?' Emma glanced up from the newspaper she had been reading.

'Well, there's Segar's wife and mistress. I'll bet they'll cash in in a big way on old Heinrich's demise.'

'They've already started,' Tim said. 'That must have been what all that secrecy was about in Augsburg. I reckon they'd got together to sell off some of the Herr Doktor's treasures before the probate came through. That would explain why they were nervous about being seen together.'

'And there's Bernard Marais in Paris,' Catherine added. 'He can now be cock of the walk among his bunch of weird friends.'

'As long as the police don't catch him for massive drug dealing,' Emma said.

Tim took the chalice from his wife and stared at it for a few moments. 'Ginny and Tris will never think kindly of it but it has finally cleared their family name – not to mention removing Julia Devaraux from their lives. It's an ill wind . . . I suppose we should be grateful to it, too. It helped to bring things to a head with Druckmann. I was really surprised how quickly he caved in. George must have got something remarkably hot on him.'

Catherine and Emma exchanged glances. By common consent, no one had said anything to Tim about his wife's abduction.

Emma stood up. 'Well, I suppose someone had better do some work.' She wandered slowly from the room.

'What's up with her?' Tim asked. 'She doesn't seem

to be her usual, smiling self. Come to think of it, you're looking a bit peaky. Anything wrong?'

Catherine, whose sleep was still punctuated by nightmares, glanced down at the banner headlines of the tabloid Emma had discarded. 'CHERRY RIPE – Pop's most eligible bachelor "plucked" by German steel tycoon's daughter after lightning romance.' She also rose and walked towards the door, where she turned to face her husband. 'Great detective – huh!'

She went out leaving Tim staring after her, a bewildered look on his face and a magnificent example of Renaissance craftsmanship in his hands.

EPILOGUE

The murderer handled the plain buff file lovingly, reverently, as though it were a crisp-lettered incunabulum from the printshop of Caxton or Wynkyn de Worde. Its owner would not have traded it for the rarest volume in the world's finest collection of early printed books. Every folio masterpiece, every treasured first edition had its blemishes and endearing inaccuracies. Here, within these bulging covers of anonymous beige, was perfection. The insoluble crime.

The murderer was glad to be allowed to keep his masterpiece. He had heard the case doctor explaining to one of the warders that it might aid recovery and readjustment. Fool! Philistine! But then one could not expect ordinary people, little people to appreciate great art.

Slender fingers opened the folder. The murderer smiled a self-congratulatory smile at the sheaf of photocopies and cuttings clipped in precise order. The top page, beautifully printed in Renaissance Italian . . .

A selection of bestsellers from Headline

OXFORD EXIT	Veronica Stallwood	£5.99	☐
THE BROTHERS OF GWYNEDD	Ellis Peters	£5.99	☐
DEATH AT THE TABLE	Janet Laurence	£5.99	☐
KINDRED GAMES	Janet Dawson	£5.99	☐
ALLEY KAT BLUES	Karen Kijewski	£5.99	☐
RAINBOW'S END	Martha Grimes	£5.99	☐
A TAPESTRY OF MURDERS	P C Doherty	£5.99	☐
BRAVO FOR THE BRIDE	Elizabeth Eyre	£5.99	☐
FLOWERS FOR HIS FUNERAL	Ann Granger	£5.99	☐
THE MUSHROOM MAN	Stuart Pawson	£5.99	☐
THE HOLY INNOCENTS	Kate Sedley	£5.99	☐
GOODBYE, NANNY GRAY	Staynes & Storey	£4.99	☐
SINS OF THE WOLF	Anne Perry	£5.99	☐
WRITTEN IN BLOOD	Caroline Graham	£5.99	☐

All Headline books are available at your local bookshop or newsagent, or can be ordered direct from the publisher. Just tick the titles you want and fill in the form below. Prices and availability subject to change without notice.

Headline Book Publishing, Cash Sales Department, Bookpoint, 39 Milton Park, Abingdon, OXON, OX14 4TD, UK. If you have a credit card you may order by telephone – 01235 400400.

Please enclose a cheque or postal order made payable to Bookpoint Ltd to the value of the cover price and allow the following for postage and packing:

UK & BFPO: £1.00 for the first book, 50p for the second book and 30p for each additional book ordered up to a maximum charge of £3.00.
OVERSEAS & EIRE: £2.00 for the first book, £1.00 for the second book and 50p for each additional book.

Name ....

Address ....

....

....

If you would prefer to pay by credit card, please complete:
Please debit my Visa/Access/Diner's Card/American Express (delete as applicable) card no:

Signature .... Expiry Date ....